Coyitito and the Stars

H. Decker

Octopoet Press
Blue Mountain, New York ✦ 2016

ISBN 978-0-692-66009-6

Design by Carol Lynne Knight
Printed in the United States

For Gari Gullo, Donna Decker, Joan Siebold,
David Bowie — and my Students

Acknowledgments

Thank you to my husband, Gari Gullo, for being a blazing Constellation of music, poetry, prayer and passion.

Thank you to my sister of Luminosity, Donna Decker, who listened (and listens) to Coyitito (and me) as he (and I) reeled (reel) into life.

Thank you to my Mother, Joan Siebold, for teaching me the words I grew to love — for her welcoming editing, and her beautiful Radiance.

Thank you to my niece, Krisanne of Light Sisto, for coordinating the cover; for being my co-coordinator in much of what we do, and for her brilliant shine.

Thank you to my nephew, Michael Sisto, for the illumination he brings into our family and this world.

Thank you to my niece, Tracy Sisto, and nephew, Krishna Upputuri, for their luminescence.

Thank you to my friend Marie (Light) Leary for graciously offering to type this book from its hand-written pages.

Thank you to Maria (Light) Goldenberg for her friendship and constant, gentle and graceful editing.

Thank you to Lynne (Light) Knight for bringing Coyitito to the readers.

Thank you to Bernadette (Light) Conroy for her compassionate, insightful friendship and editing.

Thank you to Lorraine (Light) Litwin and her daughters: Alyssa (Light) Coons and Samantha (Light) Litwin — and her son-in-law, Rory (Light) Coons and Rose of Light Carruba.

Thank you, Susan (Light) Pepitone for listening to this story (and all the others.)

Thank you to the Day Stars: Bob Boyd, Tony Calister, Karen Del Seni, Keri Gillen, Noreen Scout Howard, Judi Irving, Adam Kulak and Kathy Parrella for listening and believing in what we all do—and for believing in this story.

Thank you to the shining smiles of Jeanne D'Angelo, Joann Galli and Jackie Vitucci—

And to those of Rosemarie Catanese, Lynn Falanga, Carol French, Amelia Giorgio and Rita Palazzola.

Thank you to Eddie Pepitone: the Laughing Star.

Thank you to the glow of Gary Siegal.

Thank you to Chi'Kuang Chang, Kenny Conroy, Elise Tirado and Ken Tirado for keeping the light shining.

Thank you to the Word Stars: Bernadette Mayer, Phil Good; Herbert Leibowitz; Morty Schiff; Jo Gillikan.

Thank you to the most recent Family Stars: Evan, Nick, Elianna and Kylie Ann; maintain your magical glow.

Thank you to the Bright Star: Sandra Miller — the world is lit much brighter for so many because of You.

Thank you to the Heavenly Stars: Donald Aaron Decker; Gladys and Dominick Vuotto; Mary and Oscar Decker; William and Helen Decker; Thomas Kravitz; John Kravitz; Carmine Gullo and Virginia Ann Hawkins Gullo; Sandra Ann Gullo Sisto; Denise Simone, John Forest Meade Kress; C.F. Borgman; Gerard Anthony Rizza.

Thank you, Poets.

And Thank you to all of You who have sat in Room 243—to all my students.

All of You—Bright Stars*

This book is dedicated to all of You.

Coyitito and the Stars

Coyitito and the Stars

SNAP.

"What was that sound?"

It woke me up, so I climbed out of the bed I shared with Tio and started to move around our room.

Out of the corner of my eye, I saw something glittering on the small wooden desk. I wasn't sure what it was. I didn't think it had been there before I went to bed.

As I tiptoed over to the desk, I kept turning around, wanting Tio to wake. He didn't. The air filled with something sweet and warm. It could have been cinnamon. I really didn't know my spices too well. I didn't spend much time in the kitchen.

And there on the desk was a plate with three cookies. I didn't know from where they came. I wanted to wake Tio and say, "Tio, look! Three cookies on a plate are on the desk." I'm surprised the scent from them didn't wake him.

"Were they all for me?" I wondered. I bent down to the plate and looked closer. I very much enjoy cookies, so typically I would eat three of them in three seconds. I wasn't sure where these came from though, so I just looked at them: round circles. The top half of each was the color of dark ink. And right in the center of the darkness was a small silver glittering; it looked like a star. I think it was a star right there in the middle of the darkness.

And the other half of the cookie was also dark, like the top half, only instead of the sky, I saw the water. It would come together to a point, like a wave. Then it seemed to be sucked back into the cookie, and when that happened, I saw the same small glittering.

I know it was the middle of the night, and this might all be a dream, and maybe my eyes were tricking me, but the glittering star above in the sky of the cookie had a matching star below in the water.

I watched this for awhile, how the star appeared and disappeared with the wave's swelling on the bottom half of the cookie, and the one above seemed to stay positioned in its dark ink place.

Magdelena and Tio needed to see this.

I wanted to go back to my bed, wake Tio who sleeps there with me since his brother Juan has gone away, far, far away. I wanted to ask Tio if he had heard the *snap*.

Magdelena was sleeping. I could run to her, past Maestra Maria's room, and say, "Magdelena, three cookies flowing back and forth are on the desk, and each one has a star above and below."

I thought Magdelena would have an answer; she always knew.

She had to be part star with all her twinkling light.

But I didn't. I stayed in the room I shared with Tio, whispering to him, though I knew he was sleeping; I could tell by the way he breathed. "Tio, are these cookies with the silver stars really here?"

Tio had to be part star, too. He looked like a star when he slept: hands and legs pointed out to the sides and his head lying straight up between his shoulders: the fifth point.

Then I realized that maybe the three cookies were for each of us.

I was so excited. I didn't know how I was going to get past Maestra Maria to wake Magdelena and tell her, "Magdelena, these three cookies — I think one is for Tio, one for you, and one for me. They must be magical cookies, Magdelena, because I think they appeared when I heard a *snap* in my dream."

But I knew I couldn't wake her now. Maestra Maria would hear me and want to know what I was doing, and what could I tell her? I couldn't tell Maestra Maria about the moving cookies. Part of me didn't believe they were there.

I decided that I needed to wake Tio, but he was sleeping so soundly and had been through a lot lately; I didn't really want to wake him, even with this news.

I would whisper to Tio very gently. If he didn't hear me, I would try to go back to sleep and explore the cookies with Magdelena and Tio in the morning.

Tio slept through my whisper, so I decided to leave him be. I thought I heard the sound of water, and it lulled me to sleep, I guess, because I woke in the morning and looked at the desk. Now I could wake Tio and we could, together, check these cookies that appeared. But they were gone.

Did I dream them? Maybe Tio had eaten them. "Tio, did you notice any cookies on the desk in the night?"

He shook his head no. I believed him. I didn't know what happened to the cookies, or if they were ever there, because they weren't now. I must have dreamed them.

Maybe it was the first time Tio slept all night since what happened to Juan. The dream cookies might have helped him.

SEVERAL WEEKS AGO, we were down at the farm where we shouldn't have been. Juan climbed on the horse's back. The farm down the street from the school kept two horses, working horses. One was mean; the other wasn't; but they were identical looking, so we really had to study them to find out which was which. They were both named Working Horse, but each had a number after him: Working Horse One and Working Horse Two. They were both black velvet with deep eyes — brown eyes — almost black. Their eyes showed their differences. Sometimes the horses were worked too hard. Maybe that's what made one mean. The mean one was very good at moving backward and rearing high into the air.

Lately, we made a game out of riding the horses. Some of our friends from the town and we would pick straws as we walked the road after our school work on summer nights. We made up rules with the straw. Some nights it was whoever got the shortest straw; that one would have to jump the fence and pick one of the horses and ride. Sometimes it was whoever got the longest. Sometimes it was whoever pulled the least amount of straw with one hand. Sometimes a number was given — seven, twelve — whoever picked that number of straws — rode. Sometimes two of us were chosen to ride, depending on the rules of the game.

I used to panic. I never told anyone, but as soon as the rules were called, and it was time to pick the straws, I would become terrified and hope the game would be stopped. Inside my head I would start a request: "It is I, Coyitito, the one who is getting ready to pull the straw. Please bring the thunder. And the strikes of lightning, so none of us rides. Please let the farmers come and chase us. Please don't let us ride today."

I renamed the mean horse Ochenta: eighty times worse.

Once, Juan and his twin brother, Tio, picked the winning straws. Juan and Tio looked exactly alike.

Juan threw himself over the fence first; Tio was right behind. They both wanted the mean horse, both wanting to spare the other, both feeling the same feelings. They spent so much time together before they were even born. I wanted to yell, as I always wanted to — "Stop." But I didn't. I joined the others around the fence and waited.

I tried to figure out which was the mean horse; I studied how they moved, but it was impossible.

No one ever said this for certain, but I think the farmers sat far back in the shadows and watched us. I think they took bets; some of them won money on who picked the mean horse, or if only one of us was riding, the bet was on which Working Horse was chosen: One or Two.

They never chased us away.

This time, Juan climbed onto one of the horses, and within seconds Ochenta reared up on his two back legs — tall — tall as the roof of the barn, and Juan slid down his back. One, two … Juan was on the ground. And he didn't move. He didn't ever move again.

The farmers did not come. Juan's brother, Tio, rode the horse he was on — the kinder horse — over the fence and down the road. Ochenta ran around in circles. He lifted his head high into the air. Then he lifted his front legs and again reared, neighing wildly. When his front legs hit the ground, he started running sideways, his eyes scorching us with their fury. Though terrified of him, I snuck through the opening in the fence. I wanted to get to Juan. The mean horse might trample him in its madness.

When Ochenta galloped to the other side of the fence, I ran over to Juan. He didn't move when I called his name. I grabbed his two hands and pulled him through the dirt. I remember how the dust drew up around us. Ochenta wasn't interested in us anymore. I pulled Juan to the edge of the fence and heard galloping. I froze. But it wasn't Ochenta — it was the other Working Horse with Juan's double sitting behind Maestra Maria as she sped to our side.

Afterwards, the people in the town said Maestra Maria was drenched in sweat when she jumped over the fence and lifted up Juan. But I knew better; I knew that Maestra Maria was weeping from every piece of her. She, too, loved Juan.

When Juan died, Tio took me as his brother. He climbed into my bed at night and put his feet up to my head, and his head to my feet. Once I saw a picture in one of our books: it was twins lying in their mother's womb. (I think it would be lying, not laying. I always have to think about that or ask Magdelena.) That's how Tio and Juan were: head to foot. So I became Tio's other, his brother — and he became mine. And then we were inseparable.

The straw games were over. We never went to the fence or the horses again. I don't know what happened with the farmers. Maestra Maria and Padre Miguel reminded us every day, several times a day, that we were not to go outside of the Protected Zone, and I don't think the farm was in the protected area. They were very concerned about what had happened, but they seemed to be gentle with us instead of stern because we were so sad. I think they didn't want to push us further into our sadness, but now it seemed they and Maestra Agatha watched us very intensely.

But one time, Tio woke in the middle of the night. He was wild; his eyes flames. He grabbed my hand, pulled me out of bed and said, "Let's go." The air was thick with heat. I never questioned Tio; I just went. The darkness was so thick that every once in a while, I closed my eyes to see if there was a difference between my eyes being open or closed; then, I said, "Tio, where are we going?" I was filled with dread for so many reasons, but I also wanted to stay with Tio. He might need me to help him.

"I want to see the horse," Tio said. "No, Tio. Padre Miguel and Maestra Maria will look for us. They will be very, very angry." Tio told me he was going with or without me, and he dropped my hand. I followed him. We walked through the courtyard toward the iron-gate. It wasn't locked, so we quietly slipped out. I wanted to say, "Tio, Tio, we are breaking our trust with Maestra Maria and Padre Miguel. Tio, no," but I didn't. I followed Tio.

When we got to the fence at the farm, Tio started to climb. Working Horse One and Working Horse Two stood inside the stall. Tio crept toward them. I climbed over the fence, too. One of the horses neighed once, and then he grew louder. They knew we were coming.

The horses started to stamp. They felt Tio. He stepped onto their straw ground. "Tio," I whispered — but he was gone from me. "Tio," a slender voice called in the night. "Tio, come here." The command was strict, but Tio only stalled for a moment — then he crept on toward the neighing and the stamp. "Tio." I turned around. She was running across the field, lit by the moonlight. Magdelena looked like a constellation, and her long hair was a shadow against the night. "Tio." She sped toward him breathing heavily.

Often she was smiling.

She wasn't smiling now. Her long hair spread out behind her, trailing light, which passed me by after she did. Maybe the stars sent Magdelena to save Tio. And me. She would typically never break the rules.

"Tio, take my hand."

He obeyed her. She led him away. I followed.

I think I have been following Magdelena for centuries.

She led Tio through the darkness, back to his bed. But before we slid through the unlocked courtyard gate, I turned around. I thought that I saw Maestra Maria behind the trees, following us.

MAESTRA MARIA ASKED Tio, Magdelena, and me to stay after school the next day. Our assignment was to draw the map of the Protected Zone over and over again. We had to draw the trees and rocks and sky and river: all of the boundary lines, and as soon as we finished, she told us to tear them up and begin again. I think we must have created the maps fifteen times before she said, "It saddens me for you three to have this assignment. Padre Miguel and I were not sure what to do. We did not want to have to lock the gate. We want you to be able to travel into the woods inside the protected area. But you leave the area, putting yourselves in grave danger.

"The school has been in a protected area for a very long time. The trees give us an idea of how long. Some of the maps are hundreds of years old. We know the boundaries of the area that is protected because we were given maps just like you are given maps. We must commit those maps to memory and destroy them so that others cannot find them and use them against us. I know you know the boundaries. But you have been crossing the lines, and we need to find a way for you to stay safe without locking the woods and rivers from you. So please, understand the limitations.

"You have been delivered to us here at the school for a purpose." She didn't say anymore.

What did Maestra Maria mean we were delivered for a purpose? What was the purpose? I wanted to ask her; I wanted to say, "Maestra Maria, what do you mean?" But I dared not ask her. Neither did Tio or Magdelena. I needed to ask them later what Maestra Maria meant. Maybe they knew.

I hoped Tio understood what Maestra Maria was saying about the limitations. I understood. I'm sure Magdelena did, also. I don't know about Tio.

We ripped our drawings of trees and north, south, east and west into shreds, which Maestra Maria threw into a small barrel of flames.

I decided that Maestra Maria had to be a star.

When Padre Miguel and Maestra Maria first taught us about the protected area, we would go outside and memorize the formations of the trees and rocks. Then we would come back and draw what we saw. Every day they made sure we did this. And we would always destroy our drawings after we drew them. Even now, we participated in daily visual lessons about the Protected Zone, noticing any changes the earth might make on the rocks and the trees and the way they appeared against the sky.

"Notice," said Padre Miguel, and we would all understand his command and take notice.

MAGDELENA OFTEN TOOK TIO'S HANDS after Juan died. That's something she started doing when she led him away from the fence the night he went to do whatever he was going to do to the horse that killed his brother. She led Tio as he grieved, and I stayed behind them, ready to help if needed.

I wanted Magdelena to hold my hands, too. Once, Magdelena, Tio, and I walked in the woods toward our friend The River, and she reached for my hand. Then we three walked like that: Magdelena in the middle, and each of us at her sides.

One night, I awoke. It was very dark. We had worked hard during the day, preparing the school, inside and outside, for a large festival. The people from the town would come soon and bring their special treats, and everyone would dance. We worked hard in the garden and in the classroom.

Maestra Maria reminded us every morning in class how important it was for everything to look welcoming. She would tell us, "We want our guests to feel welcome." Everything always looked perfect, so I'm sure they would feel welcome even if we didn't do all this work. But I didn't say that to Maestra Maria. None of us complained about Maestra Maria, really. She was very kind to all of us. Strict, but kind.

When I woke up in the night, my limbs were so tired, and my eyes were sore. I looked for Tio. He wasn't there. He was often disappearing lately, and I was always trying to find him. He seemed to be able to camouflage himself, and I wasn't always able to find him. I only hoped he was staying in the Protected Zone.

Somehow, Padre Miguel knew of Tio's recent disappearances. He was very concerned. I know he called Tio into his office, the big office with the big desk, and had a talk with him. Tio respected Padre Miguel deeply, but he was so sad; that is what sent him outside at night, I think. I think he must have said, "Yes, Padre Miguel; I will do as you say." But he didn't. And I was afraid Padre Miguel would become very upset with Tio and send him away, even though Padre Miguel loved Tio and us very, very much.

I woke up alarmed. How many more chances would Padre Miguel give Tio? I thought that I would need to start breaking more of the rules, too, so if Tio were sent away, I would be, also. Maybe they would send us to the same place together. Little did I know Padre Miguel would never send Tio away. Or me.

"Where are you?" I whispered as I ran barefoot and frightened into the woods, keeping the map of protection visible in my head, checking the trees and the ground, trying to find Tio in one of his hiding places before Padre Miguel and Maestra Maria knew he was gone, not realizing that they seemed to always know where we were these days and nights. "Where are you, Tio?" I whispered, hoping he was in the Protected Zone.

One time, when I was searching for Tio, I saw red coals glowing in the darkness. "Someone is here," I thought. Tio wouldn't light a fire; he would not want to call attention to himself in that way. He would hide and watch. I heard sounds. I knew I shouldn't stay, but I had to find Tio. Men were talking not far from me. I knew I had to go, but what if they had Tio? All of a sudden, I heard a noise very nearby. I froze. Tio scurried down from a tree next to me; he grabbed my hand and ran.

"Tio, are they the Ones without Faces?" I whispered. We learned about them, the Ones called No Faces, but Padre Miguel taught us, along with Maestra Maria, that if we were in the Protected Zone, we would be safe. I wasn't sure why that was so. I didn't dare ask. I did ask Magdelena and Tio, but they didn't have the answer. "Just trust that it is so," Magdelena told me. Tio didn't respond at all. So I tried to follow the advice of Magdelena, though I often wondered if she wanted to know more, too, though something told me that she just trusted it to be that way.

"Even though it is safe," said Padre Miguel, and Maestra Maria would back this up, "one must always be very, very careful, because one never knows."

Sometimes when he was talking to us, and laughing with us, he would throw questions at us about what marking a certain tree had in the south, or which rock we should be aware of to know our limits. Then I would see how his eyes reached up and searched over the fence and out into the woods. And we knew; we were aware, that we must be cautious.

But Tio wasn't afraid, so he went out there into the woods, while I, I, Coyitito, was terrified.

Tio took my hand. He knew the woods. I was sweating with terror. I tried not to step on any branches. He led me around that night, the way Magdelena led him.

Someone was very close. I stopped moving. So did Tio. I froze behind a tree. Someone was walking very, very nearby. "Are we in the Zone?" I wanted to ask Tio. My knees knocked together. Tio was right next to me, but he seemed to disappear. I didn't. I knew I would be seen. I had to talk to Tio about hiding in the woods. It wasn't a good idea for him or me.

All of a sudden, someone was moving in the trees ahead of us. At first, it was just a shadow, but then the moonlight fell on the man's face. I inhaled deeply, making a sliver of a sound. The man did not turn to us, but Tio and I both knew that we had to follow him back to the school, so we did. We trailed behind Padre Miguel who entered the courtyard before us, leaving the gate open.

We shut it, went through the door and into our room. Tio climbed into bed and seemed to fall asleep right away. I waited for Padre Miguel. I knew he would be very, very angry, and I hoped that he wouldn't send us away — not yet.

Moments later, he appeared in our doorway.

I quickly closed my eyes and waited for him. He seemed to be as big as the door frame. "Tonight you did stay in the area of protection, Tio, keeping you and Coyitito safe. And I know that you feel the need to wander, and your friends Coyitito and Magdelena want to keep you safe, but at night you need to stay within the walls of the courtyard because the woods can be dangerous, and I need some sleep." I heard him move away. I squinted to look, and he was gone. Tio and I didn't move. I think he did fall asleep while I was wide-eyed thinking of ways to keep Tio inside the courtyard at night.

Days later, before high noon, Magdelena led us to The River. "Listen. She calls to us. Do you hear her, Coyitito? Tio, do you hear her? She tells us to visit her and swim. Get your swimming trunks. I'm all packed."

Magdelena knew The River was in the protected area, so she knew it was safe. She asked Maestra Maria if we could go to The River, and Maestra Maria must have said yes because all of a sudden, one afternoon, we were on our way. Just the three of us walked the path in the woods toward the sound of the water.

Tio let go of Magdelena's hand and ran. She released my hand to follow him. I wanted to be close to Magdelena; I wanted to keep holding her hand. "Magdelena," I called inside my head. "Magdelena," but she was running far ahead of me, so I had to run to catch up.

I still hadn't told her about the cookies, which appeared on my desk with two small glittering stars. I decided I must have been dreaming, but I still wanted to tell Magdelena to see what she thought.

When I reached them, Tio was already at the water's edge. Then he raced into the water.

Before, when Juan was still here, Tio and he would keep each other laughing in bed at night. We all shared a room then: Manuel, Tio, Juan, and I, so their laughing kept Manuel and me awake, and I think we wished that we could climb into their beds and get into their laughter. They would laugh as quietly as possible, but sometimes Maestra Maria or Padre Miguel would come in and tell them that they were keeping the trees awake.

Then Manuel moved into another room down the hall. He doesn't have to share rooms anymore because he is older than all of us. He is the oldest, and the one with the most years gets special privileges, like a room to oneself. So with Juan gone and Manuel down the hall, Tio and I share our room — and that is fine with me.

Back at The River, Magdelena looked at Tio and then me.

Then she ran into the water, yelling, "River, River I hear you calling me. I hear you calling we three." Then she turned my way and said, "Come on, Coyitito!"

I couldn't move. I was frozen. How could I run into the water where Magdelena swam so joyously and unafraid? I was so nervous to be that close to her in the water, to swim with her. Magdelena looked very, very lovely, and I felt very shy.

Maybe I would just stay out here and keep watch.

Magdelena and Tio both disappeared underwater. I shuddered. When they re-emerged, they were laughing. From where I still stood, I watched their legs kicking in the clear water. Then Magdelena's head popped up from under followed by Tio.

They both watched and waited for me to come rushing into the water, joining them. It was very difficult for me to have them looking at me, waiting for me. Tio swam off. Magdelena swam toward me — and then she did the unthinkable. Magdelena rose out of the water and headed toward me. She was coming to get me.

She glistened. Sparkled. Yes, she was a star. Her cold river hand reached for mine. "Come on, Coyitito. It is fun. The River wants you to come and play." I couldn't speak to her.

Then I said to her, "Magdelena, I will come into the water, but you must first count to ten, and then I will be there in the water with you."

She laughed herself back into the water and said, "Coyitito, if you are not here by the time I reach ten, I will be back to get you."

She splashed and swam toward Tio, and I ran the other way.

"Just keep running," I told myself. I wanted to jump into the water with Magdelena, just like Tio was there with her, but I felt more shy than ever about swimming with her.

"Run faster," I heard from inside me. Then I wondered if Magdelena and Tio would get back safely. I wondered if the No Faces had soundlessly crawled down the canyon rocks somehow breaking through the Protected Zone. I wondered if someone or something would get Magdelena or Tio, so I turned around.

And when I did, I heard it. Unmistakable. The sound of the horses: the snort, the hoof on a branch, on leaves. How many horses were there? Who rode them? I needed to hide. I hoped Tio and Magdelena were quiet. I stood silent to see from which way the sound came. I would move quickly behind a set of trees, and hopefully, oh very, very hopefully, I would blend in.

It sounded like many horses, maybe many No Faces. "Oh no," I shuddered. The other day I heard Padre Miguel talking to the man who had come, delivering two donkeys to help with the work. The man came down over the mountain, and he had many stories. Padre Miguel met the man at the gate and greeted him.

They shook hands; Padre Miguel gave him water.

They led the donkeys around the back to the field and stood under a tree. The donkeys walked the field. Padre Miguel believed that anyone or anything that came to stay needed to get used to being there right away. So he watched the donkeys as he talked to the man. And they didn't know that I was nearby. At least, I don't think they did, but it was hard to fool Padre Miguel. I think the donkeys maybe knew; they looked my way. I looked theirs. But the man didn't notice me, and I listened to them.

The man spoke slowly, and Padre Miguel listened slowly. He nodded. He let the man talk. He squinted his eyes the way he does, and he listened the way he does. Sometimes the breeze came, and the words were taken away from me but I did hear something about the No Faces and the caves. The man with the donkeys tried to travel away from the No Faces — where he thought they might be — but one time — when he was going down a steep path — riding the first donkey as it traveled as close to the edge as a piece of hair — he saw what he thought was them. Down below him. And he had no option because they seemed to know he was coming, and their horses knew, too. So he rode on the donkey toward them — filled with dread.

When he reached the bottom, it turned out that they weren't No Faces, and they welcomed him and shared food and stories about some of the Ones in the canyons who were dangerous. And they told him which way to go where he would be most safe. They gave him good advice, and he changed his direction at the crossroads, and didn't meet any dangerous Ones. He trusted them.

Padre Miguel seemed to trust him.

When he left, Padre Miguel stood by the tree in the yard, looking up into the sky. Then Padre Miguel turned my way and wandered toward his office.

I was remembering this as I stood in the woods near The River listening to the approaching hooves. Behind the trees, I waited. I held my breath. The horses would be passing me at any moment. Then the first rider appeared in front of me. Maestra Maria appeared on a horse. I was sure not to move.

She wasn't going very fast and really no one was behind her. All those hooves I heard — all that commotion was really only one horse and rider. I was very quiet, so I could watch Maestra Maria ride by on her horse. I absorbed myself into the air so I could watch her as long as possible. What was she doing? Was she checking on us?

I wanted to call out to her; I wanted to say, "Maestra Maria, Maestra Maria, I, Coyitito, am over here," but I remained silent.

Was this really Maestra Maria? It wasn't often I was able to see Maestra Maria in this way: riding through the woods.

Laughter. Someone was coming. Maestra Maria halted her horse and listened. More laughter. She quietly steered her horse into the trees, waiting behind the foliage.

The voices came closer.

I was again stunned.

Maestra Maria was across from me among the leaves. I couldn't really see her, but I saw the cloud of her horse, and her black hair. And then I realized that maybe, somehow, the protected area had been invaded, and if it were, I might need to save Maestra Maria from the Ones who were coming.

Tio and Magdelena were still wet with the river when they rounded the corner. I stepped out from the trees. "Ten!" Magdelena laughed as she reached for my hand. When I looked into the trees again, Maestra Maria was gone.

IN OUR CLASSROOM, I looked at the inkwell on my desk. Today Maestra Maria was going to teach us about poetry and how to write a poem. "How do you write a poem, Maestra Maria? How do you know if it is a poem?" came a voice from the back of the room.

Maestra Maria's eyes rose and fell on each of us. "Let us go to the place where poetry is unleashed," she said.

"Where is that?" was Manuel's second question.

Usually, Maestra Maria didn't want us calling out, but today she let Manuel bellow his questions without raising his hand.

"Today is without restriction — for you and your poetry," she said. "When we write today, we will halt the meter we have been studying in the rhythm of the classic poets; we shall let rhyme tumble down a hill. Today we want to visit poetry's living quarters, and each of you will find poetry where it resides."

I sat near the window listening to Maestra Maria. I could listen to her all day every day. I knew she said we didn't have restrictions today, and Tio was probably thinking that meant he could run out of the classroom, down to The River, and go for a swim. I'm sure we were thinking about what we could do if we were unrestricted. Then, I thought about listening to Maestra Maria and catching glimpses of Magdelena as she listened, also, so attentive to Maestra Maria or whoever was talking.

Today, Magdelena was sitting in front of me. We often changed where we sat. Maestra Maria thought it best if we changed our seats. She thought it "broadened our perspective." I always wanted to sit next to Magdelena.

Sometimes Lucinda was next to me.

★★★

PADRE MIGUEL AND MAESTRA MARIA NAMED US when they found us at the door, or gate, or on the sides of the road, or in the woods. They told us that they chose their favorite names for us or the names of their favorite people.

Maestra Maria also told us, whenever we wanted to hear the story, and sometimes Padre Miguel would repeat it, that Magdelena, Juan, Tio, and I appeared on the same day. She found Juan and Tio at the gate when she went out in the morning. "They were unmistakably identical from the very first moment I saw them." She said that they appeared to be a few days old, wrapped in the same colorful blanket, side-by-side.

Later that morning, a donkey appeared at the gate. Maestra Maria went out to investigate and found, in the donkey's saddle, an infant wrapped in a light cloth. "Who do we have here?" she asked. And there, right in front of Maestra Maria, was Magdelena, who appeared to be one month old. Maestra Maria cradled Magdelena into her arms.

While Maestra Maria and Maestra Agatha busied their morning with three new arrivals, Padre Miguel walked through the woods. On his way back to the school, he said that he heard sounds among the trees, so he headed in that direction because the sounds seemed to come from someone who was very, very young. When he was closer, he looked down to where the sounds were, and there I was on a bed of leaves. He said that I wasn't crying; it was more like I was talking, so he talked to me. He immediately said to me, "Coyitito, you have found me," and he lifted me up and carried me back to the school, where Maestra Maria yelled down the hallway when she heard him enter: "Padre Miguel, three children came to us today."

"Four," he joyfully responded to her. And she came out to meet me and took me in her arms. "Meet Coyitito," Padre Miguel said. "Hello, Coyitito," Maestra Maria said, and she kissed my head. "He seems to be one to two weeks old."

And then Maestra Maria brought Padre Miguel and me into the room where Magdelena, Tio, and Juan were.

Maestra Maria told Padre Miguel that she had named Magdelena, and her beautiful name matched all her other beauty. Then Padre Miguel asked Maestra Maria to name one of the twins and he would name the other.

"I will name you for all my favorite uncles; we shall call you Tio," said Padre Miguel. Maestra Maria agreed, and she herself had one very favorite uncle named Juan. So that's how we four found our names — and our places here at the school.

I think there was more to the story, something about finding us all on the same day. Padre Miguel stopped mentioning it, but I know I heard him talk about it when I was very, very little. He would use the word we later learned in our vocabulary unit: *auspicious*. I didn't know the word at the time, but it stayed with me, and when we learned it, I remembered that Padre Miguel used to say that: finding the four of us on the same day was *auspicious*. And my being in a bed of leaves in the woods meant something to him. And now with Juan gone, I wondered if we were still that way: *auspicious*.

Maestra Maria's voice brought me back into the moment.

"It is time to find your poems." "Go," she said. "Go visiting."

And each in our own way, we went.

I had never been there before, but I think I knew when I arrived. I felt it; I, Coyitito, felt poetry. It came in all different kinds of weather; that's where poetry lived. Some of the weather I had only read about, but never experienced. Of course I knew summer; I always lived in summer. But I had not known the cold. I had not felt the snow. But poetry lived there among the icicles. My toes had never frozen; neither had my hair or eyelashes. Yet here I was — in winter — a place I had never been — leaving footprints in the snow.

"Am I supposed to be in winter, Maestra Maria?" I whispered to her as she passed silently around the room. She dropped her ear further toward my voice.

"Yes." Yes, I was supposed to be in winter.

In the place where poetry lived, I watched Magdelena emerge on a horse from the side of a snow-covered mountain. I was an owl, perched on a pine bough. She passed right by me — right in front of me — and I watched her — watched how the snow fell onto her — watched how her black hair moved the mountains as it lifted and fell. Magdelena's dark eyes scanned the sky and the mountain but didn't find me. The snowflakes fell, and Magdelena's hair swallowed them.

"Let us share," said Maestra Maria. I froze in the heat of the classroom. "Share?" I thought. How could I share the place I visited with Magdelena, who was riding in the snow? What could I say?"

"In poetry, it is important that we all share something," Maestra Maria said. She always did this: wanted us to feel comfortable sharing. I didn't usually mind, but this time I would rather keep what I had seen private.

"Who wants to begin?"

Magdelena raised her hand.

"Where did you go, Magdelena?"

"I went to the woods. I followed two boys who walked among the trees.

"I followed them to the canyon, where a river flowed. And we three bent down to taste the water. When we looked up, the sky was filled with stars, though it was still daylight."

I thought that Maestra Maria's eyes registered the place by The River. I saw Magdelena's stars.

"And is that a place you would go to find a poem, Magdelena?"

"Yes, Maestra Maria, yes it is," Magdelena smiled.

Magdelena dipped her pen in the ink and began again to write.

"What about you, Coyitito? What can you share with us?" she questioned.

Tio was sitting at his desk traveling in his own world, but he kept silent.

"Perhaps you are not ready yet, Coyitito?" I needed more time. I was hoping I would read toward the end of the sharing and maybe I could offer just one sentence.

"Where did you go, Tio?" she asked. "You can keep it simple if you would prefer that. One word could be enough for you to share."

Maestra Maria was very gentle with Tio. I think everyone was.

"I went inside the horse. My legs were its legs. My nose grew its way. I felt its heart pump. I stood on its rear legs. And then, right before Juan slipped, I put the horse's front legs back down on the ground."

Maestra Maria stared at Tio for some moments, water in her eyes. She moved to the place where Tio sat and put her hand on his shoulder. He shook his head to one side, got up, and walked out of the room. I followed him with my eyes. Magdelena asked Maestra Maria for permission to join Tio and left the room in search of him.

We were very, very quiet. Then Manuel spoke from the last row. "I'll tell you where I went, Maestra Maria."

Maestra Maria still ached with Tio's pain; I could see it. So did I. We most likely all did, even Manuel, but I think he was trying to help Maestra Maria and us recover from Tio's visit inside the horse and the aching loss of Juan.

"Do tell us where you visited, Manuel," said Maestra Maria's voice. Her eyes were still heavy with sadness.

"First I went to Paris and drank café on a boulevard. Many people walked the streets wearing leather shoes and small hats. Then I went to Italy and ate spaghetti with a fork and spoon. I flew in an airplane above the clouds, on top of the rainstorm and over the jungle, where I saw a lion sit at the feet of a gigantic giraffe. And when my plane landed, I danced a tango down the steps, onto the pavement where you stood, Maestra Maria. I danced over to you, offering my hand for you to join me. Right there, right below the wing of the airplane, you joined me in a tango."

Manuel could say this to Maestra Maria without insulting her. He could probably even do it. She did not take offense at what he said; he did not mean for her to. And he made us smile with his vision, lifting the storm clouds, which filled our classroom and Tio's empty desk.

Maestra Maria surprised us: she put a pencil between her teeth and took two dance steps. We all applauded.

Then she continued her dance steps my way.

"Do you feel comfortable sharing any part of your visit with us, Coyitito?"

"I was in the winter snow."

★★★

THE NEXT TIME Magdelena, Tio, and I went to The River, I ran in first. When I saw that we were getting close to the water, I dashed ahead. I ran from the back of the line, ran past Tio, then Magdelena, running straight to The River's edge, and I took the plunge before they did.

Magdelena was soon behind me. Then Tio. Then we heard it: someone was coming. Tio swam fast, up and out of The River, telling us to follow; we mustn't pause. And we did; we followed him. We ran into the woods, full with The River's drops. We ran quickly as we heard the gallop. Tio was hardly ever afraid; he instead went into action.

He led us to a small cave behind layers of trees; it was almost invisible. A cave appeared before the one we entered, and I would have headed for the first one, but Tio didn't. He later told me, when I asked him why he did this, that if someone were to follow us, they would look in the first cave before they reached the second. The second cave was really very good because it had small tunnels, and if we bent down and crawled on our hands and knees, we could go various ways. We huddled into a corner of the cave. Tio entered last; his quick eyes scanned the land before he ducked among us. "Aren't we in the Protected Zone?" I asked. "I believe we are," Magdelena said, "but Padre Miguel says that we must always be very careful. Did you see who was coming, Tio?" Tio shook his head no. "Maybe it's Padre Miguel," I said. "Maybe he is checking on us."

The galloping was definitely headed to where we had been at The River. The Dangerous Ones would look for us. "Magdelena," I whispered. "Are we protected here?"

Magdelena placed her finger over her lips.

The galloping stopped by the first cave. My courage fled. Tio stood motionless. Magdelena listened. "Hello to you three inside the cave. It is safe to come out now." Tio turned and led us in another direction. The ceiling was so low we crawled on all fours.

"I am here to tell you that I am one of your protectors."

"I will wait for you in the four directions, until you come out of your hiding place. I will wait because I want you to know that I will not harm you. There are others who might not think like me, but I will make sure that when you come to The River, you stay safe.

"Yes, The River is in the Protected Zone, but you never know," said the voice outside the cave.

"I have seen you before; you three: two of you swam the last time here; one of you didn't. I kept watch for you because it is helpful to have protectors, even in the Zone. I am Don Pedro. I am your friend."

We all looked at each other, and even though we might be wrong, we decided to believe him because we were in the protected area.

When we crawled out to meet him, he told us not to believe everyone who says they are our friend these days, even in the Protected Zone.

But he was our friend; Padre Miguel and Maestra Maria said it was true when Don Pedro came back to the school with us.

SOON AFTER, it was a special moon night, which meant we celebrated with a festival and invited some guests from town. Music played, and some danced.

Manuel was already in the center of the field dancing.

Besides the tango, he loved the flamenco. So did I, really, but I wasn't good at dancing. When Manuel danced the flamenco, he seemed to become a bird that spread its wings and rose from the ground. Maybe that's why he loved airplanes. And there he was, spinning and jumping.

He began asking people to dance with him. One time, he even asked Tio, and believe it or not, for about fifteen seconds, Tio allowed Manuel to dance him around the field. I don't know what came over Tio, but he did. Manuel asked every girl or lady to dance with him. Every girl or lady who was in Manuel's presence danced with him.

His eyes focused on Magdelena. She, too, was a very good dancer. Magdelena took his outstretched hand.

When Manuel and Magdelena danced, everyone watched.

Magdelena stomped toward Manuel, and he lifted her high up into the air. He twirled her around as if she was a big beautiful bird. Maestra Maria watched keenly as Padre Miguel moved away from her and toward some of the invited guests.

I watched Tio watch Magdelena. She winked his way. I wanted her to wink at me. I wanted to dance with her like Manuel did.

Then Manuel put her gently back to the ground. And once again, she did the unthinkable: she came over to me and said, "Dance with me, Coyitito."

It was hard to deny Magdelena. I couldn't dance so well; I hesitated. "Follow me," she said, and I did; I followed her. I held her hand too tightly, but she let me, and she led me swirling around the field until we were both spinning, our outstretched hands holding each other's. The clouds swirled, the trees swirled; we laughed and became so dizzy we fell on the ground.

And we stayed like that watching the clouds take shape.

"You know what I see in that one, Coyitito? I see a door. See. Quick. Look. And look, Coyitito, look how the door is opening. Do you see that?"

Yes, I did see it just the way Magdelena did. And when the cloud moved a bit more, opening the door further, inside was a glowing star.

"Coyitito, look. Inside the door is a star. Do you see it?"

"Yes, Magdelena, I see the star." And I wanted to tell her; I wanted to say, "Magdelena, what if we could fly and go visit a star?" But instead Magdelena said to me, "Coyitito, what do you think Maestra Maria meant when she said we have a purpose?"

All of a sudden, Maestra Maria stood over us.

"Join us for the ending dance," she beamed as she dropped her hands to ours.

★★★

WHEN SCHOOL FINISHED THE NEXT DAY, Tio headed for The River. It was very hot, and swimming would be refreshing. I joined him, though I thought we should check with Padre Miguel before we left. It seemed like we should ask or tell someone, even though The River was safe.

Magdelena caught up to us. I really thought she was going to try to stop us, but instead she said that she had heard The River calling us all afternoon. "We really need to check with Padre Miguel before we go," she said. Actually, she said The River started calling us early this morning. It was so loud that she woke up early, very, very early; the sun was just thinking about starting to come out; the dogs were just settling down after a long night of yapping, and it was then, when they silenced, that Magdelena said she heard The River begin to call, and then, many, many times throughout the day, she sent invitations to us.

Padre Miguel had come into our classroom three times during the day; he rarely visits, if ever, three times. Usually he comes by once a day in the morning to wish us a good morning. Maestra Maria has taught us that always when Padre Miguel enters the room, we are to stand and say, "Good morning, Padre Miguel." "Good afternoon, Padre Miguel."

I knew it was still morning, so Padre Miguel had come by three times, and it was still morning. And even though he tried to smile, he looked troubled, and I didn't think that he was troubled because Tio, Magdelena, and I were in the woods; he looked more troubled than that.

The gates were locked when we tried to go through them.

Magdelena said we needed to write a letter to The River, to say we weren't coming. She said that when you are invited and the person inviting really wants you to come — and you don't show up — that is a big insult. She said we couldn't insult The River like that because The River began inviting us today at sun-break, and now it was hours later, and with all the fuss around the invitation, we weren't coming. We had to tell The River why; in the past, we had school, chores, and homework, but we still came. "We don't really have to write it," said Magdelena. "We have to tell it and let the breeze take our words there like it took The River's words to us."

We noticed that there was hardly any breeze, but we did what Magdelena suggested.

"Why don't you tell The River, Tio, why we aren't coming?"

"River, we are not coming because Padre Miguel locked the gates."

"Add something, Coyitito."

"River, we are not coming today because when we tried to leave the courtyard, the gates were locked. Forgive us."

Magdelena added, "Thank you, River, for your invitation. At the moment, we are locked in. Please understand."

IT TOOK SEVERAL DAYS for The River to respond. And then she did. She sent us a message.

We were in the classroom. The sky had been sunny all morning: bright and clear. Then a storm cloud moved in during our grammar lesson. Maestra Maria was working on the subjunctive tense with us. "Wish." "Could." "Seemed." "Seem."

My personal favorite was the future conditional. "If only The River would answer."

"Coyitito, will you please give us an example of the subjunctive," said Maestra Maria.

"I wish … I could … dance like Manuel."

Then the storm clouds darkened the sky. And then the thunder came booming through the open windows. Then lightning struck above the trees.

I'm sure Tio was thinking about how he wished he could be swimming.

Then, in the fierce storm, we heard it: the galloping. We all looked toward the window. Even Maestra Maria looked outside to the road. And then we heard the front bell ringing, and we knew someone had come. And I knew The River had sent that someone.

Tio knew too. His ears perked up.

And Magdelena was certain. She drew The River on a piece of paper, and when she held it up this time, Tio nodded, and so did I.

The bell rang again before someone answered the gate. Maestra Agatha usually answered the bells, and we watched out the window as she carried the big rainbow-colored umbrella and moved quickly in the storm toward the ringing.

We heard her ask, "Who's there?"

It seemed as if she wasn't sure if it were friend or other who appeared at the entrance to the gate.

The storm continued, and the horse outside with its rider stomped around. I know that the dogs don't like the storms, and they try to hide wherever they can when the storm strikes. It is also the same with some of the horses.

The donkeys didn't care about the storms, but Maestra Agatha did. She was brave to be out there. I'm sure Padre Miguel would have gone, or Maestra Maria, but Maestra Agatha was often the gatekeeper, and she seemed proud of it.

Maestra Maria's eyes were fixed at the gate. She moved away from the window.

I saw Maestra Agatha at the gate.

"What is your example for the subjunctive, Magdelena?"

As Magdelena began to tell Maestra Maria and us her subjunctive story, a voice called from the other side of the gate, "It is I: Don Pedro." And we knew The River had sent him.

Padre Miguel walked quickly into our classroom; we all stood up to greet him, but I could tell he didn't have time for this today. Once we were up, he stopped and listened to our greeting; then he greeted us back. Then he moved to Maestra Maria's ear, and he whispered her way. I watched her face; so did Tio and Magdelena. We watched her, and the calm covering of her face seemed to change for a moment.

Maestra Agatha came into our classroom.

Padre Miguel left with Maestra Maria.

Outside, the bell rang again.

"It is I, Don Pedro."

"Why does Don Pedro have to wait?" I wondered.

Padre Miguel walked to the gate. He carried the circle of keys. We saw him unlock the doors and open them. I saw Don Pedro's hat as he rode into the yard. Padre Miguel looked up at him. Don Pedro disappeared with Padre Miguel. Maestra Maria was nowhere to be seen.

"All right," Maestra Agatha said. "How many of you have finished your story?"

"Our story?" I didn't know what she was talking about. I hadn't written any story. And I knew that she would follow Maestra Maria's lesson, so soon we would all need to share, and I had nothing written.

"All right. Finish up, and in a few moments, we will share."

Manuel volunteered to go first. "I wished on Monday that it would be Sunday. I wished on Tuesday that Saturday would exchange days with it. I hoped on Friday to dance on Saturday night. It seems to me that the days blend. I wish to become an airplane pilot."

"Maybe you will, Manuel."

"And you, Juan, what did you write your story about?"

Maestra Agatha did that sometimes; she confused the names of Juan and Tio. And it was very painful, even for her when she would realize that she again got the name wrong.

I had seen her do that the first time she called Tio, "Juan". It was soon after Juan died, and Tio was still fresh in his scars. Maestra Agatha called Tio, "Juan" and he ran out of the room.

We could not find him for several hours. Magdelena and I looked everywhere.

I went to the building we use as a tool shed. In there, I saw Maestra Agatha.

I watched her for a while wishing for Tio to return. I decided to lay my head down on the cool floor, and when I did that, I saw Tio. He was under one of the benches curled up. I guess no one thought to look for Tio in there because it wasn't his favorite place to be. He wanted to be outside, so others were outside, looking up into the trees; some had even gone to the farm where Ochenta was, but the whole time Tio was lying on the cement floor in the tool shed. He knew I saw him, and he placed a finger over his lips for me to be quiet.

This caused a conflict for me because I wanted to do what Tio asked, but others were looking for him. Magdelena was frenzied, and so was Maestra Maria. Padre Miguel, himself, was outside somewhere, maybe outside of the protected area, searching for Tio.

Then Maestra Agatha turned because now she heard me. She stood up, came by me and whispered, "I have asked for help in finding Tio." And with that she left, and I was there with Tio.

So I walked out into the courtyard, and, thankfully, he followed me. Word spread; Tio was back. And his heart was heavy with the sadness of Juan, so Tio didn't get into trouble with Maestra Maria or Padre Miguel.

Back in the classroom, Tio answered Maestra Agatha's question.

"I wish I were my brother. Tio wishes he were Juan. We wished we would both be alive together, riding horses and swimming in rivers."

Maestra Agatha's face dropped.

"I am very sorry, Tio. Very, very sorry."

Maestra Maria entered the classroom. She sensed something was wrong. I wondered where she had been.

She had a way of knowing. She didn't ask what had happened, but she told us to rise, so we could take a walk in the courtyard. It was still raining some, but the thunder and lightning had left. So we stood up and found our places. Magdelena changed spots with Lucinda, so she would be Tio's partner. I was behind them. Even though we didn't need to, Magdelena reached for Tio's hand. He let her take it.

I saw Maestra Agatha heading away from us.

"Let's get some fresh air," Maestra Maria said, and "let's move from the subjunctive into the present."

So we went out into the courtyard. Don Pedro and Padre Miguel were nowhere to be seen.

And that was the last we saw of Padre Miguel for a while. He just disappeared.

People from the town heard about it and kept coming by to see if he had returned.

Maestra Maria was concerned, but I thought that I saw in her something that waited before she worried too much. I asked Magdelena if she saw this, and she said that "yes," she did see that same waiting.

I even went into the tool shed and looked under the seats to see if he was hiding there, like Tio did.

Magdelena told me she searched everywhere: she even looked underneath the donkeys just in case he was there.

And Tio, he climbed the trees. I saw him scurrying up a tree, looking through the leaves, scanning all around; then coming down, moving to a few trees over; then going up again.

Seeing Tio run through the trees made me remember how Tio and Juan climbed together; they did everything together. They lived in a world of action.

Once school was over, Tio and Juan would race each other into the courtyard, and when they reached a finish line, they would race to the library for homework. They definitely raced through homework. One of them did half the homework; the other one did the other half, and then they would race through copying what the other wrote.

"You both have the same incorrect answers," Maestra Maria would say to Juan and Tio.

And then they would race outside, down to the field where they'd kick a ball back and forth, after which they raced to the trees and climbed. Each of them chose a tree or a side of the tree and up they went — and then sometimes they would stay there — just the two of them disappearing.

And even though some of us climbed the trees too, even though we could go up there and join them, somehow we knew that this was their world. All theirs. And none of us ever climbed into their world up in the trees.

Except Padre Miguel.

He didn't look as if he could climb trees, but one time Tio and Juan were gone so long; they didn't come down, and night was coming, and the owls were getting ready, and the dogs were howling away in the distance. No one could find Juan and Tio; then Padre Miguel appeared.

"Which tree did they climb?" he asked us while we stood in the field watching. Maestra Maria and Maestra Agatha came with lanterns.

"That one," Lucinda pointed.

We knew that it didn't matter what tree they went up into; they could have hopped into other trees by now.

Padre Miguel counted three trees over and began to climb. Some of the light was still out. Maestra Agatha told him to be careful, but I could tell, once Padre Miguel started climbing, that he had climbed before. Many times — because Padre Miguel pretty much walked straight up the tree and settled on one of the top branches, one that would hold him.

And then he called out:

"Juan, Tio."

And their two heads emerged.

And down all three of them came.

For a while, no one was allowed to climb the trees, but one day someone climbed again, and Juan and Tio were back in the branches.

Someone said that Juan and Tio built a house somewhere up there in the branches, but no one ever found it.

Maybe Padre Miguel did.

But now Padre Miguel wasn't here, and people began telling stories about what might have happened to him.

Some people said the Ones called No Faces came and took him.

Others said that he might be a No Face himself and that he was training all of us at the school to be just like him. I didn't believe this. Neither did Magdelena. We didn't even ask Tio if he thought this was true.

Some said he owed Don Pedro in some way, so Don Pedro took him, kidnapped him until he paid up.

I think someone said something about Padre Miguel leaving in the night to go and find another who had also disappeared. I heard Maestra Agatha tell someone that Dona Catalina Williams had disappeared too. She was the wife of Dr. Williams. Dona Williams often came to visit Padre Miguel. She baked cakes for us, but especially for him. He was fond of the tres leche cake, and Dona Catalina Williams was known all over the town and beyond, they say, for her blending of the tres leche.

Even though Dona Catalina Williams had much money and help in the kitchen, she baked her own cakes, and she would come, she would ride her horse to the gate.

On the horse's back, along with her, was a basket. She and the basket would come down off her horse and go into the office of Padre Miguel.

We smelled her perfume when he brought her into the classroom.

"Good morning, Padre Miguel."

"Good morning, Dona Williams," we would say.

She would ask us if we wanted to hear a story. She would always ask Maestra Maria if it was permissible for her to interrupt our lesson with a story. Maestra Maria would politely allow her. I don't know if she really liked it because Maestra Maria didn't like to be interrupted.

But that was when Padre Miguel was still here. Now he wasn't, and Maestra Maria was in charge. Even when Padre Miguel was here, he relied on Maestra Maria. She was really the one who knew everything.

Maestra Maria called a meeting between the town and the school together, so we could all ask for the safe return of Padre Miguel. He had been gone several days, and I guess she was starting to worry about him. All the townspeople came.

Dr. Williams came with all his family, including Dona Williams. She was back home, so she wasn't with Padre Miguel. We didn't find out where she had been, but I am sure that Maestra Maria and Maestra Agatha knew and checked with her for the possible whereabouts of Padre Miguel. I am sure that someone besides Dona Williams knew where she had been, but we didn't.

Dona Williams brought her delicious sweet cakes and tres leche cake, Padre Miguel's favorite desserts. She told Maestra Maria that perhaps Padre Miguel would smell their aroma and come back to us.

I wondered if Maestra Maria thought that it might be the aroma of Dona Williams' perfume that would bring Padre Miguel back. Maestra Maria probably wouldn't think this, but I, I Coyitito, wondered if this could be so, and if it could, we would all be very, very grateful for his safe return.

All of us, the townspeople and the school, filled the first two benches of the building where we had gathered. This time Magdelena and I seated Tio between us. He was missing Padre Miguel very, very badly, so we wanted to keep him near us. We all watched Tio very carefully while Padre Miguel was gone.

Then someone was at the door.

I knew it was rude to turn my head and look toward the door, so I didn't.

But Tio turned his head. And so did Magdelena, much to my surprise.

By the look in her eyes, I could tell that The River had sent an invitation.

Don Pedro galloped right into the room. He lifted his hat and rode up the aisle.

Maestra Maria looked him straight in the eye as he approached.

"Forgive me, Maestra Maria," he said. "I have come to join in the safe return of Padre Miguel."

If Don Pedro had kidnapped Padre Miguel, he sure kept it well hidden.

Maestra Maria thanked Don Pedro.

We silently petitioned for Padre Miguel's safe return.

When we went back outside, Don Pedro marched his horse toward the gates. As he passed us, we followed him, and Magdelena said, ""Thank you for delivering our invitation from The River, Don Pedro. We know that she sent you." He nodded.

Magdelena said, "I will ask Maestra Maria if we can walk to The River with you, even though the guests are all here and Padre Miguel is not. Maybe The River invited us because she knows where he is." Magdelena left to go ask Maestra Maria if we could leave for a while. I saw Maestra Maria look deeply into Don Pedro's eyes from where she stood. He nodded his head toward her, and Magdelena returned saying that Maestra Maria said we could go for one hour. Then Maestra

Maria headed towards us. She said, "You three must stay with Don Pedro the entire time. You must stay next to him. Tio, do you understand what I am saying?" Tio nodded, but Maestra Maria didn't just ask him. She asked Magdelena and me, too. We both said, "Yes, Maestra Maria," unlike Tio who nodded his head.

Tio, Magdelena, and I walked alongside Don Pedro and his horse as we moved into the woods and to The River.

When we arrived at our friend, Tio ran splashing right into The River, diving underneath the water. I think he was asking where Padre Miguel was.

Don Pedro climbed onto the canyon trail above us, keeping watch, I think. He wasn't right next to us like Maestra Maria said he should be, but he was close and keeping an eye out for something. His face was strong with concentration.

Magdelena and I joined Tio in the water. We hoped The River would deliver Padre Miguel back to us. The River had called us for a reason. We swam around in her waiting for an answer.

And then out of the corner of my eye, I saw it.

On the canyon trail, I saw someone. I wanted to alert Tio and Magdelena. I wondered where Don Pedro was, and if he would save us from the approaching figure. Even though we were in the protected area, lately it seemed that something was changing. Tio and Magdelena didn't see what I saw because they were both diving under the water, hoping for news about Padre Miguel. It was during one of the times that they were underwater that the figure started coming our way. The woods silenced. Don Pedro wasn't standing in his place above us on the rocks. I shivered and was afraid.

Just as I was about to somehow tell Magdelena and Tio about the approaching stranger, I heard:

"I am on the trail of Dona Williams' sweet cakes. I will race you there."

I looked straight at Padre Miguel. "Padre Miguel!" I exclaimed. Tio and Magdelena were now aware of the approaching man. They both burst out of the water and ran to him. Then I followed.

Without turning his head, he said, "Who will win?" and I knew he was smiling when he said this. He had the Padre Miguel smile in his voice.

Tio ran after him. Tio rarely did anything like this, but he ran after Padre Miguel and said, "Padre Miguel, where were you?" Padre Miguel put his hand on Tio's shoulder and said, "I'm back." Then he ruffled Tio's hair and said, "Hurry, Tio, before all the cakes are gone."

Magdelena appeared smiling on Padre Miguel's other side.

It was said that Padre Miguel was on the canyon trails checking the area of protection. We didn't know where he had gone. But he was back. The River had delivered him to us.

And someone else, someone new.

"Meet Rojo Anita," Don Pedro told us. "Who is Rojo Anita?" I wondered, and she looked at me and smiled.

"Rojo Anita, this is Tio. Here is Magdelena, and this is Coyitito." Padre Miguel introduced us.

Some say Padre Miguel had gone to the trails to find Rojo Anita and bring her back. We didn't know if she had been captured, or if she had been hurt, or why he needed to save her, but we did know that when Padre Miguel returned, Rojo Anita was with him.

"Hello, Rojo Anita. It is a pleasure to meet you," Magdelena said. "Hello, Rojo Anita. It is a pleasure to make your acquaintance," I said. "Hello, Rojo Anita," said Tio.

We started our return to the schoolyard where many waited for Padre Miguel's safe return. We didn't ask questions, but we were so curious about where Padre Miguel had been and who Rojo Anita was. I could tell all three of us wanted to know.

Then Tio again asked him. He said, "Where were you Padre Miguel?" And Padre Miguel answered him by saying, "I went into the trails to check the lines of protection and to look for Rojo Anita, who was missing. Don Pedro came to tell me that she had disappeared, and we didn't know if she had been taken. Rojo Anita helps us by being one of the Protectors, and if she had been captured, I needed to go and help her. So I went because I would be the one who could find her, and Don Pedro stayed outside in the woods by the school where he kept watch. But Rojo Anita was very hard to find, and Don Pedro became worried that he had sent me away, and that now perhaps both Rojo Anita and I were gone.

"Then I found Rojo Anita. She was well hidden because, at one point, the Dangerous Ones pursued her. It took me some time, but I was able to find her hiding place, and together we are back.

"And here we are. And here you are."

Then Don Pedro said, "I heard The River tell me that if I brought Tio, Magdelena, and Coyitito to her, we might be able to get both of you back safely and quickly.

"Maestra Maria was worried to let them come with me, but she trusted The River."

He reached for Rojo Anita's hand. What did that mean?

"I knew The River sent Don Pedro," said Magdelena. And she did: she did know that The River sent Don Pedro as an invitation to us. And then Magdelena said, "How could you ever be taken, Padre Miguel?" I agreed. Tio was silent.

Padre Miguel looked at Magdelena.

"You never know. Changes are here. You three, in fact, may be called upon to help in this changing time."

What did Padre Miguel just say? My head was swimming.

"We — Padre Miguel — called upon to help in this changing time?" said Magdelena.

I shivered. I didn't say a word.

"We will see," said Padre Miguel. "But I do think that your auspicious arrival has had its meaning. I will be here to protect you, as always. So will Don Pedro and Rojo Anita. Do not fear. But I do believe, the signs say so, that the times are changing."

Auspicious. So this is what that *auspicious* really means? I wanted to turn around and run. Maybe, oh maybe if I went back to The River, jumped in, saw Padre Miguel out of the corner of my eye, then maybe we could start again, and he wouldn't say what he just said.

He said the word *auspicious* without italics.

Instead, Magdelena said, "You can count on us, Padre Miguel." And Tio nodded his head. Magdelena looked at me, and I nodded my head, too.

I think Padre Miguel didn't want to tell us much more because he invented a game for us to play the rest of the way back. Don Pedro walked with Rojo Anita. They played too as they continued holding hands. Rojo Anita was very good at the game called, "What Do I See?" You see something and the others have to ask you questions about what you see, trying to guess what it is. Rojo Anita seemed to win every time.

Everyone in the schoolyard cheered when we walked through the gates with Padre Miguel. Maestra Maria looked at him and smiled. She really, really smiled like I had never seen her smile before. I think, by the way I saw her shoulders fall, that she sighed with Padre Miguel's return. She must have been very, very worried.

Maestra Agatha burst into tears.

Manuel danced the tango in a circle around Padre Miguel.

And Lucinda, she dropped to the floor like a domino when it falls. Padre Miguel lifted her up and carried her, as he visited everyone who had come to ask for his safe return.

At some point I noticed that Rojo Anita and Don Pedro were no longer around.

But days later, after Padre Miguel's return, Tio, Magdelena, and I asked if we could visit The River. When we were in the water, we heard a voice call to us, "Do you want to learn to dive from up here?" At first we thought it was the voice of The River, and then we looked up and we saw her: Rojo Anita with her long hair, red jeans and shirt without sleeves. Rojo Anita's bare feet hung over the rock's edge as she looked down at us.

None of us made a move. Yes, we had met Rojo Anita with Padre Miguel when he returned from wherever he had been, so we knew that he knew her. But we weren't sure if we should climb up onto the rocks. I knew Magdelena was studying the lines of the Protected Zone. So was I. I think even Tio was studying them. We knew them so well, but maybe Padre Miguel had been out changing or adding to the protected area. He didn't tell us that, but others thought so. Rumors spread around the school, but we hadn't seen any new maps. Rojo Anita was standing inside the Protected Zone.

"I am standing inside the protected area." How did she know what we were thinking?

"All three of you are very wise to consider this spot where I am standing — and me. Yes, you are all well aware of the dangers inside the canyon trails. Padre Miguel will be happy to know that you three considered whether or not you should come up here to dive from the rocks, even though you very much want to."

Tio dashed out of the water, lifted himself onto the rocks, and climbed up a small path to where Rojo Anita stood. He was always so brave.

Rojo Anita stretched her hand out to him. "Hello, Tio," she smiled. Rojo Anita had a nice smile.

"Thank you, Coyitito," she said.

I think Rojo Anita reads minds.

She looked at me and winked.

I really, really think Rojo Anita reads minds, and that worries me.

Magdelena swam to The River's edge and started up the trail to where Rojo Anita and Tio stood. I didn't know what to do. I wanted to follow Magdelena and dive off the rock with them. I looked up. It wasn't very high. I had never dived from the rocks before, and I was worried about hitting my head or disappearing. But I couldn't let Magdelena and Tio dive without me. What if they got hurt? So I followed Magdelena, and when I reached where they all were, Rojo Anita spoke to me; she said, "Coyitito, I will not let any of you get hurt. I will teach you to dive and stay with you. The River will protect you."

So Rojo Anita does read my mind. Does she read Magdelena's mind? Maybe she can tell me what Magdelena thinks about.

"No, Coyitito, I can't." She smiled at me.

I had so many questions for Rojo Anita about what Padre Miguel said. What did he mean about the changing times and that the three of us might be called upon to help in some way? I wanted to ask Rojo Anita. Tio wouldn't discuss it, and Magdelena was also very quiet about it. I looked at Rojo Anita and she shook her head "no."

I have to stop thinking. I must stop thinking around Rojo Anita.

"First let us talk," said Rojo Anita. "I will tell you a bit about me, so you know who you are diving with." So we waited on the rock with Rojo Anita, and she told us about how she found her horse one day when she was traveling in the canyon. She was walking along a canyon trail on her way to a river far away from this spot, "But," she said, "I think that this river and that one are in the same family." And when she started going down to the river, a horse came galloping up, "In a full force gallop," she said, and she heard it, so she moved and hid behind a rock. It ran past her, then stopped, turned its head, and looked her way.

She saw no rider, but she knew that the rider might come on foot, and perhaps be dangerous, so she stayed silent, and so did the horse.

"The moon was coming," she said, and still the horse waited.

"The howling ones began calling through the canyon as the night grew bigger. I slowly crept from where I hid behind the rock. The night grew colder, and I wanted to travel back to where I had been staying in the caves. When I looked, the horse was standing as still as she had been when she stopped galloping and found me."

Rojo Anita continued, "I know the horse appears to the rider, but one never knows. So I said to her, 'Have you come for me? Are you my horse?' And she didn't move.

"So I looked her deeply in the eye, and there she was, looking right back at me.

"'All right, Senorita,'" I said. 'Let us go then.' And off we sped. We have been riding together ever since."

I didn't see Senorita now.

Rojo Anita whistled and Senorita appeared just above us.

"She is there, Coyitito. She helps keep watch. Have your horses appeared to you yet?"

Our horses?

Magdelena answered for us. She said, "Not yet, Rojo Anita. Do you think they will appear to us?"

"Each of us has a horse," said Rojo Anita.

I could see Tio's eyes grow with wonder. Did Rojo Anita know when our horses would come, or who they were?

"The horse is very specific to the rider," she said. "Your horses will come. We don't know when, or how, or where — but they will come." Then she stood.

"Are you ready to learn how to dive from the rocks?"

We three nodded, "Yes." Tio was very eager. So was Magdelena. I stayed back just a bit.

Rojo Anita stood at the edge of the rock. Her long toes moved up to the edge of the hard surface. She looked at us.

"Try this," she said. We stood in a line next to her. I was at the end. "Coyitito, come and stand on this side of me," she said. I looked at Tio and Magdelena, but they were very involved in getting ready to dive. I moved to the other side of Rojo Anita. Tio was at her other side, and Magdelena next to him.

"First let's jump, so you feel how high we are. It is not as high as you might think — but also the water here is deep enough, so you will not hit your heads. When I say three, let's jump. Tio, take my hand and Magdelena's. Coyitito, take my other hand."

I wished I were back over there holding Magdelena's hand.

"Do you want to go back over there?" Rojo Anita asked me. How was I ever going to be able to think anything? I didn't answer Rojo Anita. I know I should have answered her; she was my elder, but I realized that I just needed to think my answer. So I thought, "No, Rojo Anita, I will stay here." Magdelena said, "Coyitito, Rojo Anita asked you a question." "No, Rojo Anita, I will stay right here. Thank you."

We all held hands. Rojo Anita's hands were river cold. And strong. "Let's count to-gether: one, two, three …" And we were sailing through the air. Rojo Anita never let go of my hand, or Tio's, and Magdelena never let go of Tio's. We landed into the water all together and went down, and quickly, very, very quickly, we swam back up; all of us were excited.

"Are you ready to try the dive?" Rojo Anita asked, as she pulled herself onto the rocks and climbed from rock to rock back up to where we had begun. Rojo Anita didn't walk the trail; she climbed the rocks. So did Tio. And then Magdelena de-cided she would climb the rocks also. So there I was, worrying about how slippery the rocks were. I thought it best to take the trail and waited for Rojo Anita to read my thoughts, but she didn't say anything like that. Instead, she jumped back into the water, landed next to me, and said, "Coyitito, I will race you up the trail." And Rojo Anita quickly leapt from the water and started running up the trail. I sped behind her. She was very fast. So was I. And each of us wanted to let the other win. So I said, "Rojo Anita, let us jump into the water from here, and climb back up the rocks."

"Are you sure you want to do that, Coyitito?" But she knew the answer. I did and I didn't want to do that.

So Rojo Anita dropped her strong arms and lifted me up.

"Here goes," she said, and she threw me into the cold river, following me.

I looked at her.

"Let's go."

Tio jumped into the water next to us. Then Magdelena. The four of us scrambled up the rock surface, which was slippery with The River.

Then Rojo Anita stood at the edge of the rock; her arms were raised above her head, her knees bent, and then, within moments, she was flying down into The River. Tio leapt right behind her. Magdelena looked at me and said, "Are you ready, Coyitito?" I was ready, so she and I dove together and barreled into The River. And then we scurried out onto the rock's surface, climbed up, and dove back in again and again.

WE DIDN'T GET TO GO to The River as much as we would have liked because we were getting ready for the Gratitude Feast. Maestra Maria was very excited about it. The Feast was planned for the coming Saturday and was being held at the school in honor of Padre Miguel's safe return.

Maestra Maria thought that it would be a good idea if we all wrote poems for Padre Miguel. She led the lesson by saying, "Close your eyes." Not everybody closed their eyes because I heard her say, "Lucinda, it is safe to close your eyes."

Lucinda was always afraid to close her eyes. Even at night, when it was time for sleeping, Magdelena said that Lucinda would wake from sleep yelling. She had nightmares and started sleeping with Magdelena, who would sing Lucinda back to sleep.

I opened my eyes, just peeking out, and I saw Maestra Maria head over to Lucinda's seat in the back of the room and put her hand on Lucinda's shoulder.

"Now," Maestra Maria said, "Think about Padre Miguel." And she waited.

"Think about something he has said to you that was meaningful. Think about how he has made you laugh." Now Manuel was laughing aloud. He was in his own private world of Padre Miguel. And then I heard Magdelena's giggle. And I didn't see it because I wouldn't dare open my eyes at that point, but I knew that Tio was smiling inside because Padre Miguel had said so many funny things to Tio, and to Juan, and especially after Juan died. Padre Miguel was trying so hard to cheer Tio up. He wasn't disrespectful to the loss of Juan; he was trying to help Tio. And when Juan was still here, Padre Miguel used to make the both of them laugh at the same time.

And then Lucinda burst out, "I love Padre Miguel," and when we were laughing and smiling, Maestra Maria left us there for awhile, and I knew that she herself was smiling because Maestra Maria had a special relationship with Padre Miguel. And then gently she said, "When you are ready, open your eyes, and put down in words what you just experienced with Padre Miguel. Just write it down, and this will become your poem."

I opened my eyes and saw that Tio, who really did not like to write much at all, was bent over his page, rapidly writing. So was Magdelena.

Maestra Maria even sat down at her desk and started writing too.

Then I heard it. A slow trot. And when I looked out the window, I saw it: a beautiful brown- colored horse had arrived. And I knew someone's horse had just appeared because the horse finds the rider. Whose horse was it? Maestra Maria's ears were turned toward the sound of the horse. A horse without a rider could also mean danger.

Tio looked up at Maestra Maria, who had moved to look out the window, and he said, "How do you spell giraffe, Maestra Maria?" Tio felt excited, either because of what he was writing for Padre Miguel, or because somehow he felt this horse might be his horse. He didn't say, "Excuse me, Maestra Maria, may I use the dictionary," not that he really would say that. But he might have interrupted her differently if he wasn't excited. Lucinda answered him. "G-I-R-A-F-F-E. Giraffe."

"Thank you, Lucinda," said Maestra Maria. Tio nodded to Lucinda and wrote down her spelling of the word, while Maestra Maria kept her eyes looking outside, then inside again. Tio's pen scrawled across his paper; he was doing this for Padre Miguel.

I wasn't writing so much. I had only written three lines, but they said so much about Padre Miguel, I thought. I was fascinated with the horse outside. Maestra Maria stayed near the window.

In a little while, it seemed as if we started noticing the horse outside — except Tio who kept writing. And then I knew that Tio's horse had arrived because he was the only one now who wasn't paying attention to it. And Magdelena seemed to know it was Tio's horse too. She held up her paper to me and there was an arrow pointing Tio's way. Maestra Maria moved away from the window with a smile on her face. She, too, knew Tio's horse had come.

"Finish your poems for homework," she said. Mine was already finished, I thought. We left the classroom, and I asked Magdelena if I could read mine to her. Tio was still in the classroom writing his. I wanted to read to Magdelena and go see the horse, so I read on the way.

"Padre Miguel is like a cold glass of lemonade on a hot day: helpful and wonderful.

When Padre Miguel laughs, the whole world joins him because they believe him, and his laugh has the sound of drums people can dance to.

Padre Miguel is our light in the darkness."

"Padre Miguel will like your poem, Coyitito; it is beautiful."

"May I hear your poem, Magdelena?"

"When I finish writing it, I will read it to you, Coyitito."

When we again looked toward the gate, Padre Miguel was opening it, and a horse entered the courtyard.

Tio was standing near us, holding the poem he had written for Padre Miguel. He looked at the brown horse as it trotted in his direction. When it came near to him, it stopped moving and stood still. Tio held out his hand. The horse moved its face down toward Tio's hand. They both stood, eye to eye.

Padre Miguel watched from where he stood. I saw Maestra Maria out of the corner of my eye. Then Padre Miguel neared Tio and put his fingers inside each other so Tio could step into them. When Tio did, Padre Miguel lifted him so he could swing his legs over onto the horse's back.

Tio knew how to climb onto a horse's back.

"What do you think you might name your horse, Tio?" Padre Miguel asked him.

"Padre Miguel II," Tio said.

So Tio's horse, Padre Miguel II, had arrived.

Rojo Anita came to the Gratitude Feast in her red jeans, red wide hat and a light blue shirt over the tan one she wears when she swims. She was barefoot. I was sure glad to see her. She looked at Tio and his horse, and a smile spread across her face.

"What's his name?" she asked Tio. "Padre Miguel II," he said. She walked over to Padre Miguel II and rubbed her hand above his nose. "Come on, Coyitito," she said as her back was turned toward me. She read my thoughts. I wanted to pet Padre Miguel II, also. So I moved to where Rojo Anita stood with the new horse and Tio, and I ran my hand over the horse's side. "Hello Padre Miguel II. Welcome," I said. Then Magdelena came, and she too met Tio's horse. "Take good care of Tio," she told him. "I know you will."

Then, all of a sudden, we heard galloping approaching the gate. Everyone turned. Even though we were having a feast in gratitude of the safe return of Padre Miguel, we kept the gate closed, so visitors would have to be let in. That's the way Padre Miguel wanted it. He kept a stern eye on the activities outside the gate while he laughed with the ones who had come to join him in gratitude.

Padre Miguel walked over from where we were all eating and standing and sitting inside the courtyard.

The galloping stopped. A voice boomed from the other side of the gate. The rider wore a hat, which covered his eyes and did not let us see his face.

"I am Ramon, brother to Rojo Anita. I have come to show my gratitude to Padre Miguel for finding my sister. I have ridden over the mountain, come down the trails to see you, Padre Miguel, and to thank you."

I watched Padre Miguel, and then I noticed all the flowers we had picked for the Gratitude Feast; they really were beautiful. We had gone into the nearby fields and picked the wild flowers. Maestra Maria had led us into the fields during one of our lessons. She said it was all right to be going outside to pick flowers during our lessons because we were learning about different types of flowers and trees, and we were in the protected area, so this was a way to really get to know them. Even then, she kept looking around us.

Magdelena made a huge bunch of flowers. When I looked at them, I thought they could lift her up into the sky and float her above the canyons.

My flowers were all the same color. So were Tio's — only his were short, and mine were long.

I saw Magdelena's bouquet of flowers, and then I saw Rojo Anita join Padre Miguel. She must know her own brother. She seemed to wait a moment before she smiled and said, "Padre Miguel, my brother, Ramon, has come to thank you."

Did Padre Miguel know Ramon? He didn't seem to. And why had Rojo Anita hesitated before she smiled at her brother? Maybe they thought that he was One of those — One of the No Faces. They could trick us like that. I know they could. They were said to take on the faces of those that we loved and trusted when really they weren't. They stole pieces of the one they took.

And nobody knew how.

This is what was being said. We had to be very, very careful because maybe people we knew and loved might not be who they seemed.

This scared me terribly. "What do they mean?" I asked Magdelena and Tio. I wouldn't question Padre Miguel or Maestra Maria when they told us how careful we had to be. They didn't want to scare us; they said it wasn't to frighten us when they told us that the No Faces, it seemed, were coming out from their hiding places on the canyon trails.

It was said that they have always been around; that's why we have the Protected Zone. The No Faces have always been trying to capture the ones with faces. They wanted the children, so they could make the children their own. And they wanted the powerful ones, like Padre Miguel.

I imagine they wanted Maestra Maria and Rojo Anita. All of us. And Padre Miguel was more worried than he had been before. I could see it on his face. He wouldn't worry for himself, but for us.

So he didn't want to be rude to Rojo Anita's brother Ramon or Rojo Anita, but he needed to know that Ramon was who he said he was.

Magdelena asked Padre Miguel a question one day when he came in to talk to us about the No Faces. Padre Miguel wanted to make sure we practiced safety, so he came and tested us on the protected area. He knew Maestra Maria quizzed us every day, but times were changing. He said that again and again.

So Magdelena asked him; she said, "Excuse me, Padre Miguel, but how does one know if a No Face has stolen a face or pieces of someone? Does the person have any sign of change?"

I, Coyitito, shuddered. I didn't want to know any of this, and yet I needed to.

"We are not at all certain, Magdelena."

I knew Magdelena had considered what Padre Miguel had told her and wanted to find an answer. I wanted to say, "No, Magdelena. Do not think about this. We will stay in the protected area. We can even stay here at the school with Padre Miguel and Maestra Maria, and we will be safe. We can ask Padre Miguel if Rojo Anita, Don Pedro, and Ramon (if Ramon is really Ramon, we should know very soon) can stay here with us. And we will go about our studying and play together, and we will be safe here."

"Welcome, Ramon," Padre Miguel said.

Somehow Rojo Anita knew that her brother was her brother, and Padre Miguel believed them. I don't know if her mind-reading helped.

"It depends, Coyitito," she looked at me and said. "Sometimes."

Ramon entered the courtyard. I couldn't take my eyes off him. He looked just like Rojo Anita. He, too, wore jeans and a blue long shirt with the sleeves rolled up on his arms. But Ramon wasn't barefoot. He wore boots covered in dust.

I saw Magdelena watch Ramon. And Tio watched him too. When I turned around, I saw Maestra Maria's eyes on him. Perhaps she didn't yet trust him.

Ramon slid down off his horse. Padre Miguel said, "Ramon, have something cool to drink for you and your horse. Have some food, too."

"Thank you, Padre Miguel. I am again grateful. We have been riding long." And Ramon led his horse to the water-pail.

As he did so, I saw that his horse had packs thrown over its sides. I couldn't tell what was inside Ramon's packs, but I saw Tio looking at them. And Magdelena turned her eyes toward them too. Somehow we were all drawn to what was inside Ramon's bags.

Ramon asked me if I was the one they call Coyitito. I told him I was Coyitito, and I wondered how and why he wanted to know. He said he had something for me, and if I would come over to his horse, he would give it to me. He had something for Magdelena and Tio also he said.

I didn't know Ramon, and I was a little bit afraid of him, and I didn't understand why he knew my name and had something for me. Maybe I should ask Maestra Maria if it was allowable to receive Ramon's gift. I looked around the courtyard for her. I saw her bringing out another table for Dona Williams' cakes. Dona Williams had brought so many of her delicious cakes that more tables were needed. I thought I needed to go and help Maestra Maria with the table when Manuel appeared to help her. I guess Dona Williams was very, very grateful that Padre Miguel had returned, so she made all these cakes. We all were very, very grateful that he was back with us.

Earlier, I had heard from Magdelena that Dona Williams had made a new kind of cake, something with lemon and some kind of cheese with brown sugar on top. I saw Magdelena having a piece as she talked to Dona Williams. Magdelena most likely wanted the recipe.

Tio walked over to the cake table. I saw him reach for several pieces of chocolate cake. He handed a piece of cake to Ramon, one to me, and then he moved to Ramon's horse and his own, Padre Miguel II.

"Does your horse eat chocolate cake?" Tio asked Ramon, who said, "I never gave him chocolate cake. Does yours?" "I have never yet fed my horse cake; he is new. His name is Padre Miguel II, and Padre Miguel likes chocolate cake, so my horse must like it too." He looked at me, and I shook my head "yes" thinking that what Tio said made sense.

So Tio held the plate in front of Padre Miguel II as the horse ate Dona Williams' treat. Padre Miguel II seemed to enjoy Tio's offering very, very much.

""Can I give this to your horse?" Tio asked Ramon.

"You can try." Ramon smiled.

Tio held the plate to Ramon's horse's mouth, and within moments, the cake was nowhere to be seen.

"I think he liked it," Tio said.

Then he asked Ramon, "What is your horse's name?"

"Solamente."

"Tell them how Solamente found you," said Rojo Anita.

I didn't realize that Rojo Anita was there. "Yes, the horse finds the rider," she continued. "Padre Miguel II wandered in here and found you, Tio. Senorita came to me. Solamente actually landed in Ramon's arms. Your horses will find you too, you know," she said to Magdelena and me.

"Would they?" I wondered. Rojo Anita shook her head yes.

Padre Miguel didn't seem to ride a particular horse. That was odd. I would think that he would ride a very particular horse, but he didn't. He rode different horses when he rode, and sometimes he even rode the donkeys. When he came back from finding Rojo Anita, he wasn't riding at all. He was walking. Maybe Padre Miguel mostly traveled on foot.

Maestra Maria rode different horses, also. I've seen her on the horse in the woods, but she rides different horses. Maestra Agatha, too. Maybe they all need to be able to ride all the horses for some reason. And the donkeys. So maybe sometimes more than one horse finds the rider.

"I was a boy about your age," said Ramon, "when I met Solamente. Rojo Anita and I lived with our relatives at the end of the canyon where there was a farm and a field. I used to go to work at the farm early in the morning before the sun came up.

"One of the horses was going to soon give birth.

"After working hard all day, I was in my bed dreaming. In my dream, I rode a horse to the top of a mountain. When we arrived at the peak, we stopped. The night sky was all around us. A voice reached from the darkness and said, 'Ramon, you ride alone, yet you are fierce and protected by the spirits of the canyon.'

"Then I awoke.

"I rose and headed for the farm. I was earlier than usual, and it was still very dark outside. When I arrived at the farm, I heard noises by the barn, so I hurried. And when I got there, I saw the Mother Horse was trying to give birth, but something was very wrong. She couldn't do it, and she was suffering.

"I wanted to go up to the door of the farmers and tell them, but I knew there was no time. I had to act quickly if I was to help them. I knew it might already be too late.

"All I could do was ask for guidance, so I did, and I put my hands where I thought they should go. I blocked out all sounds and thought of my dream. I asked the spirits of the canyon to help bring forth the horse I would know as Solamente. And I said, 'Solamente, I will guide you now as you will guide me later.'

"All of a sudden, a shining horse was in my hands, and his mother was released from her suffering. Oh no, she didn't die, but she was freed from the difficult birth of Solamente.

"So I stroked him, and held him and his mother. I wrapped them in blankets and went to get the farmers. They were grateful to me and said that when he was stronger, I could take him; he was my horse. Solamente found me.

"And now he eats chocolate cake."

I again wondered about my own horse. I thought about when I would ride fast through the fields or up the canyon roads, riding in full gallop until my heels were caked with dust, like Ramon's boots.

And thinking like that, I remembered Juan, and what happened to him. Now I was thinking about Juan when Rojo Anita broke in and said, "But that horse didn't choose him. When the horse chooses the rider, the horse protects the rider."

I wished she would stop reading my mind. What if I started thinking softly about how pretty Magdelena was?

Rojo Anita looked at me and smiled. "It's safe with me," she said, and Ramon looked at me.

"Is my sister reading your thoughts?" asked Ramon, "She does that to me, too. Don't worry. She has to be near you to read you. If you go to the other side of the yard or by that table, she won't be able to hear you."

And I thought about how I would always be far away from Rojo Anita when I was thinking about Magdelena.

Then Ramon moved over to Solamente and the two bags hanging over each of his sides.

I was very excited. I knew I shouldn't really be excited because maybe there was no reason to be, but I was. I was tingling all over my arms and legs. I looked at Tio. He was wide-eyed as Ramon approached the bags. Magdelena was also very focused.

I again wondered if we should ask Maestra Maria or Padre Miguel if we could receive the gifts Ramon brought when Rojo Anita said, "Padre Miguel has agreed to let you receive these gifts."

"When did she ask Padre Miguel?" I wondered.

"When we were in the tunnel," she said.

"Tunnel? What tunnel?" I again wondered.

"Perhaps you will someday know," she said.

I didn't want to think another thought. Rojo Anita could read my mind, but I couldn't read hers, so it sounded like a one way conversation. All the others heard was, "When we were in the tunnel. Perhaps ... someday ..." How come she didn't read Tio's thoughts, or Magdelena's? Why mine? And she used my name, so everyone knew she was reading my mind.

"It's not just you," she said. At least she didn't use my name this time. Maybe Magdelena was thinking the same questions as me. I think Tio was thinking about something different.

Then Ramon moved toward his pack, untied the cord holding it together, and reached inside its depth.

His face was very concentrated.

"To the right, I believe," said Rojo Anita. He didn't even look at her, but his hand moved to the right. He lived with Rojo Anita when they were small, so he must be used to her reading his mind.

"I can block thoughts," she said to the air. I was relieved that she stopped, for the moment, saying, "Coyitito."

Ramon grabbed something with his hand and lifted it out of the pack.

Before he made it visible to us, I looked around the courtyard. Everyone was having a good time. I looked for Padre Miguel's nod of approval, but I didn't see him or Maestra Maria. I trusted Rojo Anita that she had talked to him already. Then I waited for her to say something to me, but she didn't. She didn't respond this time, and I was very, very glad to be free for the moment.

"Magdelena, this is for you, I believe. Your name is on it."

I still didn't know how Ramon knew our names before he met us — unless someone had told him our names. Rojo Anita remained silent.

Magdelena's gift was wrapped in a cream-colored cloth that seemed to be soft. Ramon placed it in her waiting hands.

"Ramon," she said. "I did not know you were coming, and so I have no gift ready, but if you can wait a moment, I will gather a gift for you." Leave it to Magdelena to think about the other, not herself.

"Thank you, Magdelena," Ramon said. "That is very gracious of you. I appreciate your offering, which is a gift itself. I must tell you though that I am the deliverer of the gifts. I was given the presents to give to you."

"Who gave them to you, Ramon?" Tio asked. Only Tio would ask in this way, and Ramon told all of us that he would tell us the origin of the gifts after we had each received them.

"Open your present, Magdelena," Rojo Anita said.

And Magdelena unwrapped her present.

A cream-colored comb slid into her hands.

Magdelena studied it with her heart. She didn't have anything like this.

Ramon moved to the other side of Solamente. This time when he reached inside, he immediately found what he was looking for and pulled it out gently.

He held a white cloth, filled with age. "Tio, this is for you."

Tio shyly reached out his hand to Ramon.

Tio reached up and placed the white cloth on the back of Padre Miguel II. He unfolded it slowly, not like I thought he might. I thought Tio might be so excited about his gift that he would unwrap it quickly, but it wasn't so. He gently took his time.

And inside the folds of the cloth was another cloth, which Tio unfolded.

Magdelena had taken her braid down and was combing her hair.

As Tio unfolded the cloth, I saw it.

From the corner of my eye, I spotted it. I looked at the others to see if they saw, but only Rojo Anita noticed what I noticed before it was gone. The stallion of Maestra Maria silently passed us by.

I imagined Maestra Maria riding her stallion with her hair hanging down her back. Did she somewhere have a comb like Magdelena's? I'm sure Rojo Anita heard me thinking my thoughts, even though she remained quiet about it. When I looked at her, she wasn't looking at me; she was looking at Tio, who had finished the unfolding, and in his hands he was holding the piece of aged cloth, staring at it. His fingers touched something on it as he lifted it. Tio's eyes didn't look up; they stayed there, right there on the fabric.

Tio held his cloth up as high as he could. And right on the top, in thick red letters, Tio's name was sewn: *T I O*. Tio. So this was Tio's cloth.

Ramon reached into his pocket and pulled out a dull metal key.

"This is for you, Coyitito."

Me? This key? What was this key? Magdelena received a lovely comb, Tio an engraved colorful blanket, and I, I get this key?

I didn't look at Rojo Anita.

Ramon said, "I was told to carry this key in my left pocket until I could hand it to you. She said the key might look deceiving, but do not underestimate it. Meme said that you, and only you, could use it. Sometimes it will work; sometimes it won't. 'It's kind of a faulty key like that,' she said. You are its keeper for now, Coyitito.

"She also said that your gifts are temperamental. Sometimes they do something, and then they don't do that again. 'You never know,'" she said.

Who is Meme?

I had so many questions, but Rojo Anita placed her finger over her lips silencing me.

Magdelena said, "Ramon, we would all like to thank Meme. We will gather some flowers and write her a note if you would be so kind as to deliver them."

Ramon smiled at Magdelena, but he wasn't finished yet. His hands opened onto three small tins.

"This one is for you, Magdelena. Tio, for you. And here you go, Coyitito."

We opened the covers. Inside were cookies. They were delicious! I'm not sure what they were.

"I met an old woman as I traveled through the canyon," said Ramon. She stopped me as I came round a corner, and she asked me if she could ride with me for her legs were weary from walking for so, so long."

We looked, and Rojo Anita was crouching on the ground, listening.

"I told her I would lift her onto my horse, but she had no trouble getting on Solamente."

Ramon continued. "'Where are you going?' I asked her, and she said, 'I will show you.' I did worry that she would lead me into danger because we never know if the person is who they say or another. But I stayed with her, and we rode along the trail. I was very alert to danger, while she seemed to nod on and off asleep.

"Solamente led us through the canyon, and when night came, I told the old woman we would find a cave, eat dinner, and sleep the night.

"'No,' she said. 'Keep riding. Do not stop. It is not safe like you think it is. Keep going. I will tell you when to rest.'

"I thought I knew better than the old woman, but I did what she said, and we traveled deep into the night.

"And then she said, 'Turn here and go up that road.' So I did. And Solamente led us up the road.

"She continued, 'Now turn here. Now here. Now here. Turn that way. Go up there. Turn here. Turn here. Go down there. Yes, yes down there. Now turn here. And go inside this cave. No, not that one. This one.'

"And we went into a very dark cave. 'Keep going,' she said, and I told her that I could not see anything at all, and she said, 'I can.' And we traveled in the complete darkness, Solamente moving slowly straight ahead.

"Then in the middle of the darkness, she said, 'Turn here. Turn again. Turn again,' and when we went up a short hill inside the cave, we stopped. She said, 'It is I, Meme,' and something moved in the darkness. A door slowly opened. 'I bring Ramon and Solamente,' she said, and we three rode inside the door, which shut behind us. 'Turn here. Go straight up and turn, turn, turn,' she said.

"And then there was light — candles burning, and someone standing in front of us.

"He came over to Solamente, reached out his hand to shake mine. 'This is Ramon,' she said, and she jumped down off Solamente. (She seemed to be a mind reader like my sister, Rojo Anita.)

"Meme said, 'Rest here, Ramon, and you too, Solamente. This is Azul; he will bring you water.'

"And so we rested. We fell asleep, and even in my dreams, I traveled the cave corridor, and I was aware that we were so far in the center of the earth. I didn't know how we would ever get back out again.

"And when I awoke, Meme came over to me with strong coffee, baked bread, and cookies warm from the heat.

"'Before you leave, I have some things for you to take back to Coyitito, Magdelena, and Tio. You will find them, or they will find you,' Meme said."

★★★

I, COYITITO, woke up in the middle of the night. The wild dogs were making all kinds of sounds yipping and yapping. I had been dreaming. In my dream, the moon climbed down the sky and kept climbing into the middle of the mountain until it lit up the entire cavern. In the moon's glow, I saw a silver stallion. I moved to where the stallion stood, and I knew it was my horse. I couldn't wait to tell Tio and Magdelena. I woke up and leaned over to Tio.

Very quietly I whispered to him, "Tio, I saw my horse in my dream." But Tio wasn't there. Tio was gone.

At first I thought maybe he went to the room down the hall, so I crept quietly toward the door, but I saw no light. I went in anyway because sometimes Tio would crawl into dark places, small spots, and hide. He wasn't in there. I wanted to tell Magdelena and see what she thought we should do, but it wasn't easy to get past Maestra Agatha and Maestra Maria. I thought of telling Padre Miguel, but I didn't want to get Tio in trouble.

I thought that he might be in the tool shed, and I wanted to go find out, but I was terrified of going out when the wild dogs were so near. I thought that Tio might be hiding under one of the benches, sleeping soundly, but something told me that Tio was gone. And I didn't know where or why.

I waited for a while, back in my bed, trying to decide what to do. I could wake Manuel, but he might say that we had to tell Padre Miguel, and maybe we did. Maybe we did have to tell him.

What if Tio were in danger?

Maybe he went to sleep at the bank of The River.

The wild dogs made my decision.

I climbed back out of bed, went into the hall, and was going to go to Padre Miguel when I heard her whisper, "Coyitito, where are you going?" I turned around and saw Magdelena at the bottom of the stairs. Before I answered, Maestra Maria said, "Where are you going, Coyitito?"

"I am going to wake Padre Miguel to tell him that Tio is missing."

Quickly, Maestra Maria was no longer in front of me; she was heading to Padre Miguel's room. He was already opening his door because he had heard all the commotion. Maestra Agatha, Magdelena, and I followed her. Then Lucinda came from her room.

I saw Padre Miguel tell Maestra Maria to go. She pulled a shawl from the door rack, slipped on shoes, and opened the door. I knew I wouldn't let her go alone.

We ran outside because Padre Miguel said we should start to look for Tio outside.

Magdelena was very frightened for Tio. She was running toward the shed because she, too, knew about Tio's hiding places. I heard Padre Miguel saying, "Tio. Where are you, Tio? Tio, you are not in any trouble for disappearing. We are all worried about where you are, so please come and show yourself to us."

I knew that Padre Miguel felt terribly guilty about the death of Juan. I knew because after Juan died, I saw it on Padre Miguel's face.

I knew that he didn't want anything to happen to Tio.

"Tio."

I heard him call Tio again, but I had already slipped through the gates, following Maestra Maria through the trees. Then she slipped on her black shawl. She didn't know I was there. I felt guilty that Padre Miguel might be frantic if I were missing, too, but I didn't intend to be gone for long.

Maestra Maria's head disappeared into the dark night. We were heading toward The River. I knew it. I could hear the sounds, and then I heard a whistle: a sharp, piercing whistle. Three times and within moments, I heard hoof beats galloping at full speed, coming down from the canyon. I watched as a silhouette of a horse stopped in front of Maestra Maria, and when the horse stopped, she took the hand that reached for hers, helping her onto the horse's back. They came my way before veering off onto the canyon trail, and when they passed me by, I saw a man who looked like Don Pedro.

But it couldn't have been Don Pedro because moments later something else happened. Two more horses came galloping my way, and just in the nick of time I moved as quickly away as I could because in the moonlight I could see Rojo Anita riding Senorita at a full gallop. I didn't want her reading my mind as she passed, knowing I was hiding behind the trees. I remembered if I were far enough away, she wouldn't be able to reach inside and find me, and right behind her, galloping paces behind, was Don Pedro.

And then I heard the voice. "Go find Tio, Coyitito. We must go and find Tio," a female voice said. I turned in the direction from where the voice came — and there — in the opening in the woods, the moon was bright, the moon was so, so bright. The opening was lit as though daylight had spread out in that spot.

Rojo Anita once told us when we were sitting by The River that she always welcomed the moon; in fact, Rojo Anita said that she saw the moon as her sister. That's what she'd say. She said that she and the moon thought alike: there were times they both liked to disappear; there were times they both wanted to let the whole world know that they were the center of attention, that they were coming and whoever was watching would see them.

Rojo Anita told us that the moon was really good friends with the sea; they did things together. She said if you traveled the canyon trail long enough, and that was very, very long, then you came to the ocean. And there, at that water, the moon came down for big conversations with the waves.

I had never been to the ocean. Neither had Tio or Magdelena.

I looked at the opening in the trees and blinked. I didn't know for sure if I was seeing things because right there, in the middle of the clearing, stood a silver horse.

I spun around, closed my eyes, opened them, and looked again — and still — the horse stood there. She was beautiful: her silver coat was gleaming in the moonlight.

Had she been talking to me? Had she been the one to tell me that we must go and find Tio?

I started toward her. She was either in my imagination, or maybe the spirit of the woods sent her; maybe she would lead me somewhere I did not want to go. I moved her way, and as I did, I saw a shadow; someone was in the woods with me. I didn't know who it was, but the horse didn't move. She stood stationary in the light, the spotlight on her.

I remembered the first poem I had written when I was about seven:

The moon is a big ball/With craters big and small/The moon is a big flashlight/And shows us the way to go at night.

Rojo Anita said that sometimes she needed to be hidden when traveling in darkness on the canyon trail. "Sometimes the moon just wouldn't go away," she said. "The moon wanted to stay right by my side, so she'd shine and shine. I'd wait for a cloudy sky or the beginning of the month to do my night travels because she was quieter then," said Rojo Anita. "She has a predictable schedule."

As I moved toward the silver horse, so did the shadow. We were near each other both moving toward the light. We were still under the cover of the trees' darkness.

"Who's there?" I boldly whispered, as I stuck my foot out into the moonlight. The silver horse gave me courage. The dream horse.

"I think we both saw her at the same time," said Magdelena.

Magdelena. Magdelena was here, shining.

And I had been hearing from the others that sometimes it happened. Sometimes, it was said that two people rode the same horse because that's how it was. The horse appeared to both of them at the same time; it was *their* horse.

Really? Magdelena and I were going to share a horse? Really? I would get to spend all that time with Magdelena. I was ready to do that.

What did this mean? Would we get to ride our horse together forever?

"What shall we name her?" asked Magdelena.

"You choose, Magdelena."

"Let's give her two names. You pick one, and I'll pick one."

Magdelena looked up. She was in my full view now. There was Magdelena standing in the light of the moon; her long hair was shimmering down her back, looking the way it looks when she unbraids it after swimming in The River, so it could dry. Sometimes she took out her braid before going into the water, and her hair would follow her when she swam from one side to the other.

Once, I watched Magdelena jump from above with Rojo Anita, and her hair flew like a magic carpet behind her.

"Senorita," she said.

Yes, Rojo Anita rode Senorita. Maybe Magdelena was paying respect to Rojo Anita and her horse.

I thought of so many names. But then I kept thinking of the word Maestra Maria was trying to teach all of us. I didn't really understand all of it, but she had been telling us about the Duende. Maestra Maria said to look for the Duende in all things: the life force inside the book, or the song, or the dance. She said it was the difference between one person's dance and another's; or the way we were moved when we read a poem. She seemed to understand it better than we did, of course, and she would say how difficult it was to explain the Duende, but when it was there, you knew. I wanted to name the silver horse, our horse, Duende.

"Duende," I said.

Magdelena smiled. She knew Duende.

Senorita Duende was what we named her; that's what we named the silver horse, who appeared to us in the light of the moon.

"Let's go find Tio," Magdelena said. As she approached Senorita Duende, the horse bent her knees, so Magdelena could easily climb on the silver back. And I climbed on right behind Magdelena.

Without a word, Senorita Duende left the clearing, heading for the canyon trail.

And then I remembered that Maestra Maria was riding on a horse with a man who looked like Don Pedro.

"When I was in the woods following Maestra Maria, I heard her whistle, and a horse came. A rider that looked like Don Pedro came out of the darkness, reached his hand to hers, and she joined him on his horse. They sped away in search of Tio, I am sure. Who do you think he was, Magdelena? It wasn't Don Pedro because moments later Rojo Anita and Don Pedro came into the woods on their own horses."

How did Senorita Duende know where to go?

"We are going in search of Tio," Magdelena said directly and softly to our horse.

"I don't know who it could have been, Coyitito," Magdelena said. "I saw them, too."

I wanted to know who he was, and how he knew to come at the sound of the whistle, but here I was, sitting behind Magdelena as we rode a horse that had come to us, riding the canyon trail searching for Tio.

"Padre Miguel will be very worried," Magdelena said. And I worried that he would worry because, for now, it seemed he had many worries. And while I was thinking about Padre Miguel, I thought about what Rojo Anita had said about traveling in the light of the moon. Just then, I heard it. So did Magdelena. And we both asked Senorita Duende to run into a cluster of trees, turning off the canyon trail, hiding us. I saw Magdelena touch Senorita Duende's neck in the direction she wanted her to go, but it seemed like Senorita Duende understood our needs, and we veered off to the right.

Our horse glistened in the moonlight so much that we had to get out of the moonlight because coming down the canyon trail were several horses: we heard them. And we either knew them, or we didn't. Either Rojo Anita, Don Pedro, Maestra Maria, and the other man were coming back down the mountain with Tio or they weren't. So we kept going into the trees, hoping the others wouldn't see or hear us until we knew who they were.

We didn't know them. We were able to decide this when they stopped nearby and looked from side to side. It was almost like the wild dogs — the way the riders turned their heads around — like they were sniffing out the trail of someone or something. They were close enough for us to listen. They didn't talk for a while. They just all turned their heads from side to side.

Then one said, "The light will show them to us. Keep sniffing them out." And then we knew they were looking for someone, most probably us. "Smell that? Follow it."

We couldn't move, not even a little bit, because they might hear the branch creak or some other sound we might make.

I began to sweat. I sat terrified as they began to move into the trees.

I took my strength from Magdelena. She sat motionless, but full of listening.

They must be the No Faces. I am sure we were out of the protected area by now.

Above us the owl began to hoot. The owls had a way of talking, and I hoped the No Faces didn't know the language of the owl. I didn't know it, so I hoped it wasn't saying, "Here they are, right below me: the boy Coyitito, the girl Magdelena, and the horse they call Senorita Duende are all sitting underneath me under the branches of the tree."

"The owl talks," one of the men said.

I thought about Rojo Anita, hiding from the moon's light as they traveled the canyon trail, looking for Tio.

I thought of Maestra Maria wrapped in a shawl on a dark horse. And of her partner: all in black from what I could tell.

And I thought about how our horse was not black at all, but silver and visible.

And then we heard a quick thrash of sound. And we bolted. Senorita Duende ran through the trees until we were a streak of lightning; Magdelena's hair was blowing in my face.

I heard them pursuing us. They were the ones who picked up the children and made the children their own. And they were chasing us through the woods.

Weren't any of our Protectors following us, or had the silver horse called "us" to find her and become "our" horse?

I had to be strong for Magdelena.

Once, when we were jumping from the rocks with Rojo Anita, I thought that the No Faces might be watching us from behind the rocks, but Rojo Anita had said, "Clear your mind of it. We are protected here. Do not even think of them," so I thought about The River water below and jumped in.

Now here I was sweating and asking for help. How could this be? I thought about Magdelena, who sat in front of me, my arms tight around her. I thought of the No Faces taking Magdelena, and that thought made me braver. Senorita Duende was moving at lightning speed.

The No Faces were very quick also, but not as fast as we were. They were still on our trail when Magdelena yelled so I could hear her, "Coyitito, take out your key," and I did as she said. I slipped one hand into my pocket, and held Magdelena with the other, pulling out my key.

Senorita Duende stopped abruptly. We jerked forward on her back, and right there in front of us appeared a door on the trunk of a tree. The hooves approached steadily behind us. One of them yelled that he thought we had stopped. Senorita Duende stood in front of the tree's door. My key seemed to be a faulty key and would not always work, Ramon had told me, but here goes. The moon's light showed us a small lock in the wood's surface. I inserted my key and turned it clockwise. The door opened. Senorita Duende bowed her head, and she walked us inside. We shut the door behind us.

Could this really be happening? Did this have to do with Meme; Meme, someone we didn't yet know?

It was completely dark in there, and I didn't know where the safer place was: outside or inside. I was shaking. I saw a glow coming from Magdelena's hair. It was like she had her own star under there. She must have seen it too because she took her comb from where she kept it hidden underneath her hair. Her comb glowed in the dark, offering a soft light.

"Right here. Here is where they went," we heard a deep voice say outside. Horses stopped right outside the door.

"Their trail ends here," One of them said. He must have been the One with the nose of a wild dog, the One who followed our scent and smelled our fear.

"Where did they go? Find them. NOW," exploded a mean voice.

Hooves pounded away. But some of them stayed. Right outside the door.

How would I protect Magdelena? Maybe another door existed nearby, and we could find a way out of this dangerous spot.

Any moment the door from which we entered would be destroyed.

Magdelena didn't say a word.

"They must be here. Keep looking until you find them or else ..."

A thrashing sound hit the tree where we hid.

Inside, our temporary shelter shook.

"They're in here. Right in here. Go in there and get them — NOW."

And we heard them outside the door. We heard horses' hooves, and then silence.

We waited.

We knew we were trapped, and they were setting the trap further. Magdelena never said a word, and I asked all the protectors from all the ages for protection.

Still silence.

It sounded as if they all galloped away — fast — and outside there was silence, but I thought they must have galloped, then walked their horses back to the place where we were, surrounding us.

After a while, though terrified, I opened my eyes, which I had shut in fear. And when I did, I saw that Senorita Duende was lit up by the light of Magdelena's comb.

I looked at Magdelena. She seemed to be covered in the night sky's lights. She looked at me and put her finger over her lips, just like Rojo Anita had done.

And then I saw it. In the corner of the room I saw a No Face, and then I knew that somehow they had gotten inside our hiding place. I shuddered and pointed, and Magdelena turned her head in the direction. How many were there? Did they all arrive? How did they enter? Was this their hide-out?

I held Magdelena tightly and decided I would do everything I could to protect her.

But she turned to me and quietly said, "What do you see, Coyitito?"

I couldn't believe it. What did I see? I looked again at the No Face in the corner. My eyes screamed terror, and Magdelena saw my fear and again she asked, "What do you see, Coyitito?" I was too terrified to talk.

I pointed to the corner.

"I don't see anyone or anything," she whispered.

When I looked again, the corner was empty.

"I think we need to stay here and rest for a bit," said Magdelena. "If the No Faces are out there, we will walk into their trap. We will stay here, and if they come in … we will just wait here for now. I think you need to rest your worry some, Coyitito."

I kept checking the corner. Was it really empty? Why had I seen someone there? But this time when I looked, it wasn't a No Face that I saw; it was a pack of wild dogs heading for me to bite at my knees. I tried to move out of their way, but they didn't stop.

"What is wrong, Coyitito? What frightens you?"

I realized that Magdelena didn't see the wild dogs; only I saw them — and they never reached me; they just kept coming.

But I did tell her. I said, "Magdelena, I see a pack of wild dogs coming to tear me apart," and she said, "Coyitito, you always feared the wild dogs, but they are not here now. The only ones here are you and me and Senorita Duende, no one and nothing else. Do not be afraid. When you see something that frightens you, ask me if I see it, too. Check with me. We will have a word, Coyitito, which we will use when we need to check with each other to see if we both see the same thing. What word shall we use? How about Cassandra?"

"Cassandra? But no one believed her, Magdelena."

"We would. We would have believed her, Coyitito. And she knew; she knew the truth. Do you want to use a different word?"

"Cassandra will be our word for checking the truth, Magdelena, for helping each other see the truth when we lose sight of it ourselves."

Magdelena seemed pleased with our plan. I was too. I thought about how I might be riding around on Senorita Duende yelling, "Cassandra. Cassandra."

"I am very glad that your key worked," Magdelena said. Me, too. I was very, very glad that my key had worked. Thank you, Meme, wherever you are.

The wild dogs of my fears had left the room we hid in and had been replaced by snakes crawling all over the floor. It didn't seem like Magdelena saw them. As soon as they disappeared, I saw a huge fire burst from the walls. I was ready to whisper "Cassandra, Cassandra," but by this time Magdelena was actually resting on the floor with her eyes closed; Senorita Duende stood near the wall, and I watched the room change from one of my fears to another while I waited for the No Faces to break down the door.

And where was Tio?

At some point I must have fallen asleep with my fears, and when I awoke, Magdelena was sitting next to Senorita Duende combing her silver mane. I looked around to see what fears might stand up to my sight, but instead I saw water and bread; I thought my fearful visions had changed.

"Coyitito, have some water and some freshly baked bread."

"Where did they come from, Magdelena?" I remembered the dream cookies.

"I saw that little closet over there, and when I opened it, a jug of cold water and warm bread sat on the shelf."

This was a No Face hide-out. I knew it, and just as I thought it, they appeared.

Six of them.

But nothing happened.

Magdelena looked at me and asked me what I saw, and I told her about the six No Faces.

"Cassandra," Magdelena said.

"Does Cassandra mean that we are safe from what we see? Is Cassandra a word of safety? If you say Cassandra to me when I am wide-eyed with fear, does that mean we are safe?"

"Yes, Coyitito; it means we are safe. The word can pull us back from where we are in our thoughts into a safe place where our thoughts are not in control of taking over and making us believe that what we think is real."

I reached for the water and bread.

When I lifted the water jug, I saw another door, not the closet door that Mag-delena showed me, but another door. I wasn't sure if the door was there or not, so I turned to Magdelena and asked her if she saw it. "Yes, I do see it, Coyitito; Cassandra. I didn't see it before when you were sleeping, but it is there now. Yes. Maybe it is time for us to leave."

We hadn't heard the No Faces since they seemed to go off in search of us. Maybe they did go in a different direction.

I tried the door, but it was locked.

Then I remembered my key.

I reached into my pocket. Senorita Duende moved closer to the new door we saw. Magdelena carried the water and bread. We weren't sure what was on the other side of this door. I told Magdelena that maybe it was best for us to go back through the door we knew, but "No," she said, "try it with your key."

"O.K

"Let's go through the new door," I said.

Senorita Duende bent her front legs. I took the food and drink from Magdelena as we climbed onto Senorita Duende. Then I searched for the lock. When I found it, I turned the key clockwise, and the door opened.

We stepped out onto the canyon trail.

Hopefully, we would find Tio and not the No Faces.

THE SUN WAS STRONG. We started heading straight, and then we turned downhill because we thought we heard The River. It was all so familiar as we moved down on the trail. Senorita Duende seemed to want to go uphill, but we guided her down because we thought that maybe we were back at our River. And I thought that maybe the door we had found led us back, and Tio was back, and we would go to Maestra Maria's class in the morning, and Padre Miguel would walk in, and we'd all stand up and say, "Good morning, Padre Miguel," so we instead moved downhill.

"Did The River send us an invitation?" asked Magdelena, and I didn't remember getting one, but I thought that maybe The River sent us the door that we opened.

So, we kept on.

Magdelena started smiling and pointing, "Look Coyitito; look, it is our River!"

"How do you know?" I asked her, and she said, ""Look Coyitito! That is how I know. There is Tio getting ready to jump. One, two, three! There he goes. Hurry down, Senorita Duende. Look, Coyitito, we have found Tio!" And she guided Senorita Duende into a gallop. But I didn't see Tio jump from the rock. I didn't see Tio at all.

"I don't see Tio, Magdelena."

And she said, "That's not very funny, Coyitito." But I really didn't see Tio, and I thought about the No Faces I saw in the room, and the wild dogs, and the snakes, and the fire, and how Magdelena didn't see any of it. And I knew this wasn't our River, and Tio wasn't in it.

So I said, "Magdelena, remember how I saw the No Faces, and the wild dogs, and other sights I did not wake you to tell you about, and how you did not see these? Well, I don't see Tio, Magdelena. Tio is not here. So we must go because this River did not invite us."

But Magdelena was persistent; she could be that way, so she said, "I hear you, Coyitito, but I really do see Tio. Here. I will call out to him." But I had to put my hand over Magdelena's mouth before she could call him because we didn't want to tell the surrounding trails that we had come.

"I'm sorry, Magdelena," I said. "I truly am." And then I remembered our recent pact, and I said, "Cassandra, Magdelena. Magdelena, Cassandra." We really had to trust each other.

"Cassandra?" Magdelena asked. She stared at the place where she thought she had seen Tio, but I saw her realize that he wasn't there. Why had she thought he was? I think she just wanted him to be there and for us to be back in the safety of our River.

And then we heard the noises coming from the trees, and we knew we had to leave quickly. Very, very quickly; something Senorita Duende knew all along.

"Let's let Senorita Duende always guide us," I suggested to Magdelena.

And Magdelena agreed. And Senorita Duende again quickly brought us into the trees. When we were hidden, we saw the horse. It came out from the trees.

How many more riders were there? The No Faces rode in packs, and this could be their leader.

Magdelena stared straight ahead of her.

We stood quiet, very, very quiet.

I wanted to tell Senorita Duende to go. "Go. Go, run fast," but I knew we had to stay where we were.

And then I thought of the room where I saw the No Faces and my other fears, and how they really weren't there — but I was so frightened because I thought they were.

The rider stopped and looked around. I think he must have somehow heard us. He gave a signal with his hand.

And they came; they came storming down the mountain. The horses came galloping.

The riders came toward us. I knew they would circle us at any moment.

Magdelena just stared straight ahead. Senorita Duende stood where she was.

I looked through the trees. They have to be No Faces; maybe at least ten of them were coming our way. I knew Magdelena saw them; her breathing said so.

All of a sudden, someone was behind us. "What are you doing here?" he whispered. "It is very, very dangerous to be in this part of the canyon. This isn't like the place by The River: here there is no protection. You should not be here."

We turned; Ramon and Solamente stood behind us. Magdelena told Ramon we were looking for Tio, who had disappeared, and so was he; Ramon was looking for Tio, too.

He came closer and kept his eyes all around.

"So I see that your horse has arrived to you. Whose horse is it? Who saw her first?"

"We both did," Magdelena said.

"Ah, sometimes that happens," said Ramon.

"What did you name her?"

"Senorita Duende," we said at the same time.

"Senorita Duende?" he asked.

All of a sudden, Senorita Duende broke into a full gallop. Without any warning, she was speeding through the trees.

Ramon was behind us, keeping pace. We were very, very fast, climbing up a trail. As we neared the top, Senorita Duende stopped and stood behind a cluster of trees. We must have gotten to this spot in seconds because we were at the very top — and moments before — we were at the bottom.

Ramon pulled up behind us. He didn't say a word. He knew as well as we did that if Senorita Duende dashed us up the canyon trail at lightning speed, she knew we had to leave in a hurry.

When we looked down, we saw the group of horses cluster together. At any moment, they would climb our way.

I looked at Ramon. He saw it too: so did Magdelena.

But Senorita Duende had a plan. We were on the top; they were on the bottom; we saw them; they hadn't reached us yet. Senorita Duende walked out onto the rim with Ramon and Solamente following us.

Ramon whispered for us to stay back, so he could lead. We listened to him, and Solamente and he narrowly passed in front of us.

The No Faces must have seen him do it, because all at once, we heard a shout.

"There. Up there. Go and get them. GO!" a fierce voice yelled below us.

"GO. Get them. NOW."

Hoof beats pounded.

Ramon turned straight towards a rock. I didn't see any opening, but there must have been one because all of a sudden, he disappeared.

"Where did he go?" I wondered. Senorita Duende then slipped between two rocks, and we were no longer in the sunlight. Inside it was very, very dark. "But won't the No Faces follow us, Ramon?" I asked him.

"I know the caves," he said.

It was pitch black inside. Ramon lit a light. "I carry this light with me. Follow me."

I don't think he realized that Magdelena's comb could light the darkness.

"Do you know this particular cave, Ramon?" I asked him. And he told us that he did know this cave, this cave he knew very, very well, because this is the cave where his horse brought him with Meme as his rider.

"How did he know that this was that cave?" I wondered.

Ramon was fixed on the way he was going. He didn't talk to us for quite a long time. And I just kept trying to remember that the shadows on the sides of us and in front were nothing to be afraid of, even though they scared me.

We followed along.

And then I thought: I had the terrifying thought that maybe Ramon wasn't Ramon, but maybe he was a No Face.

I froze behind Magdelena. I needed to check with her, but how could I?

Then I knew it; I knew we were being followed. I knew we were. It wasn't just that I was afraid. I knew someone was there, behind us, as we went further into the cave. I felt the cool air, and I knew that someone was behind us, just out of the rim of the light. I didn't know what to do. I sat behind Magdelena, closest to the clutches of the one or ones that followed us, and I started to panic.

Ramon stopped abruptly and pointed his light behind us; a shadow dissolved.

"Who's there?" Ramon asked. "Who is following? Show yourself."

No one came.

Ramon rode us further into the darkness. "Trust that Senorita Duende knows a path in here," I thought.

Ramon stopped again and turned in a circle, his light shining around as he spun. His hand dropped to his side.

"Ramon," a voice called him.

"Ramon. It has been a long time."

And standing in the light was the oldest woman I had ever seen.

"Are you looking for the Little One, for Tio?"

"Yes, Meme; we are searching for Tio. Have you seen him?"

Meme had very long silver hair. She wore many bracelets.

She nodded as she looked into Magdelena's and my eyes. I felt her look into my eyes, and it seemed like she looked even further than my sight. It seemed like Meme looked into me from my head to my feet and then above me and below me, and I couldn't stop looking at her.

Her finger pointed at me as I started to shake behind Magdelena. I watched her finger as she dropped it, and as she did, I heard it. I heard the *snap*. I knew my eyes widened. It sounded like the sound that woke me up from my sleeping, the sound that brought the cookies.

"Coyitito, Magdelena, Senorita Duende, come. I have been baking," she said.

Meme joined Ramon on Solamente's back.

Meme just said she had been baking after she snapped. What did this mean? How did she know us? I was too afraid to ask Magdelena any questions.

We thought we would get to Meme's baking room within moments, but we didn't. We kept going for a very, very long time. All of us were quiet.

And then we arrived at a door. Finally, I was very, very hungry, and I couldn't wait to get inside Meme's place. But she didn't open the door. She just stood at the entrance. And so did Ramon. In fact, Ramon, too, slipped off Solamente and moved to the edge of the wall, leaning there with his foot up. Meme was now standing on the ground. And she stood. And stood. And stood. Meme stood for so long I thought she had become a statue.

Every once in a while, I looked at Magdelena, stretching my neck a bit to see if I could see her. But she just stared straight ahead. Magdelena's manners kept her quiet.

At one point, I became very scared. Why wasn't anyone moving? I thought maybe they had all become stone somehow, and they all had left me. But Magdelena was breathing against me as she sat on Senorita Duende.

Then, finally, Ramon moved. He shifted his legs from one to the other. I waited. He didn't move further.

I looked at Meme. "Please open the door, Meme. Please," I thought.

And then I had another thought.

I slid down off Senorita Duende. My feet hit the ground. No one moved except me. I inched toward the door, moved to the side of Meme, reached into my pocket and took out my key.

It fit into the lock, and the door opened when I turned it clockwise.

I couldn't believe what I saw inside the frame. My eyes continued blinking.

Magdelena and Senorita Duende moved close behind me and saw the vast vision on the other side of the door.

"Tio! Tio! Is he really there, Coyitito? Is that him? Do you see him, too? Cassandra?"

I did see him; I saw Tio too, and I turned to tell Ramon and Meme the news, which they already must have known, but Ramon, Solamente, Meme, the door, and Meme's baking room, which we didn't get to see, were gone.

WHEN WE WALKED through the door, we were somewhere we had never been before. In our books, we had read about it and seen pictures, but we had never been to the ocean. Now Senorita Duende galloped onto the sand. I didn't know if she had ever seen the ocean before. It was so different from The River.

"Magdelena." The wind carried her hair to my face.

"Cassandra?" Magdelena asked.

"I see a tremendous blue ocean with waves. Cassandra," I told her. And she nodded. She saw it too.

The ocean looked like the dream cookies on my desk.

Meme said she had been baking, but I didn't see any treats.

But I did see what I saw when I first opened the door. And Magdelena saw him, too. Tio was riding on an ocean wave, which delivered him to the shore. We watched him come crashing onto the sand, then getting up and running right back into the ocean to do it again.

At first he didn't see us. And then he did. And when he did, he stood there frozen, and I thought I might have to use my key to unfreeze him. But we started shouting and waving and galloping straight toward him. He picked up his hand and waved to us. He must have wondered if we were real.

We went straight to the water's edge and jumped off Senorita Duende. The water licked our feet. We all looked into each other's eyes. Then Magdelena hugged Tio, and I did too, and we all hugged each other.

And then we introduced Senorita Duende to Tio; she headed over to where Padre Miguel II stood watching Tio. Padre Miguel II moved his legs back and forth on something large and white. I ran over to say hello to Tio's horse. Magdelena and Tio followed me.

Padre Miguel II bent his head for us to pet, and we noticed that he was standing on a large white cloth. Magdelena asked, "Tio, is this …?" He nodded his head "yes." Magdelena knelt down on the sand, examining the cloth with her eyes. "This is your cloth, Tio? The one you received as a gift from Ramon?" "Yes," Tio said. "My two cloths are one now; kind of like Juan and me: he lives inside me instead of outside. It changes sizes." "It changes sizes?" I asked. How did it change sizes? "How does it do that, Tio?" I asked him. He shrugged his shoulders.

Then Tio ran back to the ocean with Magdelena following him. And I ran after them.

How long had it been since we left to find Tio? I didn't know. Perhaps I could ask Magdelena.

Then I saw that Tio seemed to understand the ocean in a way Magdelena and I didn't. We knew The River. We had all learned The River together and missed her. But this water was different. There were no canyon rocks from which to dive. The water stretched out and out far, so far. I didn't know where the ocean ended and the sky started.

So I asked Magdelena as we stood at the edge of the ocean. "Do you know where the sky starts?" Tio, who was jumping about in the waves, said to us, "I'll race you to go and find out." And he swam toward the horizon, and then changed his direction. A wave brought him to shore and left him at our feet.

Magdelena watched in wonder. "Tio, teach us how to let the ocean carry us like that," and we followed Tio into the water.

The ocean was so very different from The River; it knocked us down and spread salt on our skin.

"Come over here," Tio said. "You have to wait here, and when the wave comes, you ride with it, or duck down. Do one of those. I'll tell you to ride or duck."

Magdelena and I joined Tio in his spot. He kept turning around to watch the waves. Then he yelled, "Ride!" He threw himself onto his stomach, stretched out his arms in front of him, and the wave rushed him to shore. When he got there, he stood up dripping with sand and water and ran back toward us. Magdelena and I just stood where we were. We were both a bit frightened by the ocean, though we all knew how to swim in The River.

"Ride!" Tio yelled to us.

Magdelena put her hands out in front of her.

I did the same.

The wave poured over my feet, my head, my arms, and led me to shore. Within moments, I was next to Magdelena and Tio, lying on my stomach in the sand, laughing as another wave covered me.

Tio sped back into the water. Magdelena too. Me too.

So we did it again, and again. All daylight we swam out, and the ocean brought us back until we were hungry and tired. Tio said he had food for us up by his blanket. He said that he had found food over by a cove. Bread, water, and cookies were left in a small cove.

Cookies. I wanted to ask Tio about the cookies, but he was running ahead of us toward his blanket and the horses.

I said to Magdelena, "Magdelena, didn't Meme say she had been baking?"

"Yes, Coyitito, she did, and I am grateful because the ocean has made me hungry. What about you?"

I wanted to say, "But Magdelena, how did Meme deliver the food to Tio, and where was she now?" But Magdelena had run ahead of me, turning and yelling, "Come, Coyitito, hurry."

★★★

TIO SPREAD THE BREAD and cookies onto his white cloth that grows and shrinks. The cookies were dark ink colored, like the top half of the ones in our room that night when I had heard the *snap*. White powder was sprinkled over them, and it seemed like in the center of each one was what looked like a pearl.

"These cookies are almost too beautiful to eat," said Magdelena. "Don't you think so, Tio? Coyitito? Look at the shine in the middle. Is that a pearl? Or a star? And look here how the color is so dark, like ink, and then seems to move." I hadn't noticed until Magdelena said that. These cookies were so similar to my dream cookies.

"Cassandra?" I asked Magdelena.

She lifted one of the treats. "Cassandra," she said.

"What's Cassandra?" Tio asked as he reached for a cookie.

"We must eat dinner first," said Magdelena as she placed one of the cookies back on the cloth. We followed her, but I am sure that Tio wanted to first eat his cookie as much as I did. Three cookies — one for each of us — again. I hadn't told Magdelena about the dream cookies because I thought I had dreamed them.

"Cassandra means that I see what you see, Tio. Coyitito and I saw people who weren't there, but we thought they were. So we created a word, which means that, yes, I see it, too."

Tio stared off into the distance. We both knew he understood.

We three tore off pieces of bread from the fresh loaf left on the beach in the cove.

"Tio, how did you get here?" Magdelena asked.

Tio looked at us and said, "I don't know. I left in the night because I had a dream, a very real dream. Juan came to me and told me to go to the ocean. Go the way Ramon went, find the woman, and she will bring me to the ocean.

"In the dream, he told me that he would help me. 'First get on Padre Miguel II and ride.' That's what Juan told me. So I did. I knew I should have told Padre Miguel and you two that I was leaving, but I was in my dream, and I thought Juan might not wait for me, so I left. I went to my horse, Padre Miguel II, and said, 'Follow Juan.' And he did; he followed Juan through the darkness, up the canyon trails.

"I kept telling Padre Miguel II, 'Follow Juan,' because I didn't see Juan, but I knew that he did.

"I couldn't see much in the night; the moon was not out, but somehow the stars were. You'll see them later. Somebody must be shooting them from an arrow because they keep leaping across the sky.

"But Padre Miguel II knew just when to turn. The stars lit the sky, but on the ground there was much darkness. Then I saw a glow, a large light, and it was a fire, so I knew someone was near. I trusted Juan to lead us. Then Padre Miguel II started going backwards. I didn't know he could go backwards like that — but he did. He didn't turn his head, but he started moving down the trail."

I, Coyitito, listened to Tio's story. I couldn't believe he was telling us so much. Quiet Tio was really talking. I thought about so many things as he talked. I thought about how Tio and Padre Miguel II might have fallen off the rim in the dark, or how the No Faces were behind them, or might, at any moment, come running in front of them, taking them into their caves and making Tio one of them. What would they do with Padre Miguel II?

As I listened to Tio's story, I wondered how he left the school unnoticed. Maybe he left in his dream.

I was lifted from my own thoughts back into Tio's story. "Padre Miguel II took me down the trail backwards. And then they started coming on their horses.

"And then he jumped. We were falling down in the dark. I hoped he knew what he was doing. We fell; I don't know for how long ... but then I felt his hooves hit the ground. He started walking again, right inside a cave, like he knew exactly what to do. I guess Juan was helping. For some reason, he wanted me to come to the ocean. Padre Miguel or Maestra Maria didn't hear me leave."

"Wasn't the gate locked, Tio?" Magdelena asked him.

"Padre Miguel II jumped over the wall."

"But the wall is very, very high, Tio."

"I know. I didn't know he could do all this jumping.

"Then we were in a cave; it was dark, but Padre Miguel II kept walking. Juan must have been talking to him. I was very tired, but I didn't go to sleep. And then I thought that somebody was following us."

And Magdelena and I knew who was following them.

Tio never talked this much, and I could see he was growing tired. So were we. And before we knew it, we were on our backs, lying on Tio's blanket, watching the amazing archers shoot the stars across the sky, and we must have fallen asleep with the waves coming to shore and the salty air our cover.

It has been said that the No Faces never ever come to the ocean because they don't know how to get there and don't know how to swim. So we were not afraid of sleeping in the open, out on the sand, under the sky.

I don't know which one of us awoke first, but all of a sudden, we were all awake. In the dark night, under the sky's light, Padre Miguel II and Senorita Duende started neighing. I think it was low at first; I thought it was part of my dream. Then the sound grew louder, and Magdelena asked Senorita Duende why she was neighing the way she was. Senorita Duende and Padre Miguel II moved their legs backward and forward, staring straight out into the ocean. And when we looked to where they were looking — we saw them! Shadows and outlines appeared out on the water.

We realized that somehow the No Faces had found a way to the ocean, and their horses, who could swim, swam them toward shore. There must have been a piece of land out there that we didn't see because somehow they were coming!

We stood up on the sand. There was no way we could outrun them. They were still out on the water, but their horses rode the crests of the waves right toward us. We had to leave. Quickly.

Tio was already on Padre Miguel II's back. Senorita Duende bent down to let us climb onto her, something we learned that she did when we might need her to. Now what? Now our horses would dash us away to safety. But they didn't move; they stood right where they were; Tio's blanket was underneath us.

"Maybe they want us to get the blanket, Magdelena," I said. And as I said this, Senorita Duende bent her head, opened her mouth, and swallowed one of the three cookies on our blanket. Then Padre Miguel II opened his mouth and the second cookie disappeared. But neither of them ate the third.

"Senorita Duende, we must go, please," I said, but she didn't move. Then Tio jumped off Padre Miguel II's back; he grabbed the third cookie, split it three ways, and handed a piece to Magdelena and me.

"Let's do what they do," Tio said.

Magdelena, Tio and I ate. A salty sweet taste squirted into my mouth. I looked at the ocean. The No Faces were almost at the shore. We did what the horses did, but soon we would be captured. Then both horses took an end of Tio's blanket and picked it up in their mouths.

The first group of No Faces had now reached the shore. The wave spilled them onto the sand. I sat frozen behind Magdelena. She sat as still as I. Tio seemed to be waiting, his eyes on the figures who started galloping towards us.

"We must leave," I said to all of us as the shadows became clearer and closer. I sat staring in terror as I heard the approaching gallop of the horses. They headed straight to us. I thought Tio might do something, but he sat there on Padre Miguel II holding steady.

All of a sudden, we rose quickly into the air as the No Faces pounded toward us. We soared high, all of us on Tio's blanket, flying, flying high over their heads.

"Get them; go and get them now. Right NOW!" We heard the shouts from the fierce One who speaks orders. I looked down, and he was pointing at us as we flew far away. I saw something reach up into the air; it looked like a rope, but we were so far away from their hands at that moment.

I couldn't believe it. I held fast to Magdelena's waist. I didn't want to move because I thought we might tip the blanket. Padre Miguel II and Senorita Duende stood still with the three of us on their backs. I was afraid to talk thinking that I might unbalance the blanket with my voice.

"Cassandra?" I whispered. Tio and Magdelena both nodded "yes."

"The cookies?" I asked. And they both nodded "yes" again. Somehow the cookies that the horses knew they should eat had lifted us, but I decided not to talk anymore because Magdelena and Tio were quiet.

Finally, when I looked around, we were right in the crush of stars. One of them passed right over Tio's head. He turned his eyes to follow the trail of light.

I was mesmerized in the land of stars. "Look at this, Magdelena. Tio, do you think we can stop here and look at the stars?" I asked him. I wanted to slip one of them right into my pocket. Manuel would love this flight.

Then I became mesmerized by one of the stars. I was drawn to the star and its light. I very much, very, very much wanted to see if I could go inside the star. Would I be able to visit the inside of the star?

"Tio, can we stop here by this star?" We floated among the five pointed lights. Below us, the No Faces scrambled on the beach. Tio nodded and spoke to Padre Miguel II. The blanket stood still. We were right next to a luminous star.

I decided to take out my key and place it as close to the light as I could. Maybe I could go inside! I thought the star would be burning hot, but it wasn't; it was cool. As I turned my key clockwise, a sliver of light moved to the right and an entrance appeared. I waved at Magdelena and Tio, Padre Miguel II, and Senorita Duende, knowing they would wait for me.

Before I was completely inside, Magdelena cautioned, "You may not want to come back out, Coyitito; it may be too beautiful."

"I'll want to," I told her.

And I meant it.

I expected light when I went inside the star, but it was dark, very dark.

Then I heard a voice in the darkness, and it said, "What do you want?" and I thought the star might give me what I wanted, so I started thinking of things I wanted. I thought of combing Magdelena's strong hair, and I saw Magdelena and me, and I was combing her hair. I wanted fresh milk, and I was drinking fresh-milk. I wanted to tell Maestra Maria where I was, inside a star, and that we had found Tio. She appeared with her hair hanging down, riding a sable horse, and I said, "Maestra Maria, you have found me here," and she said, "You have found me here, Coyitito." And I wanted to swim in The River with Tio, and The River appeared, and Tio was diving from the canyon rock, and I was next, ready to jump. And then I stopped, for a single moment, and I saw nothing. And I said to the star, "What are you? Whatever I think appears. What are you without my thinking?" and the star said, "I'm a star."

So I turned around to leave. And I stepped out into the open sky, my foot ready to fall on Tio's waiting cloth, but Tio and Magdelena and Padre Miguel II and Senorita Duende and the cloth weren't there in the sky, so I started falling. And I fell; I fell for a very, very long time. I slid down the sky in total terror. I, Coyitito, was very frightened.

I tried to stop. I even tried to pull my key, but I was falling too fast, and I couldn't reach it.

And I fell right through the darkest sky.

Plunge! Then I was in water, falling, and then I stopped falling and swam toward the surface. I had no idea where I was or what was waiting for me when I finally raised my head out of the water, but I did know I wasn't in the ocean because it wasn't like that. It didn't have that salty taste. This was different. This was some-thing familiar, something I knew well.

I'm not sure how it happened, but somehow The River had sent me an invitation, and I guess I answered because as I swam to the surface, I knew that I was in The River. Our River.

I looked around underwater for Tio and Magdelena, for Padre Miguel II and Senorita Duende, but I didn't see any of them when I popped my head above The River.

I wasn't sure who would be waiting for me, but sitting in the sun was Rojo Anita. "You have finally come, Coyitito." I looked at her; my eyes filled with my friend. "Rojo Anita, is that really you?" I felt so many feelings. I wanted to run to the surface rocks and put my arms around Rojo Anita and tell her about the No Faces finding the ocean and Tio's changing cloth, and everything, but I wasn't sure that she was really Rojo Anita or really there.

Maybe I was still inside the star, and Rojo Anita was just in my mind.

"Are you just in my mind?" I thought, and Rojo Anita said, "No, I am not just in your mind, Coyitito; I am here," and with that she dove from the canyon rocks, dove straight down into the water where I was.

Next to me in the water, Rojo Anita rose up.

"So what about this star?" she asked.

I told her that I flew in the night sky on Tio's cloth, and I asked him if we could stop, and I used my key. My key. I reached into my pocket, but it was gone. My key was no longer there.

Rojo Anita knew as soon as I did. And just when we were both getting ready to go under the water and to look for my key, a shadow crossed the sun. We looked up and sailing above our heads, coming slowly down from the sky, a white cloth floated. And on it, Magdelena, Tio, Padre Miguel II, and Senorita Duende appeared.

"Where did you go, Coyitito?" Magdelena yelled from above. "You were gone so, so long. We couldn't find you. Your star disappeared."

Tio peered down over the side of his cloth, looking at Rojo Anita and me.

The cloth landed on the surface of the water. Tio, Padre Miguel II, Magdelena and Senorita Duende jumped down and landed in The River. Tio took the cloth, pulled an end, and it became small again. He must have been practicing with his cloth. Or maybe it just had a mind of its own: temperamental.

Magdelena jumped from Senorita Duende's back, and our horses waded to The River bank. I saw Rojo Anita exchange glances with them.

Rojo Anita swam to Magdelena and Tio and hugged them tightly. I was going to dive underneath the water to find my key, but up rose someone else: Don Pedro's head appeared, dripping from The River. I wasn't sure where he had come from, or how long he had been here; I only knew that it was good to see him. Here I was with Rojo Anita, Don Pedro, Magdelena, Tio, Padre Miguel II, and Senorita Duende. If only Maestra Maria and Padre Miguel were here.

And then I saw it. I saw the sable stallion through the trees. Rojo Anita knew I saw it, and she called to me. "Coyitito, come over here. We must all talk," but I didn't go right away; I lingered, and she called me again, "Coyitito." And out there riding the other way, away from us, I saw the stallion, and on it, I saw a long black haired rider, and I believed that it was Maestra Maria, and behind her, sitting behind her, like I sat behind Magdelena, was another rider. I couldn't see him well, but he looked like Don Pedro, and he held his arms around Maestra Maria's waist. And I saw how they shared their horse like Magdelena and I shared Senorita Duende, the horse who had come to us both at the same time.

And I wanted to run to her. I wanted to run to Maestra Maria and tell her how we had found Tio and had swum in the ocean; we had found the ocean — and the No Faces. I wanted to tell her all about the cave and the star visions. I wanted to tell her, I wanted to say, "Maestra Maria, I went inside a star, and I saw you there. I saw you inside the star. And then I fell from the sky, right into The River," and I know she would have said, "Coyitito, what did you learn from the star?" And I would have said, "When you wish upon a star, Maestra Maria, in the subjunctive, you can change it to the present. Wish is subjunctive, yes? So 'when you wish upon a star' can change to 'When you are a star.' And she would have nodded and said, "Yes, Coyitito, your star is your present; your star is a gift."

And I watched her ride away and knew I should not mention that I saw her because, at that moment, Rojo Anita swam to me and said, "I'll race you to the rock; whoever gets there first wins." "Wins what?" I asked her. "Who knows?" And it was enough to take me from the sight in my eyes, but before I raced Rojo Anita up the canyon trail, I lingered a bit longer, staring into the trees. And I wondered why Rojo Anita didn't want me to go to Maestra Maria and tell her about Tio.

Rojo Anita and the others were already on the canyon rock getting ready to jump, and I hurried out of the water, ran up, turned around several times to see if Maestra Maria's trail was visible, but when I reached the top, they had all jumped already. So there I stood, ready to jump by myself. I looked down to make sure no one was beneath me. I waited for them to call and shout and say, "Come on, Coyitito. Jump!" But no one was beneath. No one called. They were all gone. All of them. Even Senorita Duende and Padre Miguel II. And I thought about how probably none of this had happened and that I was probably still inside the star. I had no Magdelena or Tio to check Cassandra with, so I jumped.

And I landed in The River.

"Coyitito, oh my, where have you been?" Padre Miguel boomed from the trees. I looked up, and there he was coming down from the branches. "We have been looking for you!" He scrambled down to the ground, and I swam to meet him. There was so much I had to tell him and ask him, but as my mind raced with all these words, I saw Rojo Anita, Don Pedro, Magdelena, Tio, Senorita Duende, and Padre Miguel II standing under the trees. I quickly looked for Maestra Maria, but she wasn't there.

Rojo Anita smiled. "You took too long, Coyitito. You didn't win." And I thought that maybe, maybe, they really were there. She nodded and said, "You know you have to find your own way of knowing what an illusion is." I wasn't sure what she meant, and I wasn't sure if Rojo Anita was reading my mind. I was so overcome with seeing everyone and Padre Miguel that I splashed my way out of The River and right into Padre Miguel's arms.

"Cassandra?" I readied to ask Magdelena.

"Cassandra?" Rojo Anita asked. Then she must have read me because she said, "Cassandra." And Magdelena smiled at me, and Tio nodded.

But even though Padre Miguel was so glad to see us — and very, very joyful to see Tio — something was wrong. Very wrong. I thought maybe he was still very angry that Tio and we had left, but something else seemed to upset him.

And then he told us:

"We believe the No Faces came and took Manuel. He was missing for school in the morning. Maestra Maria reported it right away. No one heard anything in the night. He was just gone. Like you three — gone. But with Manuel, there was a foul odor that lingered. We have no idea where he is.

"We didn't know where you were either. For a very long time, we didn't know. Rojo Anita couldn't see you. She couldn't get in touch with any of you. And then she came riding with Don Pedro. And they rang the bell in a coded way in the middle of the night, and I jumped out of bed and went to the gate. Maestra Agatha was behind me, and Maestra Maria, too.

"Rojo Anita said, 'Padre Miguel, I am sorry to wake you, but I see them in my mind's eye. I see Magdelena, Coyitito, and Tio. I have found them.' And Maestra Maria behind me sighed a deep sigh and said, 'Where are they, Rojo Anita? Let us go and get them,' and she was ready to run to where you were. And I, too, was already leaving. And Rojo Anita said, 'We can't go to them. We have to bring them to us.' And with that she lifted her head toward the sky.

"She pointed her finger. 'There,' she said.

"We looked up. The stars were all over the sky. 'There?' Maestra Maria asked. And Rojo Anita pointed at one of the stars and said, 'Yes, I see them there by that star. That star right next to the Big Dipper. Do you see the Big Dipper?' And we all nodded that 'yes, we did' because sometimes that's easier to see than Cassiopeia or Capricorn, so I am happy that you picked the star you did because at least we had an idea where you were. And then Rojo Anita said, 'I will try to make it even clearer for you,' and she took her two hands and held them just a bit apart and told us, 'Look through here. Look through my hands.' And we did.

"Then we saw it. Rojo Anita's hands were like a telescope. We saw, very small, very, very tiny, the white cloth with horses and riders stopped outside a star. Rojo Anita said it was the star on the bow of the archer. He might shoot that star at any moment, so we must act quickly. She said we must all go to The River and ask her to send an invitation, inviting all of you for a dip in her streams.

"So Maestra Maria and I joined Don Pedro and Rojo Anita, riding with them, and we all went to The River. Maestra Agatha locked up the gates. We rode through the darkness, allowing the horses to lead us. I kept looking up to where you were. So did Maestra Maria as she rode behind Don Pedro.

"Then we arrived at The River. All of us waded out into her depth on the horses because we thought the invitation required the strength of all of us to reach you.

"We gave The River our request. We told her that we had finally found her friends, and could she please invite them for a swim. We pointed to where you were above her.

"She became powerful and started moving rapidly. She quickly took the legs of the horses and moved them along. We had no choice but to follow her direction, and when she stopped her strong movement, she placed us in one of her river pools, which was very calm, barely moving. From there, the stars reflected on the surface. We were surrounded in the pool of stars. We looked for the star where you had all stopped, but it must have been released from the archer's bow in those moments because we saw its reflection shoot across the pool's surface, and when we looked up, it was flying across the sky.

"But you, Coyitito, were inside that star as it sped. And the others were outside. But thankfully the invitation had arrived before you separated, Coyitito. So you all received the invitation, but you arrived from different directions."

I could tell that Padre Miguel was offering gratitude for our safe return.

"We must find Manuel," Magdelena said sharply. "We must go and find him now."

And Padre Miguel, Rojo Anita, and Don Pedro knew this was true.

"How did he disappear?" Magdelena asked.

"Just like you all did. But Rojo Anita can't see him. And we believe he was taken."

"We also know that it is up to you three to find him," Padre Miguel continued.

"You three have been chosen to help in the fight against the No Faces. From the moment you all appeared on the same day, to the special gifts you have been given, your ability to fly and go inside the stars, and to your seeing the No Faces when they found the ocean — all this means that you three have been selected for this most important task. We would rather protect you, but we know that it is you who will ultimately protect all of us."

I SHIFTED MY FEET.

Protect all the others against the No Faces? Find Manuel? Did Padre Miguel know what he was saying?

"When do we begin, Padre Miguel?" Magdelena beamed at him. Leave it to Magdelena to think this was an honor. He smiled back at her. Then he looked at Tio who stared him straight in the eyes. Tio nodded his head once into Padre Miguel's gaze. When Padre Miguel turned to me, my knees were knocking. He winked at me.

"You have already begun," he answered.

We stayed at The River, thinking about what Padre Miguel had just told us.

Rojo Anita and Magdelena emerged from the water. Magdelena's hair was a fountain streaming down her back. Tio and I were still in The River water while Magdelena and Rojo Anita sat on the rocks.

"Tio, what do you think about what Padre Miguel said?" I asked him. But Tio was not in the mood for words, so he shrugged his shoulders telling me, in his own way, that he did not want to think about it or talk about it.

So I watched Magdelena in awe. Her comb glowed cream white in her hand, and it sank into the depths of her hair. When it reappeared at the tips of her black carpet, it brought with it rivulets from The River.

Mostly Magdelena's hair was in a braid, and it sat right in front of me when I rode behind her on Senorita Duende. I watched Magdelena's braid ride up and down with the rhythm of our horse's hooves.

Sometimes I dared myself to think of taking the small band from the bottom and watch as her braid would slowly unwind as we moved. I thought how it could take hours for Magdelena's hair to unweave right before my eyes. Or maybe I could just reach out and help it move faster every once in a while. Or I could ask Senorita Duende to go faster, make more of a breeze, and maybe Magdelena's braid would get caught in the breeze, and all of a sudden, her hair would explode into my eyes.

But I didn't touch Magdelena's hair. I just rode behind it and felt it from afar.

Now it was drying in the sun.

I looked at Tio to see what he was doing, but when I turned to him, Tio was gone, and I thought he was probably underwater because he loved being under the water. He spent as much time down below as he did above when we were at The River. Or that time at the ocean: Tio kept going under the waves.

I returned my gaze to Magdelena's hair when, all of a sudden, something grabbed me from the rock and pulled me under the water. I couldn't escape. I was underneath the surface, being held by something or someone. It was too long. I was splashing and struggling. No one came to help me. I knew it wasn't Tio; he wouldn't think this was funny. I didn't know why Rojo Anita and Magdelena weren't coming to help me. I asked The River to please release me.

And just when I thought I couldn't stay another minute under the water, I was released and came up gasping, looking for who held me and why no one came to help. But Magdelena and Rojo Anita still sat on the rocks; I saw Tio swimming from upstream; Padre Miguel II and Senorita Duende stood under the trees. But Senorita Duende caught my eye, and I knew that she knew I was struggling. And then I thought I saw something in Magdelena and Rojo Anita — something that said they knew too.

I looked toward Tio, who was on the surface at the moment, and then I saw him, all of a sudden, being pulled under just like I had been. I knew he was pulled under by the way he went down: he was quickly sucked under, and I started running and swimming to help him.

I yelled to Rojo Anita and Magdelena that something was in The River, pulling us underneath, almost drowning us, but they just looked my way and didn't move toward us.

Tio was still under, but he was used to it. He always lasted long at the game we started playing — who could stay under the longest — so I thought that he might be able to survive longer than I. But there was no sign of him. I couldn't tell where he was.

Soon again I had the opportunity to look for him underneath the surface because, all of a sudden, it happened again: my legs were pulled out from me, and someone held me while I squirmed and moved my arms and tried to get free.

My eyes opened as I struggled. I did see Tio's legs, so the rest of him must have been above water, but he wasn't coming my way. I tried to call to him, hoping The River would carry my voice to his ears, but he did not turn around or swim my way.

Then, just again when I thought I could not stay one more second under the water, I was released.

I whipped my head around.

Then down I went.

This time it was different. Instead of being held under the water, I was taken on an underwater river ride. Someone behind me held my legs by the ankles and pushed me like I was a wheelbarrow. (All of a sudden, I thought about the poem we read where so much depends upon a wheelbarrow.) I was being pushed very, very fast. In front of me was a large rock; I was heading straight for it. I tried to change my direction, but whoever had me steered me right for the rock. I cried out underwater, stopped abruptly, and was let go. I faced the river rock in front of me. I started to try to climb out onto the rock, to catch my breath, look for Tio, and see where I had traveled in those few seconds.

I thought about how the No Faces found the ocean. Somehow they had found the way to the ocean, and I thought they must have broken through the Protected Zone here too.

Then I saw Tio — way, way upstream, and I called to him. "Tio! Tio!" I was afraid to go back into the water all the way. My legs were still dangling from the rock.

Tio didn't hear me, but the force did because my legs were pulled; I slid into the water without breaking my nose on the stone, and I was being pushed upstream; within seconds, I was passing Tio who had been far away from me.

I don't know if he saw me as I sped by, but now I knew I was far from him because more seconds had passed. Then I was steered right up against a canyon wall. I was left there.

I knew whoever was playing with me would be back. I knew I was far from the others. I knew I wanted to get back to them. But here I was trapped by the canyon and The River.

"River, please help me." My intruder was back and rushed me downstream.

And when I got there to where my friends were, I stood up at the bank I knew so well, shaking and terrified, while Magdelena's hair welcomed me, and Tio swam my way.

I panted my way to Rojo Anita and Magdelena, yelling to Tio to get out of the water quickly, but it was too late. He was gone.

"Rojo Anita, quick! We must save Tio from the No Faces. They have gotten in, like they got into the ocean when we were there without you and you couldn't see us. They were almost drowning me. How come you couldn't hear my mind calling you? Was I that far away? We must save Tio," and I ran back to the water, but no one followed me.

"Senorita Duende, help me save Tio! Padre Miguel II!" but even the horses just looked at me, so I went myself into the water, dreading each step. And then I swam the way I thought Tio went, but before I got very far, Tio appeared in front of me, laughing. Laughing. Tio was laughing. And I didn't know why.

He stood up with a big smile on his face, and behind him, out of the water, someone appeared whom I had never seen before. I stared at him, not understanding. And the man was laughing.

"Coyitito, I am sorry I frightened you. It is the way it is. You must learn as much as you can if you are going to come against the No Faces. I have been sent to teach you. So here I am to teach you the ways of The River. I am Canyon Joe."

Canyon Joe disappeared under the water, taking Tio and me with him. This time I was less afraid. He pushed us both upstream, fast, taking us right up to the rocks, then veering one way or the other. And when he thought our lungs had enough, he lifted us to the surface to breathe.

"Notice the rocks," he told us. "Study them. They look similar, but no two river rocks are the same. The River rocks are a road, a trail in The River. And sometimes you might need to travel underneath her surface. She protects us right here, but the safety zone soon ends. Some new configurations have appeared, I am told. See this line on the canyon wall, the place where the rocks split; that is where her protection ends on this side. Notice the spot. Do you both see it?"

And we did. We nodded that we saw it. But what about Magdelena? She wasn't here to see this new line in the Protected Zone. And I said, "Canyon Joe, I see it. And Tio, you see it, yes? But Magdelena's not here to see it."

"Yes, I am Coyitito," and there was Magdelena next to us, her dried hair again soaked as she rose out of the water. And behind us was a woman I had never seen before: a short woman, small, just a little taller than Magdelena when they both stood.

And I was amazed that Magdelena appeared, and so did this Lady, and Magdelena's hair was unbraided, clinging down her back. And the Lady's hair was turquoise, and it fell far down under the water.

"Meet my wife, Marina Teresa," Canyon Joe said.

Marina Teresa already knew our names because she called them out loudly; "Coyitito. Tio." And the canyon river started calling us by name after Marina Teresa. All of a sudden, the canyon called us and kept calling; first, it called loudly, then lower and lower; "Coyitito. Tio." And as our names traveled through the canyon, Marina Teresa called "Magdelena." So the canyons called us: "Coyitito. Tio. Magdelena. Coyitito. Tio. Magdelena."

"This way," Marina Teresa whispered.

"This way."

"This way."

And we were all under the water again.

UNDER THE WATER, Marina Teresa's turquoise hair floated past her feet.

She pointed her finger up, and we all followed her to the surface and watched Canyon Joe climb up the rocks until he was high above us. "Come on up here," he called, and we scrambled the rocks.

"Let's dive. Put your hands over your head like this with your head between them. You are an arrow. If your hands are straight, when you hit the water, they can guide you far down. Your hands reach the water before your head in case there are dangers. Jump out and point down. Your hands will guide you back up if you point them that way," said Canyon Joe.

None of us told Canyon Joe that we had dived before with Rojo Anita.

And Canyon Joe raised his hands above his head, bent his knees, and he made himself an arrow. Whoosh. He was in the air, traveling down into the water — down, down; he disappeared, and then he reappeared on the surface.

"You go," he called up to us.

All three of us stood together. "On three we go," Magdelena said. "One. Two. Three." We were flying.

I was traveling far down into the water when I remembered to point my arms upward, and when I did, I reached the surface to find Tio, Magdelena, and Canyon Joe.

"Now let's try something else," he said. And he climbed back up the rocks, and we followed him onto the trail. All of a sudden, a shrill whistle filled the air, and a horse appeared below us. It ran up the canyon trail. We had never seen this horse before, and we had to move out of its way as it sped. It rode to the top of the rocks where Canyon Joe stood, and when it got there, he jumped on it.

"This is Midnight. Midnight and I have been riding together for a long, long time. Right, Midnight? And another thing we've been doing — we jump off the canyon rocks from up here — down into whatever is below us. You have to know how to jump with your horse." And Canyon Joe touched Midnight right between the eyes.

Senorita Duende could jump, I'm sure. Padre Miguel II was a jumper! We didn't tell Canyon Joe that, either.

It didn't seem like every horse could jump, but I was always being surprised. And he said, "Now watch. It's simple." And in a second, Midnight and Canyon Joe were gone. We were afraid to watch, but then we heard a splash, looked over the rock, and Midnight was riding Canyon Joe to land.

We were alone on the rocks when all of a sudden we saw Senorita Duende and Padre Miguel II climbing on the trail. "Ask them if they want to jump with you," Canyon Joe called to us.

We stood on the edge of the rock, getting ready to jump when, all of a sudden, a rumbling began. The rocks started moving back and forth. We stumbled where we stood. The whole canyon started shaking and moving.

"Oh no," I thought. "Is this what I think it is?"

"What is going on?" I yelled to Magdelena and Tio, but all of a sudden, The River got very, very high and was pounding, and rocks fell around us. The River got so high that it climbed onto the ledge where we were, grabbed the horses' legs, and pulled us in.

"What is going on with The River?" I yelled into Magdelena's ear, but she couldn't answer because we were being carried with force. I was very, very frightened. And then I heard a noise behind us. It sounded like a huge wave, nothing like what we had known in the ocean, was coming our way. We felt it. We felt it behind us. We were being lifted high, high up, and I knew we would have to get down from this height, and it worried me. We were getting too, too high in the sky when all of a sudden some creature came. Some sleek, slippery creature arrived and slid under Senorita Duende, so now we were riding on something that was still under the wave. And Tio too, was being carried by something. And then Marina Teresa appeared on her horse, followed by many shiny swimming *ones*. She rode the wave right between Tio and us, and her horse, her horse was very, very different from our horses.

Her horse stood straight up on the wave, and Marina Teresa was inside a pouch that stretched across its middle. She rode her horse on the waves, and these swimming *ones* surrounded her. She had a big shell in her hand, and as we rode on the top of the wave, she blew the shell, and all her swimming friends started leaping out of the water, jumping, except the *ones* who carried us on their backs. The wave still was very, very high as Marina Teresa, her horse, and the shiny ones steadied themselves and us from toppling or dropping.

And then the rumbling stopped, and the wave started to get lower and lower and still lower. And then we were getting closer to the banks of The River.

"Marina Teresa, what happened?" Magdelena asked.

"An earthquake," she said. "Sometimes Canyon Joe throws rocks around; that is why he is Canyon Joe."

She asked us if we were all right, and I was bewildered. But we were fine, and I didn't want her to think we didn't appreciate her and her friends.

"I have never seen a horse like yours, Marina Teresa," Magdelena said. Tio was mesmerized as he gazed at Marina Teresa's horse. He kept his hand on Padre Miguel II's head. I put mine on Senorita Duende's side, hoping our horses were steady after that frantic ride. This must be part of the training.

"This is Aphrodite. She is a sea horse. And these are my friends: The River Dolphins," said Marina Teresa.

Some of them were pink. "Look, Magdelena, some of the dolphins are pink!" I exclaimed.

We had never seen real dolphins before!

"Here we go!" Marina Teresa announced. Then she rode on the water with her dolphins behind her, and we were again carried downstream.

Canyon Joe stood on The River bank with someone. It didn't look like Rojo Anita or Padre Miguel. It did look like a familiar form. He waved for us to come his way, and without us doing any steering, we were deposited near the waterline and walked through the shallow path to shore.

Canyon Joe jumped onto Midnight. "See you soon again. Keep practicing." And Canyon Joe rode away while Ramon stayed behind with us.

"Ramon!" We were so glad to see him, and we had so much to tell him. We would tell him all our stories and ask about Meme.

"Let's take a ride on the trail," Ramon said, and we rode together into the canyon.

★★★

RAMON MUST HAVE BEEN TESTING us with the limits of the Protected Zone because I knew, and I think Magdelena and Tio also knew, that we were continuing out of its boundaries. I hoped Ramon was Ramon and knew what he was doing as we traveled the trail. We followed him because we didn't want to insult him, but I kept turning around to see what was behind us; it was in front of us that the No Faces appeared.

Many, many No Faces lined the canyon trail below us.

I pointed when I saw them but Ramon, Magdelena, Tio, Senorita Duende, and Padre Miguel II saw them before I did.

"They're not real," Ramon said.

"What do you mean they're not real?" asked Magdelena.

"They're decoys. I've been noticing as I ride that the No Faces make decoys of themselves out of material and post them as lookouts. From a distance, they look real. They always make them standing with their backs facing the trails. They line them up like that, sometimes fifty of them. But they're tricky. Sometimes they put a few live No Faces in between the decoys, so when you come riding, and you think, 'Oh look, the No Face decoys are out,' the real No Faces, mixed in between, start coming your way. You must be very careful."

Finally, Magdelena asked, "Ramon, why are we riding this way?"

All of a sudden, before Ramon answered her, he turned us quickly inside a cave; it was complete darkness. We turned and turned again and again, seemingly following Ramon and Solamente. I hoped Senorita Duende knew where Ramon and Solamente and Tio and Padre Miguel II were going ahead of us. I hoped Ramon was our Ramon.

And then all movement stopped. I heard three knocks upon the stone. A door slid open; light shone behind it; we all entered; the door shut. And there was Meme. She had a fire roaring.

She looked up at us, her face glowing from the flame.

A puddle grew under the stones on the other side of the room. Tio and Padre Miguel II neared it.

"Taste this, Tio," Meme said.

He reached for the cookie in her hand.

"Coyitito, Magdelena, taste; I just finished these. I have a different batch for you, Ramon. Remember that sometimes your horses will appreciate the cookies too."

I watched Tio bite into his cookie. His face twisted in a strange surprise. I bit into mine. Was this caramel in sea salt? Or fudge covered in sea salt? Magdelena bit into her cookie.

"Sesame," she stated.

Meme smiled as a door appeared where Tio stood.

The door opened, and the ocean was again on the other side. Tio galloped toward it; we followed him.

I turned to thank Meme, hoping that Ramon, Solamente, and she planned on joining us, but they were gone.

I waved at the closed surface anyway and said, "Thank you, Meme."

Our horses ran to the water.

★★★

I COULDN'T WAIT to go into the water. But, all of a sudden, a wave came out of nowhere, rolling right to us. It wasn't very high, but it was powerful. The water took Senorita Duende, Magdelena, Tio, Padre Miguel II, and me. Then something big and powerful came underneath us, and we were flying through the water, far, far away from shore. When we were far, far away, we stopped, just like that. We stopped moving and sat far, far from shore. At first, I thought that Canyon Joe had joined us in the ocean.

I started to become nervous when he didn't appear, and we were just sitting out in the middle of the water, waiting.

And then — I heard it. The rush of water. It wasn't a waterfall though it sounded like one; it was another wave coming our way. It wasn't as big as The River wave, but it was high, and rolling toward us. I didn't know if we could ride a wave like this one, or if we would duck and it would go over our heads, but as I was thinking about all this, I looked at the wave. Riding on its crest, right in front of us, was Marina Teresa on her rainbow colored sea horse, Aphrodite. And all around them were dolphins, not just pink, but blue, too. The dolphins came rushing in, their faces peering out from the wave.

Just when we were lifted high into the sky, the force of the wave left, and a gentle drop brought us closer to the shoreline.

The dolphins jumped out of the water, spinning in circles, smiling. And Marina Teresa sat right before us. "So, Rodeo and Juna found you!" Rodeo and Juna? "They are the dolphins that rode you through The River when the water came," Marina Teresa said. "And they never forget you once they have met you."

Rodeo and Juna were still underneath us. "Marina Teresa," Magdelena said. "Who rides with Rodeo?"

"You two do. And you, Tio, you ride with Juna." Marina Teresa raised her hand and cast it around in a circle. When she arrived at the twelve o'clock mark, she pointed straight ahead, and the water followed her lead, taking us somewhere. The dolphins swam along, and Marina Teresa and Aphrodite were the leaders.

"Where are we going?" I asked Magdelena, but she said, "I don't know, Coyitito."

The water moved quickly, but calmly. It moved toward the shoreline, and it brought us up on the sand toward the rocks. Then it brought us inside a cove. Marina Teresa disappeared into the opening first; all the dolphins were gone from sight; then we entered and were engulfed by darkness.

We were still in the water, but we couldn't see a thing.

And then something jumped into the air, and with it leapt a trail of light. Another dolphin jumped, and light followed. The dolphins began jumping and jumping, and the cave where we traveled exploded in trails of light. As the dolphins dove back into the water, the light followed them underneath, illuminating our legs.

Then the jumping dolphins stopped, and darkness again appeared.

Magdelena gasped; I looked around. On the bottom of the cave, inside the water, the night sky lit up. Stars were everywhere, glowing constellations underneath us.

"Look," Magdelena said, and suddenly Tio was surrounded in stars. They moved through the water toward him and then made a circle around him.

"Oh," said Marina Teresa. "Tio, you have been invited by the starfish. If they invite you, you may go."

"Go where, Marina Teresa?" Magdelena asked.

"To the Cave of the Departed," Marina Teresa said.

"Will Tio return from The Cave of the Departed, Marina Teresa?" Magdelena asked.

"I believe he will," Marina Teresa said.

Magdelena and I waited to see if we were invited, but no invitations came.

"Can Padre Miguel II come?" Tio asked.

"He will join you. Juna will swim you there."

Tio looked at us. He glowed in the light of the starfish.

"At the moment, we are in the Cave of Luminosity," Marina Teresa said. "As long as movement occurs, there is light and the darkness dazzles."

I moved my legs back and forth in the water and watched a show of light traveling in front of and behind me. Magdelena dropped her hands into the water and lifted them. Droplets of light fell from her fingers.

We watched Tio swim away on Padre Miguel II and Juna, half covered in light.

"What will happen in the Cave of the Departed?" I asked Marina Teresa.

"He'll tell you," she said, and then she and Aphrodite dipped under the water. We only knew where they were by the luminance they spread as they swam. And then the dolphins started playing, and Rodeo brought us quickly, very quickly, deep into the darkness of the cave and back again to where all the dolphins and starfish glowed.

When we were still for a moment, I jumped right off Senorita Duende. Underneath the water as I descended, stars flashed past my eyes. I thought about the star in the sky, the one I entered, and I wondered if I could go inside one of these large starfish, but just as I was thinking that thought, a flash of light struck the water next to me, and Magdelena glowed. She was moving her arms back and forth, and lightning streaks flowed from her; Magdelena lit the darkness.

Moments later, a voice traveled from within the cave.

"Magdelena! Coyitito! I saw Juan. I went swimming with Juan."

Tio was very excited as he appeared from the dark, his legs in light as he neared us.

"I saw Juan. We dove together in the water. I introduced him to Padre Miguel II and Juna. And he, he introduced me to his dolphin. Juan's dolphin is a departed dolphin named Dulcinea. And I couldn't really see her, just a little bit. Like lines. And I asked Juan if Dulcinea was pink, but he said that really she's more red than pink."

"How were you able to leave him?" Magdelena asked gently. I was wondering the same thing, but Tio was so happy, I didn't want to interrupt him, but Magdelena, she was always so gentle with him.

"I can see him again. Every time the full moon comes, I can see him."

"Will you swim with him in the Cave of the Departed?" I asked him.

"Juan and Dulcinea swim in the ocean waters of the full moon. So I just need to be near the water when the moon is full, and he will find me. Dulcinea will bring him. And Juna will bring Padre Miguel II and me."

"I am so happy for you, Tio," said Magdelena. And so was I. I said, "I am so happy too, Tio."

"How was your visit, Tio?" Marina Teresa asked. I'm not sure where she had been.

"I saw Juan, Marina Teresa. He was my twin brother. I swam with him in the cave, and I met Dulcinea, the Red Departed Dolphin."

"Ah, Dulcinea. Dulcinea, the Red Dolphin. She is more red than pink: she was popular among the dolphins and very, very strong," Marina Teresa told us. "She was a leader among the dolphins. She jumped high and swam fast. Your brother must be very special for Dulcinea to have come his way."

"How did Dulcinea find Juan, Marina Teresa?" Magdelena asked.

"They found each other," Marina Teresa smiled.

"Now we are going to show you the ways of the ocean water," she continued.

We floated out of the cave and into sunlight and the ocean. When we arrived, we saw, behind Marina Teresa, a very, very large black shape approaching. I started to become terrified. I remembered how the No Faces had come the last time we were at the ocean. Marina Teresa saw my face and asked, "What is it, Coyitito?" I couldn't even answer. The shape got bigger and bigger and bigger — and all at once — it leapt from the water, flew through the air, and dove underneath Marina Teresa.

Tio's eyes widened. I'm sure Magdelena's did also. Then the shape came again, spiraling up to the surface, lifting its hugeness out of the water — flying — and splash! I saw small islands around Marina Teresa, who did not appear to be frightened as these small islands started jumping, flying, and diving.

"Ah, Mermer has brought the whales; you can always feel the whales coming. They say, 'We are coming; we are coming,' and then they are here!" Marina Teresa laughed to see them. Aphrodite spun around so Marina Teresa could see the whales and their show. Then the dolphins joined and started jumping, and a huge wave came roaring far out from the ocean. We could hear it before we saw it. It rolled quickly our way. The whales dove under; the dolphins got ready to ride. We watched the wave come in, lifting Marina Teresa right toward the sun, then picking us up and taking us into its hold. Rodeo and Juna kept us steady as we sped along the ocean, heading straight for the beach, with the rocks beyond it and the canyon trail.

The wave fizzled into shallow water and left us on dry ground. Tio, Magdelena, Senorita Duende, Padre Miguel II, and I landed.

Marina Teresa, Aphrodite, the dolphins, and the whales vanished as we stood on the sand. Just like that, they were gone. I didn't know where they had gone.

I looked at the rocks in front of us. Someone was up on the higher ridge. I thought I heard a *snap* of fingers. Senorita Duende and Padre Miguel II sped toward the sound.

"Hello, Tio, Magdelena, Coyitito, Senorita Duende, Padre Miguel II. Did you like the ocean?" She raised her eyebrows.

"Look," Meme said, and she snapped her fingers. Something appeared over her right shoulder as Meme sat there on the rock, her legs crossed.

Just above her shoulder, in a kind of cloud, No Faces looked at us. No Faces had faces, but the faces they wore were stolen from others. They turned their backs to us, standing in line formation, just like we had seen them with Ramon — as decoys.

"Are these decoys?" I asked, but Meme silenced me by putting her hand over her mouth.

"Shhh," she said, as though they would hear us, and I thought that maybe they were closer than we thought.

Then we saw, from the line of No Faces, some moved away and started walking. So they weren't all decoys; some of them were real, and the hairs on my arms stood up. I went to whisper to Magdelena, but Meme said, "Shhh," so I stopped.

I wanted to say, "Cassandra?" I didn't. Meme said to be quiet.

We watched.

Meme looked at us.

"Coyitito, sometimes when I *snap*, I want to surprise you, so I don't always make it clear that the *snap* coming your way is me."

She *snapped*.

Above her other shoulder, the woods appeared. Only trees, and then we all heard the galloping horses. I turned my head; so did Magdelena and Tio. But the horses weren't behind us; they were in front above Meme's left shoulder. We watched as the trees swayed, and the galloping grew louder, and we waited, listening to the hooves.

The horses' hooves beat louder. I was distracted and looked over each of Meme's shoulders. On one side, several No Faces stood among the decoys; on the side of her other shoulder, trees swayed and horses ran. Closer and louder.

Then Meme *snapped* and the visions disappeared.

"Be aware," Meme warned.

"Do you know how to call the water?" she then asked. "Did anyone tell you how to call the water?"

And then she was gone.

And I realized that none of us, not Tio or Magdelena or Senorita Duende or Padre Miguel II, not one of us knew how to call the water, or so we thought.

BUT MEME wasn't really gone because I heard her return with a

Snap!

She must have been the one who had come to the room I share with Tio back at school and who had delivered those dream cookies, which had disappeared in the morning.

How did Meme come and go? I thought I should talk to Magdelena about this, and Tio. But they wouldn't know. None of us knew anything about any of this. Maybe Rojo Anita knew, or Marina Teresa. Maybe Ramon.

So I accepted that Meme appeared and disappeared, and I only hoped she would come if we needed her.

This time, Tio looked up over Meme's shoulder. So did Magdelena. And when I looked up, I saw the No Faces slowly turn all at the same time, the way the clock turns. They didn't show the front of themselves; they again turned to the back, and there they were, backs to us, standing on the edge of the canyon trail, looking down at something. Their necks lowered; their heads bent, and there they all were, looking at something or someone.

And then one of them moved; I only saw one of them do this, but it was enough for me to know; one of them shuffled his feet a little to one side, then a bit to the other. Then he went a little faster, just a bit, almost unnoticeable. He was the last No Face on the line. Then he picked up speed, just a bit, enough to move out of line by shuffling backwards, then forward. Magdelena saw it, and Tio saw it too.

Then the No Face next to him, he moved just a bit, too. He moved the same way the other one moved, and this movement was picked up by the other No Faces in the line. The No Faces were shuffling their feet, and started, just a bit, swinging their hips. We saw maybe twelve No Faces doing this, and we knew. We knew what they were looking at down below them: it had to be Manuel. The No Faces were dancing because he was showing them how to dance, or he was dancing on his own. Either way, Manuel was moving, and this was a sign that he was alive and dancing.

Then we heard the barreling thunder. All of a sudden, it was so loud I covered my ears. And I didn't know if the thunder was in the cloud above Meme, in back of us, or both. Then we saw what made all the noise. No Faces on horseback appeared. Their horses were big and strong, breathing heavy, nostrils flared. They had been riding long enough and hard enough.

The first No Face turned to the side. I thought he would look right at us, but he didn't. He turned his back. And he shouted very, very loudly; he shouted, "CEASE!" And all the dancing No Faces stood straight and tall. All movement stopped as the speaking No Face took his horse right up to the backs of the Ones standing on the canyon trail.

I knew they weren't behind us at the moment, or maybe they were, but the No Faces in the cloud above Meme stopped. All at the same time.

Then he, the speaking No Face said, "JUMP."

And Meme *snapped* her fingers. They were gone.

We had so many questions for her.

Magdelena asked Meme if Manuel was all right. We stared at Meme wide-eyed waiting for a response. Tio wanted to know if they jumped at Manuel. I wondered where they were, and how we were ever going to get Manuel back.

Meme *snapped* her fingers again.

The courtyard at our school appeared, and I felt such deep stirrings. I so wished I could be there in my chair at my desk in school, listening to Maestra Maria tell us about verb conjugations and read us poetry. How she would get us all to write. I remembered that one time when she had us close our eyes; she closed hers too because when I peeked out of mine, Maestra Maria was standing up there in the front of the room with her eyes shut.

"Now we are going to go to a place where we feel safe. We feel loved. We feel inspired. We feel free," she had said.

And I imagined now that Maestra Maria must have gone to the woods that day.

"Gong. Gong. Gong." The sound pulled me back. The bell in the courtyard was ringing in the vision above Meme. We couldn't tell who rang it, but we saw Padre Miguel … Oh, Padre Miguel. When Tio saw him, he started as if Padre Miguel was right there in front of us. Tio yearned for Padre Miguel; it was all over him. He actually said, "Padre Miguel! Magdelena, Coyitito. Look, it's Padre Miguel," and Tio reached out his hand just as Padre Miguel reached out his to unlock the gate. And it was almost like, for that split second, Tio held hands with his horse's namesake.

Padre Miguel looked right into our eyes. He stepped up to the open gate. Who was there? "Magdelena, who's there? Who's ringing the bell?" I asked her just in case I somehow had missed who it was. But she shook her head to say she didn't know.

Padre Miguel stepped out onto the road. All of a sudden, behind him was Maestra Agatha. "Maestra Agatha," Magdelena said, "Maestra Agatha." I yearned to see Maestra Agatha. "Who's there?" Maestra Agatha asked Padre Miguel.

Then the sight of her sent my heart pounding. I wanted to yell out from deep inside me; I wanted to yell, "Maestra Maria. Help us. I am so very, very scared. I want to help Manuel, I want to save him, but I am so very, very scared, and I need you to tell me that everything is all right, and we will be safe. And we will find Manuel, bring him back, and we will all be safe."

Lucinda came running down the courtyard. Lucinda said, "Are they back? Have they come back?" And Maestra Maria reached out to hold Lucinda's hand.

"Look at Lucinda," Magdelena said. "Oh, she must be so worried. First we were gone; now Manuel."

Padre Miguel must have come back off the road because he appeared in front of us above Meme's head.

"I don't see anybody. I don't know who rang the bell; no one is here. I don't know. Then he, Maestra Agatha and Maestra Maria stood together with the others, looking straight into our eyes.

"Padre Miguel! It's Tio!" Tio yelled to him. But Padre Miguel didn't hear. They didn't hear Magdelena as she said, "I miss you all so very much." And I didn't think they saw me either when I waved my hand in front of their faces.

Before Meme *snapped* away the vision, two things happened. Loud, thundering horses' hooves approached. We turned. So did Padre Miguel and all the others with him — and before the vision was gone, Maestra Maria looked right at where we were and said, "Go where you feel safe, loved, inspired, and free."

"She knew we were here. Maestra Maria knew," I said to Magdelena, Tio, Meme, and our horses.

Magdelena said that yes, somehow Maestra Maria knew we were somewhere to hear her. Magdelena said we must have been the ones to ring the bells, one gong for each of us.

"Were all those horses going to the school, Meme?" I asked her. Where were all those horses and their sounds going?

"Maybe it's foreshadowing; maybe not, Coyitito." That is how Meme answered me.

With a *snap* of her finger, Meme had a new vision over her head: The River — our River.

And it was right there — flowing as gently as it flows when it does. And that was all; The River flowing in front of us.

We followed with our eyes.

Then Magdelena said, "The River must be sending us an invitation." We continued to watch. It didn't stop its stream. It was like it wanted to tell us something, so we watched as long as the vision stayed — being grateful to be lost in its comfort.

Then we heard a rush of water; a loud *snap*, and Meme and her visions were gone.

The three of us sat on Senorita Duende and Padre Miguel II. We were filled with so many different emotions after having seen Padre Miguel, Maestra Maria, Maestra Agatha, Lucinda and Manuel. We three were now each in our own worlds.

Then I saw Tio lurch forward. "Look," he said. "Look!" And right there, where Meme had been moments ago, was a shell.

The shell sat exactly where Meme had been, so I thought, and I think we all thought, that she had left it for us, but we didn't know why.

Padre Miguel II led Tio to the rock with the shell in its center. When he picked it up, it was as big as his hand and had a string on it — from one side to the other. Tio slipped the shell over his arm. It hung there, right in the middle of his chest.

Magdelena said it. "Marina Teresa had a shell like that; do you remember Tio and Coyitito?" We remembered and shook our heads.

"Do you know why it is here, Magdelena?" I asked.

"I don't, Coyitito, but perhaps we will find out."

Padre Miguel II started moving. So did Senorita Duende. "We must get to Manuel," I said out loud. "He is somewhere in the middle of the earth," Magdelena responded. "We will find him." But I knew, and so did they, that finding him meant finding the No Faces, too.

WE STARTED TO MOVE; Tio was right next to us. I had no idea where we were going until we came to a clearing, and at the end of the clearing was the canyon trail — one way went up — the other way was flat, but that could change at any moment. The trails did that; they were flat, and all of a sudden, they started to climb.

Our horses stopped at the crossroads. It seemed like we were now the ones making decisions about the directions, instead of them. Maybe this was also part of our training. Our training! That really frightened me. But we had to save Manuel and get back to the school. We didn't know what was happening there.

"Which way should we go?" I asked. "This way," Magdelena pointed, and Tio nodded. I was so glad they both chose the same direction. I wanted to go that way too, but I hadn't said anything.

We turned left.

And started to climb.

"You know when that fierce One came riding in the vision over Meme's shoulder, and he told the Others to 'Cease' and 'Jump;' from where did his voice come?" I asked. I hoped he wasn't anywhere near us now.

But Tio and Magdelena didn't answer me.

They just looked straight up the trail, and when I leaned over Magdelena's shoulder, I saw what Tio and she saw.

No Faces stood, backs to us, looking down at something or someone. And then the last One standing in a line with others, very, very slowly started to move; then just a bit quicker, he started going back and forth. Then the One next to him starting doing the same, and soon the whole line was moving together. They were dancing. Then we heard the thunderous hooves, and the horses came. They came down from the trail, and we didn't know if anyone had seen us yet, and we tried our best to hide. And then the fierce One rode up next to the line of No Faces, and he said, he said what we had heard him say before in the cloud above Meme's head. He yelled, "Cease!" and all the No Faces stopped moving. Then he yelled, "JUMP." He turned his head a bit to one side, and he saw us and let out a howling yell. "THERE! Right THERE! Get them NOW! GO!" And the No Faces who were about to jump, and the Ones behind them on horses, and the fierce One started for us.

They were quick and loud, and we hurried as fast as we could. Senorita Duende and Padre Miguel II turned around in a flash, heading back down the canyon trail. The fierce One was gaining on us. "THREE! THREE!" he kept yelling, and I think he was adding us to his numbers.

This part wasn't in Meme's vision for us. I was terrified. My heart raced. I called upon Maestra Maria and Padre Miguel. I called them loudly, right out loud. I said, "Maestra Maria and Padre Miguel, we are in danger. The No Faces are right behind us. I am almost in their grasp. Please, help us."

Senorita Duende galloped so fast that her back hooves slid on the stones, and we almost went over the ledge. Tio and Padre Miguel II were sliding as they veered. Where was safety? I knew we were in grave danger.

And then the earth started moving. We felt it tremble. Then we saw some of the stones split. We kept riding as the trail began separating. The No Faces felt it, too; I knew they did, but I thought they might be able to ride through it.

"An earthquake!" Magdelena yelled. Canyon Joe? And then I saw Tio lift his hand, reach for the shell, and blow. And before we could do anything to change it, Padre Miguel II and Senorita Duende jumped.

We were falling fast, very, very fast. In the split seconds of falling, I thought that maybe down here, somewhere, was Manuel. I didn't know that we would ever see him again because the fall was steep, and I didn't know how we would survive it.

I also didn't know if it was our River.

Then The River came and met us. It rose up high, high, high to meet us. The River caught us. Senorita Duende and Padre Miguel II landed on its surface, and then we sank down into her depths. It was good to be there, feeling The River on our fear and pounding hearts. The River washed away the canyon dust.

"Go somewhere you feel safe, loved, inspired, and free."

But where were the No Faces?

We knew they couldn't swim, but their horses could.

We surfaced in The River. I was terrified to turn around because what if the No Faces were following us? What if somehow they knew the jump, landed into the water, and were coming? So I turned around and looked. I didn't see anything behind us. Clouds covered the sky above.

Then The River took us. The force was strong, and it carried us as night arrived. I kept turning around. Tio and Magdelena didn't bother to turn. They concentrated on looking ahead. I turned for probably the hundredth time, and, yes, definitely there was something or someone in the water. Yes, definitely a figure, and yes, the figure was on a horse. I thought it could be Canyon Joe, or Ramon, or Rojo Anita, or maybe even Maestra Maria. Maybe she knew and heard us in Meme's vision and in my call to her — and maybe she came looking for us.

But then I realized who it was, and within moments, many other shadows appeared; many, many shadows, and I knew the fierce One who yelled "CEASE" and "JUMP" was behind us; and right behind him were the many No Faces. I didn't know where all the horses came from, but it looked like they were riding two on a horse, except for the fierce One; he rode alone.

I could tell he knew that I was turned and looking his way, just by the way he sat higher on his horse.

"Magdelena! Magdelena! The No Faces are behind us!"

"Are you sure, Coyitito? Are you sure they are coming?"

"Yes, I am sure."

"How far away are they?"

How would I measure? How far away were they? Twenty, thirty, forty trees away? From that cloud to that cloud?

"See that big rock up there on the left? It seems like they might be that far. Cassandra? Magdelena?"

She turned her head. "Cassandra," she said.

"I wonder if they will move faster," Magdelena said.

"So do I."

We both knew that Senorita Duende couldn't go faster. She was being carried like we were. She couldn't swim, or change direction. The River moved us.

"We must trust The River," Magdelena said.

And I did agree with her, but I was still terrified and kept turning around. It didn't seem that the No Faces were getting nearer, but I knew that that could change at any moment. Neither Magdelena nor I mentioned this, but we both knew that neither one of us would tell Tio about the No Faces because he seemed to be resting. His head rested on Padre Miguel II's head, and his body lay straight on the horse's back. He had his arms around Padre Miguel II's neck, and The River carried them that way, horse and rider.

The sky grew dark, and something in me chilled. I caught a chill inside me, and I shivered. It may have been the water, but I felt like something else happened, and it had. Something else had happened.

I must have registered the sound before I really heard it. But I heard it. And I knew Magdelena heard it because her back arched in front of me. And I wasn't sure if Tio heard it because he didn't change positions, but I heard it; now it was loud and clear. When I turned around, I saw the No Faces turning their horses to The River bank, toward the trail. I don't know how they were finally able to break their horses from the strong current, but they were, and the fierce One, he had already gotten out of the water. Some of the others were struggling, and The River pulled some of them back in, but some must have been very, very strong because they were able to move against The River's stream and get onto the trail. And they had started galloping toward us, moving very, very quickly, quicker than The River.

"Magdelena, the fierce One has reached the Canyon Trail, and he is heading for us."

"It will be hard for him to reenter The River," Magdelena said, and maybe she was right. I hoped she was right because now he was really, really gaining on us. I only saw his outline with several horses behind him — two riders on each. They were coming on both sides of The River, quickly coming toward us. I heard him yell several times, "You. YOU. You. CEASE!" He was pointing at us. "CEASE!" I didn't know why he told us to cease when he knew we couldn't, or maybe he thought we were stronger than that.

Then he roared, "GET HIM!" And I knew he meant me. The fierce One wanted me first. I would rather it be me than Tio or Magdelena.

And then the clouds moved; the stars popped out, and so did the moon. I didn't know if this was good because now we were all lit up for the No Faces to see. Their galloping increased; they were almost parallel with us when something else happened.

I thought I had seen it before when the canyon rock shook, and we were taken into The River. I thought I saw a lone horse without a rider jump. I thought for a moment I might know that horse, and I didn't want to think that. I didn't want to know the horse without a rider; it could not be good. So I put it out of mind, but I did see the horse jump. And I didn't know what happened to it.

The No Faces called wildly, and the fierce One took out a long rope. I knew he could throw the rope our way and bring me right off Senorita Duende's back. And then I had a tremendous fright; "What if it were Tio? What if he wanted Tio?"

Tio rose from Padre Miguel II's back. "No, Tio. No," I yelled, thinking it was better if Tio lay stretched. I thought it would be harder to wrap the rope around Tio. But what if the rope snared horse and rider?

I felt Magdelena shudder in front of me. She bent to Senorita Duende's ear. "I know you are going so fast, Senorita Duende. Is it possible to go faster in order to help Tio?"

But the fierce One didn't want Tio right now.

Alongside Magdelena and me — there was a rush. Someone arrived. I didn't know how the No Faces had gotten to us so quickly.

But it wasn't a No Face; maybe it was Manuel! I guess his horse had found him because here was horse and rider. And I didn't think it could be good because in the light of the moon, I looked into the horse's eyes, and I saw a horse I recognized. And I knew. I knew what I had known when I saw the horse jump. Manuel was riding on the back of Ochenta.

Manuel stopped next to us, right next to us, for a second. His breath was heavy.

"Coyitito! Magdelena!" and then he was gone. Within seconds, he passed us by, sped right up to Tio. We saw him look at Tio for a split second. He must have said Tio's name because Tio looked at him. Then Manuel was gone. Tio yelled, "Manuel! Manuel!" I don't know if Tio knew that the horse was Ochenta.

The fierce One was right behind us. I looked his way. Tio was still staring at Manuel's path when the rope flew from the fierce One's arm. It looped over our heads. I saw how wide it was, and I realized that it was wide enough to catch the three of us. I looked up, and through the circle that was coming down to grab us, I saw the full moon. And then I heard something. Magdelena stayed steady. She heard it, too. So did Tio. We all knew we were headed for a waterfall. Danger on all sides. As the lasso fell from the sky, pointing at us, we saw Tio disappear right over the edge of The River, right in front of us. And we were right behind him.

I wasn't sure what terrified me more: the lasso or the fall. And where did Ochenta take Manuel?

I wrapped my arms around Magdelena's waist. I wanted to tell her things I had never told anyone, just in case I never saw her again. I didn't think I would ever see her again, so I held her tight and waited.

The beginning of the fall was steep and fast. Then, all of a sudden, it became slower, and slower, and even slower.

"Magdelena, what is happening?"

And all of a sudden, we landed gently into the ocean.

As soon as we did, very close by, very, very close by, something huge leaped out of the depths and sailed across the sky.

"So, you rode the waterfall!" Marina Teresa said and beamed from Aphrodite. "The name of that waterfall is Oscar," and the huge shape jumped again out of the water, close enough to send us rocking in waves.

"Oscar has a huge water spout on the top of his head, don't you, Oscar?" Marina Teresa laughed. "See?" And Oscar, the huge whale in front of us, disappeared again, and all of a sudden, Tio, Padre Miguel II, Magdelena, Senorita Duende, and I rose way high up in Oscar's water spout in the sky. Oscar lowered us gently.

And when he did, Tio and Padre Miguel II disappeared. "Where's Tio? Where's Tio, Marina Teresa?" and she pointed way, way out, way out in the ocean. "We need to go get him." I was alarmed, but no one else was.

"Remember the Cave of the Departed, Coyitito?" Magdelena asked me. Yes, yes I remembered the cave, but we hadn't been there. And then I realized that Tio had been there, and that is where he saw Juan and met Dulcinea, the Red Departed Dolphin.

"That's one of Juan and Dulcinea's favorite places to swim: way out in the middle of the ocean," Marina Teresa said. "And the moon is full, so they can be together."

Tio was just a dot in the light of the full moon. "Dulcinea and Juan are protecting Tio out there," said Marina Teresa.

"And what about us?" I thought.

Then Marina Teresa lowered her voice in warning. "You must be careful of the sea eels."

"The sea eels! Where are the sea eels, Marina Teresa?" I started looking around underneath me. My legs moved in the water. I noticed Magdelena move her legs also, and I felt that she sat up higher in front of me.

She, too, spoke to Marina Teresa about the sea eels.

"Marina Teresa, what must we know about the sea eels?"

"It has been said," Marina Teresa said, "that the elders from the line of No Faces, a long time ago, had certain powers the No Faces do not now have. The No Faces you saw are from a heritage trying to get back the power they lost. The elders were powerful on land, but they were weak when it came to water. Even so, they wanted to conquer land and sea.

"They made very strong, very potent ropes. It is said that they must have taken minerals and ingredients from the sea and braided them into the weaving. Maybe they captured fish or swooped seaweed up with their hands. No one knows.

"It seems that the elders sent their ropes out into the water. The cords were drawn in by the surge of the sea, and the transformation happened: they became sea eels. We don't think the current No Faces know how to make water ropes, because we do not see such an increase in sea eels over the years.

"The eels worked like the ropes of the No Faces on land: they circled their victim, and hauled him or her to shore where No Faces waited.

"Then the No Faces lost track of the way to the ocean. They were lured to land until they found you at the ocean. All of a sudden, they were back in the realm of the water. Their horses can swim, like yours, but their horses' legs are made best for the trails. The sea eels squirm around the ocean floor. If we see them coming, we can stop them. They can't grasp our slippery ocean skin. Their roping action slides off Aphrodite or Oscar or Rodeo or …"

Marina Teresa stopped talking. She turned around on her sea horse.

Moving toward us, in the light of the full moon, was something that split the water into two sides: a line down the middle. It wasn't a very wide line, maybe the size of a tree trunk. The water separated, barely. I shuddered. Marina Teresa lifted her hands. The water silenced. Magdelena didn't move in front of me. The water was almost not moving when, all of a sudden, something took us. Something took Magdelena, Senorita Duende, and me. We zipped through the water with the full moon in front of us, then behind us.

"Magdelena," I cried into her ear. But she sat in front of me, straight and alert. So focused, Magdelena was always so focused.

I felt the water push at my thighs, then pull. We spun in circles. I looked for Tio out there, hoping he would come with Juan and Dulcinea, the Red Departed Dolphin. Where was Marina Teresa?

And then I saw — I saw we were heading toward shore. What waited there for us?

A blockade. As we zoomed to land, something happened. All of a sudden, we stopped short. The stop was so fast, so strong, I slipped off Senorita Duende and landed in the ocean. Marina Teresa and Aphrodite appeared next to me. She reached for my hand and guided me into Aphrodite's pouch. I looked at Magdelena in the moonlight. Aphrodite swam up next to her. She turned to look at me.

"What happened, Marina Teresa?" she gasped.

"Look," Marina Teresa said. Then she clapped her hands three times. All at once, the blockade came alive. So many dolphins! Oh, so many dolphins jumped from the water. And Oscar — there was Oscar — and he had friends with him — just like him — but not as big. Oscar seemed the biggest of all. And some others — some we hadn't seen before.

When we had seen the blockade, it looked like rounded and sharp pieces. We knew the rounded ones, as soon as they leapt. But what were the sharp ones?

"Sharks," Marina Teresa said.

"Sharks!"

"They won't hurt you," she told us. "Will you, Blanca?" And the big shark in the moonlight seemed to grin. I thought that Blanca would love to eat us, but Marina Teresa wouldn't let her and her friends feast on our legs and arms.

"Marina Teresa, look!" I said. "Blanca will swallow us!"

Marina Teresa laughed as Blanca swerved away from us in the moonlight.

"Marina Teresa, were we captured by a sea eel?" Magdelena asked.

"That was a drill. We haven't had sea eel drills for such a very, very long time. I wasn't sure if we knew how to assemble."

Didn't the ocean have a Protected Zone? Maybe it never needed one before.

But I thought about that line in the water coming our way, and Marina Teresa lifting her hands — and the way we were sped through the water.

And something in Marina Teresa told me that the sea eel had come, and it had gotten close.

Then our own protector dolphin, Rodeo, joined us.

"Rodeo came for you," Marina Teresa said. I felt so much safer in Marina Teresa's pouch than I did riding on Senorita Duende with legs submerged in the ocean where the sea eel roamed. But I knew I had left Magdelena alone for too long, so I asked Marina Teresa if she would mind if I returned to my horse and to

Magdelena. Marina Teresa opened her pouch; I swam out onto the surface of the sea. I felt a chill.

And then I was sucked down below the surface.

I was spiraling around and around. My breath was somewhere; I wasn't sure where. How could this happen? Oscar, Marina Teresa, Rodeo, where was everyone?

"Do not panic. Hold your breath lightly. Let tiny pieces of air escape from your nose. Go right up against the surface of whatever you encounter. Then turn." I heard Canyon Joe in my mind. He taught us these ways when we were in The River.

But he didn't tell me about spinning, spinning, spinning, and spiraling in a vortex and being sucked down.

Where was everyone?

Where were my protectors?

I couldn't move. The force wouldn't let me move my hand.

"How am I ever going to survive?"

"Rodeo!" I tried to call.

Rojo Anita must have heard me because I saw her. Was she somehow close by me? I don't think that she was inside the vortex with me; and she had to be close to hear me — because there was Rojo Anita.

And then she was gone.

I was alone in the dark, spiraling water.

I didn't know if my eyes were open or closed until I saw the first streak of light. Then I saw another streak, and soon the whole spinning world was spun in light. And I was covered. Illuminated. And I was no longer spinning.

My head was lifted above the water. I took deep gulps of breath. Stars surrounded me — moving me ever so gently, so, so gently — but quickly. Was I dead? They escorted me to the cave. But it wasn't the Cave of the Departed; it was the Cave of Luminosity; the starfish had come to save me. I thought they only brought people to the Departed place, but here I was, in another cave, and my friends were there — glowing!

"Coyitito!" Magdelena shouted — and she and Senorita Duende were a streak of light as they came into my arms. I wrapped my arms around Senorita Duende's neck, and she lifted me out of the water. I dripped light as I hung from her, look-ing straight into her eyes — then Magdelena's.

"Cassandra?" I asked Magdelena.

"Cassandra, yes, Coyitito!" Magdelena took my hands.

"Oh, my, Magdelena!" Senorita Duende slowly lowered me into the water. I submerged myself, so I could thank the starfish. I looked at them glowing in their pools. "How do you thank a starfish?" I thought. And then I knew. I lifted my head out of the water, and began to softly sing to them. I didn't know what to sing, so I started making *whooshing* sounds, then added "thank you, thank you, fish of star. Whish. Thank you, thank you, fish of star. Whish." Magdelena joined me. And we sang. And the starfish gathered, rose to the surface, and swirled.

"Coyitito," Marina Teresa spoke. "Are you all right now, Coyitito?"

"I am, Marina Teresa. Yes, I am. Do you know what happened to me?"

"Yes. I know what happened to you. It is very dangerous what happened to you. Very, very dangerous. Excuse me."

Marina Teresa dipped underneath the water. She spread out, and the stars lit up her blue hair. Some of the starfish were still by my side — but at this moment, many of them surrounded Marina Teresa and pulled her away. Aphrodite floated behind her.

Magdelena said, "Marina Teresa must be going to the Cave of the Departed. I wonder who she'll meet there." And as Magdelena said this, another vision appeared in the darkness of the cave's tunnel, turning it into light.

"I rode the waves with Juan! He rode Dulcinea, the Red Departed Dolphin, and I rode Padre Miguel II and Juna, and we rode all these big, big waves way out in the middle of the ocean." Tio was so lit up even his teeth shone. "I won't see him until the next full moon, but I will see him then, or maybe before that. Maybe I will somehow get to see him more than once a month."

"That is so wonderful," Magdelena said.

"Where did you and Juan leave each other?" I wanted to know. I thought of the sea eels out there in the ocean — and the vortex — and Tio.

"Dulcinea, Juan and Juna swam with us to the entrance to the cave. Juan told me not to worry, that I was entering the Cave of Luminosity, and I would find both of you here with Senorita Duende, Marina Teresa, and Aphrodite. Hey … where are Marina Teresa and Aphrodite?"

"We're right here! Welcome back, Tio. How was your full-moon visit with Juan and Dulcinea?"

I looked at Magdelena. She raised her eyebrows. Neither of us knew nor saw when Marina Teresa returned.

"Marina Teresa, there are many waves out there in the middle of the ocean, and Juan and I kept riding them."

"Yes, I know about those waves, Tio. They are the waves of the Full Moon."

I was surrounded by starfish. I again looked at Magdelena. Though we were both floating on Senorita Duende, the starfish only surrounded the area where I was sitting on Senorita Duende's back.

All of a sudden, a sea horse floated from the way of the Cave of the Departed, trailing streams of light.

"Ah," said Marina Teresa.

The sea horse floated right toward Senorita Duende, Magdelena, and me. The starfish around me floated me to the pouch of this horse. I didn't want to leave Senorita Duende and Magdelena. I didn't want my own horse, different from the one Magdelena and I shared.

Marina Teresa must have known my thoughts — not like Rojo Anita but different — just because of the way I looked.

"Eclipse has come for you. She will join the starfish in escorting you into the Cave of the Departed. Later, she will bring you back again to Senorita Duende and Magdelena."

"Marina Teresa, who has invited me?"

"I do not know, Coyitito. When we are invited, we are invited by someone specific, who invites only the one or ones he or she wants to talk to."

I was already being guided into the pouch of Eclipse, a tall seahorse, where I again felt the safety I had felt in Aphrodite's pouch before the vortex sucked me down.

"Marina Teresa, why was that vortex very, very dangerous?"

"What vortex?" Tio asked.

But Marina Teresa placed her finger over her lips, and we were silenced as I floated into the darkness, which lit with Eclipse and floating starfish. I really wasn't used to being alone. I spent all my time with Magdelena, Senorita Duende, Tio, and Padre Miguel II. Who invited me? I was frightened to find out. Maybe something had happened to Maestra Maria, and she had departed. Oh, no. I couldn't bear to lose someone I loved.

The circle of starfish surrounding us began to disappear one by one until a half circle was left around us. It was no longer light in front. And then we too disappeared. I couldn't even see Eclipse. I became very, very frightened. "Eclipse! Eclipse!"

I felt her pouch. I was still in it, but I couldn't see anything. And then ...

Stars were everywhere! They were leaping from the water and somehow, somehow, I don't know how — they were sticking on the ceiling of the cave. It looked like thousands of them. And they were below us — all over the water under Eclipse and me.

"Eclipse, this is so very, very beautiful. I wish Magdelena and Tio could be here." I looked up and down and sideways, and everywhere, everywhere I saw stars.

Eclipse stopped moving. I felt her bow, and I was bent toward the water. I thought this meant that I should swim out of her pouch, but all of a sudden she lifted up again, and I was treated to the stars everywhere.

Then she bowed again, and as I was lowered toward the water, I looked at the stars beneath me. I was lifted up again. I wasn't sure what Eclipse was doing, but within moments, I saw the stars all around me, and as I watched them, Eclipse lowered into another bow and released me from her pouch.

I looked up at her.

I wanted to ask her if I was safe here, but I felt that I must be safe with all these stars around me. I started to swim in the star-filled cave when the starfish came my way and surrounded me from head to foot, to fingertip, side to side.

And then they lifted me up. They lifted me standing into the water. Only my head was out of the water, and I tried to see if it was covered in stars. I looked straight up at the ceiling light, and then I saw it. I didn't know what it was, but there were very, very tiny stars gathered in something. They clustered. I wasn't sure what it was, but something was white — and lit up.

I kept watching.

The tiny star cluster grew.

I thought how this must be a constellation. Where was Eclipse? I wanted to turn around, but I didn't — somehow I didn't. I stared right in front of me.

The glow moved up and around, leaving a black circle in the middle. What was this? A long cluster of stars hung like the grapes in the grapevine, circled up and around with a dark circle in the middle, and then the circle stretched. It grew. And the stars around it grew within. Then it closed in again.

I thought I had been invited by someone to the Cave of the Departed, but so far no one appeared.

When the circle widened again, it released a rush of stars — and words.

"I am Melaquiades, Coyitito. I have been silent for one hundred years, but there is something, something very important, very, very important I need to tell you.

"You, Coyitito, you have brought the No Faces to the ocean. Their sea eels have tried to lasso you into their forces — tried to trick the ocean after the drill Marina Teresa and the others had — that quick moment when you slid from the pouch of Aphrodite. That's how the No Faces operate. Quickly. They seize the moment. But not in a good way. Not for the benefit of others."

Who is Melaquiades? Why is he telling me all this?

"One hundred years," I thought. I kept thinking, "You, Melaquiades, haven't spoken for one hundred years. And you talk to me. You invite me to the Cave of the Departed. Me! I'm sorry, but I really don't know you, so why, oh why, why, why did you invite me? Are you sure I am the one you wanted to invite? Me?"

"Yes, you, Coyitito."

Oh no. He has the ways of Rojo Anita.

"Yes, Rojo Anita was given the power to read thoughts," he said.

I did not want to think about anything ever again.

I tried not to, but I kept thinking about how he said I brought the No Faces to the ocean, and I felt very guilty, very, very guilty. Then I looked up and the eyes of Melaquiades were lit by stars.

"Rojo Anita stays busy," and the black hole, which was his mouth, spread into a star-lit smile. "There are so many thoughts," he said. "How does she do it?" And I realized that he read every thought I thought.

"I want to answer them all," he said. "But there is much to tell you before you return. So you keep thinking, Coyitito. But I will need to talk to you at the same time. Perhaps what I have to tell you will take you from all that you have on your mind."

I looked at Melaquiades, looking for the rest of him. His face was there, but I didn't see the rest of him. He didn't comment on my search for him; instead, he said,

"At one time — we were all stars, Coyitito. At the very beginning, before there were people — there were stars.

"And the stars were above — in the sky — and below — in the ocean. Every star in the sky had a twin star on the ocean floor. If the one above moved around the sky, the one below moved. It was like a magnetic force, keeping them connected. In the beginning when there were only stars, all was fine. The sky and the ocean filled with light in the blackness of the night."

Melaquiades looked up at the ceiling, and so did I. Stars were twinkling and moving, and I realized that in the cave water where I was, the stars were twinkling and moving also.

"How do you get those stars on your ceiling, Melaquiades?"

"That is the sky, Coyitito."

"The sky?"

"Yes, the sky."

I wasn't sure how the Cave of the Departed was out in the open sky like that, but Melaquiades didn't want to tell me that because he didn't. I wondered if Tio saw this sky when he was here with Juan.

"Then some of the stars from the ocean washed up onto the shore, and instead of being brought back to the water, they stayed there on the shore," Melaquiades said. "But they didn't move for a long time, a very, very long time.

"And then the stars on the shore started to move. They didn't go back toward the water, and the water didn't come for them. The sand became their domain, and the particles in the sand fed the stars, and as they ate from the sand, they started to change. Their forms grew longer; they grew into lines: long lines. And their five point tips became what we know as arms and legs. And one of the tips grew into a head. And the weeds of the sea turned dark and plaited, and grew into hair. And the ones who had grown from the sand stars began to move. And to stand straight. And walk. And evolve differently. So much happened with their fingertips, which were closest to the tips of the stars.

"The ones that stayed on the land were different from the ones in the sky and the ocean. As they grew into a new form, they moved further away from the ocean. And the ocean moved away from them. As the ocean pulled away from them, land grew, and these No Faces were now part of the land. And they traveled on foot, forgetting how to swim. They moved further and further away until they were so far that they found the rock and the stone. And they went inside, into caves. And in the caves they grew. And it is said that in the caves they discovered gold and gave it value. And they mastered the way of the land.

"Their doubles in the sky followed them, but the No Face doubles on land lost their glow. So the ones in the sky, without the balancing magnetic pull, started to fall out of the sky and land somewhere. And the stars that landed from the sky grew into ones like you, Coyitito. Similar to the No Faces in shape, but very different. The stars that fell from the sky matched their double in size and shape, but the burst of light that fell with the falling star continued to beam inside you, giving you a face. And feelings of compassion and love.

"For every No Face has a double with a Face. And the ones without faces wanted to take the ones with faces and make them their own, but not because they wanted to reunite with their other. They forgot they once had another. They just wanted to own all the forces in the land. They wanted to round up all the Faces and own them. They grew with desire; they grew selfish and mean. They forgot the ways of the sky and the ocean. But one day, they came upon the ocean, and when they did, they wanted to own it, taking it like they took the Faces that they found. But they couldn't. Even though they were once ocean stars, they had lost their way and discovered greed.

"So they stooped before the great ocean taking their ropes, their ropes which they used for capture. And they worked the ocean's ingredients until their ropes were ready and released. And the No Faces knew; they saw the ropes come alive and spin circles in the ocean.

"And the sky — they used her. They used her moon — and the stars — those stars they once knew so well — for direction and light.

"Many of the stars are settled into place — above and below. And others are still moving around.

"The No Faces turned away from the ocean after releasing their ropes and headed back toward the canyon. And they stayed in the caves waiting for whatever and whomever they could take.

"And they never went back to the ocean. Ever again.

"Until you.

"Tio has been given the white cloth, Magdelena the comb, and you the key, which has been lost in The River. At some point, you might find it again.

"You, Coyitito, have met the star in the sky! And you have gone inside.

"You are the one I have heard about: the one who will help reunite the stars that fell from the sky with their ocean others."

Melaquiades told me too, too much. I was very, very concerned by his story. And then I grew even more concerned when he told me again:

"You have the signs, Coyitito."

I was very, very frightened. I didn't know what Melaquiades thought I could do.

"One more thing, Coyitito. The No Faces have the power to take on the faces of their double or another — it seems. If a face is close by, the No Face can take it — and the one with the Face loses it. We are not sure if this is permanent. And we don't know how to tell a No Face from one with a Face."

This frightened me even more.

"We need you to find out how this happens, Coyitito, and stop it from happening. How can the No Faces take the faces of the other?

"They have their secrets."

"You must be very careful, Coyitito — very, very careful."

"How do I know that I have never met a No Face with a Face?"

"You don't; you don't know. But there must be a way to know the difference. You need to be very careful of the one you are talking to. Find out, Coyitito, and when you know you must tell all the others."

"The No Faces have grown in their numbers."

"But isn't there some way, Melaquiades? Something you can tell me to look for, so I know?"

"Be careful on your way out of the Pool of Relocation."

Now I was getting frightened of all this that Melaquiades was telling me. How would I ever know? I must always know Magdelena, and Tio, and Maestra Maria, and Padre Miguel, and Rojo Anita, and Ramon, and Meme, and Azul. And Manuel, and — oh — oh — could any of them have ever been a No Face with a Face I knew so well?

I started shivering.

And what was the Pool of Relocation? "What is the Pool of Relocation, Melaquiades?"

"It is a pool in the waters of the cave. The pool is filled with desires. If you enter the pool, when you are filled with wants and desires, it relocates you. If you enter the pool without desire, then you stay where you are. But if you are wanting of someone or something and you enter the waters of the pool — then you are relocated."

"Where?"

"To your desire in one form or another."

"But isn't Eclipse going to guide me back to the Cave of Luminosity where Magdelena, Senorita Duende, Tio, and Padre Miguel II are?"

But when I looked up at Melaquiades, he was gone.

I looked around the Cave of the Departed, but all I saw were stars — and where Melaquiades had been only moments before, there was a constellation. And when I looked into the water, I saw the same lit-up pattern — and where I thought I had seen Melaquiades' eyes when I talked to him moments ago, there were two twinkling stars above and below.

And then Eclipse floated over, and the starfish gathered, and we all sailed out of the Cave of the Departed.

I was relieved to be with the starfish. What could they possibly desire? They would get us past the Pool of Relocation without falling in.

The passage ahead was dark and chilly. I didn't see stars above, like I had seen moments before in the Cave of the Departed with Melaquiades. Maybe I would see Magdelena and Tio soon.

I thought of both of them. I thought of Magdelena's long dark hair in front of me as we rode Senorita Duende. Even in the blackness of the cave, I reached my hand out just a bit to touch the dark air, reaching for Magdelena. I didn't venture my hand too far out because I didn't know what was out there. I listened — alert. Tucked into Eclipse's pouch, I felt somewhat safe, but I knew, oh, I knew … I wanted to see Magdelena and Tio so, so much. Too much.

I started spinning. Where is Eclipse? Where are the starfish? I spun in darkness, but it was very, very different from my spinning in the ocean with the water rope.

And then I stopped spinning.

Suddenly.

And I was cast there.

Right there.

Right on the ground.

I looked around.

It was dusk.

I saw bats fly into the sky.

Where was I?

The trail ran both ways — up and down.

So, I was on the canyon trail. But where?

And I didn't have a horse. And I didn't have Magdelena or Tio. And night would come, and I was very, very frightened. Why didn't Melaquiades help me more, tell me what to do?

I started to walk up the trail. Somehow I felt going up was safer than going down. I kept picturing terrible things in my mind — and I tried very, very hard to make them stop. I remembered how my mind could make terrible things happen, and Magdelena and Tio weren't here to check with.

I told myself, "Coyitito, you are walking here right now on the canyon trail. Nothing else is happening." Yet. Nothing else is happening yet. What if the No Faces are behind that turn, or if they jump from that cave? What if the big lasso falls from the sky? What if …"

"Coyitito. Coyitito."

It wasn't me this time talking to myself, calling myself by name.

"Coyitito. Shhh … Come here. Come here."

It wasn't the first time Rojo Anita called for me. When I fell from the sky into The River, Rojo Anita was there waiting for me — and here she was now. I didn't remember thinking about Rojo Anita as I passed through the Pool of Relocation.

But wait. Oh no! What if this Rojo Anita was a No Face? How would I know?

"It is the one you know, Coyitito. It is I — Rojo Anita — the one you know."

And then I thought that this might be my Rojo Anita because she may be reading my thoughts.

So I went toward her, where she sat at the entrance to a cave. I went up to her. I had no choice, really. And I didn't want my Rojo Anita to feel sad that I would distrust her.

"You must be very, very careful. Yes," she said. "So — you have found out more about the Double? The No Face?"

"Yes, Rojo Anita. I have found out. Why didn't you tell me?"

"Because you must find out on your own. Whatever you discover, you must discover on your own."

"Rojo Anita, I left Magdelena and Senorita Duende and Tio and Padre Miguel II back at the cave. I fell into the Pool of Relocation, because I wanted, I wanted so much to see Magdelena, but I don't know how to get back to them, Rojo Anita. I don't know how to return.

"You always help me. Will you help me now?"

"Of course I will always help you, Coyitito."

"Did you send for me for any reason? Did you invite me because you have more to tell me?"

"Yes, Coyitito. There is more to tell you and show you. There is much we have to tell you."

"Did you send for Tio and Magdelena and Padre Miguel II and Senorita Duende?"

"I did. They should be coming shortly. Come, Coyitito."

Rojo Anita had three extra horses.

"Who are these horses?" I asked her. "Whom do they belong to, Rojo Anita?"

I didn't want to change horses. I wanted to ride on Senorita Duende with Magdelena in front of me. I didn't want a new horse. A new horse. What did that mean? What did it mean about my horse? My horse — the one I shared with Magdelena.

"I don't want a new horse, Rojo Anita."

"You don't have a new horse, Coyitito. These three horses appeared when I was coming down the canyon trail, but none of them is your horse. None of them came toward you when you approached. None of them is for you. But we will ask one of them if you may be a Guest Rider as we travel. We can ask."

Rojo Anita approached the first horse and asked her gently, very gently. Rojo Anita laid her hand on the horse's snout and looked into her eyes and said, "Will you be a Guest Horse for my friend, Coyitito? He rides Senorita Duende, and she is on her way, but may Coyitito ride you until she gets here?"

The horse backed away from Rojo Anita. She backed up, and without warning, she rose onto her two hind legs, rose up high. I looked at her hooves in the air, as she shook her head, neighing and shimmying. And when she hit the ground with her hooves, she galloped away.

Rojo Anita looked at me.

"I guess she is not taking Guest Riders," Rojo Anita said.

I was frightened.

"Don't be frightened, Coyitito," Rojo Anita said, as she approached the second horse.

The horse was beautiful. Its pattern looked like the land. It was brown and white.

"A palomino," Rojo Anita said. I liked the horse just by the way it looked. I never wanted to leave Senorita Duende — ever — but I would like to be a Guest Rider on this horse.

Rojo Anita again asked this horse if I could be a Guest Rider. The horse didn't move. Rojo Anita looked my way.

"You can ride this horse, Coyitito."

"How do you know, Rojo Anita? How do you know that when I get on this horse, it won't throw me off like Ochenta threw Juan? Remember he died, and now he rides Dulcinea, the Red Departed Dolphin, and Tio sees him on the full moon. How do you know?"

"Because I know, Coyitito."

And I believed her. I believed Rojo Anita knew, so I climbed onto the palomino, and she accepted me as her Guest Rider.

I looked at Rojo Anita, and she smiled at me. "See, Coyitito."

AND THEN I HEARD IT; I heard the galloping, and I thought the first horse was coming back. But there was more than one horse. There were several, and they were still far enough away, but they were coming. And Rojo Anita knew. She heard them. She quickly jumped onto Senorita and told me, "Hurry, Coyitito. Hurry." And Rojo Anita galloped into the cave.

"We must get off the trail. We must go through the caves, Coyitito. Stay very, very close behind me. Stay close."

I couldn't see.

"Rojo Anita, I can't see."

"Your horse will follow behind me as long as you stay close. Listen to the hooves."

The third horse was behind us.

I was so very, very frightened.

"Are you all right, Coyitito?"

"I am very afraid."

I hoped Rojo Anita knew where to go. And she did. She always did. And I knew that soon, very, very soon, we would be at The River. And Padre Miguel would be there — oh, Padre Miguel. And maybe Maestra Maria, maybe Maestra Maria would be there too. And Magdelena and Tio and Senorita Duende and Padre Miguel II would come.

This Guest Horse was much smaller than Senorita Duende.

"Rojo Anita, Rojo Anita, are you there?"

"Shhh, Coyitito, sound travels in the caves. I am here."

And sound does travel in the caves because, all of a sudden, I heard the sound of hooves gathering somewhere behind us. And I heard one word travel through the darkness — and echo and re-echo so many times until it was almost silent again, and I knew, I knew we were in grave danger.

"CEASE!"

That was the word.

"CEASE. CEASe. CEAse. CEase. Cease. Sseee. Sseee. See ..."

"Hurry, Coyitito, Hurry!" I heard Rojo Anita pick up the pace ahead of me. She knew too. She knew that the One whom I saw tell the No Faces to jump — the mean One — the One who swam against the force of The River — and ran faster on land — the One who built his lasso over our heads before we got to the waterfall — he was gaining speed ... (I wanted to tell Rojo Anita that we found a waterfall — and it was Oscar the Whale's water spout — but Rojo Anita knew all that) — Behind us the hooves were gaining — and again — "CEASE!" It was much closer now — and again it bounced off the cave walls growing fainter.

"Ssseee ..."

But the sound of the hooves was excruciating. I couldn't tell how many there were, if they were all coming fast like that, or if some of them were echoes, and I broke a sweat, hoping that Rojo Anita was still in front of me, because it got so loud. I didn't know where she was. I knew I shouldn't talk, but I had to, and the Mean One was already on our trail, so I yelled in front of me; I yelled, "Rojo Anita, are you there?" And before she could answer me, I saw the strangest thing. As I was galloping by in the darkness, surrounded by all these hooves, I saw just a crack of light. It was a line of light up ahead on the right side, and I didn't know what it was. I thought maybe, just maybe — oh maybe there could be a door to open there. I didn't want to stop, not even for a second, so I yelled, although I should have just thought it, "Rojo Anita, are you there?"

"Yes, I am here, Coyitito. Shhhh. Hurry."

So I hurried, and as I approached the light, I yelled, "Rojo Anita, should we go into the light? Should we go …"

And the hooves were so close that I heard the snorting of the horses.

The Mean One again released one word, and I thought that this time, I could help us. I could help Rojo Anita and me. I know she knew best, but I thought I would help too. So I bent to the palomino's ear and whispered, "Stop." Then I called to Rojo Anita and said, "Rojo Anita, let us go here," and turned into the line of light.

"Coyitito! NO," Rojo Anita yelled. The "NOoooooo" echoed down the cave, colliding with "CEAssseeee!" And the light grew open, and I thought that I had made a grave mistake, and I wished I could change it.

But I couldn't. And just as the Mean One appeared around the bend in the cave — I turned to look for Rojo Anita. And I saw her; I saw her turn my way. And I said, "Rojo Anita …" but I didn't say another word, because when she turned toward me —

I knew she was a No Face.

I saw it in the way she looked at me. Her eyes reached to take me. She steered Senorita at me.

She was not my Rojo Anita.

Then I heard a large banging sound. It sounded like the kitchen pans when they were struck together.

I shuddered and galloped into the frame of light, which dissolved behind me.

INSIDE, MEME WAS BAKING.

"Just in time, Coyitito."

Just in time? Just in time for what? Who was this? Was this Meme?

"Meme?"

"Who can bake like Meme can bake, Coyitito?"

I thought of Dona Williams.

I was very, very shaken. I decided to trust Meme. I didn't know if Meme was Meme or not, but I did know that I was just in the cave, and I really thought, I really, really thought that Rojo Anita was Rojo Anita, but she wasn't.

"Meme, I am so very, very frightened. I saw Rojo Anita as a No Face, and I didn't know. I really, really didn't know. I really thought that Rojo Anita was Rojo Anita …"

"Have some sponge cake, Coyitito. It will soak up your fears."

So I got off the palomino and sat down by Meme and decided to eat her sponge cake.

Meme asked, "Did you hear me calling, Coyitito?"

I thought how I had only heard the sound of pans.

"That was me, Coyitito! What does the word *pans* spell backwards?"

"Oh, Meme!" I didn't say anything out loud. I didn't need to.

"What do I do with the palomino Guest Horse, Meme?"

"Keep the Guest Horse here with me."

Meme's sponge cake was delicious.

"I've been baking all day," Meme said, "waiting for you, Coyitito."

I watched Meme. What if she weren't Meme? I almost wished I didn't know about the No Faces or the Double, but, I did. I did know. So I watched her as she lifted one of the boards in the floor, and then I heard her go down some steps, and she was gone. She disappeared.

But I still heard her. "Where is the blue flour? I know I put that flour down here — oh — I need to go down another flight. Coyitito, come down here and help me."

So this was it! Meme would lure me down, down into the bottom of the cave, and then she would be One of them.

"Coyitito, come down here. My face isn't going to disappear," but I wasn't sure. So Meme came back up and said, "Here. I will show you that I am Meme. I will give you a vision."

Snap.

Above Meme's shoulder, I saw them. They were sitting on the shore next to each other.

"I wish Coyitito would come back. I hope that he is safe."

"Me too, but I think that he is fine, Magdelena."

"I hope he is fine, Tio."

"He is."

"How do you know?"

"I can just tell. Coyitito is fine. He's coming."

Tio was comforting Magdelena about me!

I must tell them about Rojo Anita when I see them again.

Snap.

The vision was gone.

"So do you see that I am Meme. A No Face Double couldn't bring you the visions."

"Is that true, Meme? The Doubles can't do what the other can?"

"Mostly."

"But moments ago, Rojo Anita read my mind."

"Did she read your mind, Coyitito, or did she just read you?"

I had to think, but Meme left no time for thinking. "Come on, Coyitito. I need your help downstairs."

So I followed Meme.

I had no idea we would be going so far down. We went to the first staircase and then another flight down the skinny wooden steps, which were like a ladder. Meme ran down; she was so fast. I was frightened because the steps were steep. After climbing down many more steps, I thought we arrived. But no, another landing. And another. How far down were we? I wanted to ask Meme when we were going to stop — and then she said, "Ah, here we are, Coyitito. Get off the ladder and come this way. Come over here."

So I got off the ladder steps.

It was damp where we were, but I followed Meme. The room had a soft glow, almost a blue light. I saw that the walls were covered with drawers, some big and some little.

"I'm looking for the blue flour, Coyitito. I couldn't find it all morning. Now I know it's in one of these drawers in the blue room here, but I don't know which. You start over there, and I'll start here."

There were so many drawers.

"Blue flour, Meme?"

"Yes, Coyitito — well kind of blue with a tinge of green. You'll find indigo, navy, teal — it's kind of a turquoise — but more blue than green. It needs to match the color of the ocean, the one you have swum in. It needs to be that color blue."

Meme started opening and closing drawers. As she shut them, puffs of flour dust clouded over her hair. Soon she was covered in blue flour dust.

She clapped her hands.

"Coyitito, get to work."

I opened the first small drawer. As I pulled it toward me, I saw that this was not the blue of the ocean where I swam. I pulled the drawer out a bit more and then a bit more, and the more I pulled the drawer, the more it kept coming.

"Coyitito, that is a different ocean color than the one we need."

But I couldn't stop pulling the drawer.

"What ocean is this, Meme?"

"It depends on the color."

I had never seen an ocean this color.

"Push the drawer back in. Hurry. We must hurry."

So I pushed the drawer back in and walked a few rows down. I looked around at all the different drawers, and then I reached one that I thought must be the one. This had to be the one. I knew this color.

"Meme, I think this is it."

She came over, looked, and said, "Keep pulling. Pull until the water comes."

I had no idea what that meant, but I pulled and kept pulling until the drawer was all the way across the room. Meme stood waiting, watching for the water.

"Here it comes, Coyitito."

I walked to where she was, and I saw it. A stream of water came running down the middle of the blue flour.

"Here. Take this pail. Fill it with the flour and water. I'll meet you back upstairs."

I didn't want Meme to leave me alone down here, but she turned and went back up the stairs.

I started filling the pail, and as I did the stream of water grew. It started getting larger. The more flour I took, the larger the stream grew. And then it was more than a stream; then the waves started coming. At first the waves were very, very small, but then they grew larger. Soon, they were getting very large and covering all the flour. Then they reached a very high peak. I looked up at the waves as they rolled into the drawer, and soon all the flour dissolved into the water.

The waves never left the drawer.

They never spilled over the sides, but inside the drawer, the sea was casting what seemed like ten foot waves.

"Fill the barrel," I heard, and it must have been Meme because, all of a sudden, a large barrel appeared, and I lifted it, filling it with the sea.

"Close the drawer."

I started pushing the drawer shut, and as I did, the ocean waves grew smaller. I pushed — and pushed — and the drawer was completely shut when Meme called down, "Bring the barrel and the pail back up here."

I didn't know how I would ever carry them, but when I lifted them, they were both very, very light. I placed the pail over my arm; the barrel I lifted into my other arm, and I started lifting myself onto the first step.

"Hold on tight!"

The steps started lifting themselves straight up into the air. All the way up — a breeze against my face; I realized how far down we had been when I saw how far away Meme was.

And then I landed in her kitchen, where she took the pail and barrel from me.

"Now I know you have learned ways to breathe underneath the water, but these submarine cookies of Meme's can also help. Eat the cookies, and you will be able to stay underwater for as long as the cookies let you."

"How long is that, Meme?"

"It varies for each person. But you'll know. They give you a warning before they stop supplying you with breath. They send you a warning message."

"What is the message?"

"We never know ahead of time. You'll know when it comes. Now, I need three parts water to this one part flour; I need a little of this; I need ... Coyitito, will you please hand me that bottle. Yes, that one. Thank you.

"Ah! The submarine cookies are ready. Here — taste."

I don't know how Meme bakes them so quickly, but here they were, sending their cookie scent through the room.

"Baked in lava," Meme said.

"Lava?"

"Coyitito, you give Magdelena this one; give Tio this one, and this one is for you. Eat what Meme baked, Coyitito! Now!"

I nodded.

Meme looked straight at me and said very seriously, "*You* are the necessary ingredient, Coyitito.

Now, step inside the barrel."

I looked at Meme, and she raised her eyebrows, so I lifted myself over and down into the barrel.

And then I felt the water at the bottom of the barrel. My feet were wet — then my knees, my shoulders, and my head was covered in water as I slipped out of the bottom of the barrel and into the sea.

I thought I would find Magdelena, Tio, Senorita Duende, and Padre Miguel II right away, as soon as I left Meme, but I didn't. I was in the ocean by myself, and I knew that at any moment, that slimy, viscous water snake would be at my side. I listened and looked. I really couldn't see much in the water until, all of a sudden, it was as if I had headlights in my eyes. My vision was full force light, and I spun around looking. I hoped no No Face would come into the ocean to find me. I thought my breath would be gone any moment now, so I started to swim to the surface, and I realized I was breathing steadily. I had eaten one of Meme's submarine cookies.

Next to me was a huge patch of seaweed. I watched it wave back and forth with the ocean's movements. I yearned, oh how I yearned, to be with Magdelena and Tio. Then I heard something in the water. I went behind the seaweed and realized that if my eyes were open, they were two beams of light. And if I shut them, I wouldn't be able to see. So I drifted behind the seaweed and half opened, half closed my eyes.

Where was Rodeo? I thought our Dolphin protectors were always around in the water. Maybe Rodeo didn't know I was here. Maybe Rodeo was with Magdelena.

And then I saw what made the noise. Thousands of bubbles floated past me. Round, perfect, clear shining bubbles all floated together toward somewhere. I didn't move. I watched them, and when I thought the last of them had passed by me, I decided to follow them, to find out where they were going. They looked so safe to me.

They turned right and left. So did I and the seaweed. They turned often. The light from my eyes was hidden in their glow, or at least I thought so. And then the bubbles stopped moving. All at once, they came to a halt. So I halted, too, and then the bubbles started disappearing. Something was happening. A group of bubbles formed a circle and was taken somewhere.

Oh no! I thought about the spinning cyclone of the water snake, the lasso of the rope, and now circles of bubbles — gone! I needed to get out of there — quickly — but before I could swim away, I was caught in the circle of bubbles and escorted somewhere. I was held pinned against the bubbles and brought to an underwater cave entrance. It couldn't be. It really couldn't be — the Underwater Cave of Secrets! I squirmed and twisted and tried to break free when someone said, "What. Is. This? What kind of bubble. are you? You are a very. very. DIFFerent kind of bubble. WHAT. are you doing Here? Are YOU. Trying. To. Gain. Access. to the Underwater Cave of SECRETSS?"

And with that, I was whisked by what felt like a rope and brought in front of the One behind the voice.

"Did. YOU. think that somehow. YOU. would get past ME?"

I looked up to where the voice started. So many ropes! Moving in and around the entrance to the cave were all these — tentacles! They were tentacles.

"NO. ONE. gets past. ME. I. AM the QUEEN. of the Secretsss. Come bubbles, come — deliver YOUR secretss into the cave. (I will whisssper for a moment.) Stay with your secretss, bubbles; guard your secrets. from the ones who try to take them. Like YOU! YOU are here to. steal secretsss. COME.HERE."

And I was whisked again by one of the tentacles right close up to the speaking One. I was caught in the arm of a giant octopus.

"Sooo — OOOOO — whose secret. do YOU. want to STEAL?"

I felt like I was turning blue. The squeeze was too strong on me. Perhaps the submarine cookie was wearing off. I was suffocating, I thought.

"COME, GIRLS. FASTER." Then the octopus was whispering. "Get the bubbles inssside fasster. More secretsss are alwayss on their way. Hurry. Hurry. Hurry."

And through the light of my own eyes, I saw another octopus, not as large as the one whose grasp held me breathless. I couldn't move.

"YOU — stay here! Ha! Ha! HA!" said the one whose name I hadn't yet caught. Where was I to go?

I thought I would perish here — and thought to send out a secret, but before I could, the One who held me unrolled me to the tip of release.

"Would you. Like. To. Leave. NOW?"

I would. I most certainly would.

I shook my head "yes."

"Ha! HA! HA!" And I was swirled back into her arm, wrapped up until I was curled right outside her voice.

"Of course you. would. BUT, SWEETIE! YOU. CAME TO ME. Shhhhh … I didn't. come. Looking. For. YOUUUUU. Ssso now — you must stay. HOW WOULD YOU. like a job. LASSOing. bubbles, and bringing them back to me. ME. ME? How many? ARMS? Do. YOU have?"

She uncurled me, so she could count.

"One. TWO. How much do you. Think. YOU could do with TWO arms? HA! HA! Ha."

I was breathing better each time she released me, but I could tell the submarine cookies were wearing off. I suppose my warning would come, and I would miss it wrapped up in the arms of this Giant One.

"Look. OVER. There," she said, and she stretched her tentacle and again released me to its end, but she never let go.

"NO, I. meant over. THERE," and she plucked me into another of her arms.

"No. no. no. OVER. There," and she handed me over to herself three times.

"Ha. Ha. HA."

"DIZZY. FELLA?" she asked.

I thought I was about to pass out when she dipped me down into the depths of the ocean, then lifted me right above the surface — yes — air — and pulled me down again, drawing me up close to her.

"Pleased. To. Make. Your. Acquaintance." she said. "Whatever. YOUR. NAME. IS. I'M. Marleena. THE. GREAT. MARleena. Ha! HA. Ha."

And then I felt it. All of a sudden, something started to happen. I felt it inside me; it came up and out. And I started to hiccup. First, it was slight. And then it became really fast, and I didn't know what was happening. I didn't know what was going on, but each time I hiccupped, a bubble came out of my mouth.

I felt the first one rise, and I couldn't keep my mouth closed because it was right there, right inside my mouth, pushing my mouth open — and I saw it — a big bubble popped out.

Marleena the Giant One saw it. "CATCH. That bubble. GIRLS. THere's a bubble. On. Its. Own. CATCH. IT. And bring it. Into. The. CAVE."

And then another bubble was released from my mouth.

"Oh. Oh. OH. Here's another. Bubble ON its. Own. Where AREthese bubbles. Coming. From? GIRLS. Are. You. Doing. Your. JOB? Get this. ONE. BEFORE IT ESCAPES."

And then the bubbles started coming faster — until they were escaping from me so fast, I almost couldn't keep my mouth closed.

Was this the warning Meme mentioned? And if it was — what next? What was going to happen next?

"Hurry. HURRY. Hurry. GET. Those bubbless." Tentacle arms reached out for the bubbles.

"Don't. Let. ANY. Get. Away. Don't let. ANY. OFtheSECRETS. Escape. STAY CLOSE BY. Oh. Oh. OHHHHHHHHHHh. Look. at that one. there. Look. GO. GET. IT. KAROLEENA. GO. Get that bubble. THERE. YES, yesss. There. WAIT. I. GOT. It."

And one of Marleena the Giant One's arms grabbed the glossy bubble as it floated in the ocean.

She was so busy with my bubbles that she forgot about me for the moment, and I was so busy watching the bubbles, letting them out of my mouth, watching her and her Girls, I didn't notice something very important — very, very important. I was shrinking! (Meme!) As the bubbles left my mouth, I was getting smaller and smaller.

At some point, the bubbles came speeding out of my mouth, and Marleena the Giant One started getting frantic and was almost whispering when she said, "GIRLS. Girls. GIRLS. DoN'T — LOOK. LOOK. LOOK. Some of the. BUBBLESS. ARE. ESSSCAPING. CATCH the BUBBLES. HURRY. All ARMS areNEEDED. NOW! All ARMS. GIRLS. Takeout allyour ARMS and corral THOSEBUBBLES. HURRY. KaroLEENA — hurry. Hurry. HURry. NOW!"

And Marleena the Giant One struck out several of her arms, and caught as many bubbles as she saw. Her great arms drifted in the path of the floating orbs, wrapping around as many as she could find.

I was in one of her arms as it slid through the water. Some of my bubbles seemed to be getting away, and she hurried to capture them, and when she did, what was left of me slid from her grasp. I was so tiny, so very, very tiny, and she hadn't been thinking about me with all these bubbles floating around, so I swam in the tiniest form as far away from her as I could. I looked around for a place to hide.

Then the shrill alarm sounded. It was like the sound of a high pitched whistle. My ears hurt. I didn't know how much longer I had after the warning. I knew I had to get to the surface quickly, or I would need air and not be able to breathe.

Then everything seemed to stop. The whistle sounded again. I saw the Girls Marleena had been talking to. They lined up in front of her — their long arms pointing down. None of them moved their arms as they hung in the ocean.

The shrill whistle blew again — then Marleena the Giant One spoke:

"He. Has. ESCAPED. FIND. HIM. Karoleena, you. stay here. and guard the Cave. Pick two. Girls. to stay with you. Keep YOUR. EYE. OUT. FOR. HIM.

"The others — GO AND FIND HIM. YOU HAD BETTER FIND HIM OR ELSE — you know what happens. You. Will.......... Lose. Your. arms — and then what? Then, how will YOU. FUNCTION? How will. YOU. keep your job. at the Underwater Cave of Secrets. IF YOU HAVE NO ARMS? KaroLEENA. YOU. And. Your. Girls. GO check all the bubbles. THAT just. Arrived. Make SURE. HE. didn't float in. With THEM.

"Find him. FIND. Him. FIND HIM. NOW. Whoever. Does. Not. FIND. Him. Iss. Sssuspect. GO!"

And then Marleena the Giant One spun in a giant circle as her Girls opened their arms and took off in different directions. Karoleena and the others swam into the Underwater Cave of Secrets. I was hiding behind a coral shell, right at its corner. I was right there at its base.

"Come OUT.ComeOUT. Wherever. You. ARE! You know. WE. WILL. find YOU. The ocean is OURS. And. We. Will. Find. You. We see. In the DARK! We know. The ocean. It is better. that YOU SHOW yourself. If. You. Show. Yourself. Now. I will. Have. Mercy. Mercy. MERCY. on you, but if YOU don't, if you. DO. NOT. COME. OUT. NOW — you will be. sorry. You. Will. Be. ... GIRLS. FIND. HIM. NOW."

Marleena the Giant One spun steadily. Her giant arms were moving quickly, and though I was still very small, I knew I had to get out of there. I had to keep moving. I didn't know where to go; I had no idea.

"KaroLEENA. DID. YOU. FIND. HIM???️ Did. Your. Girls. Find. Him. YET?"
Marleena the Giant One's shrill voice sounded.

And then Karoleena spoke. I was not prepared for the sound of Karoleena's voice.
When she answered Marleena, she had the softness and the sweetness and the
sound of Maestra Maria. And for those moments, I was mesmerized and I didn't
understand. And it frightened me because the No Faces stole faces — all right —
wasn't that enough? But down here in the bottom of the ocean, the keepers of the
secrets of the cave — the ones with eight arms — they sounded like the ones I
knew and loved. That really, really added to my worry.

The soft voice said, "We are sorting through the bubbles, but as of yet, we have not
found him, but we will, Marleena."

All those words of hers mesmerized me. I hung on to each word with longing. "Oh,
Maestra Maria," I thought. I even started to swim out toward her voice — when I
noticed something.

"KarolEENA. Did. You. FIND. Him YET?"

Before Karoleena answered, I looked up. The ocean above me was lit and swarm-
ing with arms. Arms cut through the water, reaching straight up, then curling fast.
When they knew they were empty, they unfurled to the tip and curled furiously to
the center, released and searched again. All these arms were in search of me.

Marleena the Giant One continued to spin. And before Karoleena answered her,
she yelled, "KaroLEENA. SING. UsAsong. Why don't YOU. Sing. To us as you.
SEARCH?" And I knew then that I was doomed. I knew that as soon as Karoleena started to sing in the voice of Maestra Maria that I would be drawn to her
— follow her into the Underwater Cave of Secrets, need to breathe — not be able
to — and somehow, in one way or another, Marleena would win. I would be hers.

"I WANT. Him. Alive," she shrilled. "Now. SING, KaroLEENA. SING.SING.
SING."

And what I had noticed, before I heard about the song — was that I had started
to grow again. It was a tiny growth at first, very, very tiny. I almost missed it, but it
was happening. I looked at the giant coral shell next to me; it lost its size. It wasn't
giant like Marleena, but compared to me — it was large. She was enormous and
vast — even when I was full size. But the shell started to become smaller as I grew
larger, and I knew, oh how I knew, I needed to get out of there — quickly.

And then the song started. At first, Karoleena just started humming. That was
already too much for me. I heard in the humming that sweetness. I thought of
Maestra Maria, eyes closed in front of the classroom, telling all of us, "Let's start

today's exercise by humming." And all of us started humming. We were shy at first; I was very shy, Tio too, but Lucinda, Lucinda was not shy, and she started humming — loudly. I opened my eyes just to see what Maestra Maria was doing with Lucinda's loudness, and the rest of us kind of quiet, but Maestra Maria was smiling as she hummed, and she said, "Close your eyes, Coyitito." I don't know how she knew because her eyes were closed, but I closed my eyes, and soon we were all humming, and it sounded very calm — very, very calm.

So when I heard the humming, I started to close my eyes and drift — drift into the sound. I tried to remind myself. I said, "Coyitito, stop. Remember, this is not Maestra Maria. You are in a dangerous, a very, very dangerous place — terribly, terribly dangerous. You are growing; you are running out of air; Marleena the Giant One wants to make you her victim — Coyitito, Coyitito, snap out of it; snap out of it," but I was drifting, and I started moving toward her voice.

Marleena couldn't stop herself. "KaroLeeNa. SING. SING. SING." Marleena didn't know that the humming had already caught me, but her shrill voice broke the spell for a moment. And before Karoleena could start her song, I again realized that I was growing. So I did what I could. I swam into the shell. I knew sometimes that there were certain shells that walked. I think we had read about them. I think maybe there were some crabs that walked with their shells on top of them, so I thought that maybe I could start to walk with this shell on top of me until I was too big for it. And I thought that maybe, oh maybe, it would stop the sound of Maestra Maria's voice coming from Karoleena. I heard the first words escape from her as I swam inside the shell, and when I did, the beautiful voice, which I longed to hear, was muffled.

"Please, Shell, let me take refuge here inside you. I hope you don't mind if I move you. I don't know if you have a family or friends around here, but if you do, can you somehow send them a message — that you will be moving for a while — that you are needed to do a good deed? Can you please tell them that and come with me? I don't know how long I have before I'll outgrow you, but until I do, you're my only chance of getting out of here." I hoped the shell understood.

And before I could wait for an answer, I put my feet down and started to move. At first, it wasn't easy to move the shell, but then we started to go. I didn't know if the shell had decided to help me or if I was getting bigger quickly, but we started going. I didn't know where we were going — I had no idea. The ocean was filled with arms and snakes and all kinds of horrors where I was. I didn't know where Marina Teresa was but I figured I must be far from her. This wasn't her part of the ocean.

Oh no! I could tell my breath was starting to change. And as I started to breathe differently, I started to grow more quickly. And the shell covering me became smaller. And smaller. And smaller, and soon, oh very, very soon, I had to duck my head out from the shell because my head was getting too big for it. And then I looked at myself, and I was carrying the shell in my hand, and I started to gasp a bit when I heard — not that far from me: "SEIZE HIM! SEIZE. HIM! SEIZE. HIM!"

I struggled hard, very, very hard, struggled to swim upwards. And I waited for the big thrashing arm to wrap around me and pull me toward the shrill voice of Marleena. My breathing was hurried. I was trying very hard to swim fast. But nothing, nothing happened. I heard the sound of many arms slipping through the water, but none of them, not one of them, reached for me. I swam as fast as I could, swimming up, up. And now I was using my breath the way Canyon Joe had taught us. The submarine cookie's power was finished. I needed to surface as soon as possible. I saw a slit up above me, and I thought it must be the surface. I knew, oh I knew, the slimy water snake would find me — or something else would happen — but whatever was going to be — I needed air. I swam toward the opening, my lungs bursting — I needed to practice more. Oh, if only Senorita Duende and Magdelena — if only — I was almost there. I saw the surface — almost — almost —

Whoosh.

It came.

All of a sudden, the strong arm was right next to me, ready to strike.

"SSSOOOOOOOOOOOOOOOOOOO — YOU. THOUGHT. YOUwouldget- away from. MARLEENA??? YOU. THOUGHT. YOUcouldoutswim,outsmart. MARLEENA??? HOW. CUTE! BUT. I. Have arms ... for you! I. Have. Arms. All. Around. You. Come. Let. MarleenAAAAAAAAA. Hold. YOU. In. her. ARMS."

She moved quickly. I was at the surface. I took a gulp of air as she spread and curled her arms.

I was plucked into them.

And then the drawer shut with great force. I turned around to see Meme with a large stick and a key. Panting, I wondered if this key belonged to Meme. Mine was still missing. She held the stick and key in one hand; me in the other. She dropped me, put the key in the lock, turned it, and then stood in front of the drawer wait- ing. Banging and thrashing sounded from the other side of the lock. Meme raised the stick over her head. I lay on the floor gasping. She waited while the thrashing continued. Her eyes watched the drawer. I could tell it was not time to talk to her.

I didn't say a word. I knew that Marleena was still in the drawer — that she hadn't yet left.

So it was Meme who had plucked me from the ocean. And I must have been right there, right at that drawer where I had been earlier, the one we used to get the water for the submarine cookies. The surface I saw must have been Meme's drawer opening.

The thrashing stopped, but Meme didn't move. She stayed right there — until Azul came in with a pot of tea. He bent down to where I was and said, "Drink this, Coyitito; you will feel better."

I hoped this was the real Meme and the real Azul, but I didn't have enough energy left to think about it for too long.

I drank the tea.

Meme, without taking her eyes off the drawer, handed the stick to Azul. He stood where Meme had been, and he held the stick the way she did.

"Come upstairs, Coyitito."

Meme sped up the steps, telling me to climb onto the bottom step; then she lifted the steps the way she did before. And I rose up the flights to where Meme was.

"I've been calling you, Coyitito. I was calling you to come back."

"I didn't hear you, Meme."

"I told you twice to snap out of it — *snap* out of the song you heard. Did you not hear my *snap?*"

I recalled the voice in my head telling me to *snap* out of it.

"That was you, Meme?"

"*Snaps* are me, Coyitito."

"But those snaps weren't italicized, Meme."

IT FELT LIKE SECONDS before Meme woke me up.

Snap.

"Here you go, Coyitito."

"Where, Meme?" She didn't answer. She turned from the oven. "Here, Coyitito.

These are for you. Now let's see: we have these. These and these. Now — these are whish cookies, Coyitito."

I looked at the cookies. Whish cookies?

"Meme," but she was busy arranging the cookies to give me and didn't answer.

"Meme," I called again, but she still didn't answer.

"Meme." She opened the door and walked through it. When I followed her, I found the ocean, and Meme was gone.

And a huge wave came roaring my way. On its crest sat Magdelena, Tio, Senorita Duende, and Padre Miguel II speeding toward me.

"WHERE HAVE YOU BEEN, Coyitito?" Magdelena yelled to me. Tio looked at me from out of the corner of his eye. I waved at Tio.

I had so much to tell them, and I wanted them to get out of the ocean. We needed to ask Marina Teresa about whether or not the ocean, like the land and The River, has protected areas.

Where were Marina Teresa and Aphrodite? I was going to ask Magdelena and Tio this question when I, all of a sudden, saw Tio, wide-eyed, staring at the canyon trail.

Then I saw it. And I'm sure Magdelena did too because her eyes moved the way of Tio's and mine. We all saw the figure up against the rocks.

And all of a sudden, the rocks above where the person stood swarmed with riders and horses. In unison, they headed our way.

The No Faces were galloping toward the ocean. Somehow I seemed to be the one who brought them out. I hoped they didn't know how to swim yet.

"Turn around," I yelled to Magdelena, Tio, Senorita Duende, and Padre Miguel II. And as soon as Tio turned around, I yelled, "Stop!" The No Faces were coming our way, but we had a few moments. I remembered Meme's cookies and gave some to Magdelena, Tio, Senorita Duende and Padre Miguel II. I didn't know if these were submarine cookies, whish cookies, or earlier cookies of Meme's.

"Meme made them," I said.

I knew the No Faces were getting close. The cookie I ate tasted like one I had before. I thought it best to turn to the water and see what happened. Tio did the same. I thought somehow Meme's cookies would help us.

The No Faces rode into the water, too. I turned around and saw them; they were chasing us and getting closer and closer. The long lasso flew up into the air.

"Coyitito! What are we doing?" Magdelena yelled in front of me, but her words dwindled as she shrank. We all shrank and became very, very small. Tiny. So, more of Meme's submarine cookies must have been in the batch filled with a tiny amount of something, because all of us were very, very tiny as we descended underwater.

As I shrank, I thought that it was Manuel whom I saw on the rider's horse; the rider with the lasso. "Was that Manuel?" He must have been the one whom they picked up on the rocks. Was he trying to escape?

The lasso hit the water above us, but we were free from it. We were so small that the No Faces couldn't see us. I watched their horses' hooves cut through the water right above us. One horse was there with two riders. The legs of one rider were shorter than the legs of the other, and I believed this was Manuel.

Tio rode right next to Magdelena and me. His tiny eyes were wide open. I knew Tio would like this part very, very much — this shrinking and all. I knew Magdelena would be wondering all about it, but we needed to keep moving because I didn't know how long we had.

So we went along in the darkness that arrived. I wanted Magdelena to take out her comb and light the way, but I knew that was dangerous. But Meme made sure her cookies had lights somewhere inside too because once our eyes adjusted, we could see.

And then I heard the sounds: the thrashing. Maybe the No Faces couldn't swim, but their eel snakes could. I heard them cutting through the water. I knew they knew we were around, and they were searching for us. It would take them some time to find us when we were this tiny. If we were full size — I didn't even want to have that thought — but I had to have it. Because I felt it. I knew the signs: I already started growing: we all did. It was very slow, but it started happening, and when the submarine cookies wore off, the snakes would come, and we wouldn't be able to breathe underwater.

I wanted to make sure Magdelena and Tio weren't afraid, but they knew too; they knew we were starting to grow. And then another dreaded thing happened. All of a sudden, I heard it. I heard the shrill voice of Marleena, and I knew we were doomed.

I pointed down, and Senorita Duende went that way. Tio followed. I thought we might have a chance down there. I didn't know how we could get out if I pointed up. Either way … we were doomed. The eel snakes were around us, sniffing and circling. Marleena was shrilling, "GIRLS! GIRLS. GIRLS! The. SSSNAKES. Are. OUT! Watch. All. Around. YOU. KarolEENA. Arms. Out. Keep. Your. ARMS. On. the Girls. KAROleena. Ohhh . SSOMETHING OR SOMEONE IS NEAR! WE. Will. WE. Shall. OH. WE.will. Find. It. It. Hass. To. Be. HIMmm! It. Has. TO. BE. Ohhh. This. TIME.HE. Will. NOT. EScape. GO!"

I looked at my size and panicked. And then I slipped my hand into my tin. Arms spun circles around us, searching for us. I took out another cookie. I didn't know what would happen, but something would … something needed to.

As I reached the cookie, the water became filled with cords. They were everywhere, whipping around, lassoing; they knew we were here. Tio looked at me. He looked at the size of himself growing. He came very close to me, ducking from the ropes. Magdelena sat frozen in front of me. I handed Tio a cookie, and motioned for him to give Padre Miguel II some. Magdelena gave Senorita Duende a piece, then ate hers. I ate mine. The water snakes started their cyclone.

"WAIT!" Marleena shrieked. "WAIT. GIRLS. How can. You. let these bubbles. get awayfrom. YOU? KAROLEENA. How could those GIRLSletTHESE-bubblesDRIFTawAY? WE. MUST. NOT. LET THE. SECRETSSS. FLOAT AWAY. FROM. USS. We must. COLLECTall the SECRETS. WE can. GIRLS. Who. Did. ThiSSSSSSSSS? KaroLEENA. FIND. FINDOUT who did. ThissssSSS."

And there we were, being escorted by Karoleena directly into the Underwater Cave of Secrets. Meme's cookies made us into bubbles and kept us tiny and invisible.

"NOW.NOW.NOW. ContinuewiththeCYCLONE," Marleena yelled. And they did. But they must have lost our scent because no one followed us into the cave.

Karoleena kept us in her circular arm and drifted us into the cave. We floated along. The cave was lit with a bubble light, only we didn't see any bubbles as we drifted. We did see the Girls, the ones who worked in the cave. They kept their arms spread from side to side. Karoleena looked at them as we sailed past. Then she stopped and said, "Girls. Listen. Marleena is very upset. Terribly. Some bubbles escaped. I don't know how it happened, but she wants someone to blame. What will we do?"

The Girls started talking.

"Who was on duty, Karoleena? Who was positioned over where the bubbles escaped?" one of them asked.

"Did they escape from inside? I always get blamed for everything."

"It wasn't me, Karoleena. It wasn't me. I was guarding Family Secrets at the time."

Magdelena was a tiny dot in front of me. Tio was next to us in another bubble. I wondered how Marleena and her Girls knew what the secrets were. How did they know Family Secrets from other kinds of secrets? I shuddered.

"I did it. I."

We watched as one of the Girls came from behind a crevice.

"I was the one who did it. I was ocean-dreaming when I had this pile of new bubbles that had just arrived, and I fell into a kind of languor, and I knew I should have been more diligent; I always know I should. But, hey, I let it happen. I'll go face the music. I'll go see what Marleena's punishment will be for allowing some bubbles to escape."

"But, Occupia-Cema, weren't you here the whole time?" We heard Karoleena whisper. "Weren't you guarding …"

Occupia-Cema floated right up to Karoleena and whispered.

"You are the only one to know me as Occupia-Cema, Karoleena. That name is for us only: our secret. Please try not to use it around the others. You understand."

Then Occupia-Cema (I won't use her secret name) — then Occupia answered Karoleena more loudly and said, "I was guarding the …" and as she spoke to Karoleena, all the other Girls started coming over. One of them said, "But, Occupia, I saw you guarding …" and another said, "You couldn't have, Occupia. You … you were over there," and one of the arms pointed down into the cave. And as the Girls talked about where Occupia had been and how she couldn't have been the one to let the bubbles escape — the strangest thing happened. Magdelena saw it, and Tio, too. The bubbles that were guarded inside the passageways started coming out from their places. They started floating out of all the entranceways. At first, the others didn't notice. They were all so involved in figuring out where Occupia had been.

"Marleena is very angry!" another of the Girls said.

"Marleena …"

And we drifted from Karoleena's circle, blending in with the other bubbles.

"Noooooo," one of the Girls cried.

"Oh no," Karoleena sighed. "Hurry, Girls, Hurry. Catch them. Catch the bubbles. Don't let any of the bubbles get back to …"

"KAROLEENA!" the shrill voice of Marleena set all the Girls still. "OHHH —

HHH. KAROLEENA … WE. SEEM. TO. HAVE. A. LITTLE. PROBLEM. HERE …"

We floated with a group of other bubbles straight down the cave's middle. "How do we steer our bubbles?" I wondered. But then we drifted a bit from the group.

"KAROLEENA. Are. All. The. Bubbles. Where. They. Are. Supposed. To. Be.? Is. everythingall rightinthere??? Something. Tells. Me. That. The. Bubbles. Are. Not. In. Their. Caves. AM I RIGHT. KAROLEENA??? Something. Tells. Me. That-thebubblesaregetting. OUT! Something. Tells. Me. … SOMETHING LIKE THISSS …" And we weren't sure what happened, but we felt the long arm thrust its way toward Karoleena. We heard the Girls gasp, and then we heard the one named Occupia say, "That's all because of me, Marleena. May I come out to see you?"

"WHO. IS. THAT? WHO? Occupia. IS. That. YOU? KAROleena. Is. That. Occupia?"

I hoped Occupia would be all right.

We steered our horses by shifting our tiny weight around, moving away from the group. We knew at any moment we would all be lassoed up and brought into one of the Cave's entrances, so I steered for the crevice where Occupia had been. Tio followed, and just in time because the arms of the girls started grabbing for the floating bubbles. The arms sped through the air gathering as many bubbles as they could hold.

I heard Karoleena say, "Start filtering the secrets, and get all the bubbles back where they belong. And count them; check your numbers."

"KAROLEENA. Come. Outtttttt. HERE. WITH.Occupia.Now."

The arms grasped and grabbed. The cave was silent except for the sound of the arms grabbing for bubbles. "Count and filter. What did that mean?" We needed to do something; only I didn't know what. Then it dawned on me. Maybe, maybe Occupia was guarding the secret, the big secret.

I hadn't told Magdelena and Tio about the secrets. I had no time to tell them. And we needed to get out of where we were before Marleena realized that three bubbles were missing.

"Maybe we should wait for Karoleena to come back before we start. What do you think?" one of the Girls said.

"What do you think Marleena will do with Occupia?"

"BE QUIET IN THERE. STOP TALKING AND START WORKING,"

Marleena hissed from the top of the cave.

Silence.

And then I heard the sound of arms in the water, dropping and lifting. It sounded like so many arms. I wanted to move out from the crevice hole we hid in, but I knew if they saw us, they would lasso us into their numbers. So — we didn't move, but I did hear the soft, soft whispers. I had to; I had to move closer to see. Magdelena felt me going, and she stopped Senorita Duende. I don't know how Senorita Duende knew which one of us to listen to. I felt badly about putting Senorita Duende in the place of choosing whose direction to follow, so I let Magdelena lead. But I felt pulled back to the other side of the crevice where the Girls were whispering in the smallest voices, "Tell me your secrets. Tell me your most precious secret." I wanted to turn around, float right into one of their arms, and tell my secrets.

I thought about my most precious secret. Which one was that? Was that the time ... ?

Magdelena steered Senorita Duende around the side of the crevice. I didn't have time to think about my secrets because we started moving fast, very, very quickly. Tio was right next to us. We must be in some current, I thought, just as we were spun and lifted. We floated in the soft light down a tunnel. I kept checking to make sure Tio was next to us. So far, he was.

We passed entranceways like the ones the girls guarded, only no bubbles were down here. No one was down here. There wasn't any activity where we headed.

And then we saw it. Really, we had no way to change it at this point. I tried to steer us away, but I couldn't. We were stuck in a current and heading straight ahead into a huge sheet of glass. We were moving faster and faster — and I knew — oh, I knew that we were going to crash and shatter right into it. Tio knew, too. I saw him trying to change direction, but he couldn't either.

Magdelena sat in front of me. I knew she was trying to change our direction, but she couldn't do it either. The glass came closer and closer. "Please do not let us crash into the glass," I pleaded.

And then there we were — seconds away. I braced myself. We all did. Senorita Duende didn't try to turn away. She just rode the current straight, the only choice we had. She didn't even flinch.

I counted in my head — 5,4,3 ... Magdelena put one of her hands behind her, and took one of mine. I looked at Tio. 2.1. CRASH! We crashed — and slid down the surface of the glass. The bubbles made us slide! We didn't even feel the crash.

"Are you all right, Magdelena?" "I am. I am. And you, Coyitito? And you, Senorita Duende? And Tio? Is Tio here?"

And yes, there was Tio sliding along with us. We landed in the water of the cave. And it carried us along the glass. And when we looked, we saw passageways. The current moved slowly now. It led us to a point where the glass seemed to end, but then it continued. And when we looked around, the glass was everywhere!

All of a sudden, I saw it. I looked to my side, right at the glass, and I saw two tiny bubbles floating along. And I knew that inside those bubbles sat Magdelena and I on Senorita Duende, and Tio on Padre Miguel II. "Look, Magdelena. Look." She turned and saw us floating.

"Coyitito, this is a giant mirror. Look. Look. As we drift along, we drift along in the mirror too. Look at Tio. There he is." And when we turned to look the other way, we saw more glass, more mirrors. Mirrors filled the space everywhere. We floated to what we thought was the end of the mirror, and it turned and curved. And so did we. Then we saw that there were rows and rows of glass reflectors: mirrors, mirrors everywhere.

"It's like a labyrinth, Coyitito. Remember that story Maestra Maria read with us about the labyrinth? What was it called? Do you remember, Coyitito?"

And yes, I did remember, but I didn't want to remember, and I didn't want to tell Magdelena what I remembered because in the story, the labyrinth was dark and dangerous, and I was already getting the feeling of doom.

"Coyitito, wasn't it … ?" But I spoke to Magdelena very gently, very, very gently; I said to Magdelena, "Maybe it is best that we do not talk; we don't want Marleena to hear us."

But Magdelena was already taken with something else.

"Coyitito, look," Magdelena whispered to me. "Look." And she pointed into the mirror next to us. I looked and watched as we floated along; I saw Tio right behind us. And I kept looking because Magdelena kept looking, and then I saw what I thought she saw. We were growing. It wasn't at a very slow pace; it was faster than I would have hoped. As we grew, our bubble stayed the same size, so soon we were getting bigger than our bubble-home. I watched the tops of our heads burst through the top of the small orb we had been floating in for how long? I didn't even know how long. Then our arms and legs grew through the sides and the bottom. I glanced behind to Tio's image in the mirror. He and Padre Miguel II were also growing.

"Coyitito! Magdelena!" Tio called when his head was free. I placed my finger over my lips telling Tio to please, please be quiet. "Please be quiet, Tio," I thought, because I didn't want Marleena to hear us. Or maybe she already had.

Tio hushed. Magdelena still stared into the glass.

"Magdelena, what do you see?"

"Look, Coyitito. Look."

And I looked. I looked very, very hard, but I didn't see anything.

"Look at the light, Coyitito. Look at the way the light is. Look at all the stars."

I looked more and more into the glass.

"And look at that one."

But I didn't see any stars. I saw, instead, an arm, one of the arms of the Girls, or an arm of the Giant One herself. I saw just the end of the arm dash inside the mirror, then dip down into the water.

"I think they have found us, Magdelena."

"Look, Coyitito, look how bright."

"Magdelena, Magdelena, I think they are coming to get us."

I looked inside the glass. Yes, yes, I saw the arm again. I turned to look at Tio. The arm was in the mirror behind him. I turned my head the other way. The arm was there.

I watched it disappear down into the water.

"Magdelena, we must get out of here," but she was transfixed by the mirror.

"Magdelena."

"Coyitito, look, look how bright. Look how amazingly bright."

Tio sped up next to us.

"What is wrong?"

"Tio," said Magdelena. "Tio, look. Look at that bright star."

Tio looked to where Magdelena pointed. I thought that the labyrinth was playing tricks on Magdelena.

"Tio, we must find a way out. The arm is coming for us."

Tio and I steered the horses while Magdelena looked into the mirror.

"Hurry, Senorita Duende. Hurry." But I had no idea where we were hurrying. "Hurry." I thought hard, very, very hard. I kept turning around. My legs dangled in the water. All of our legs did. I kept feeling the water, waiting for the change, waiting for the grasp. I wanted to yell very, very loudly. I wanted someone to come to help us. I hoped for Meme to snatch us into one of her drawers. "Padre Miguel, where are you? Maestra Maria, it is I; it is Coyitito. Please help us, Rojo Anita. Rojo Anita, the Real One, where are you? Canyon Joe, Marina Teresa — help. Help us!"

But no one came.

We were trapped.

Magdelena kept looking in the mirror. I whispered, "Tio, we must find a way out of here. One of the mirrors must be the way out. Let us hurry. We must look for the different mirror before they catch us."

And I didn't say more to Tio other than these whispers, but I thought about what Marleena would do to us; how she would deliver us to the No Faces or something else — something more horrible, and I wanted to yell. I wanted very, very much to yell when, all of a sudden, I saw Tio reach into his pocket. I wished I had my key. Tio's white cloth reflected in the mirror when he removed it. Maybe Magdelena's comb would help.

Maybe, oh just maybe, the gifts we received would help us in this room of mirrors. Maybe we could open the mirrors and find a passage out of here.

"Splash."

I heard something in the water. I felt ripples. Tio was wide-eyed. Magdelena fixed her gaze on the glass.

"Magdelena, take out your comb. Hurry."

Magdelena didn't move.

The temperature of the water changed.

"Cassandra, Magdelena." Tio said it.

It seemed like the mirrors moved, but I don't think they did. I think the water moved.

"Swish."

I heard the water swishing.

"Magdelena, please, take out your comb. Quickly. Cassandra!" I leaned into Magdelena's ear.

Magdelena returned from her transfixed state. She reached behind her head and lifted her hair, sliding out the glowing comb. "See if you see an opening when you look through its glow. Does it show a way out of here? Tio, is your cloth blanket telling us anything?"

I knew something was moving in the water.

Tio let go of his cloth. It floated ahead of us. Magdelena's comb kept a small light around us. I was filled with chills, knowing the water was crawling with arms that would reach us and pull us down at any moment.

Tio's cloth slid on the surface; we watched it very, very closely in front of us. I looked in the mirror, and there it was, right in front of Tio. Where was it going?

The water behind us churned. I knew Magdelena felt it; Tio, felt it too, but neither said a word. I looked into the mirror. I, Coyitito, saw myself over and over, drifting in a row of mirrors, riding Senorita Duende with Magdelena in front of me holding her lit-up comb, and Tio next to us riding Padre Miguel II. And as I looked at this image, I watched Tio's cloth sink.

"Tio, your cloth; it is sinking." I was alarmed. Losing my key was a regret of mine; we couldn't lose Tio's cloth, too.

Tio slid off Padre Miguel II into the water. His shell floated away from him, and then it sunk. That too — gone.

Our gifts sure do come and go.

"No, Tio, no," I called to him. But he was already under the water. We couldn't see him, but we saw his white cloth lit by Magdelena's comb.

The cloth was gone, too. Padre Miguel II disappeared after Tio. I was thinking fast. I needed to save Magdelena and follow Tio, but for the moment, I was frozen.

Then it happened: what I dreaded came true. We were grabbed and sucked underneath the water. Quickly. All three of us. One moment we were on the surface of the water in the room of mirrors; the next moment we were captive.

"Hold your breath," I told myself. I knew Magdelena and Tio would hold their breath the way we learned from Canyon Joe and Marina Teresa, but at the end of our breath, Marleena waited.

Down, down, down we were pulled. And all around us I watched our falling in mirror after mirror after mirror with Magdelena's comb still glowing.

How far would Marleena take us before she showed herself? Magdelena and Tio had never met her. I shuddered to think of how she would treat Magdelena. I know Marleena would envy Magdelena's kindness, courage, and hair. Her hair floated in front of me as we sank.

Further down. Now it was getting difficult to hold my breath. Had Marleena already taken Tio? He would give her a hard time.

I needed to breathe. I knew the others did also. How was Senorita Duende doing?

Then our reflection was gone. Something flew over our heads. An arm? A rope?

All of a sudden, we were being pulled along by something behind and in front of us. I couldn't see it, but it wrapped around us. I waited for Marleena's big squeeze.

And then I saw that we were covered in a large white cloth. It circled around us: top, bottom, and sides. We floated in its center and were able to breathe. Our legs hung in midair from Senorita Duende as we were pulled swiftly along.

"Magdelena, Magdelena, are you all right?" I panted.

"Yes, yes, Coyitito. And you?" I answered "yes" to her, and we asked Senorita Duende the same question. Then both of us wondered about Tio. Where was Tio?

"I need to go and find Tio," I told Magdelena, but when I tried, I couldn't get out of the white circle.

"I am here," we heard a voice say. It sounded like Tio's voice, but we didn't see him.

"Padre Miguel II is steering with me."

"Where?" I asked Tio, but all of a sudden, we dipped quickly down and flew through the water.

We were moving fast, and I wasn't sure where we were going. Then I caught sight of them: Tio and Padre Miguel II, riding right ahead of us. Padre Miguel II's nose pushed the white cloth with all of us in it through the water.

"I see my shell," Tio called back to us.

"I see it down there. My shell is holding something open. Do you think we can make it to my shell and the opening, Coyitito? We can, Coyitito. We can."

I wanted to say "Cassandra" to Tio. I wanted to ask Magdelena if she saw Tio's shell, but I didn't have time. Tio's cloth shrank, and flattened against us. Padre Miguel II moved like lightning, and I felt it. I felt us slip under an opening, which crashed shut behind us. I didn't know if Tio's shell survived, but I sure thanked it as we passed through the opening it made.

And then we heard it. We all heard it. It was very, very loud. The alarm rang through the caves and echoed. The shrill, slimy voice shrieked through the darkness.

"SOMEONE. SOMEONE. SOMEONE. Has just EXITED! THE.CAVE. OF.SECRETSS.SECRETSS.SECRETSS.Through. THE ROOM OF MIR-RORSS.MIRRORSS.MIRRORSS. No one EScapeSSs. No one eScapeSSS. No one EScapesss. GO.GO.GO."

We were still in water; now our heads topped its surface.

But now Marleena was on us — and so was her *army*. SSOMEONE.SSOME-ONE.SSOMEONE."

All of a sudden, we veered quickly to the right. Then we veered quickly again. Then we were headed for a hole in the wall. It was barely visible, but Magdelena's comb lit the way. And there it was. Right in front of us. We had no idea where we were going, but we had to go somewhere. I thought of that character we read about with Maestra Maria: the one named Alice who followed a White Rabbit she met, and the hole she fell through. I hoped this hole in the wall would help us.

We were in a dark black tunnel of water, heading down, again holding our breath.

And then the thrashing arm came. Even through the water, we heard her:

"NOW. I. AM. GOING TO GET YOU."

And she uncurled her long arm right toward us. I felt it unroll and dash through the water.

"NOW. IAMGOING TO ..."

But she missed. Her arm just missed me. I felt it right above our heads, thrashing and dashing and searching. Magdelena turned around. Her comb lit the water above us. We saw the giant arm pointing straight down, but it couldn't go any further toward us.

Marleena shrieked, "I.MIGHT.not.FITTHROUGHTHISSSSHOLE.BUT. otherSSSS.WILL.TRIA. COME NOW!" And we knew within seconds Tria would come, and we figured Tria must be one of the eel snakes, because Mar-leena's arms were attached to her GIANT BODY, and she couldn't fit through the hole we found, but Tria could.

"OHTRIATRIATRIA. GETTHEM! NooneEScareSSSS.MARLEENA!"

And we felt the arrival of the snake. We felt Tria parting the waters in front of itself, arrowing its way toward us. Tria could make a cyclone in the water or — or just come straight for us and —

I thought of all the terrible things. And then there it was, so close behind us. We felt the rush of water as Tria neared our ankles. We kept moving but there was no way, no way that we could outswim the water snake. Magdelena held her comb.

"HURRYUPTRIA! You. Should. Have. Gotten. THEMBYNOW. TRIA. You. Have. 1,2,3 secondSSS." We heard Marleena's voice further from us.

1 …

2 …

And then the strangest thing happened. All of a sudden, we started to be lifted out of the water. We started rising out of the water and into the air of the cave. Tio was right next to us as we started to rise. I caught his hand just in time. I looked to see if his cloth was what brought us up, but it was something else.

Tria raised its long neck from the water, ready to strike us down as we sped away. I heard it behind me. But we were a second ahead of Tria as we shot up straight into the air.

"Tria. If. YOU. DON'T. Have. THEM. BACKhereINtwoSECONDSSS. Tri-AAA."

But we lost Marleena's voice as we rose higher. And higher.

Magdelena still held her comb in front of her.

"Look, Coyitito. Look. There is the star — just like the one I saw in the mirror. Look," Magdelena said.

And I shuddered because I thought that Tria was still behind us, and Marleena's arms would pluck us from the sky, and the labyrinth had somehow caught Magdelena into thinking she saw a special star. And then Tio's white cloth was underneath us, helping us. Senorita Duende, Magdelena, Tio, Padre Miguel II, and I were riding the cloth through the sky, heading for the star Magdelena kept seeing.

I thought about the star I had visited and wondered what this star had in store for Magdelena and us.

It seemed that Tria hadn't reached us; neither did Marleena.

I knew the No faces were on the land, and now in the water, but I didn't think the No Faces were in the sky.

I LOOKED AT TIO and Magdelena again. They were mesmerized. And then I looked at what they were looking at. In all that black velvet sky, bursts of light shone. I turned my head from side to side. Where were we? We had been in the sky before, but where were we now? Straight in front of us, getting closer and closer, a big, bright star lit up the night. I looked at it: the tips of its points were almost a shade of light purple.

I looked below — and there — below us were clouds. Not scary clouds, not storm clouds, but floating cotton lit by the stars and the moon.

"Look at this show," I said to Magdelena and Tio. "Look at that rush of stars!" I thought of Melaquiades. But Magdelena was still mesmerized by the star we were heading toward, and Tio was quiet as he stared wide-eyed at all the stars.

And then we stopped in front of the star Magdelena didn't take her eyes off as we rode through the night, free from Marleena's grasp. I thought about the star I had stopped outside of the last time we were in the sky, and I wondered if this was that same star. But, no, this visit belonged to Magdelena. We were pulled right in front of the five pointed light. Without saying a word, Magdelena, still holding her comb, stood up on the white cloth, as if she had done this before. She held out her hand. The star slid open. Then she disappeared.

Tio turned to look at me. I went right up to where Magdelena had just been, but I saw no entrance, no way in. I told Tio that we might need to wait a bit and see if Magdelena returned. We didn't want to open whatever door she went through and fall through the sky. I had done that when Rojo Anita saw us, and The River sent an invitation. But with Magdelena, I wanted to wait.

Was this the star Magdelena saw in the cave's mirror? I think Magdelena thought so. Maybe the star had called us.

Then I saw something to the right of us. I looked several times to make sure — but, yes — there it was. There was, I think it's called, the dorsal fin Marina Teresa had showed us in the water. The tail rose up in the sky in what looked like small haloes.

"Look, Tio! Look! It's Juna or Rodeo, or Dulcinea, the Red Departed Dolphin, in the sky!"

We both watched the dolphin. Was this a constellation in the sky? Did this dolphin match a dolphin in the ocean — or all the dolphins in the sea? And then we saw something very, very amazing. As Tio and I and Senorita Duende and Padre Miguel II watched from Tio's cloth, the inside of the dolphin, where the dark sky was, filled with all these stars. I don't know where they came from, but all of a sudden, right in the middle of the dolphin, right where its stomach or its heart might be, right there — the stars started coming. They rushed in — kind of like a big breeze blew them — or as if they were shot out of one of those big iron cannons we saw when Maestra Maria showed us photographs of a fort. The stars burst forth right into the middle of *this* Dolphin, and then they started to spread out in the dark spaces. Stars moved up into the Dolphin's head and all the way to the tip of its tail. They filled in the Dolphin's outline until all at once the Dolphin, which only moments ago had only been dots, now gushed with stars!

But none of the stars leapt outside the Dolphin. They all stayed inside the lines, filling the Dolphin, but not falling or escaping.

Tio pointed, and it seemed, oh, I didn't think it was really happening, but it seemed as if the Dolphin started to move. I thought I saw those thousands of small stars join together and start to move the Dolphin constellation from its place in the sky." Coyitito, the Dolphin is moving," Tio said. I thought so too.

"Cassandra, Tio?"

"Cassandra, Coyitito. When Magdelena comes back, let's follow it. Let's follow the Dolphin."

All of a sudden, the star in front of us opened, and Magdelena appeared in its middle, beaming as she stepped out onto the white cloth.

She shone very, very brightly.

"Coyitito, Tio, oh my!" Magdelena said. She clasped something in her hand. I didn't ask her what it was; I waited for her to tell us. Tio asked her; he said, "Magdelena, what do you have in your hand?"

"I will tell you. I will tell you what happened."

But before Magdelena started talking, I saw in the sky where the Dolphin was filled with stars — I saw that the stars left the outline of the constellation and flowed back into the sky, kind of like our River. I heard them; they sounded just like The River did when it was flowing.

"Look," I said. "Look at all the stars. They look like the stars by our River. Don't they look like our River, Tio, Magdelena? Look!" And we all looked as the river of stars headed right for us.

I wasn't sure what to do. That many stars!

"Let's go. Hurry, let's turn around and go. We must hurry."

But Tio and Magdelena watched wide-eyed as the stars flowed toward us.

Tio stood up on his cloth.

"Wow," he said. "Coyitito, Magdelena. We will ride the stars, just like we do the ocean waves. It will be different on our horses — but they can do it. They can ride the waves with us."

And then we saw it happen. If Magdelena and Tio were not with me, I don't think I would have believed it, but there they were, and they saw it too.

"Cassandra?" we said together.

The Dolphin constellation left its spot in the sky and followed the flow of stars.

And then, just like that, the stars veered away from us. "Look. The stars went the other way," Tio said. "Let's follow them. Let's go." But before we could even think about following the Dolphin and the stars, something grabbed hold of us. And it started to pull us.

"Let's go follow the stars, Coyitito. Magdelena, look, look at the Dolphin." Tio didn't realize we were starting to be pulled, but Magdelena did. I felt her stiffen in front of me.

"Magdelena, what is happening?" I asked her. "Do you know what is happening? Did your star tell you?"

But Magdelena did not answer me, and Tio then felt the pull too.

What was happening? I imagined the eight arms of Marleena reaching way up into the sky and pulling us. I could see her grabbing Tria, and lassoing Tria into the sky until the creature found us. And then I imagined the slimy moving rope pulling us, pulling us into the water. Into Marleena's cave.

What did we find out anyway in her cave? I didn't know any more secrets than before we went there. I shuddered thinking that someday I might have to go back in there. I would like to see Karoleena and Occupia again. They weren't at all like Marleena. Maybe they knew something about the secret.

Magdelena didn't move in front of me. I felt her sit straight. I didn't find out what she had clutched in her hand. I wanted to ask her, but I felt like I shouldn't.

"Where are we going?" I gasped to myself. We were moving slowly; someone was pulling us out of the sky.

When I looked around, I saw, far away from us now, the river of stars with the Dolphin back in place.

And then we landed. It was pitch black. It didn't feel like water; it seemed to be hard, like ground. "Are we on a canyon trail?" I wondered.

Is Marleena here? The No Faces? Even though Marleena is in the water, and the No Faces are not, they are the same. Maybe in the beginning, the beginning Melaquiades told me about, maybe then, before they all wanted something, maybe then Marleena was kind.

And then I asked. I said, "Magdelena ..."

"Shhh."

That was all Magdelena said. And I knew Tio wouldn't talk. And Senorita Duende and Padre Miguel II wouldn't make a sound.

So we sat there in the dark, dark silence and waited. It seemed like we were waiting too long, and I wanted to move, and I know Tio wanted to move, but we knew that Magdelena didn't want us to move, so we didn't.

And when it got too much for me, sitting somewhere in the dark, dark night, I lightly tapped the side of Senorita Duende, but she didn't budge. So I did it again. Magdelena didn't tell me to stop, but we still didn't move.

"Magdelena," I whispered very, very, very softly.

"Magdelena, how come we aren't moving?"

And she said very, very softly, "I don't know."

And then I started to panic. We were stuck. Very gently, I tapped Senorita Duende, and I asked her very softly to please move an inch, but nothing.

I became very, very frightened.

"Magdelena, we are stuck."

"Yes, we are stuck, Coyitito."

I couldn't tell from looking around if we were on a cliff, in a cave, surrounded by No Faces or snakes. The sky was covered. No light. None of the Dolphin stars were above us. Where were we? Why couldn't we move?

I felt a chill on my skin.

And then we heard it. We heard something. What was it? The hair on the back of my neck stood in fear. I think Magdelena's did too, but I couldn't tell. I didn't dare reach out and touch Magdelena's neck.

We heard it. We all heard it, but we didn't talk at all. We all knew someone was coming, and we couldn't move. The sound seemed to get closer. We heard the twigs break in the darkness. It sounded like just one horse and one rider. But we couldn't be sure. We could never ever, ever be sure.

It seemed like the rider and the horse started coming our way. And we froze. We couldn't move anyway, but we froze inside ourselves.

I felt Magdelena freeze, and I thought Tio was probably frozen solid, not because he was afraid, but because he was listening. My breathing was heavy, so I tried to quiet it. Senorita Duende and Padre Miguel II were very, very quiet.

The rider and the horse were so very close, closer and closer. If only we could see. Please, please let us see.

But nothing. No light. Magdelena didn't dare take out her comb.

And then we heard it.

We heard the sound so, so near us. They had to see us. Somehow, whoever it was knew we were close to them.

One horse. One rider. I thought about Solamente and the first time Ramon came, and how he had come again and sat on the rocks by The River and traveled alone. I thought about how Ramon had brought us the gifts. I wondered if we were still standing on Tio's blanket. I thought how I would love to see Ramon.

I felt Magdelena move her arms. I felt her turn slightly.

And then the darkness broke with sound. It said, "Coyitito, Magdelena, Tio, Senorita Duende, Padre Miguel II. Where are you?"

And I knew, I knew Ramon had come, and I lifted my head and opened my mouth, and I started to say, "Ramon, Ramon, we are here. We are stuck. There is no light. We can't see. I am frightened, Ramon. Ramon," but Magdelena quickly covered my mouth with her hand, and no words came.

"Coyitito. Coyitito. It is I. It is Ramon, the one who rides Solamente. Tio, hello Tio. Magdelena, it is I. It is I, Ramon, brother of Rojo Anita, protector of you all. Where are you? You are in grave danger. Come out from where you are hiding."

My heart ripped. I yearned to see my friend, Ramon. Magdelena kept her hand over my mouth.

"I saw you land somewhere around here. I know you are close by. Come out. Come on out. I will lead you safely through the canyon trails back to The River, where Rojo Anita and Padre Miguel are waiting for you. Come out; hurry. There is great danger around you."

And then we heard the great danger. We heard hooves and hooves. We heard so many hooves coming, and we knew that the No Faces knew where we were.

"I want to help you. Show me where you are. Quick."

And the hooves kept coming.

"Come out, Coyitito, Tio.

"Coyitito, come out now.

"Magdelena."

Magdelena looked at me and uncovered my mouth.

And the hooves were pounding above us. And then we didn't hear Ramon.

And we knew; we knew he had brought the No Faces to where we were.

And Ramon must have joined them.

Could it be?

Did Ramon become a No Face?

And where was Meme? Why didn't a door appear with Meme on the other side? I kept listening for her sound, but I didn't hear her.

I kept realizing that we had no control over anything. We never knew what was going to happen next.

They were right above us. So we must be below them. They circled the ground. The hooves of the horses came running, and then we heard it. We heard the one word — the one that said, "CEASE!" He yelled the word loudly, very, very loudly. And everyone stopped moving. Just like that, all movement stopped above us.

And now I grew very, very frightened. Now I didn't know what to do. But something seemed to happen — something — because Senorita Duende took a step backwards — a very, very small step back, and I knew whatever it was that held us had changed. And Magdelena gently tapped Senorita Duende backwards. She was very, very careful not to make a sound.

We heard them all around us, but it seemed that we were somewhere hidden — and then I realized that we were in a cave below them, and they were above us on the ground.

And Tio and Padre Miguel II took a step back.

Two more steps back. Slowly. Quietly. Two more back. We would step back. And wait.

"LISTEN," we heard the Mean One yell. "LISTen." And Senorita Duende and Padre Miguel II stopped moving.

And we sat there. Completely quiet. And then, above us, all was quiet. No one moved.

I was petrified.

And we didn't take another step.

And then we heard a sound — a single solitary sound in the darkness. Someone was close by.

Magdelena knew. We all heard it. It was the quietest sound, but it was a sound. And we stayed unmoving. Waiting. And then we heard another very quiet sound. Above us, they waited. And someone, someone was inside the cave. Near us.

"LISten," the Mean One yelled.

And inside the cave, the movement stopped, and we didn't hear anything for a long, long time.

And then we heard shuffling above us. Not a lot, but a little. One or more of the horses starting moving, and whatever was near us in the cave moved quickly while the noise was above us. All of a sudden, between Senorita Duende and Padre Miguel II, something arrived. We couldn't see, but we felt it. It whispered very softly, so softly we could hardly hear, "Follow me." And I think it held the tails of the horses and guided us slowly. "Oh no," I thought to myself. Who was this?

"CEASE!" And we all ceased moving. Above and below, the shuffling stopped. And we stopped right where we were; in the middle of the blackness, we stopped. And we didn't move for a very long time.

Then we heard the Mean One yell above us, "SEARCH!!" And the horses' hooves boomed, and we knew they were on our trail.

Whoever was leading us took the moment of all the movement to hurry us somewhere. We were moving through the darkness. We felt the one moving us stop. "Turn around," a voice said, and our horses turned.

"Shhh," the voice said. "Be very, very quiet." And we stopped.

Above us, but further away, we heard, "You. STAY. You. STAY. You. SEARCH. And FIND THEM. GO." When he yelled, he sounded like Marleena. Oh!

And more horses' hooves were released.

I shuddered.

When the horses above broke the ground with their sounds, we moved quickly. Whoever this was didn't yell to the ones above us, saying he had caught us. Our guide, who we decided to trust because we were in danger, didn't talk but led us silently. When the movement above stopped, we stopped. And then very slowly, very, very slowly, we started again — but slowly and silently.

Then we turned. And we turned again. We hadn't met the one who led us, and we didn't know if we could really trust this one, but we knew that we were moving away from the Mean One because the next time we heard him yell, "Cease!" his voice was much further from us.

Was this Meme?

Had Ramon left them before they arrived? Maybe he was still our Ramon.

We traveled slowly through the darkness. No one spoke. No one said a word. Every once in a while, we stopped moving completely. We just stood and listened. Then we started moving again for a short while.

I wanted to whisper into Magdelena's ear. I wanted to ask her who she thought was leading us, but I didn't. I thought it could be Meme or Azul; I hoped it wasn't a No Face Ramon leading us right into danger; maybe someone knew us, and we didn't know them. I didn't know. I felt and heard Tio and Padre Miguel II next to us. And we kept moving and turning until we heard the distant sound of the Mean One yell — and it was far away. We almost didn't hear him. And we stopped when he yelled, listening for hooves, but we didn't hear any, and we kept moving until we didn't hear any sounds at all.

Our guide knew the caves well, or at least we thought so, because we were still in darkness and moving.

And then, all of a sudden, the voice spoke, in a whisper; it said, "I think we have gotten away; we will keep going, but I think we have gotten away from them. Let us listen."

And we sat listening.

And I knew that voice. And I knew Magdelena and Tio knew it, too. And I wanted to yell; I wanted to jump off Senorita Duende and say, "Manuel! Manuel." But I didn't. And neither did Tio or Magdelena. We just all sat in the darkness, making sure there was silence above us.

And if it were Manuel, was he a No Face, or still our Manuel?

And after another long time, the voice said, "I am going to strike a match and light a candle, so we can see each other. I think we are far enough away. I will make a small light." I thought about Magdelena's comb, but I didn't say anything.

And then the small circle around us lit. And there he was; there was Manuel. I was so, so happy to see him. But he looked tired and frail and worried. I knew Magdelena only saw his weakness, and I knew she felt his troubles and wanted to help him. I did too. I, Coyitito, wanted to help him too.

"Manuel, Manuel," Magdelena said.

Tio looked at him.

"Manuel." I looked at him.

But Manuel put his hand over his lips and said, "We must be aware of all the sounds. We must be careful. Let us keep moving. I just wanted to see you all." And he looked at us. His eyes filled with tears. "Coyitito, Magdelena, Tio."

Was he a No Face now?

I decided to believe this was our Manuel; he looked so sad he must be ours. Our Manuel wasn't usually sad, but after what he must have been through, he would be sad. I didn't think that No Faces could be sad.

"Let us keep moving. We will find a place where perhaps we can sit for a little while, and I will tell you my story."

"Manuel, how did you escape the No Faces?" Magdelena asked. Manuel seemed to shudder.

"Come ride with me," Tio said, but Manuel said he would rather walk. He said he could feel vibrations in the ground, so he wanted to keep his feet there. He said that perhaps he could feel the No Faces on their horses by the vibrations in the ground.

"Manuel, what about your horse?" I asked. He didn't answer my question, but said instead that we should keep moving as quietly as we could. He kept a small light lit, and we traveled through the cave.

"Follow me," Manuel whispered.

Then he stopped — suddenly.

"Shhh. Listen. Shhh."

And we didn't hear anything. But he did. He heard and stood frozen. Then quickly and suddenly, he turned around, and we followed him. His head moved from side to side. Entrances and turns appeared, and I had no idea where we were, but Manuel must have because he turned right, and we traveled very quietly with the small light still lit. We traveled for what seemed like hours but probably wasn't. We kept moving.

And finally, finally Manuel stopped in front of us. I didn't know if he heard something else, or if he was just stopping, but he looked relieved.

"I think we are far away from danger. We never know, but I think maybe we are because I don't feel the vibrations in the ground. Do you hear anything?"

We all stopped and listened.

Then Tio quietly came from Padre Miguel II's back and did something I had never seen him do. He got on his knees, then slid onto his stomach, and he lay on the ground with his ear against the dirt. Then he lifted his head, turned it to the other side, and listened again.

"I don't hear anything," he said. "Sometimes I think I hear better with one ear than the other, but neither ear hears anything."

Manuel smiled.

We all did.

And we dropped down from Senorita Duende.

"We must always be very, very careful," Manuel said. "We must never let our guard down. The No Faces — they have ways. They truly do. We must listen and if we hear any sound — any sound at all — we must go from here."

"Where will we go, Manuel? Where are we going? If we hear anything, where is it we are going?" I asked him.

"Away from the sound."

"How did the No Faces get you, Manuel?" Magdelena asked. "Are you all right? Padre Miguel sent us to look for you — and instead you found us. But what happened? What happened to you when they caught you?"

At first, Manuel was quiet. Then he said, "Oh, they are mean, Magdelena, very, very mean. There is one who commands all the others, and he is mean — very, very mean. They all must follow what he says. But really they are all mean — except for one. One of the No Faces isn't as terrible as all the others. I think he is a little bit soft — just different from the rest of them. I could see it. When they told him to get me and bring me, he was different about it."

"What did they do to you?" Tio asked Manuel. "We saw their big ropes. They tried to take us by The River."

"Yes. They tried to take you. And they are going to keep trying. They will keep trying until they have you. Especially you, Coyitito."

They wanted me most of all? That made me very, very scared. I mean, I knew they wanted me, and I would rather me than Magdelena, or Tio, or any of the others, but I, I, Coyitito, was very, very scared.

"That is how it is with them. I watch them — how they practice their lasso to catch the young ones and make the young ones their own. I shudder each time I hear them going out to search. I am always thinking that they are coming back with one of you.

"One night I was missing you all so much, so I crept out to the gate, and I decided I would leave and go to your favorite place — The River. Maybe you would all be there.

"It was dark and late, and I thought I might be caught, but I did it anyway because I had a dream. I had a dream, and you, Magdelena, and you, Coyitito, and you, Tio, were there in my dream. We were in the field, like we were at the party, and it was dusk. The sun was setting and the moon showed, and a bright star shone in the sky. Have you seen the bright star?"

Did we know the bright star? I was just going to tell Manuel about the bright star that I met and Magdelena met. Manuel said, "Coyitito, do you want to say something?" but Magdelena interrupted and said, "This is your story, Manuel. Coyitito can wait until you finish. Is that true, Coyitito?"

"Yes, that is true."

I looked at Tio. I could tell he was thinking about The River and the full moon — and something else was on his mind. He waited for the full moon, so he could ride in the water with Juan and Dulcinea, the Red Departed Dolphin. (Was that Manuel who passed us in The River? I had to wait to ask him about that. Magdelena would tell me to wait — not to interrupt him again.)

Manuel looked at the three of us.

I wondered if he heard something. He remained silent — listening. He looked around, but then he continued his dream.

"The music was playing, and I was stamping my feet. Then I saw you, Magdelena — from the back. Your hair was unbraided. I started to go over to you when I saw Coyitito and Tio. I saw your faces — and they were happy and laughing.

"And then I saw — guess who I saw; I saw …"

And he stopped. Completely. He lifted one foot, then the other.

"Let's go," he whispered.

We lifted onto our horses. Manuel still went on foot, but he could ride on Padre Miguel II if he needed to do that.

Manuel moved quickly — so, so quickly. His dancing made him very fast and able. I'm sure he could tango through the cave-ways, dodging the No Faces. But he hadn't dodged them; they had caught him before; I'm sure they could catch him again. I'm sure they could — and if they did, they wouldn't only catch him; they would catch us, all of us.

I became terrified. All of a sudden, just like that, Manuel took away the light. Pitch blackness. He whispered, "Just follow me. I know the ways of the caves somewhat from traveling with them. We must be quiet."

I shuddered to think how we would see. I couldn't help it; I had to ask. I whispered, "Manuel, how will we see?"

And Manuel answered, "Coyitito, you worry too much."

I do. I do worry. But it was pitch black, and I couldn't bear it.

I told myself, "Just trust, Coyitito. Trust." But I was having a hard time trusting. And I knew, I knew that right in front of me sat Magdelena. And I knew that right underneath her coat of black hair, hiding underneath was her comb, which glowed in the darkness. I knew that if I just lifted her hair — just a bit — just a little, I could slide the comb out from her hair. But I knew it was her comb, and I best not do that, even though I very much wanted to.

I thought of so much, and I became more and more terrified. We moved so slowly, so slowly, because I'm sure Manuel was feeling walls and floors, making sure we didn't fall into a hole. What was that slithering? How did Magdelena remain constant? I kept picturing — or was it real — the slithering? What was that? I knew Tio was nearby. So was Manuel. Magdelena was right there. I heard them breathing. And what else was it? What else did I hear? Was it a hoof? Something sliding? Something in the air? I wanted to cry out. Why wasn't anyone else saying anything? Didn't they hear it? Didn't they …

I couldn't bear it any longer. I moved my hands out from my sides, whispered, "Excuse me, Magdelena," and quickly lifted her hair. Her comb glowed underneath. I lifted her hair high. Manuel was in front of us. He turned in the light.

And I heard Tio turn around behind us. He was swift. He called to us; he yelled, "Follow me," and Senorita Duende turned around following Padre Miguel II. I had to turn to look behind me.

Manuel started to run with us. He was fast, but very quickly, very, very quickly, we were faster, and very soon the glow of Magdelena's comb faded, and the place where Manuel's face should be faded into the darkness.

"Was he a No Face?" I asked.

Tio didn't answer.

We were not safe.

Manuel had taken us far, far into the caves. Far into the darkness. And hooves up ahead approached. And the slithering sound was somewhere.

Tio was in front of us. He turned quickly.

"Stay next to me," Tio said.

And he started to go very, very fast. We had just run from Manuel so quickly; now we were going even faster.

Where did Manuel go?

Was that Manuel, or was that One of the Ones who had stolen him?

I wanted to ask Magdelena. I wanted to say, "Magdelena, oh, Magdelena. Was that the real Manuel?" But we were moving like the air moves during the big storms, so I didn't say anything. I didn't talk to Magdelena as she held her comb, and we galloped through the darkness.

Tio laid his head on Padre Miguel II's head. I thought maybe we should do the same; maybe the ceiling became lower. As I thought this, Magdelena bent her head and placed it on Senorita Duende's, and then I bent my own head and put it on Magdelena's shoulder. My head rested right there. I hoped this was all right with her; it seemed like it was. I couldn't believe I could put my head on Magdelena's shoulder like this.

And we rode like that through the cave, lit by her comb.

At any point, anything could happen, but I could have stayed next to Magdelena that way for a very, very long time.

But it wasn't very long because, all of a sudden, we felt something above our heads. And we knew, we knew what it was. So quickly, we veered to the left and started going down the dark corridor. Tio led us. They were upon us — behind us. Somewhere. Somewhere so close. So close that at any moment — any moment at all, we wouldn't be able to outrun them.

We moved fast. Our hooves were loud, so loud that we couldn't tell where the other hooves were. And they knew the caves. They knew the caves better than we did, so I knew that, at any moment, the lasso would fall on top of us, and we would be theirs.

I heard the sound before I saw it. So did Tio because he took an entrance to the right, and we turned before the rope fell down on us.

How far could they throw? How close were they? How many?

And then the rope landed. Right next to us, but not on us. We waited for that one word. We waited for him to yell, CEASE!" But instead we heard, "Will you stop already. Please stop. It is I. It is Ramon. Stop."

And then he quickly rode up to us. He was behind us. "Coyitito. Magdelena. Tio. It is I. It is Ramon who rides Solamente. Look. Look. It is I."

And we heard a splash. And Tio and Padre Miguel II disappeared in front of us. And then we saw them. The starfish had come for Tio. They had come here in the cave to take them to the Cave of the Departed.

And then Magdelena and I ran with Senorita Duende into the water. And the starfish waited to escort us too.

We saw Ramon stop with Solamente. We didn't know if he was our Ramon or not.

I waited to hear if Ramon was invited, but he didn't follow us. No starfish appeared to guide him.

"I will see you when you get back, Coyitito, Magdelena and Tio," he called to us. We didn't know what would happen when we returned. And though that thought worried me, I was most concerned about why we were heading to the Cave of the Departed.

We floated along.

I didn't know how the starfish found us, or where the caves met, but I did know that all three of us were on our way to the Cave of the Departed, and that meant that someone who is Departed wanted to see us. And I wondered who that was.

"Magdelena, whom do you think we are going to meet?"

"I don't know, Coyitito. I hope no one we know and love has passed into the Departed. Maybe we will meet someone from the past who has departed."

Tio was silent. He had lost Juan; he couldn't lose someone else. I thought his blanket might offer him comfort as we sailed into the Cave of the Departed.

"Tio, take out your cloth blanket," I suggested to him. "Maybe we can use it if it gets cold on our way." I really thought Tio might need it for comfort because someone in the cave was calling for him — and us.

"It's not here. Maybe I dropped it in the cave where we landed after we rode in the sky," Tio said. I thought his mind must really be elsewhere at the moment. After all, the starfish came for him first.

I also thought about how our gifts did whatever they wanted to do — just like Meme. They appeared and disappeared — just like her.

I knew Tio was frightened to find out who was in the cave. Someone had been calling him. Someone had been guiding him through the cave. And now we were going to find out who it was.

The Cave of the Departed was crowded as we approached. Eclipse had come to meet us. From what I could tell, I didn't know any of these Departed people.

"Magdelena, I don't know anyone."

"I don't know anyone either. But someone must know us," she said.

I turned to Tio who was next to us. His eyes scanned all the Departed Ones. I thought that he was probably looking for Juan — and also for whoever else had called for him. I thought that he was worried. I was.

All of a sudden, all the Departed Ones stopped what they were doing and turned our way. Eclipse and the starfish led us closer to them. They hovered; some stood on the rock surrounding the water. The Ones in the water parted a path as we slowly glided toward the rock surface at what seemed to be the end of the cave. I never knew anymore where things ended and things began, but I did know we were being led to a spot on the rocks. As we approached, I looked at the faces, dreading whom we would meet.

From the back of the crowd, he came.

I looked at Tio.

Tio jumped off his horse — jumped right into the water, and stomped his way toward him.

From the back of the Departed Ones, he came toward us — and Tio ran to him. Tears streamed down Tio's face. Magdelena shuddered this time and dropped herself into the water, walking toward him.

I didn't move.

My heart was pierced.

This could not be.

This loss we could not live with.

Tio ran to him.

He smiled at Tio. He wrapped his arms around Tio's head — holding him as Tio wept.

"No. No," Tio wept.

"No."

Magdelena wept too as she approached them, and he opened his arms to include Magdelena in his comfort. She put her head on top of Tio's, comforting him as she was comforted.

Then he raised his eyes my way.

But I couldn't move.

So two of the Departed Ones came to me and led me to where he stood. And when I got there, he opened his arms, and I too fell into them — and we three: Tio, Magdelena, and I wept until he spoke, and when he did, he said,

"This is how you greet me! Aren't you supposed to say, 'Good morning, Padre Miguel' when I walk into the room?"

And in my heart, I started to smile because he would want us to. And I knew that Magdelena did too, but I don't know that Tio did.

"What happened, Padre Miguel? What happened to you?" Magdelena asked.

And Padre Miguel opened his arms again to include another. And Juan looked at Tio, and Tio shook his brother's hand.

"Juan. Juan. You and Padre Miguel died. You both died, Juan. You were enough for me, for Little Tio. Padre Miguel watched out for me after you died. Padre Miguel protects me. My horse is named for Padre Miguel. And now Padre Miguel has left me, too."

Padre Miguel's face turned into pain.

"Tio, I will be here for you just like I was. I have been calling for you, and you have heard me. You have heard me calling. You have work to do. Very, very serious work. You, Magdelena, and Coyitito, must get busy. You know how I am, Tio. Time for tears — and then we have work to do. So tell me when you are ready to hear what must happen. We don't have all that much time. We must act quickly.

"Look at me, Tio. Look at me."

I watched Tio lift his eyes into those of Padre Miguel.

"Ah, there you are. There is the fierce, courageous, funny Tio whom I know. Look at me. I will not — I promise — I will not desert you. I will do what I can to protect you from where I am — here in the cave. I don't really understand the ways of the cave yet, but I will learn them.

"I recently arrived."

"You recently arrived, Padre Miguel?" Magdelena asked.

And Padre Miguel said,

"Ah Magdelena. Dear, dear Magdelena. I will protect you too, Magdelena. I will learn the ways of the cave, and I will protect you."

"And you, Coyitito."

I lifted my eyes to him.

"You, Coyitito. I will protect you, Coyitito.

"You are all my children.

"You are all my children.

"Juan, I think you are protected here, but I will continue to teach you grammar and poetry, for the sake of Maestra Maria, while we are in the cave together. Maybe I could hold a morning class for all the Departed."

Juan backed away.

And we all knew that Padre Miguel would hold grammar lessons, and read and write poetry in the Cave of the Departed. But that's not why we were sent for.

"I don't know how it happened," he said. "I don't know if it's ever happened before, but I departed because a No Face took all of me and somehow kept me. Somehow, I never returned. I don't know how it happened, but I do know that I was taken when I was walking in the woods. I had been to The River hoping she would send you three an invitation for me when I thought I heard something. I wandered out of the protected area at that point. I wandered away looking for you out in the woods a bit, and I felt something. I felt as if there was an animal stalking me. It gave off a very, very bad odor. Then I felt a wind lifting the leaves. I thought I might become faint with the stench, so I did what I do: I climbed a tree, so I could see better and perhaps escape the odor and the animal. And when I climbed the tree and looked around, I didn't see anything at first. But then I saw the movement of the branch and felt the wind. But I didn't see anything else, and I stayed there for a very, very long time. I stayed there through the night and listened to all the sounds I know.

"But I knew that something stayed all through the night also. The stench remained, and so did the wind. And then the sun came up. The odor lessened, along with the movement of the leaves. And at one point, I slowly, slowly left my perch. And when I got to the ground, the wind came — a very, very harsh wind had arrived, whipping right up to me. It delivered the horrible scent. The trees bent next to me, and the wind whistled; I felt it all around me. I was caught in the wind as if I was caught in a funnel. I was spun round and round until I was so dizzy I could not think or know who I was.

"When I came to again, I was here — at the Cave of the Departed. As soon as I arrived, I asked the others how I could reach the Living Ones. I told them that I am Padre Miguel; I am in charge of one of the Protected Zones: I am in charge of the school. Great danger would approach the school because the No Faces had taken me over; Maestra Maria, Maestra Agatha, and the others would think that the Imposter there was really me. The school would no longer be safe. I needed to get in touch with you three, so you could warn the others.

" 'Ask the starfish to find the Ones you are looking for,' they told me here inside the cave.

"So I did. I asked the starfish to locate you and bring you to me.

"Here you are. You must leave, and tell Maestra Maria. You must warn Maestra Maria. She will not know that I am not me. You must tell her."

My heart sank.

Maestra Maria in the hands of the No Faces. Padre Miguel in the Cave of the Departed.

I wanted to cry out loud.

But we must be strong.

We must be strong for Padre Miguel. For ourselves. For Maestra Maria. For the others.

"Padre Miguel, how do we know the No Faces from the Faces?" Magdelena asked.

But Padre Miguel's eyes opened very, very wide — wider than I had ever seen.

Tio turned to look at what Padre Miguel saw. And Magdelena. And I thought that I knew what they were looking at because I had already seen all the Departed Ones turn toward the vision. Padre Miguel's mouth opened.

The vision was filled with stars. And the voice of Melaquiades said, "Has Magdelena told anyone what happened in her star?"

"Coyitito, have you found out what happened inside Magdelena's star?" Melaquiades asked.

I looked at Melaquiades. He twinkled. I looked at Magdelena, and Tio looked at Melaquiades. And when I turned my head to look at Padre Miguel, I saw that he was bowing in the direction of Melaquiades, and I thought that I didn't bow when I met him — or even now — so I began to bow when Melaquiades said,

"Magdelena, will you tell us what happened inside during your visit with the star?"

I knew all this was very important, but Padre Miguel had already told us about how the One who had stolen him was on his way to the school, and when he got there, he would take the ones there and make them part of the No Faces. They would take the others like they took Manuel. We needed to go. We needed to leave in a hurry.

"Coyitito. It is very important that we hear what happened inside the star," Melaquiades spoke.

I looked at Tio. He stared at Melaquiades. He didn't take his eyes off him.

"Tio."

Melaquiades held out his hand.

"Tio, pleased to make your acquaintance." Tio took tiny steps toward the hand that reached out to him. And then Melaquiades' arm started to extend until it was right next to Tio. And then Melaquiades took Tio's hand and shook it. And Tio stood back, but he kept his eyes right there, right with the eyes of Melaquiades.

"And you, Magdelena. It is so very good to make your acquaintance."

And he took his hand from Tio and gave it to Magdelena, who shook it and smiled at him.

"I am Melaquiades."

"I am honored to make your acquaintance," Magdelena said.

And then he took his hand and reached across the others to where Padre Miguel stood. And he reached for Padre Miguel's hand and said,

"Welcome to the Cave of the Departed, Padre Miguel. You have been doing great work at the school, keeping the children protected from the No Faces. For years, you have been shielding the children from harm. For years, you have protected so many — so, so many. And one day these three got out and went down to The River and other places, and they survived. They heard The River — the way she calls, you know the way she calls, Padre Miguel. How many times has she called you?

"And then we all knew," he continued.

"You knew — we all knew that Coyitito, Magdelena, and Tio would help us fight against the No Faces and discover secrets about them.

"You had to give your physical life up in this fight, Padre Miguel. At one time or another, we have to do that; we have to give up the world of form as we know it at the time. But there is a whole other world here.

"And the Cave of the Departed has its own secrets. I see that you already know that. You were already able to send the starfish out to bring these three back to you."

"You saved us from Ramon," Tio flashed at Padre Miguel. He stomped over to his Dear Departed Friend and said,

"Ramon was coming. He said he saw us come from the sky. He came to save us. Then Manuel came, Padre Miguel. And I listened to the ground — listened for the horses. But Manuel, he was a No Face — we think he was — and then we fled — and the lasso came next to us, and Ramon said he was Ramon. He said, 'Coyitito, Magdelena, Tio — it is me, it is …'"

"Did Ramon say 'Me', Tio? Did he really say 'Me'?" Padre Miguel asked.

"No. No," Magdelena said. "He said, 'I,' Padre Miguel. Ramon did not say 'me.'"

I thought about how we needed to leave.

"Was it Ramon?" Padre Miguel asked.

"We didn't know, but he threw the lasso, and it landed next to us."

"Ramon doesn't miss," said Padre Miguel. "If the lasso did not land on you, it was not meant to."

"How come Ramon uses a lasso if he's not a No Face?"

"Get them with their own weapons," said Padre Miguel.

"I want to know the lasso," said Tio.

And Melaquiades handed Tio a rope.

"So Magdelena," he said. "Your star?"

Padre Miguel took the rope from Tio and started curling it into a small circle.

"My star," Magdelena said.

"I met Lena inside my star."

"Lena?" said Melaquiades.

"Ah, Lena. How is she?"

Padre Miguel let the rope go, and a circle leapt into the air and descended to the group. Then he pulled it toward him. Tio looked at him, smiling.

"Show me," Tio said, and Padre Miguel gathered the rope.

"She is well. She said she had been waiting for me. I didn't know how she knew me, but she said that she had always known me, from the very beginning, and she was so grateful that I had come."

"Did she give you any gifts?" Melaquiades asked Magdelena.

Yes, she did give Magdelena a gift. I saw Magdelena had clutched something.

"Yes, she gave me a gift, Melaquiades," Magdelena said.

And she reached into her pocket, and the lasso flew from Tio's hand, right over Magdelena and me. It landed onto both of us. Tio was learning the lasso quickly.

"This."

Magdelena took out what looked like a black velvet box. It looked like midnight. I kept my eyes on the box. Then she opened up the middle, like a door.

Tio brought his circle to a close around our feet. I picked up the rope and tossed it over our heads, and Tio brought it back to him. Magdelena and I studied the rope tossing as she began to open her gift from Lena.

We could learn the rope.

"Before you open that, Magdelena; Coyitito, did you discover any secrets in the Underwater Cave of Secrets?"

"The Underwater Cave of Secrets!" Padre Miguel exclaimed. "The Underwater Cave of Secrets."

"Bubbles and mirrors are there. So are Karoleena and Occupia-C; (I remembered not to say Occupia's whole name. Melaquiades probably heard my mind. He looked straight at me.) And the terrible Marleena," I answered him.

Before I could say anything else, the light suddenly shifted in the Cave of the Departed. Something was happening. The light grew brighter and seemed to come from way, way, way up above us. It was as if a thin piece of light fell into the cave.

"This." We looked at what Magdelena was holding.

Magdelena opened her box, and inside was a mirror.

"Keep your mirror close to you, Magdelena," Melaquiades said.

Then, Melaquiades handed us ropes. "These are for you, Coyitito, and you, Magdelena. Show them the way of the rope, Tio."

Tio had just learned the rope, but he was very, very good at it. Excellent, really. I didn't think I would ever be able to do that. I knew Magdelena would, and she did; she picked up the rope and was a natural with it, but I, I, Coyitito worried.

"Throw it, Coyitito," said Magdelena. "Throw it." So I threw it, and it bounced off the wall.

"Try again," said Padre Miguel. "Concentrate."

And I practiced the rope, and more quickly than I would have thought, I understood its ways. We three all became very good with the rope in a short, short time. I wondered about these ropes of Melaquiades.

At the moment, no one asked any more about the Underwater Cave. Padre Miguel's voice was urgent when he said, "Return to the school. You must warn them," Padre Miguel said. "Be very, very careful. Keep practicing. You all always learn very quickly."

We didn't want to leave, but we knew we had to. Juan stood next to Padre Miguel. Melaquiades turned. The starfish approached us, leading us away. The Departed Ones waved as we drifted back to the Living.

It took longer than we thought it would, and as we moved along slowly, we grew hungry, even though we worried for Maestra Maria and the others back at the school. "Always eat for energy, even when you are not particularly hungry," Maestra Maria would instruct us. I remembered that I had some of Meme's cookies, so I took them out, offering one to each of us.

"Magdelena, have some of these. Here, taste these. Magdelena. Here, Tio." I offered some to Senorita Duende and Padre Miguel II.

They were very tasty, the cookies left from the ones Meme packed. I wasn't sure what the taste was, but I wished I were back at The River, heading to the school to help. If only we could be at The River first, I knew, oh, I knew it would all work out. It would work out — wouldn't it?

"I wish we were at The River and heading to the school. Don't you wish that, Magdelena?"

I wasn't sure if that was Magdelena's wish. Maybe she wanted to be in the sky visiting Lena.

"And you too, Tio. Don't you wish we could just be at The River — on our way to the school from that spot? Our River?"

And Tio nodded, but maybe he really wished for Padre Miguel to come back or for Juan to come back — or something else — something I didn't even know about.

But Tio must have wished what I wished, and Magdelena must have wished for something else because, all of a sudden, I was at The River — so was Tio — but Magdelena wasn't there.

"Where is Magdelena?" I asked Tio, and I knew he was thinking the same thought. "Where is Magdelena?"

I was overcome with so much. Here we were, back at The River. Hadn't I just wished for this? It must have been Meme's cookies. I didn't know what they were, but they must have been whish cookies.

"Tio, do you have any of your cookie left? They must have been whish cookies. If you have some left, maybe we could wish for Magdelena. Maybe we could wish for help, for the No Faces to go away, to be gone. Forever! Maybe we could wish for Manuel ..."

And all of a sudden — just like that — a small wind started. I picked up a scent coming our way — an odor. Maybe this is what Padre Miguel was talking about. Then someone appeared above us on the canyon rock.

The figure rode a horse — and stopped — stopped above us.

And then leapt off the rock — horse and rider.

Tio saw it too. We both watched as they fell through the air. Not everyone could do this. Maybe it was Canyon Joe: he could leap like that. Maybe he was on his way to help us.

But I didn't think it was him. He would have called our names. He would have said, "Coyitito. Tio. Magdelena."

Oh, Magdelena, where was she?

"Tio, let's hide."

And Tio and I, and Padre Miguel II and Senorita Duende moved into the trees.

I was very nervous. Where was Magdelena? We had to go — we had to move very, very quickly to get back to the school.

"Tio, let's go!" And we sped through the trees toward the school.

But the figure was soon upon us. I heard the horse behind me. So did Tio. So he did something I had never seen him do before.

He stopped Padre Miguel II in his tracks. He turned around, and then I saw it. I saw something fly from Tio's hand, and I knew he had the rope Padre Miguel used to show Tio how to lasso. The rope flew into the air. I stopped when Tio stopped, and I watched the rope over my head — going toward the rider coming our way.

But then something strange happened. Something very, very strange happened. The rope landed around me. And when I turned around, I knew this wasn't my Tio; somehow he had been stolen.

"Tio," I yelled, hoping this would return him to me.

How had Tio disappeared so quickly? Weren't we in the protected area? But no, no — we had passed the protected place of The River — and there I was. A rope was around my waist. I was captured, caught. A No Face had stolen Tio in the wind, and I was lassoed by this rider who a moment ago was my friend.

He was behind me.

And facing me was another rider — another No Face? — another one I knew and loved.

I shuddered.

The rider passed by me, rode toward Tio, took something into his hands, freeing me, and yelled, "Go. Go, Coyitito. Go."

And I went.

Within moments, the rider was behind me. I didn't know which rider it was, so I did what I thought was best. I headed back to The River — back to the protected part. That was all I knew to do. I asked Padre Miguel; I said, "Padre Miguel, please help me. A No Face has taken Tio — and Magdelena is missing. Please get me to the safety of The River, and help me to get back to the school so that I can let Maestra Maria and the others know that there are No Faces inside the gates."

How long will they wait before they take over the school? I must hurry.

And Senorita Duende almost flew me back to The River.

And when I got there, we both went into the water.

Behind me, someone galloped fast.

And above me, someone dove from a rock.

"Coyitito, are you all right?" she asked as she lifted her head out of the water.

I was so frightened of her. Last time I saw her, I believe she was a No Face. I just looked at her and listened to the splashing behind me. Was The River really protected — or had the No Faces taken over the area the way they take over the faces and the bodies? How do they do that?

And how come sometimes when the No Faces take over faces, I can tell, like with Tio. And Manuel. Did Manuel really lose his face? Was he a No Face or not? And Ramon. And …

"There seems to be a transition period as it happens, Coyitito."

Not with Tio, I thought.

And the one chasing me came up close behind me. And the one in the water said that several things can happen during the transition. And I thought that maybe she was reading my mind. But hadn't the other One done that? The One who had earlier borrowed Rojo Anita's face? Which Rojo Anita was this?

I turned around. Manuel was in the water with me. "Oh no." Both of these could be No Faces. Both of them.

I looked Manuel in the eyes. Nothing was revealed. But when I looked his horse in the eye, I saw something very, very familiar — something I had seen much, much earlier. And I knew it was Manuel; I just didn't know which side he was on.

"Yes, Manuel rides Ochenta," Rojo Anita said. "Ochenta is paying for throwing Juan and killing him. Now Ochenta rides with Manuel. Is that so, Manuel?"

Manuel shook his head yes and said, "Yes, Coyitito. Our horses appear to us as you know. And when Ochenta appeared to me, I knew he was my horse, but I was terrified of him and didn't want to get on him to ride. But I knew: the horse appears to the rider. So I climbed onto him, and he took off. He was so very, very fast. And off we sped.

"I kept waiting for him to throw me, but he didn't. In fact, he keeps me on him — even when we jump from high places. He keeps me safe when I ride."

I thought about the time in The River when I saw the horse and rider jump, when the No Faces chased us in the water and then rode to the land where they were faster. And they gathered their ropes above us — and then the horse and rider passed me by. And when I looked into the horse's eyes, I saw something familiar... and then I asked. I wasn't sure if Manuel and Rojo Anita were No Faces or not, but I asked anyway. I asked, "Do No Faces take over the horse when they take over the rider?" But I didn't get an answer because, all of a sudden, Rojo Anita said, "We must go. Now."

I didn't know where we were going or if I should be going, but I and Senorita Duende were stepping from The River. We, all of us, were soaked with The River water.

I still looked into Ochenta's eyes.

Still I wasn't sure, so I began to say to Rojo Anita, "Rojo Anita ..." but she stopped me and said,

"Coyitito, we must get to the school. We must find Magdelena and Tio. I have been listening for them, but I haven't heard them yet.

"When we get out of the protected area, be very careful — very, very careful. It is very dangerous. Stay close."

I shuddered.

"Be brave, Coyitito."

I wanted to tell Rojo Anita — I wanted to say, "Rojo Anita, Padre Miguel has died," but she must have already known, for she said, "I am very, very sorry for you about Padre Miguel. For Magdelena. And for Tio. Tio must be very, very sad. You are the only ones who know he is gone. Where was it that you found out?"

And I tried to block my thoughts about the Cave of the Departed just in case Rojo Anita wasn't Rojo Anita. But I couldn't stop the thoughts.

And Rojo Anita said, "I hope that someday I will be invited to visit the Cave of the Departed because I liked Padre Miguel so very much."

And then she said, "Shhhh."

And we stopped. And waited. Manuel was ahead of us on Ochenta. But it was only Senorita, Rojo Anita's horse, coming through the trees. She had been in the woods, and now she came for Rojo Anita.

But something else came too.

"Who are you?" I asked. I knew I probably should not have said it like that. Maestra Maria had taught me my manners, but I didn't use them when I saw her. I guess I was startled with everything going on: Tio was a No Face just moments ago, and where, oh, where was Magdelena? Padre Miguel was in the Cave of the Departed, and a No Face had taken over the school, and Maestra Maria and the others did not even know — so when she appeared, my manners were not within my grasp.

"I am Dreamer," she said.

She said it softly, so, so softly that I wasn't even sure she said it. I didn't lift my eyes from her.

Then Rojo Anita spoke. I had almost forgotten that Rojo Anita was there. Rojo Anita said,

"Hello, Dreamer. I am Rojo Anita. I ride Senorita. This is my friend Coyitito. He rides Senorita Duende."

"Along with me," someone said.

And almost from out of the thin air, Magdelena appeared behind Dreamer, riding on Dreamer's horse.

I was overwhelmed. Here was Magdelena. Here was Dreamer with a glow all around her. And her horse.

"This is Gold," Dreamer said.

Gold. I looked at Dreamer's horse. At her. At Magdelena. I worried about whether or not they were No Faces, but I thought they couldn't possibly be No Faces. They were lit in a golden light, and they were very still, very quiet.

Magdelena slid down off the side of Gold.

"Dreamer brought me back."

"Where were you, Magdelena? Where did you go?" I asked her.

"I was so tired that I wished I could be sleeping in a warm, soft bed for a moment, with a soft pillow and a blanket; and then I was. I was in a bed just as I had wished, and I was dreaming. I wished that I could be dreaming," Magdelena said.

I wanted to mention the whish cookies, but I didn't interrupt Magdelena.

"Then in my dream, I saw a golden light. First, it was in the distance. And then it became brighter and brighter, and all of a sudden, a voice spoke from the center of the light and said,

"I am Dreamer. And this is Gold."

And as Magdelena said this, I turned to look at Dreamer again. But she was gone. A golden light still stayed about the trees, but Dreamer and Gold were no longer there.

"She lives in the Dreamtime," Magdelena said. "Dreamer almost always stays there. But I told her that I must come back to you, that there was grave danger. I told her about the No Faces taking over the school, and she listened. And I told her about Padre Miguel. And Melaquiades.

"And when I mentioned Melaquiades, she bowed her head slightly and said, 'Magdelena, I will take you where you need to go. Where is that?' And I told her, 'The River.' And she brought me here."

"We have to get to the school, Magdelena," someone said. I turned around. There was Tio. Tio was right there on Padre Miguel II talking to Magdelena.

I hadn't had the chance to tell her. She didn't know. I looked at Rojo Anita, who watched Tio intensely. She kept looking him in the eye and reading his thoughts

— or trying to. I was very, very nervous. I wanted to yell to Magdelena; I wanted to say,

"Magdelena, moments ago Tio was a No Face," but I didn't get a chance to because, all of a sudden, a golden light swooped over the trees. And Dreamer was back with Gold.

"Gold flies! Magdelena, Dreamer's horse flies!"

"Gold needs to fly me back and forth between Dreamtime in those rare moments when I come here," Dreamer said.

I stared at her. So did Tio. He was wide-eyed.

"This is my friend, Tio," said Magdelena.

Dreamer turned her head toward him.

"Tio. Tio, have you ever been to the Dreamtime?" she asked.

He couldn't answer. No words came out.

Magdelena said, "Tio, Dreamer is asking you a question."

I thought that Dreamer must think we had no manners at all, but all of a sudden, Tio answered.

"No," he said as he shook his head.

"Everyone comes to the Dreamtime," Dreamer said. "But not everyone remembers. I thought I saw you there recently. Very recently. Do you remember any of your recent dreams, Tio?"

Tio seemed to ponder for a moment, then shook his head back and forth.

I still wondered if Tio was really Tio, but I thought he was; I believed he was. How did the real Tio return so quickly if he was the real Tio?

"Magdelena," Dreamer said. "I came back because I saw that you left this in the Dreamtime, and I thought you might need it."

Dreamer opened her golden-lit hand. Inside was the black velvet case. Magdelena reached for it gently the way Magdelena would. Her manners were always with her.

For a moment, Magdelena and Dreamer held hands. They looked deeply at each other; then Magdelena said, "Thank you, Dreamer," and moved to stand in front of Gold.

"May I?" she asked.

Both Dreamer and Gold nodded "yes," and Magdelena reached her hand above the nose of Gold and stroked the horse.

I didn't want to be rude again, but we really needed to leave; we needed to go now, but no one made a move.

Then Dreamer said, "Have your friends looked inside the mirror?"

Magdelena reached her hand down and into the velvet pouch. She pulled out her mirror. In it, the reflection of Dreamer and Gold shone brightly.

I squinted.

"Walk around with it," Dreamer suggested. "Let each of them see themselves."

Magdelena moved over to Rojo Anita, and she looked into the glass. Rojo Anita's expression did not seem to change as she gazed into the mirror. Then Magdelena headed toward Tio.

And when she approached him, he ran the other way.

"Tio," I yelled.

"Magdelena, why did he do that?"

"Tio!" I yelled again.

But all of a sudden, we heard it. We heard a lasso zip through the air, and within moments, Tio was being led back to us; a loose lasso was around them; it was tight enough to keep him and his horse from escaping.

"I caught him," Ramon said.

There was Ramon. And Solamente. But was he the No Face we thought we had seen before?

Rojo Anita was reading her brother, trying to know what I was trying to figure out.

"Hello, Rojo Anita. Hello, Magdelena. Hello, Coyitito. Hello," he nodded as he studied Dreamer and Gold.

"I am Dreamer. And this is Gold."

"I am Ramon. I ride Solamente."

"Tio," Dreamer said. "Why did you run from the mirror?"

I'm sure Magdelena wanted to ask Ramon why he had Tio in a lasso.

"I don't know," Tio said. "I don't know why I ran."

"Do not be afraid of the mirror, Tio," Dreamer said. "Magdelena, bring Tio the mirror."

And she did.

She walked over to Tio. But Magdelena would never want to frighten Tio — or me — so she was very gentle when she said, "Tio, is it all right with you if I hold the mirror, and you look?"

I didn't understand all this fuss with the mirror anyway. Dreamer seemed to know something about the mirror that none of us knew. Maybe Magdelena knew.

I thought about that room of mirrors in Marleena's cave. I thought about how we drifted around in all those big mirrors — and now here was a small, small mirror that meant something.

"How about if you look in the mirror first, Ramon?" Rojo Anita said. "Magdelena, would it be all right with you if Ramon looked in the mirror first? Maybe that would help Tio look in the mirror."

Magdelena said it would be fine with her; Dreamer nodded, and Magdelena moved a bit to where Ramon was sitting on Solamente. As she approached, I watched Rojo Anita and wondered what she had seen and why she wanted Ramon to go next. I wondered if the mirror showed different people different things.

Rojo Anita watched Ramon intensely, and she heard everything my mind had just said. As Magdelena reached her arm up to give Ramon a glance, I watched Rojo Anita on Senorita. Ramon still had Tio in a loose lasso. Magdelena didn't let go of the mirror, so she was still holding on to it when Ramon caught a glimpse of himself.

"We must go," Ramon said.

I glanced toward Rojo Anita, who was watching him in the way she watches when she is studying. I knew she could read his thoughts — or I thought she could.

I looked his way and for a second I saw Ramon look into Rojo Anita's eyes. He only looked at her for a moment; then, he headed toward her.

I wanted to look in the mirror. And Tio — what about Tio looking in the mirror, but I thought it was better not to ask.

Ramon drew his lasso from Tio, who just looked at everyone. He seemed like Tio, the Tio we knew, but we weren't sure.

Then Tio lifted his lasso from his side and let it fly. It fell snugly onto Ramon. Ramon jerked for a moment; he was very strong, but Tio had learned quickly. I wasn't sure this was my Tio.

Tio asked, "What did you see in the mirror, Ramon?" I didn't think my Tio would ever do anything like this.

Magdelena looked at him. She wasn't sure what this was all about. She wanted to say something when Rojo Anita said, "Wait."

She addressed Ramon.

"Tio asked you a question, Ramon."

I thought that Magdelena and I should get out of there as fast as we could. I motioned for her to come my way. "Come here," I motioned to Magdelena, but she didn't move.

Tio held Ramon in his grasp.

"Magdelena, can you please bring the mirror to Ramon," Rojo Anita said.

Magdelena moved from where she stood near Tio and came closer to Ramon. He did not try to move.

"Magdelena, will you please hold the mirror up for Ramon to see," Rojo Anita said.

"You already know what I see," he told her. "You already know."

"But what about the others? Maybe they should know. Maybe you should let them know."

Magdelena approached Ramon. I knew she was frightened. "Don't be afraid, Magdelena," I thought. Rojo Anita knew too. "Don't be afraid, Magdelena," Rojo Anita said.

I looked at Tio.

Who was he?

And what about Rojo Anita?

Magdelena reached the spot where Ramon sat on Solamente. I looked at Magdelena's feet as she stopped moving. She did not show her fear. Magdelena said to Ramon, "Ramon, I hope you do not mind me bringing the mirror to you."

And that was all she said as she stretched her arm toward his face.

"Turn around so they can see," Rojo Anita said. "Turn around, Ramon."

I could tell he was getting ready to bolt, but Tio kept him tight. Could my Tio ever do this?

Tio moved the rope in a circular shape, so Ramon and Solamente could move, so we too could see in the mirror. Tio kept the rope tighter as he came nearer. I moved in closer. If Tio were a No Face, he would catch us anyway if we tried to move. And Magdelena didn't seem to be going anywhere.

Ramon moved his head from side to side. He didn't want to look in the mirror again. Tio was next to him, a bit behind Magdelena. I went and stood next to her. Her arms weren't shaking at all as her outstretched hand moved to a place where Ramon could look at himself.

Even though the mirror was small, we could see as Ramon stopped moving his head from side to side and moved toward the mirror. He held his head still, and there he was. There was Ramon. I didn't know what all the fuss was about until Magdelena gasped, and Tio pulled the lasso even tighter. Solamente didn't make a sound. Rojo Anita waited.

And then I saw it. All of a sudden, I saw what Magdelena saw, and Tio, and what Rojo Anita knew. His right eye was nowhere to be found in the mirror. The area where his eye should be was covered over in skin.

"Ramon, where is your eye?" Magdelena asked.

Then I looked. And shuddered. What did this mean? What did all this mean?

"What happened when you looked in the mirror, Rojo Anita?" a voice asked. Standing among the trees was a man. He rode out slowly.

"What happened when you looked in the mirror, Rojo Anita? I saw you shudder. Perhaps you should look again with Magdelena." Don Pedro was the one whom Rojo Anita couldn't always read.

We hadn't seen Don Pedro in a very long time. Whether he was Don Pedro or not didn't seem to matter at the moment. I was very, very glad to see him. Maybe he could help us know what was happening.

"Hello, Magdelena, Tio, Coyitito. Hello, Ramon. Hello, Padre Miguel II, Senorita Duende, Solamente, Senorita … and … I do not believe we have met. I am Don Pedro and this is my horse."

"I am Dreamer. This is Gold."

Dreamer and Gold. I had forgotten that they were even here. What did Dreamer think about all of this? I wanted to ask her. I wanted to say, "Dreamer, what …" but I was interrupted by Rojo Anita.

"Please bring the mirror to me, Magdelena."

And Magdelena drew back her arm from Ramon and moved over to Rojo Anita. Rojo Anita turned, so we could see her. And when she did, Magdelena stretched up and held the mirror so Rojo Anita could look inside.

And there it was. Rojo Anita's right eye was missing — just like Ramon's.

I couldn't stop shivering.

I shivered, and then I spoke; I said, "Rojo Anita. Ramon. What does this mean?"

And it was Dreamer who answered.

"Have your faces ever been borrowed? Sometimes in Dreamtime we see that happen — where faces of Dreamers are borrowed for other people's dreams. But they are returned."

And yes, yes. Maybe they didn't know, but we did. We knew Rojo Anita had been a No Face. And Ramon we weren't sure about, but he could have been borrowed.

And then I thought it — and wished I hadn't because Rojo Anita heard me and said, "Tio, Magdelena, and Coyitito, will you look in the mirror?"

I didn't want to look in the mirror, but I knew I would.

Magdelena brought her arm down and lifted it toward her own face. And there she was. There was Magdelena just like we knew her. And when I lifted my eyes to see if her eyes were where they were supposed to be — I saw her left eye — and where her right eye was supposed to be — it was right there. Her right eye — in all its softness, in all its courage, was right there.

I was next.

Magdelena moved toward me. First, I closed my eyes because I didn't want to know. I didn't want to know if my eyes were both there. Then I opened them slowly and moved toward the mirror.

I saw them — both of them.

I blinked up and down several times to make sure they were there. They were — my eyes. I reached up to touch them — and it was then that Tio fled.

"Tio, come back," Don Pedro called.

"Tio. It is all right. Come back," he shouted.

And Rojo Anita and Ramon, who was now free from Tio's rope, ran after him.

"Rojo Anita!" Don Pedro called.

"Ramon."

But they were gone; all three of them were gone.

"Tio's right eye is probably missing too," said another voice behind us.

I turned.

Manuel was standing near us, riding Ochenta, or so we thought. Manuel, he had been a No Face, too. Or we thought he was. He led us through the caves straight to the No Faces. And then Ramon came.

Had Manuel been a No Face?

"Manuel," Magdelena said. "Will you look in the mirror?"

He hesitated.

"I am afraid to, but I will. I shall look in the mirror, Magdelena."

And he rode over to where we were — then stopped in his tracks.

He saw the golden light.

I don't know how long Manuel had watched us, and I wondered if he had seen her already — but all of a sudden — he stopped where he was and stared straight at her.

"And how about you? Did you look in the mirror?" he asked as he slid off Ochenta.

"If you looked in the mirror, you would see a lovely, lovely sight."

I couldn't believe that Manuel was saying this to Dreamer. My manners and Tio's were one thing — but what was Manuel doing?

"I am Manuel, and I love to dance."

She looked at him.

"I am Dreamer."

Then she turned in a circle. Her horse lifted its wings from its sides — slowly. As Dreamer spun, Gold grew wider in wings.

"And this is Gold."

Manuel was transfixed.

We all were.

Don Pedro was too but not as much as we were, so he said, "Manuel. Please look in the mirror."

And Manuel took his gaze from Dreamer and moved toward Magdelena.

"Hello Magdelena. It is good to see you again," he told her.

"It is good to see you also, Manuel."

And she lifted her reflector.

We all moved closer.

Manuel looked straight into the glass and smiled.

His right eye showed his joy.

So did his left eye.

How did they not take Manuel?

"Manuel, Manuel, in the caves, I thought you were a No Face," I said.

"I know," he said. "And I wasn't sure about you three either."

And then we heard the fierce galloping headed our way.

"Are we in the protected area, Don Pedro?" I asked.

"The way things are going, who knows? But I believe so.

"Hide in the trees!" Don Pedro said firmly. And we scattered. And hid — as best we could.

I looked for Dreamer and Gold, but I didn't see them anywhere. Maybe they were now gone.

Dreamer had taught us about the mirror.

But I did see the three riders as they sped through the trees. And then they stopped in the clearing where we had just been.

"Coyitito!

"Coyitito.

"Come out. Come here.

"Don Pedro, Come.

"Come, Magdelena.

"We have found our eyes.

"Come. Please bring us your mirror.

"We have found our eyes and need to put them back in their places. I think your mirror can help us. Come, please."

I looked at Don Pedro. I whispered, "How are they in the protected area? And before, they were too? If they are No Faces, then what is happening to the protected areas?"

"They are still more themselves than No Faces," he said.

And he looked at me and stepped into the clearing.

"Don Pedro," Rojo Anita said. "I understand your concern. But we have found our eyes. And perhaps we can put them back. Here. Look."

And I watched Rojo Anita open her hand, and inside, I saw an eye. Rojo Anita was holding an eye.

Then Ramon opened his hand, and Tio opened his — and all three held an eye. That is why they were allowed in the protected area: they had most of the pieces of their whole selves, their good selves.

"Perhaps if we look in Magdelena's mirror, perhaps we can place our eyes back where they belong," Rojo Anita said.

Don Pedro called out, "Magdelena, what do you think of this?"

Magdelena moved from where she was standing next to me.

"Yes, yes, let us see if the mirror will help you place back your eyes," Magdelena said. "And then maybe you too will be back — all of you."

"Where did you find those eyes?" Manuel asked as he emerged from hiding. I wanted to know too, but I was afraid to ask — and afraid to come out from my hiding place.

"Come on out, Coyitito," Rojo Anita said.

So I did.

I came out to hear the story.

Tio looked at me. He rode over to where I was and uncurled his hand.

"Coyitito, look. Look at my eye. I didn't even know it was gone until I looked in the mirror. Look."

I didn't want to look, but I did. On Tio's face was an eye, right where his right eye would be. I studied it, looking at it, but I really couldn't tell the difference. The only difference was that he was holding an eye in his hand, and it seemed to belong to him.

"Where was it, Tio?" but then I saw my Tio change into the other Tio, the one without his right eye. He caught himself before it happened completely, but for a moment, I saw him reach for his rope. I saw his hand drop down and grab the rope. I shuddered, knowing that, for a moment, Tio thought about once again lassoing me into capture.

"It comes and goes," Rojo Anita said. "The feelings come and go. We're not completely back, and sometimes, I think, we can still feel like the No Faces do. We can get their impulses. Like just now — Tio reached for his rope, and I thought,

"Yes, we can round them up and take them with us, meaning you, Coyitito, and Magdelena, and Manuel.

"But we are strong enough to fight against these feelings. I think if we can put our eyes back, we won't have those feelings," Rojo Anita said.

Ramon stayed quiet. He was very, very quiet. "Why is Ramon so quiet, Rojo Anita?" I asked.

"Ramon, why are you so quiet?" she asked.

"Because I am so very disappointed, Coyitito. I never thought I was weak around the No Faces. I would never want to put you or Magdelena or Tio or Manuel or anyone in danger.

"And maybe I did.

"Maybe they were able to take me — and maybe I would have brought you to danger — and that is unbearable for me — to think that or feel that.

"For me, Coyitito …"

And then, in a flash, Ramon reached for his lasso and swung it right over my head.

Tio was fast, too.

So was Rojo Anita.

And Don Pedro.

But it was Tio who caught Ramon's lasso first. He caught it with his own rope, snatching it from Ramon's grasp.

"See," Ramon cried out.

"See. Look. Look at what I am capable of doing. Look. Tio has more control than I do. Tio didn't let his lasso fly; I did.

"It is unbearable.

"Magdelena, may I ask you to please bring me your mirror. Please." And when she did, he grabbed her outstretched arm, pulled her onto his horse — and sped away.

The others were fast.

But I, Coyitito, I was faster.

Senorita Duende and I ran through the trees. What could I do? I ran as fast as Senorita Duende would take us. I ran after Magdelena.

Tio came up next to me.

He rode fast, too.

I didn't know if he was my Tio or the other one when he reached for his rope.

I heard the others behind me: Manuel on Ochenta. Rojo Anita and Don Pedro. Tio stayed close to me, but I was in the lead, and then Tio yelled. He yelled, "Rope!" and I thought it was time to let the lasso fly. But he meant something else: a rope was spread out among the trees. My face would crash into the rope in a matter of seconds. I saw it now in front of me. We were moving so quickly; the rope was bound to take me right off Senorita Duende's back, maybe taking some of my flesh with it.

Then I saw him. I saw Ramon to my right holding the rope that curled several trees down from where I rode. It was held there, clasped. It looked like the clothesline back at school.

If it didn't get me, it would get Senorita Duende.

It was stretched far, far across the trees.

I veered Senorita Duende to the left. It was there too, so I did something I had never done on Senorita Duende.

I had seen it happen before, and I knew that it was dangerous, but I did it anyway.

I pulled on Senorita Duende, and she reared.

She pulled straight back and rose up into the air.

I felt her lift and lift — and it felt like she would never stop lifting. I clung to her neck. I knew that if I slid from her, I might wind up in the Cave of the Departed, so I clung tightly to her.

I heard the neighing. It didn't sound like Senorita Duende. Her broad, strong stomach hit the rope first. She pulled the tree down where the rope was attached. It bent and bent — and then she let her front hooves fall onto the ground, and raised her back legs over the rope before it sprang up again.

I turned her around, built the lasso in my hand, and let it fly.

I caught Ramon and tied his arms down to his sides. Magdelena was outside the rope. I approached. He tried to move, but I held him firm in my grasp.

Our ropes seemed to help us.

Then I started to realize what had just happened.

"Coyitito!"

Magdelena jumped from Solamente's back.

"Coyitito!"

Then Tio came. And Rojo Anita. And Don Pedro. And Manuel.

"Please help me," Ramon said.

"Please help me."

And when he opened his hand, we saw something we hadn't seen before. It wasn't just Ramon's eye; it was the side of his face that he held in his hand.

Magdelena moved closer to Ramon with her mirror. When he looked into his reflection, he saw what we saw: the right side of his face — his nose, his mouth, all of it was missing, and was in his hand.

"How did we not see this before?" I asked Magdelena. "How did we miss this?"

And then Rojo Anita said, "Maybe the No Faces are taking more of Ramon right now. Quick, Magdelena, bring the mirror to me. Let me see myself."

And Rojo Anita looked into the mirror. And there she was, without her right eye, but the rest of her face was there. "Pass the mirror around," she said.

And Tio was still missing his eye, but the rest of us had all the pieces of our faces. And after the mirror went from each one of us to the other, Rojo Anita asked for it back.

I held onto Ramon the whole time.

His struggle was visible.

I looked at him.

His eyes were cast down; his body had given in; it seemed he was sad and broken-hearted. Then I would feel the rope tighten. He would start to move around, trying to break free. His eyes would look at us; they had fire in them. He spit on the ground. I could feel him want to take us with him, take us to the No Faces and their leader, the one who yelled, "CEASE!"

And then his eyes would look wild with wonder. I knew he was fighting against himself.

So was Rojo Anita. She was fighting, too. Tio too — but not like Ramon.

Ramon, who had brought us our gifts, who had led us to Meme, who had brought

Padre Miguel II, who loved me — and Magdelena — whom he had just tried to capture — and Tio. Here I was, Coyitito, holding Ramon in a lasso, holding him trapped to keep us safe from him, to keep him safe from himself.

How did I do that?

How did I throw the lasso like that?

"Magdelena, will you come here with your mirror?" Rojo Anita said.

"I am sorry, Rojo Anita. I apologize for asking you this," said Magdelena, "but will you please come down from Senorita and come over here to my mirror?"

After what just happened with Ramon, Magdelena wouldn't take any chances.

"Do not apologize, Magdelena. Of course, I will come off Senorita and come to you," said Rojo Anita.

Rojo Anita approached Magdelena's mirror. She opened her hand and lifted her right eye with her fingers. Very gently she raised her eye to the place where it belonged.

Magdelena held her mirror steady. Rojo Anita was ready. Her right eye was just outside its home when Ramon yelled, "No. Do not return your eye. No!"

And when he yelled like that, Rojo Anita dropped her sight.

Ramon moved in his trap.

The horses were uneasy. I pulled on the lasso, but I was distracted when Ramon yelled, so he was able to move some — and that was enough for him. Quickly, he was free from my rope, jumped off Solamente, and started running toward Rojo Anita. But Tio was quick. He caught Ramon before he stepped on his sister's eye.

"Stop it, Ramon," Rojo Anita yelled at him. "Just stop it. Stop it now! I know you are being pulled between the two worlds, but you are getting on my nerves. I have had it with the way you are acting. If you will just stop it, maybe I can help you put your own face back.

"By the way, when we found our eyes before, and you found yours, did you find just your eye or half your face? It is important to know if the No Faces are taking you now, or if they already took you?"

But Ramon was on his knees.

And Rojo Anita looked at him, got to her own knees, and said,

"Ramon. Let me help you.

I will help you." And she helped him, along with Magdelena, as he replaced what I think was half his face.

And then Rojo Anita's own flash of meanness overtook her. She lifted her knee just above the place on the ground where her right eye was, and then she let her knee fall.

Don Pedro's arms rounded Rojo Anita's chest and lifted her, pulling her from the spot where her right eye lay.

"Not your right eye. Don't crush your right eye," he told her.

Magdelena stayed steady with her mirror. Don Pedro held onto Rojo Anita.

"Are you safe enough to try and get your eye back?" he asked her.

She nodded. He stayed close to her as she bent. She picked her eye up from the ground, stepped toward Magdelena and her mirror, and looked inside the glass frame.

Rojo Anita studied the place where her right eye should be, placed her hand on her eyebrow, stretched her lids apart slightly over the empty socket. That seemed to please her somehow. She stretched the lids open further and slipped her eye back in. Just like that. Simple.

"My eye is back."

That must mean that Rojo Anita was back. I looked at her. She looked the same.

"Tio, it's your turn," Magdelena said.

But Tio, during all the commotion when Rojo Anita tried to crush her own eye, threw his into the woods.

For the moment, Ramon was back to his old self again; so was Rojo Anita — at least we thought so.

Ramon sped on Solamente, stopped short, got down off his horse, and approached Tio. He didn't want to hurt Tio; he never wanted to hurt anyone when he was Ramon, but he had to take Tio into his arms, so Tio's eye could be returned.

Tio needed his eye back in order to be free of the No Faces.

Tio pushed with all his strength, but he couldn't move in Ramon's grasp.

I was very, very sad to see Tio grasped like that, but I knew, I knew he could not be trusted at this moment. I looked at Magdelena; in her own face she was worried, and I could tell that she too couldn't bear to see Tio torn between his two worlds. So she did what Magdelena does: she went over to Tio and said to him,

"Tio, you are torn between two worlds. The Tio we know is a good Tio, a strong and kind Tio, loving. The other one, the one the No Faces took a piece of — he is mean and he will harm even his friends. The mean Tio, he would harm Coyitito; he would harm me, Magdelena.

"I know the mean Tio doesn't care what I am saying — but the other Tio, the good one, the one we have known for most of our years here on earth — that Tio I am talking to right now. Please be calm while we try to find your eye. You need it to be free of the No Faces. And we must hurry to get back to the school. You know that.

"Now — where were you standing when you threw it? Perhaps I can trace its path."

And then Rojo Anita spoke.

She said, "Why don't we all go forward and search for Tio's eye?"

And Magdelena said what Rojo Anita then realized: that if we all go searching, then purely by accident at this point, one of us might step on Tio's eye — and then he might stay as part No Face.

I agreed. I thought that if we all went searching, one of us might make the mistake of crushing Tio's eye.

And then the clouds came. They came rolling in, black and thunderous. The booms started in the sky, and I knew, so did the horses — that the electric lights in the sky would sharpen their points above us at any moment.

The trees bent with the coming wind. Was this the wind of the storm? Or was it the wind of the No Faces? This was not a good time for the storm. Don Pedro said, "Quick. Go take shelter where you can. Rojo Anita, lead them to shelter."

Senorita Duende seemed nervous. So did Padre Miguel II. He was already scared, seeing what was happening to Tio. He started neighing and moving his hind legs back and front legs forward. Solamente did the same, and Ramon, still holding onto Tio, grabbed the rope hanging from Solamente and wrapped it around the tree. Solamente dug his heels in the dirt, dropping and lifting his head.

Rojo Anita rode on Senorita. The sky boomed.

Don Pedro said,

"Rojo Anita, take them to shelter. Take them now. Look for a place for the horses and the children. Now."

I looked at Tio. His eyes were wild in the storm. I wanted to go to him, but Senorita Duende had other plans. She started turning in circles. She knew I did not want her to go; the horses always knew, but she was frightened, and so was I.

Then I turned to Magdelena, but Magdelena was not there.

"Magdelena," I yelled into the wind. "Magdelena!"

All heads turned quickly to see where Magdelena was, but none of us saw her.

"Magdelena."

Maybe this is why Senorita Duende had other plans. Did she know Magdelena planned on leaving?

The sky was very, very dark. The thunder crashed above our heads, telling us how close the lightning strikes were. One more crash of thunder like that, and I knew the horses couldn't stay.

Above us, the trees bent, and I looked up in the sky; I saw the darkness, and then I saw the rod of electric light fill the dark cover.

We had to go.

The horses knew.

I looked at Tio.

Ramon kept hold of him and reached for Solamente's rope.

"Magdelena!" I yelled into the wind.

I begged Senorita Duende not to go, and she tried very hard to stay, but she felt the ground move under her hooves, and her ears filled with booming sounds — and she bolted — with me on her back and Magdelena gone.

"Please Senorita Duende, please wait for the others," but she couldn't, and she ran so fast I thought I would fall. She made sure no trees hit me in the face — or almost made sure. Sometimes I had to duck down as she sped, trying to outrun the storm.

"Where are we going, Senorita Duende? Where are we heading? We need to find Magdelena and get back to the school."

But she would not hear me. And we rode away from the storm, which followed us, quivering over our heads.

I thought she was bringing me to Magdelena.

Snap.

I heard the sound.

I heard the snap.

It must have been a branch where Senorita Duende stepped. But all of a sudden, she stopped running.

Oh no. I hope the *snap* wasn't … I hope it wasn't her leg. I hope Senorita Duende didn't break her leg by running so fast through the trees.

"Senorita Duende, oh, Senorita Duende, powerful and wondrous horse. Are you all right? Are you hurt, Senorita Duende?"

"Coyitito, *snap* out of it!"

I heard the command.

How was it that Senorita Duende spoke to me like this?

The thunder boomed behind us, but where we were, it was calmer. I wanted to check Senorita Duende's leg. She stopped moving.

I slid down off her back.

"Coyitito. The horse is not talking to you. I am."

And when I looked this time, I saw, in front of us, just a few paces ahead, Meme stood.

"Meme!" I was so very grateful to see Meme. Of course it was Meme!

"Meme."

She held open a door, and Senorita Duende and I went inside.

"Coyitito, you must get back to the school. You are needed there. And you must hurry."

"But Meme, I have been trying to. But just now, just moments ago, Tio threw his eye into the trees. And he needs it to be free from the …"

"I know. I know all about it, Coyitito. Here. Come here. Come in here."

And I followed her. And she was in her kitchen, pulling straw down from a shelf. Freshly baked cookies were laid on a counter.

"Take these. And these. And these."

"What are they, Meme?"

"Cookies — for you, Magdelena, and Tio."

Did this mean I would be seeing Magdelena again soon? I didn't dare ask.

The cookies were still warm. I did ask Meme if I could taste one of them. She said, "Yes." I bit down. She watched me.

"Well, Coyitito, what do you think?"

"I think … I think they are delicious, Meme. I taste chocolate, blueberry, strawberry, maple sugar." And then Meme sprinkled the cookies with something and wrapped them in straw.

"Leave them like this for a while."

"How long, Meme?"

"A while."

She opened a door on the other side of the room and said, "Coyitito, share these with the others," and she was gone.

Senorita Duende and I were back in the storm. But this time, we headed into the storm, back to our friends.

Magdelena was standing in front of Tio. Ramon still held onto him. She held her mirror up to his face. He jerked his head from side to side.

"I know. I know, Tio. But we must. You must be complete."

Rojo Anita stood behind Tio and Ramon. She reached out to Tio's face.

"I don't want to grab your face and hold it, Tio, but I must. I must assist in putting your eye back," said Rojo Anita.

"Yes, Rojo Anita, help me with my eye. Please," Tio responded.

And Rojo Anita found the place for Tio's eye while Magdelena held the mirror.

"LET'S GO," Manuel erupted.

"Let's go now. Now. The No Faces are already at the school. We can't wait any longer. Let's go."

And Magdelena jumped onto Senorita Duende. Ramon steered Solamente. Rojo Anita rode to the front on Senorita. Don Pedro stayed behind us. And Tio, Tio rode next to Magdelena and me as we ran through the trees.

"Magdelena, how did you find Tio's eye?"

"Coyitito. I went down on my hands and knees and started crawling slowly on the ground. I was very careful as I went. The sky was so dark it was hard to see — but then — over there — next to a big log, I saw something shining in the darkness. And I slowly crawled toward it. And when I got up close to it, I knew it was Tio's eye. So I gently put it in my hand, stood, and ran back to where Ramon and Tio and the others were.

And that's when you came."

"Meme gave me cookies."

"What kind?"

"I don't know. But she gave me a couple of bags. She said they are for you, Tio, and me." And we ate some of Meme's cookies. Tio did too.

All of a sudden, Manuel halted in front of us.

Ochenta bucked back with the release of all that speed.

Ramon stopped too.

We all stopped. Fast.

We saw our school through the trees. We had arrived. I started to shake a bit. I became frightened. This time we knew the No Faces were there. We knew the one who yelled "Cease" was right across from us, right on the other side.

"What is our plan?" Manuel asked.

Don Pedro came from the back. He moved next to Rojo Anita. She seemed very busy as she sat there on Senorita.

"What is it?" Don Pedro asked her.

She did not answer him.

Ramon came around.

"We need a plan," he said.

Don Pedro had a very serious face.

"What is it, Rojo Anita?" he asked.

"I am hearing something. They are looking for us. Wait. Shhh. Come …" Either Rojo Anita's hearing increased, or they were closer than we thought.

And Rojo Anita turned Senorita into the trees. We all followed.

"You wait here. All of you … wait right here. The protected zone has been invaded here. I need to be closer to listen. I will be right back. While I am gathering what I can — think about the best plan," she said.

Rojo Anita turned Senorita toward the school but stayed deep in the cover of the trees.

I looked to Ramon and Don Pedro. They would know what to do. They would have a plan.

And then, without warning, Manuel broke into a full gallop on the back of Ochenta.

"Manuel, No." Don Pedro yelled firmly.

"No."

But Manuel kept going.

And so did Ramon's rope.

And it pulled Manuel to the ground and rolled him toward Ramon. And quickly Ramon pulled a cloth from his own back pocket and tied it over Manuel's mouth.

Had Manuel been invaded?

Rojo Anita came riding our way. And then it started to happen. I felt it, and I looked at Magdelena. I could see she felt something too. I looked at Tio. He looked at me. Magdelena said, "Coyitito. Coyitito."

And Rojo Anita said, "Don Pedro. Ramon. Look. Look."

And they looked.

And Don Pedro said, "What is that, Rojo Anita? What is happening?"

And I saw Ramon shake his head up and down and start to smile. A little. He was a bit scared, I thought, but he just waited.

I turned my glance to Manuel. He was very, very wide-eyed. Very much so. He started trying to move, but he couldn't. He shook his body the best he could — but he couldn't do much.

And then it was over.

I didn't feel much really, but I knew; I knew that it had happened.

Don Pedro and Rojo Anita just stood staring. I know she was trying to read us, but we didn't have any answers. I looked at Tio. I looked for Magdelena. At first I didn't see her, but then I did. Then I saw her right next to me. Directly next to me. I didn't really see her with my eyes, but I knew; I knew she was right there at my side.

The cookies, I thought. Yes, Meme made us this way for a reason.

And I thought I might know the reason.

No one would recognize us, and we might be able to get onto the school grounds without anyone noticing us.

I looked at Tio.

He was a wondrous horse.

I wondered what we looked like.

I didn't know why or how Meme's cookies made Magdelena and me one horse, but maybe it had something to do with our sharing a horse. Or maybe three horses seemed suspicious. I don't know, but Magdelena and I were one horse, and Tio was another.

And we knew what to do.

We knew we needed to head toward the school, so we did. Tio ran ahead of us, and Magdelena and I followed, leaving Don Pedro, Rojo Anita, Ramon, and Manuel.

I think Rojo Anita started to read us because she said, "You're moving just fine," when I worried that maybe Magdelena and I couldn't run at the same pace.

But we did.

I felt and didn't feel Magdelena next to me.

Then Tio neighed. He neighed just like our horses did. And I understood him, and he asked if I thought Senorita Duende and Padre Miguel II were coming along, but they didn't follow us. And anyway, our horses might be noticed — somehow — someone might know.

And I neighed back. And he understood me. Then Magdelena said something, and we both understood her, so we knew we could all talk to each other. We knew we must be careful, but we could communicate.

Being a horse wasn't much different from being on one.

We raced through the trees until we got to the road.

Then we slowed. We started trotting. And before we turned toward the school, we stopped completely.

Magdelena said, "We must try to stay together."

"I won't be leaving your side," I said. And she said, "Very funny, Coyitito. Tio, stay close to us."

And he nodded. Then his hooves hit the road; he turned right, and we moved next to him, but a little back, the way horses travel when they travel together.

My heart was beating fast, or was that Magdelena's heart? I seemed to be on the left side, so I think it was my — or — our heart. I guess it was our heart.

In a very low neighing sound, I said,

"Tio, are you all right?" And he nodded yes.

And then I became very scared, very nervous, because I didn't know how long Meme's cookies would last. I remembered being in Marleena's place under the sea, and at one point, I started growing. When would we stop being horses?

But I had to stop thinking because we were at the gate, and the gate was open.

We turned and walked in.

I am sure they were waiting for us as humans to arrive because the gate was open. When we were at school recently, the gate was never open anymore. Before we left, the gate started to be locked. And here it was — open. Wide open.

We walked through and headed toward the water trough. I don't think anyone recognized us because we just moved along as horses might, thirsty and tired from the heat.

We walked toward one place where water is kept, and we saw that decorations were hanging. Tables and chairs were moved into the big yard. We knew this meant they were getting ready for a feast. But what feast? What were they getting ready for?

Then Tio moved to a different trough of water, the one that sits near Padre Miguel's office. And we followed.

I didn't dare make any sound to Tio or Magdelena because I felt that this was very dangerous, what we were doing. At some point, we would be discovered.

And when Tio got there, he did what horses do, and he started to drink. So we went up next to him and did the same.

We dropped our head down, and when we raised it — I stopped in midair. I looked into Padre Miguel's office. There he sat — in Padre Miguel's chair — right behind the desk. The No Face imposter sat right where Padre Miguel sits, drinking water just like Padre Miguel would, and sitting across from him, her face turned toward us, sat Maestra Maria.

Magdelena must have felt my response because she kicked up her back heel. I tried to quell my quivering, but how could I? Maestra Maria was in grave danger right there, right in front of me, and I couldn't tell her.

I knew Tio was very, very upset. Here was the man who took Padre Miguel away. Here, right in front of Tio, was the man who was the reason that Padre Miguel was in the Cave of the Departed.

"So Maestra Maria — I think it is best if we bring the others to the west side of the lawn — furthest from the gates. It is safer for them there. And then we can keep all the guests off in the same area. It has been rumored that perhaps those who want to capture the others will show up, but we will be ready for them. Yes, Maestra? We will be ready. We will keep the others safe."

"Yes, we will try. It seems that we weren't able to keep Tio, Magdelena, Manuel, and Coyitito safe. We haven't heard from them yet," Maestra Maria said.

"Yes, Maestra Maria. We don't want any of the others to fall into the wrong hands."

"Do you think — Padre Miguel — do you think Coyitito, Magdelena, Manuel, and Tio are somewhere safe? Or do you think they have been captured? Or something else — something worse? Sometimes I wake in the night and think I hear them."

"Hear them?" the imposter Padre Miguel seemed very, very interested.

"What do they say?"

"I don't hear them like they are actually in the room. I "wish hear" them. I wish for them to be here speaking, and in that way, I hear them. Don't you, Padre Miguel? Don't you hear Tio?"

And when she said that, Tio lifted his head and looked inside the room. Maestra Maria noticed. And he — the Padre Miguel imposter — noticed that she noticed something, so he came over to the window, but when he got there, we were gone.

We moved slowly toward the door where Maestra Maria would come from Padre Miguel's office, and we were standing there when she came out into the sunlight.

I wanted to yell to her. I wanted to say, "Maestra Maria. Maestra Maria," but I didn't. I just stood there. It was Magdelena who called her. And Maestra Maria heard it as a horse's sound and thought we were hungry, so she walked us over to where the hay is kept for the horses. And when we got to the hay, we all knew we somehow had to tell Maestra Maria about the danger surrounding her and the school.

If the Padre Miguel imposter was to do what he planned, move everyone into the west part of the yard, they would be so far from the gate that they wouldn't be able to get out and away from the No Faces. The stone walls were all around. So everyone, everyone would be trapped. And he was planning a feast, so many would come. Dona Williams would bake her cakes, and then when everyone was there, the No Faces would take everyone. They would steal them, and maybe they would do to them what they did to Padre Miguel; maybe they would start taking people's whole bodies, not just pieces and faces anymore.

Magdelena knew. So did Tio.

And when Maestra Maria stood with us by the hay, she touched our heads, looked into our eyes, and smiled.

"You two remind me so much of my dear beloveds: Tio, Magdelena, and Coyitito. But you — you remind me of Coyitito and Magdelena together. And you, you look like Tio.

"Oh, it saddens me to look into your eyes. I am sorry to be saddened, but you so have their eyes, their tender and loving eyes."

Then Tio moved away from her touch. He came around to Magdelena's side. Maestra Maria looked at him; so did we.

"Oh, I am sorry I hurt your feelings, Dear Tio Horse. Please. Do not think you only make me sad. I am happy that you are here, happy to meet you."

Tio put his long nose into Magdelena's side. I kept quiet. So did Magdelena. Tio's nose and mouth seemed to be doing something. And they were. He was opening the bag that hung on Magdelena's side. Magdelena's bag came with her when we changed into horses. His teeth pulled the string, Magdelena later told me. He grabbed the bottom of the bag and turned it over, and the contents fell out into Maestra Maria's hand.

When she saw the black velvet pouch falling, she caught it.

"What is this?" she asked.

Then she looked at Tio. She looked at him deeply. Then she looked at us.

She slid the mirror from its pouch and looked inside. She looked confused. I guess Maestra Maria only saw herself in the mirror. It seemed like she had her own face. Then Tio rode up behind her, standing in back of Maestra Maria. Maybe he wanted to see if she had her own face, but when he stood behind her, something else happened, something we didn't expect.

In the mirror, Maestra Maria saw something. She was very quiet about it. She then took the mirror, put it back into its velvet case, placed it in the sack hanging from Magdelena's side, and said, "So it is you, Tio. Hello, my Dear Tio. And I suppose that is you, Coyitito. Yes? And Magdelena, is that you? I see it in your eyes.

"Tio, I saw you in the mirror — not as horse, but as the dear Tio boy I know. Hello. So here you are, you three. Here you are as horses!

"Why is that?

"I don't want to keep the mirror exposed. Perhaps it will attract attention. But it does mean something, doesn't it? It does mean something.

"The mirror shows the person. Is that so?"

When she said this, we all nodded our heads and kept nodding our heads.

"Does the mirror show, yes, it does reflect a face. So that mirror you have, I wonder where it came from. Does that mirror also reveal a No Face?"

Tio's hooves hit the dirt hard.

We remained motionless.

Soon someone would see, if they hadn't already, Maestra Maria's long conversation with two horses: us. Someone would become suspicious; we needed to go. Very, very soon we needed to leave because we didn't know how long we had before we turned back into Tio, Magdelena, and Coyitito.

"Oh my," Maestra Maria said.

"And you have come here, come here as horses with your mirror. That is very, very powerful of you. Someone has helped you. Someone has sent you with a strong message. So — we are in grave danger. And the No Faces have come; is this so? Are the No Faces here now? Are there No Faces inside the gates now?"

We all nodded yes.

"Who are they?"

And when she said that, when she asked, "Who are they?" the Padre Miguel imposter appeared with several men.

He said, "Maestra Maria, we have heard information that we need to protect the school for the woods might be crawling with the ones who want to capture the others.

"I am sending these men who have come to help from the neighboring town to find out more information about what is happening and to protect us from the ones who might be traveling the road."

I guess Maestra Maria had no reason to distrust Padre Miguel.

"Do go and get your horses. And you two, ride these two horses, the ones that wandered in here. You, take that one; and you, Carlos, you take that one."

Maestra Maria turned her eyes to us. They told us to be careful. And we knew that Maestra Maria knew. She didn't ask us, but she knew; now she knew that her Dear, Dear Padre Miguel was an imposter; he was a No Face.

CARLOS JUMPED onto Tio's back. I wondered how it felt, if Tio felt the weight of him. He was a big man, very, very tall. He wasn't so very wide, but he was very high; it looked like his feet would almost touch the ground when he sat on Tio's back.

And then our rider jumped on our back. We didn't feel his weight so much; well, at least I didn't, but I did feel him when he kicked into my side, and I know Magdelena must have felt him too. And this made me very mad. When we rode our horses, we talked to them; we would say, "Senorita Duende, please go faster." We didn't kick her, and Tio didn't kick Padre Miguel II, but Carlos kicked into Tio's sides, and our rider kicked ours.

"Wait!" the imposter Padre Miguel called the horses. And we were stopped suddenly. And on my spine — my horse's spine — I felt a chill. And I knew Magdelena felt something, and Tio did too. Oh, Tio. I watched him as the imposter came toward us. Tio's mouth foamed, and he kicked his hind legs in the dirt. Carlos said to him, he said, "Hey, cut it out. Stop moving," but Tio couldn't stop. He was almost like one of those dogs you see in the street, and they're foaming, and that's what Tio was like. He was like that, and Carlos didn't like it, so he kicked Tio. But that didn't help.

Then Magdelena neighed, just a small sound, and she told Tio to please stop. "Please stop, Tio," for Magdelena knew that these men were mean, and Tio could get hurt. But I think Tio disagreed because he knew that horses could kill people with their strength. Tio knew that he could bolt down the road at full speed, then stop, rear, and throw Carlos to the road.

We knew too. We knew that we could do that too. Magdelena wouldn't want to do that. Neither would I. But we could if we had to.

The imposter neared us. Tio was agitated. Carlos was not happy with the horse. The imposter came up to us. We looked right into his eyes.

I watched him. I watched Tio watch him. I knew Tio wanted to run right into him, knock him down, stop him, but he didn't. Not yet he didn't.

And then I felt something. I felt it somewhere inside me. And I knew that Magdelena felt it too. I didn't know exactly what it was, but it reminded me that we wouldn't be horses for long, that Meme's cookies would wear off.

I needed to talk to Meme about this. Why couldn't she make cookies that lasted longer? I felt it again, then looked to Tio to see if he was changing back, but he was still a horse.

Padre Miguel's imposter's sweating face leaned toward Carlos, our rider, and the others.

"Go check The Closet. See if their eyes are still there."

The Closet? The eyes! Whose eyes?

"Make sure you check for their eyes — and part of that one's face, and for him. Make sure he is there — intact. Do you hear me?"

The men nodded.

He looked straight at Carlos. "Carlos, you go to the canyon. Take them with you. The rest of you ride into The Closet.

"The feast will begin. Everyone should be here by then. We can surprise everyone. Should we wait until the sun goes down? Should we close the gates then and overtake them? Or should we do it in broad daylight?

"The ropes are ready behind my office. We will keep them there until we need them. Tell the others the plan when you meet them. Tell them the whole town will be here — for miles around they are coming to the feast.

"Tell that horse to stop moving, Carlos. I am talking. Make him stop!"

And Carlos pulled on Tio's neck very, very hard, but I learned that horses have very, very strong necks. Carlos said to the horse, "I'm warning you," but Carlos didn't realize, I guess, that he was on a horse. He didn't really know what could happen on the horse he was riding. It was really Tio. Carlos didn't know. He thought he did, but he didn't.

"The feast," the imposter continued. "We petition for the safe return of — what are their names? — Manuel, Tio, Magdalena. And Coyitito — the ones that everyone talks about. Imagine — those four will bring everyone here for the petition, and then we can get them — and him. Did we already get that one — Manuel? We will get him again. We hear about them so much: Manuel, Tio, Magdelena, and Coyitito. We have been waiting for them!"

The imposter was here, right in front of us, saying our names. He was going to use us to bring everyone together to petition for our safe return, and then they were going to capture everyone.

I wished Tio, Magdelena, and I were one horse. It was so very difficult watching Tio while the imposter spoke.

"Oh, they create quite a stir. Do you hear how Maestra Maria goes on about them, how her heart has broken since they are gone? Come on now, Maestra Maria!

"How she has told everyone, how she has passed the word around that we are going to have a petition for their safe return. She has told everyone who has come by here; she has told them to tell everyone they see. 'Keep passing the word,' I told her. And she has. She has been telling the ones who ride by on the mules to tell the ones they see walking to come to the petition feast to help with the safe return of the 'dear, dear children.'

"How about when she says, 'Oh Padre Miguel, do you think this petition will bring them back?'

"I want to laugh in her face when she says that."

This I could not stand. I, Coyitito, ran from the imposter taking Magdelena with me. The man on our backs shouted and kicked and told "us" to stop. "Stop! Stop!" But I didn't stop. I ran straight to the road, to the trees, but then I realized that Tio was still there with Carlos on him. Tio didn't leave. Tio stayed to find out whatever he could. I knew we couldn't leave him alone, so I stopped. The rider kicked us hard in the sides. He raised his rope. "Please do not hit Magdelena's side," I thought. "Do not let the rope fall on Magdelena's side, for if it does, I will throw this man from our back."

The rope fell on me — lashing me. The man on our back raised the rope and it dropped on me. Once. Twice. And I wasn't the one who first raised our front legs, stepping back on our hind legs, rising up, up, up toward the trees. I watched the trees getting closer to our eyes. He went to lift the rope again, but when he did, we rose even higher until we were one straight line in the sky, and then we started to shimmer, and he started to slide.

He grabbed hold of our neck as we came back down to the ground, and just when he thought he was safe, Magdelena started the front leg lift again — high up into the sky, and when we came back down, she bolted.

We left Tio behind us; we did. And we were free to talk now, so I said to her, "Magdelena, we left Tio behind," and she said,

"Not for long. Here he comes."

And it was true. Tio came riding up behind us with Carlos on his back. And the other riders were close by him.

Carlos yelled ahead,

"Pepe! Hey, Pepe! What was that? What was that with your horse? What was your horse doing? Do not take that from a horse, man. Later, when we are finished, we will teach that horse a lesson."

And Pepe yelled back,

"We will teach this horse a lesson," but I knew that we frightened Pepe very, very much. We were still running him.

"Slow down," I told Magdelena.

But she was filled with fire and found it very, very hard to slow down. I tried to slow us down.

It was interesting to observe how this being one horse worked. It seemed that if one of us felt something very strongly, very, very strongly, then it happened. Like when Magdelena took over back there.

And now I felt strongly that we should slow down and get together with Tio if we could.

So I guess Magdelena understood because we slowed down.

Pepe started to breathe differently. At the moment, he didn't dare try anything.

"You will go out into the canyon with me. When we get out there, we will split up and tell the others. Alert them about this petition thing. Tell them to come to the front of the trees, across from the school, and to wait for the signal.

"Then they should surround the school. And when they hear the next signal, they should come marching into the gate. All of them. One after the other. Let the people see how many of us there are!

"Once they are lined up inside, they should wait for their orders."

And the riders rode off.

Tio was among them.

I turned our head to look over my shoulder at Tio leaving. He didn't make any movement to let me know he saw me watching him. And then I saw it; I saw his tail twitch, and I knew he knew I was watching him. And then I saw something else. I saw something I didn't really want to see. I saw halfway up Tio's leg, where the horse's fur was, something else was there; something that looked like skin. And I knew, I knew Tio was starting to change back into Tio. And Magdelena and I must be starting to change back into ourselves too.

Pepe jerked my side of our head back.

It angered me.

I dug my hooves into the dirt.

He knew I was mad.

I wanted to get a look at my own legs.

I said to Magdelena,

"Tio is starting to change back."

I said it in one neigh.

Magdelena didn't answer.

She dropped our head down.

And there I saw it: skin on our legs.

Pepe kicked us in the sides.

We were angered, but we moved ahead. We wanted to find out about The Closet.

"Let's go to The Closet and check for them. Let's check to see if the parts are still there. And him."

I knew what we had to do.

As soon as we could, we had to get rid of the other riders. But I didn't know how. And once we did, how would we get out of here without horses?

Pepe picked up our head. I dropped it again. I wanted to know, I wanted to see how much we were changing. I just started to look at my leg when he jerked on our neck.

"Keep your head straight."

I knew Magdelena was getting angry. I don't think I had ever seen her angry until she rose on our hind legs and gave Pepe a great fright.

We were going into the woods.

"The Closet door. There's The Closet door."

I looked for The Closet door.

"Hurry. We have to check, and then get back to the road and back to the school for the partition thing," said Pepe.

I neighed, "Petition," along with Magdelena.

"We take them over tonight!

"Tonight they lose their faces — and more — tonight.

"Now turn. Turn inside.

"Let me go first," and Pepe rode us right up to a cluster of trees.

"Look. Look at the rocks over there. No, No, no, no, no. No, no, not there. Look — look where my finger is pointing," Pepe told the other men. "There. See the rocks. See how they jut out. Follow that line to here. See those trees. Keep going. Here. See those three trees. Follow. Follow now — and here! This is The Closet door. Let's go in."

Magdelena had been close to this area before. None of us knew about The Closet, but we had been very, very close to it when Magdelena found the missing parts of our friends. These No Faces must have gotten clumsy and dropped what they had stolen. I could imagine them doing that.

Magdelena neighed to me, letting me know that she had been outside The Closet.

"You better be quiet, horse," Pepe told us.

For the moment, we quieted, not for him, but for us; we were concentrating on the path to The Closet.

We entered through the trees.

Pepe said to the men, "Stay very close to each other in here. If you don't know The Closet, you will get lost. It is a maze inside there. I used to be one of the ones in charge of The Closet, so I know the turns.

"Here we go. Here. Here. Right here."

I felt a chill as soon as we entered. It didn't really look any different from the woods outside the door, but it felt different. Very, very different, and the light started to disappear slowly. The hair on my horse's body stood up. I knew Magdelena felt it, too.

I dropped my head because I felt the chill, and on my leg, it felt different. And I saw that where my leg felt the coldest was where my skin appeared. My Skin!

I looked over to Magdelena's leg. I couldn't see, but I knew. We would have to do something soon — very, very soon. Soon we would have to do something.

I wanted to ask Magdelena. I wanted to say, "Magdelena, what do we do?" But I couldn't ask her. I couldn't bring myself to ask her because I didn't want to scare her. I didn't want her to know that our skin was coming back, covering our fur.

Pepe jerked our head again.

"Take it easy — easy," he told us as we rode deeper into The Closet.

"Everyone be quiet. I need to pay attention to the directions, so don't interrupt me. We turn right here — yes, this is it — then we turn left here — and again left — right — right — right and left."

I knew Magdelena was memorizing what we were doing. I was trying to, but I kept thinking about how, at any moment, we would be Magdelena and Coyitito — and here we were with a band of No Faces.

"If we turn left here — we should — be — there. Yep — here we are."

We were in The Closet.

I lifted our head.

It was dark — very, very dark. There was no light in The Closet. There had been some light as we traveled in, but now — now there was none.

"Look and listen in the darkness. Get down off your horses, go over there, and look to make sure the pieces and the eyes are where they are supposed to be. Ernesto delivered the pieces, and sometimes he doesn't do a good job. Now it's more important than ever; we are getting more powerful; we can't mess up. And if we do, he'll dismiss whoever messed up. And who knows how he will choose to get rid of the ones who messed up. Go check. And make sure *he's* there."

And then I saw it.

I saw in the darkness these glittering lights. It looked like the sky with all these twinkling lights. Not like all those stars — all those stars we see in the sky — or the cave when Melaquiades appears — but there were many, many glitters in the pitch black.

"Where do we go?" one of the men asked Pepe.

"Get off your horses. You can't ride in there. Walk."

Then he took out a lantern of his own. When he turned it on, some of the glittering disappeared, but then I still saw them. I knew Magdelena saw them too.

"There. Go over there. I'll point my light to where you need to go. Go there."

All of a sudden, I started to feel the weight of Pepe. He started to get heavier and heavier. I wanted to see my leg — but I already knew. I knew our bodies were coming back. I was terrified, but I didn't want to scare Magdelena. I neighed to her, but she was quiet.

"Be quiet," Pepe yelled. "Be quiet, horse. There. There. You need to go — no, look where I am pointing ... see if he's there. See if he is all there. No. In there ... go. Oh. Do I have to do everything myself? Look — is that his arm? He's the only one who should be there like that."

Pepe weighed much more than I thought.

We had to get out of here fast.

"No, no, no, no, no — go over there. There. Look."

And Pepe jumped off us to go show the man where to turn.

Magdelena and I acted together — and quickly.

We turned around and ran. I let Magdelena lead us because she knew; she knew which way to turn.

"Hey. Hey. Get back here. Hey, when I get my hands on you ..."

But we were turning left and right, and right and left. We were back in the light, and when I looked at Magdelena, I saw her; her face was made of skin and so was mine.

"Coyitito, you are back!" Magdelena exclaimed.

And I guess I was because all of a sudden, Magdelena and I were separate again. We were standing side by side.

"We need to get out of here. They will come back to look for the horse, and who knows what they will do with the horse — with us," she said.

And then we both had the same thought. I knew we both had it. I could tell by the look on Magdelena's face.

If we were back — then so was Tio. And he was in grave danger somewhere on the canyon trail; he was in terrible danger.

Then we heard them coming: Pepe and the other men were galloping from The Closet.

Pepe was yelling, "Let's find that horse. Now!"

Pepe was riding another horse now, and two of the men were riding together.

Magdelena and I moved into the trees, hiding, as the hooves headed our way. We watched through the trees as they came towards us. They were moving fast. Pepe was riding in front.

They came toward us.

"I will find that horse and teach it a lesson. I am going to find that horse and make that horse sorry that it ever met me."

They were close enough to see, and they were moving fast. At any moment they would pass us by, and Magdelena and I could start weaving through the trees, trying to find our way back to Rojo Anita and the others. They were passing us by, and I was getting very, very nervous because soon night would come, and we didn't have any horses, and the No Faces were everywhere, and they were going to take over the school, and Tio, oh Tio was probably Tio by now. And what were they doing to Tio? We needed to get back to the school. We … please …

And then the horses stopped.

Right in front of Magdelena and me … they stopped. Pepe pulled the horse to a stop — right there — right in front of where we were hiding.

He turned his face to us.

"Do you smell that horse? Does anyone smell that horse?"

He looked right into the trees.

"Pepe, we need to get back. We don't have time to look for the horse … we need to …" said one of the men.

Pepe let his rope fly right over the man's head. We saw it. We saw him unleash the rope and let it out right over the other one's head, and then he drew it back.

"Next time I won't miss. Do you understand? Next time I will take your head into my rope, pull you down off your horse, tie you up, and leave you here. Do you understand? Do. Not. Ever. Question. Me.

"Now, as I was saying, do you smell the horse? I was sure we were following its scent, and this is where I lost the scent. This is where — right here.

"Down. Get down off your horse and look for its tracks. Get down."

And the men came down and started searching.

And then Pepe turned his head from side to side. I couldn't believe he sat there on his horse knowing that we were there. He knew we were there. And he just sat there, watching, waiting … and then he unleashed his rope. But it didn't come our way … it went across from us into the trees. His rope snatched a few leaves, curled around a branch, took the branch down to the ground. He pulled it toward him, and then released his rope. Then he turned our way.

"Well, not there. The horse isn't over there. I'm surprised that didn't start that horse whining. Where are the tracks going? Don't make me get down off this horse. Where …"

And then his rope was flying through the air — in front of him this time. He caught another branch.

"I keep catching branches, but no horses. I smell that horse. I smell it. It's hiding around here somewhere."

This time he caught a bigger branch and pulled it toward him.

"Not here. No, no, not here.

"But I'll just keep on going until I find that horse. And that horse will be sorry.

"Where are the tracks?"

He unleashed his rope right next to the feet of one of the men.

"Find that horse."

The dirt around the man's feet made dust from the rope.

And I knew we had to get out of there as soon as possible.

And Magdelena knew it too because she reached for my hand and started moving.

I knew we had to go. I wanted very much to hold Magdelena's hand, but I was very, very terrified because we might make a sound, and they might hear us.

But I had to follow Magdelena.

And I had to be as quiet as I could because I knew, I knew Magdelena would be very, very quiet.

We tiptoed, and I hoped Magdelena knew what she was doing and where she was going because I didn't; I didn't know.

But I did know, I knew very, very well, that at any moment that rope would fly our way.

And then it did.

I heard it.

I heard the tree branch break. It had to be a bigger branch this time because it started cracking and breaking, and as it did, Magdelena started running. I followed her. While the branch was breaking and making all those sounds, we ran so no one would hear us. They wouldn't know the branches we stepped on from the ones being pulled by Pepe's rope.

And right where we had been just moments before — right there where we had just been, that's where the branch came crashing down.

I turned around just to see, but Magdelena pulled me, and I followed her.

"I know that horse was there. I know it was. Get over there. I know it was. Let me try here," yelled Pepe.

And I knew, I knew the rope went flying again, but we were further away now.

And when I looked up to where we had run, I saw that Magdelena had led us back to — The Closet.

I hoped Magdelena knew what she was doing. I didn't remember the directions, and I didn't know that it was a good idea to go back in there.

What was in there, really? I know we saw the glittering, and they talked about *him*, but would we get back to that spot? And so what if we did? So what if …

"Magdelena, why are we going back in here?" I whispered to her.

"We have to see what's back there. What's back there is very important to them," she said.

"But we have to get back to the school and to Rojo Anita, Don Pedro, Ramon, and maybe Manuel. And we have to find Tio. And … Magdelena, do you know the directions, because I don't. I don't remember most of them."

We were far enough away from Pepe, but really we weren't very, very far. We heard another branch fall. And then I realized, I realized that Pepe might figure out that 'the horse' headed back for The Closet. And I must have been right about that because, all of a sudden, I heard it clearly. And I knew Magdelena heard it clearly too: the hooves; they were coming.

"Coyitito, I know you said you don't remember this, but do you have any recollection at all if we turn left here, go straight or turn right? I believe we turn right, but I just want to check with you and see what you think."

Didn't Magdelena hear how close the hooves were?!

"Magdelena, Magdelena. The horses! The horses! Turn right. I believe it is right. Perhaps we should go the other way and throw them off."

"Coyitito, I think it is better to head into the scent, if that is what they are following, than away from it. Perhaps we are still giving off the scent, and if we don't go the way we came, they will find us right away. Do you think we turn right again?"

The hooves were getting closer and closer.

At any moment, the hooves would enter The Closet. Pepe knew the turns. In just a few moments, they would be here.

"Turn right, Magdelena. Turn right!"

I was very, very nervous.

"Are you sure?"

I knew Magdelena was nervous too.

We started running.

Perhaps if we could get to The Closet, we could hide there. We could hide in the darkness. But we were far from there, and the hooves were close.

The sound of the horses' hooves was inside now. I knew the horses were inside. I knew if we left the path we were on, we would be lost forever. And Magdelena was right. Keep going into the scent. Go into the scent.

And now they were just a few turns behind us.

"Turn left, Magdelena.

"Magdelena, should we leave the trail we are on? Should we … Magdelena!"

The horses were behind us.

I pulled Magdelena's hand.

They were right behind us.

I wondered if Pepe would use his rope. I wondered if he would pull Magdelena. I couldn't bear it.

And then I heard the rope above our heads.

I pulled Magdelena off the trail.

And just as I did so, the horses ran past us. They ran right by.

I thought we had a chance. I wondered if we should turn around and head back the way we came when, all of a sudden, the horses stopped moving. The galloping stopped, and it was quiet.

They knew we were there.

I pulled Magdelena when I heard him.

"Don't go in there. Don't go in there.

Come back out here. Hurry. Come back out."

I looked at Magdelena. My eyes were wide. She pulled my hand.

We ran.

Sitting high on his horse, right there, right in front of us, was Tio. And Padre Miguel II. And next to them, riding alongside them, was Senorita Duende.

"Tio. Tio!" Magdelena was so excited to see him.

"Tio!" I was, too.

"Senorita Duende," we both said, and we went over to her.

"I am so glad to see all of you," Magdelena said.

"And you are well, Tio? You are fine?" she asked him.

He nodded. "You?" he asked us.

And we said that we were; we said that we were fine and that we must hurry.

The No Faces were nearby, and we had to get back to the woods, but we also wanted to tell Tio about The Closet and ask him how he came here and where he found our horses, but Tio said,

"Hurry. We must go into The Closet and get back as soon as possible."

I wanted to ask Tio what he knew about The Closet and how he found us, but I knew that we did have to hurry, so Magdelena and I greeted Padre Miguel II, hopped onto the back of Senorita Duende, and started to ride.

I was sure glad to see her.

And to see Tio with Padre Miguel II.

And I wondered why Tio had let the rope fly when he saw us, and I asked him. I said, "Tio, why did you let the rope fly?" I thought that maybe, just maybe, Tio wasn't himself, really. Maybe we couldn't trust him as Tio. Maybe, just maybe, he was a No Face, and he would take us further into the maze, and then we would be trapped. Maybe.

And Tio said, "I didn't know if I could trust you. I didn't know if you were you, or maybe you were No Faces, and you would overtake me. But when you ran, I thought that it must be you because why would the No Faces run? The No Faces, they don't run in fear."

And I agreed. So did Magdelena. And I thought that maybe, and probably, Tio was Tio, and we were all who we were for the moment.

Being horses might have saved us from them.

But I kept an eye on Tio anyway because I wasn't sure how he knew about The Closet, or how he escaped from the others.

Then Magdelena asked him. She said,

"Tio, how did you know about The Closet, and how did you escape from the others?"

"First let us hurry to The Closet. We have to hurry there and back."

Then Tio turned right. Left. We followed him. Either he knew the directions, or he was taking us somewhere else. But I knew Magdelena must know the directions too, and I think I knew them better than I thought, and there we were outside The Closet when Tio stopped.

"Have you been inside yet?" he asked us.

We both shook our heads up and down.

"So you saw *him* then. When you were inside, you saw *him*?"

"Saw whom? Whom do you think we saw, Tio?" Magdelena asked.

But Tio had already entered, and we followed him to where it grew dark, and the glittering glittered.

Magdelena reached underneath her hair and took out her comb. A glow of light lit up the darkness.

"So those are the ones," Tio said. "Look, look at them. Those are the eyes and other pieces they steal."

"The eyes and other pieces?"

"They borrow the Faces; they take eyes. You know, like they took mine and Rojo Anita's. They took our eyes. Our right eyes. But somehow the No Faces are getting stronger. Somehow. They don't even know how, but they are. Remember how they took part of Ramon's face? They took more than just his eyes. And when it came to Padre Miguel, they took all of him. Not just his eye or his face, but they took all of him. Every piece of him, and that is why he is in the Cave of the Departed.

"But when I rode with them, they talked about The Closet. I will tell you, but we must do this. We must do this and then go.

"They store the pieces they take inside The Closets. This one is here. There are other Closets inside the canyons. This is one of the most important to them because of its location. Some powerful faces are kept in here.

"The man, Carlos, he talked all about it. He kept talking about it, going over the directions again and again in case anything happened. He wanted the others to know the way into the maze. He said there are guards inside, but sometimes they leave or go explore the maze. He said sometimes even the guards get lost coming back because it is so, so exact. That is what he said. Exact. And because of that, sometimes there are no guards.

"But I listened to the directions. I remembered and remembered. I put the turns in my mind." Tio was still talking; I was amazed that he said so much, and I knew Magdelena was, too.

"And then Carlos started to be heavy on my back. And then I knew; I knew I was becoming Tio, and I had to do something fast because Carlos was becoming very heavy.

"So he kept on talking to the others; he never stopped talking, even when they weren't listening. They rode in front of him, so I kept moving slower and slower. He didn't notice at first because he kept talking and talking. And then the others were ahead, then more ahead, and when I couldn't see them, that is when I think he started to notice.

"He said, 'Hey' and kicked his heels into my sides. And I did what horses do. It was a bit hard for me because I was more Tio than I thought, but I had enough horse in me to act fast, so I threw myself onto my hind legs. One of my legs was much more Tio than horse, but it worked.

"He slid down my back before he could grab my neck. He was on the ground, and I was running as fast as I could. I heard him screaming at me to come back, and he was yelling for the others to come to him, but I was still fast enough without his weight on me. And I ran fast through the trees until I was running as Tio. Soon I was no longer a horse; I was Tio running through the trees.

"And then I heard them coming after me. I knew they would find me, but I kept running anyway. I wanted to find a place to hide. I kept running and running, and they kept following me. So I said to myself, I said, 'Tio, stop running. Go find a hiding place,' and I did. I saw a spot where I thought I could squeeze. But then I thought that they would see the same spot. So I stopped running and noticed a hole in one of the trees. I ran toward the tree and started climbing up toward the hole when I heard them right behind me. So I hid behind the tree. I knew it was not a good place for me to hide, but that was all I could do.

"They stopped right next to the tree. I didn't know how they knew I was right there, but they did."

I, Coyitito, listened to Tio and wanted to tell him how it seemed that they could smell the scent of the horses, but I didn't want to interrupt him, and we needed to go. We really, really needed to hurry, and I didn't know why we were here anyway, and I guess Tio really needed to talk because he was really talking. It wasn't often that Tio talked, so I didn't want to interrupt him, but I thought about how Pepe and the others could come back at any moment, and how there were guards some-where; somewhere in this maze, guards roamed about on their horses.

"We need to go," I was going to say. But Tio continued talking, so I listened like Magdelena did. She listened to Tio with every piece of her. All of her listened to him, so I did what she did. I went back into Tio's story. And he said,

"I waited. They sent their horses first. I listened to the horses snort and come closer to the tree. At one point the horses were so close to the other side of the tree, I felt them. You know how they get after we ride them? They sweat and they have the way they smell, so I was on the other side of the tree, and their smell was so strong from running, I smelled them. Then one of their noses bent around the tree and hit my shoulder. I knew this was it.

"And I turned my head.

"Padre Miguel II was staring into my eyes, and on the other side of him, stood Senorita Duende.

"I touched both of their noses, jumped onto Padre Miguel II, and rode the way to The Closet. I didn't know I would find you here, but I'm sure Senorita Duende knew I would. She was coming this way with or without me."

And then, as Tio finished his story, we heard it.

From deep in the darkness, we heard the sounds. From back behind the trees in the pitch black night, someone was coming. Magdelena hid her comb behind her hair. The glittering eyes watched us.

The darkness grabbed us. I couldn't see. Magdelena held my hand as she walked slowly. I held onto her. It was so dark.

And we heard them. I knew we all heard them. It was more than one. They were trying to creep along quietly, and I knew, I knew very, very clearly that soon they would grab us and take us. I knew that they were the guards and they knew The Closet.

I shuddered.

We inched our way into the darkness as they crept toward us.

"Magdelena."

"Coyitito, shhh."

That was all she said.

I looked up. Glittering orbs peered from behind the trees. They scared me as we moved closer to them. Were they the guards who watch over The Closet? Were they the ones who were coming to get us?

Everything went quiet. All sounds stopped. We stood in the darkness. It seemed to be breathing with me, heavy. I held tightly onto Magdelena's hand.

Then — whoosh.

Something came my way. Someone grabbed me, put something over my mouth, and wrapped me in rope. I was captured. I tried to yell to Magdelena, but I couldn't. They tossed me onto a horse. Someone climbed behind me. I tried to move, to yell. Where was Magdelena? 'Tio, where are you?' Where was Senorita Duende? They started to ride me into the darkness, further and further, and then the voice said, "Get him." And I knew they had taken Tio. He had probably tried to run like Tio does, but they said, "Get him," and I'm sure they did.

I listened deeply for Magdelena. Any sound from Magdelena would let me know she was with me. But I didn't hear anything. Maybe they had left her back in The Closet. Maybe they had left her there. Maybe they didn't know about Magdelena, or maybe they did, and they took her another way.

I needed to get free. I tried to, but I couldn't move at all. I think my eyes were open, but I really couldn't see anything — only darkness.

Then, then I heard other hooves, others. I heard them coming from a different direction. And then we started moving — fast. Very fast. I felt the night on my eyes as we moved. I had to close them for they burned with the speed.

Behind us, from where we had come, I heard laughter. Men were laughing loudly, and the hooves hit the ground.

Were they coming toward us? With us? How could anyone see? How did this No Face I was riding with see? Maybe the horses did the seeing for them, too.

I remember asking Magdelena, "How do the horses see? When they are riding at night, how do they see, Magdelena?"

And she told me, she said, "Coyitito, the horses don't use their eyes to see. They see with their noses. They smell danger. They sniff out the trail. They see with their ears, listening to the way the branches lift in the breeze, the way the ground changes under their hooves. Their strong bodies are their eyes.

"And they see with the spirits of the ancestors, Coyitito. The ones who came before them guide them at night on the canyon trails."

I, Coyitito, I wondered who was guiding us now.

And then, up ahead of me, over in the distance, I saw something else. It was faint, but I knew it was there. Up ahead of me, not far, coming my way was light; light was coming. Finally, I would be able to see.

And then, just like that, my sight was wiped away. A cloth was tied around my eyes, so I couldn't see; I couldn't see at all unless I started to see like the horses.

But I couldn't see like the horses. I could only see like Coyitito.

But then I thought of Maestra Maria, and how she would tell us, all of us, to close our eyes. And we would pay attention with our eyes closed. We would listen and practice paying attention to our other senses with our eyes closed.

And I remembered listening in the classroom. And then, when I closed my eyes, the sounds changed. I opened my eyes immediately, but Maestra Maria whispered, "Close your eyes," and I didn't know if it was just me, or if all of us opened our eyes at the same time when we heard the sounds change.

At the moment, I had no choice but to keep my eyes from seeing, And the thought of Maestra Maria made me want to burst free and go to her, save her and the others from the danger she was in at the school.

I turned my head, wanting to find Magdelena and Tio, wanting our horses to guide me. I couldn't move my body, but my head could turn. Then I realized if I listened, I could hear. So I did. I listened, and I knew there were several horses. I couldn't tell how many, but I knew there was the one I rode. How did I ride?

Someone was behind me, and I sat in front of him. Or her? Maybe it was a her. How big was he or she? How rough?

I turned my head to the side.

Yes, I heard another horse. And another. And maybe another. Then I heard the horses snorting. Then I heard one of them snort. Only one horse I knew snorted like that: Padre Miguel II. So Padre Miguel II was with us. I listened for Senorita Duende, but she was usually quiet, very, very quiet.

Was Magdelena with us? I turned my head the other way when, all of a sudden, we bolted. We had been running along, but all of a sudden, just like that, we shot so fast I fell back against the rider.

I heard the rider whisper fiercely, "Go. Go." And I knew, oh, I knew we were being chased. "Please let them catch us and rescue us from these who hold us captive."

We were galloping — strong and fierce. I couldn't see, but I knew the dust was gathering up around us from the horses kicking their hooves into the dirt, lifting and speeding. It was as if we were flying, but I knew how the hooves hit the ground and stirred it; I had been a horse not too long ago.

"Here. Here," he said. It was a him I could tell from when he said, "Go."

I felt a sharp turn. And then I noticed it. I could feel it. The air was different. We must have gone under the tree cover. Or into the canyon rocks.

And then we ran even faster.

I heard the horse I was riding breathing heavy. I heard the other riders. Where were the ones chasing us?

And then — just like that — we stopped riding. The one behind me said, "Is he there? Is he still there?" No one answered.

The rider jumped down off the horse. I sat alone. I couldn't move, but I could whisper into the horse's ear, and I knew he would listen. My mouth was covered, but I would try. I leaned my tight body as close to his ear as I could, and then I heard her.

"Do not leave, Coyitito. Do not go anywhere."

I froze.

It sounded just like her.

"Shhh."

He got back onto the horse. We sped away.

I heard her in my head: "Do not leave, Coyitito; do not go anywhere." It had to be her. No one spoke like that. No one said my name like that. No one.

And then we stopped moving.

I heard the horses gather.

"Take these covers from my face; take them. Take this rope from me," I thought.

When we stopped moving, the horses' heavy breathing filled my ears.

And we walked, then slowly. Very, very slowly.

I listened to hear her voice again.

"Take him down and put him here."

"Will this work?"

"I do not know."

Other voices arrived.

"Were you followed?"

"Is that him? Look — is that him? Give him to me. Let me guide him."

"Will this work?"

"I told you I don't know. We have never done this before. But in my dream, she said, 'I will guide you there. Then open The Closet door, and find him among the eyes in the trees. Then take him to The River; take him to The River you know so well, and guide him into her waters, and see if he fills up with himself again.' So — here we are."

I knew Rojo Anita was one of the ones talking. She wanted to guide him into The River. I started shouting in my mind, "Rojo Anita! Rojo Anita. Free me. I can't see or move. Rojo Anita, I can't see or move. Free me! Free me! It is I, Coyitito, Rojo Anita."

"I hear you, Coyitito. Wait a moment. You must wait."

And I knew I had to wait, so I decided to test out if I could see like a horse.

I listened as one of the horses was led to the water.

"Come here. Come with me," she said. It was not Rojo Anita; it was the other one.

"Come. Come here with me."

Then I heard her enter the water.

"Come with me."

And it sounded like the horse followed her.

Then Rojo Anita said,

"Let him drift."

And I guess they let him drift.

Now I wanted to know where Magdelena and Tio were, so I started shouting in my mind.

"Rojo Anita. Rojo Anita. Where are Magdelena and Tio? Rojo Anita. We need to get to the school. Rojo Anita! Rojo Anita!"

And just then, just at that moment, someone untied the cloth from my eyes and mouth, and then untied the rope that bound me. I could see! And speak! And move!

And all in a flash — all in a sudden flash, I saw Magdelena and Tio and Rojo Anita … and then I saw her. There she was. She had swum out, so her head and shoulders were out of the water. Her arms were guiding one of the horses.

"Maestra Maria! Maestra Maria." I wanted to yell, to shout her name. "Maestra Maria!"

But I just watched as she led the horse to the middle of The River.

And then I saw him: the body of Padre Miguel was draped over Tio's horse, Padre Miguel II.

Coming from behind me, a footstep broke my vision for a moment. I looked down into the face of Don Pedro. He looked up at me.

"Don Pedro, what is happening?"

I jumped off the horse I had been riding. Don Pedro caught me. He knew the sight of Padre Miguel was vicious on my eyes and heart. He caught me, lifted me down. I ran to Magdelena, to Tio. Magdelena stood holding Tio's hand. She reached for mine — and the three of us, Magdelena, Tio, and I, stood at the edge of our dear friend, The River, and watched Maestra Maria lead Padre Miguel II into deeper water. We watched the body of Padre Miguel, which was draped over his namesake. They moved toward Rojo Anita, who was waiting for them in the deep water.

"Coyitito. Magdelena. Tio. Dive. Go up on the rocks and dive down here. Right here. Come to this place when you come up," said Rojo Anita.

Tio was swimming across The River in a moment. Magdelena and I were right behind him. We swam quickly across, climbed the rocks just as quickly, and stood at the edge on the cliff high above.

I looked down below us.

Across The River, Don Pedro was talking to ... Don Pedro.

"Magdelena. Tio. Look. Look. Don Pedro is talking to himself. How can this be? Maybe ..."

"Three!" Tio counted. And he and Magdelena leapt from the rock. I was just a second behind them flying through the air, heading toward Rojo Anita, Maestra Maria, and Padre Miguel.

And then I hit the water.

And I kept going into The River's depth like we always did when we dove. And then I started swimming toward the place where Rojo Anita asked us to join Padre Miguel. I didn't know why she asked us, but I'm sure she had her reasons. So I swam toward them.

Then all of a sudden, as I was swimming, I was pulled down and deeper down.

I looked up above me. I saw Magdelena's legs kicking through the water. She seemed to lie on the surface. And Tio swam next to her. The legs of Padre Miguel II, Maestra Maria, and Rojo Anita moved as they kept their keepers afloat, treading water. Padre Miguel's legs lay motionless above me, and I was sucked down.

Then I heard the voice. Unmistakable. The shrill sound of her sent chills along me.

"Girls. GIRLS. GiRLS. Come here. HURry. I mean hurRY. Do. I. Always. HAVE to come and. GeT YOU. Mysself? Hurry means THISSS.

"There. Now YOU are in front of ME where I wanted. YOU. to be.

"BE STILL. Stop that. CHATTER. YOU. YOU over there. COMEHERE."

How did I get here?

I thought I was in the protected area of The River. How did I get to Marleena's cave? I needed to get out of the area quickly, but I couldn't move against the force that pulled me.

"Girls. Kar — o — LEENA. Now I have been given information. THATisveryimportant. YOU must all be on. HIGH ALERT. Every ONE of YOU MUST be more than ALERT.

"YOU. Do YOU know what aLERT. MEANS?"

I heard Marleena's arms reach through the water towards the Girls. I knew she must be reaching for them with her arms, pulling them right up to her face and yelling at them.

"KAR — o — LEENA. ComeHERE.Right.NOW.RightHERE.rightnoWWW."

"I have a SPECIAL job for YOU. I will tell YOU about it inafewmoments. All the GIRLS — YOU are to listen to Kar-o-leena like YOUwouldlisten to ME. No one is ME, except ME, but YOU will all follow the orders of Kar-o-LEENA. I. Will. Give. Her. those orders, and YOU WILL ALL listen to her.

"KAR-o-leena, turn around. Face them. FacetheGirls, so. THEYCANSEEYOU. All OF you — look at Kar-o-leena. LOOK AT HER! You, YOU in the back. YES. YOU. Get up here. Get over HERE NOW! Right here.

"Were you listening to what I was saying? What WAS I saying? WHAT? RE-PEAT what I was saying. What was I ….oooooohhhh. What. Do. WE. HAVE here? What is THISS?"

I knew it.

Marleena knew I was there. I knew one of her giant arms would reach for me. I heard it coming through the water. I heard her call her troops. The sound went out.

"THE INTRUDER IS HERE! HE IS HERE!"

It sounded like she was jumping up and down, snapping her arms in the water.

An arm grabbed me, locked around me.

I closed my eyes.

And when I opened them again, I was face to face with Meme.

"Meme!"

"Coyitito! I have been trying to find you. Where have you been? I've been looking everywhere for you."

"Meme! Meme. I have so much to tell you, but Marleena is coming. Marleena is right out there with all her others and all their arms. Meme!"

"Coyitito, where have you been? I have this for you."

"Meme."

"Stop, Coyitito. You are safe in my kitchen. Now, here. I made this to give to you. You might know someone who would like it."

"What is it, Meme?"

"Pumpa ..."

"Pumpernickel. You made a pumpernickel cookie."

"No, no, not pumpernickel. Pump a something. I don't know, Coyitito. I took some of this from this here jar. I can't even see what it says. But I threw a dash of this in it."

I looked at the jar.

"I only could make one, Coyitito, because that's all that was in there. The jar is empty. So I made this one cookie and knew I had to give it to you. Here."

I looked at Meme's empty jar. It read "Breath." Breath. "Pump a breath, Meme?" But Meme was gone. And I was back in the water with a cookie in a tin, and Marleena and the others were close enough.

I swam. I wasn't sure which way to go, but I swam the way I thought. I listened for the sounds of Marleena and her arms, but the sounds didn't come. I didn't hear her shrill voice.

I knew at any moment she could use one of her arms or ropes to fetch me and bring me right up to her face like she did with the Girls, so I kept swimming.

And then I saw them above me: I saw the legs of Magdelena, Tio, Padre Miguel II, Rojo Anita, Maestra Maria, and Padre Miguel's limp legs hanging in the water.

I swam as fast as I could — up to them. I lifted my head out of the water, gasping for breath.

"Coyitito, where have you been?" Magdelena asked. "Coyitito, we need you to complete the circle. Padre Miguel hasn't stirred; he hasn't come back. We need you."

I looked at Padre Miguel lying on Padre Miguel II's back. I looked at Tio, who seemed so sad. Rojo Anita stared at me when I turned her way, and Maestra Maria, oh, Maestra Maria watched Padre Miguel so intensely. I knew she was waiting for him to move.

And then I knew what to do. I reached for the tin Meme had given me, opened it, took out the cookie, and crumbled it inside my hand. I moved to Padre Miguel, nodded to Tio as I lifted myself onto the horse's back, opened Padre Miguel's mouth, and dropped the pieces inside. Everyone was quiet. We waited.

Suddenly, Padre Miguel sat up.

"Ummmm ... this tastes wonderful," he said. I watched Padre Miguel; then, I looked at Tio who was wide-eyed.

"What is this? It has the taste of pumpernickel, which I love. But there is something else. Something I can't quite detect.

"Tio, do you know what this is?"

Tio stared at Padre Miguel and shook his head no.

I wanted to tell Padre Miguel that I dove from The River with Magdelena and Tio, and we all dove at the count of three. And when I was in the water, I was pulled by a force, and then I heard Marleena, and then Meme pulled me inside her kitchen and gave me this cookie, which was pumpernickel, and now here we were. And he was back and …

But Maestra Maria stopped my thoughts when she spoke.

She said,

"Padre Miguel, welcome back. We are so grateful that you have returned."

"Returned? What do you mean returned? Where have I been?"

He looked at each one of us.

"Tio, have I been somewhere?"

Tio nodded his head yes.

"Well," said Padre Miguel. "Well, where was I?"

I guess he didn't remember.

"We will tell you in due time, Padre Miguel," said Maestra Maria.

"But now we must go," she continued. "My sister and the others at the school are in grave danger."

Her sister? Did Maestra Maria just say she had a sister at the school? If she did, her sister at the school looked exactly like her. If this was not Maestra Maria, then who was this?

Was this the one I had seen riding among the trees, the one whose hair hung down her back — the one who rode with another who shared her horse?

Who was this?

"This is Raina," said Rojo Anita. "Maria's twin sister. She rides with Don Luis — Don Pedro's twin brother."

Rojo Anita sometimes needed to keep some things private. I thought all my thoughts quickly, so Rojo Anita couldn't read them, but when I looked at her, she was smiling at me.

Raina. She looked just like, I mean exactly like, Maestra Maria.

"What do you mean they are in grave danger?" Padre Miguel asked.

"We turned into horses, Padre Miguel," Tio told him. "I was one horse, and Magdelena and Coyitito were another horse. We went to the school as horses. The No Faces are there. We found out if you look in the mirror, you can see the part they've stolen. Sometimes it's an eye. That happened to Rojo Anita, Ramon, and me. But sometimes they've stolen more.

"And sometimes, they take over a person completely; they take the whole person. Like with you, Padre Miguel. Do you remember we met with you in the Cave of the Departed, and you taught me the lasso?

"Then they place what they've stolen from the others; they put the pieces in The Closet. And when we were horses, we found out about The Closet. Then we went back to The Closet, and Raina and Don Luis came, too, only we didn't know that. They came to get you, too, and we were there, so they took us here. And that's why we're all here, Padre Miguel."

I looked at Magdelena, who looked at me. Sometimes Tio would get these bursts and talk like this. It amazed me.

Padre Miguel moved towards Tio. When he was close, he reached for Tio's hand, and we all followed them out of the water.

"Are you any good with the rope?" Padre Miguel asked Tio.

Tio nodded.

Yes, it seemed that Padre Miguel had forgotten.

"You ride with me, Padre Miguel," he said.

Padre Miguel sat behind Tio on Padre Miguel II; Rojo Anita rode Senorita; we rode Senorita Duende, Don Pedro joined us, and Raina and Don Luis rode the horse whose name was Hummingbird.

"Where are we going?" asked a voice behind us.

We all turned. Ramon, Solamente, Manuel and Ochenta caught up to us.

"Where are we going?" Ramon asked with a smile on his face.

Were they who they seemed to be?

"Follow us," said Padre Miguel and waved his hand for Ramon to follow. I guess Padre Miguel thought so. How did he know?

And we did. We followed Tio, Padre Miguel, and Padre Miguel II through the trees. We walked slowly in single file. Every once in a while, the horses behind us would stop. Everyone was behind us except for Tio and the Padre Miguels. I kept wondering if we could trust each other.

Then Tio's horse stopped moving. We all stood still.

From somewhere further out, we heard the thunder of hooves. Many, many horses were pounding on the ground. How many?

"Magdelena, how many horses does that sound like?" I whispered.

She shrugged her shoulders, listening.

I wanted to yell, "How come we are not moving? Why are we standing here?"

And then all of a sudden, Tio started disappearing along with Padre Miguel and Padre Miguel II.

"Tio!" I couldn't stop myself. I didn't know what was happening.

"Tio!"

But then I saw that Senorita Duende moved forward following Tio and the others. Right in front of me — directly in front of me — they were gone, but we kept heading where they had just been.

And then I knew what had happened.

We were inside an underground tunnel. I would never have known it was there. But Padre Miguel knew.

Right inside the trees, where we were moments ago, a stampede was coming.

I don't know from where the tunnel came; I never saw it appear, but somehow it did.

I wanted to ask Tio what happened, how we moved from the trees to where we were now, but I didn't because it was very quiet, and it was very dark, very, very dark. I only knew it was a tunnel by the way it felt and by the way Senorita Duende was traveling. We were heading downhill.

I listened to see if the others were behind us, and I heard them. I heard them coming.

Then Senorita Duende stopped moving.

I heard sounds in front of us.

I wanted to call out, "Padre Miguel. Tio," but I didn't. I sat in the darkness on the back of Senorita Duende behind Magdelena.

Then the tunnel lit up.

Standing in front of us, Padre Miguel held up a glowing lantern, and when he did, I saw there were other lanterns.

"Is everyone here?" he asked.

"Rojo Anita, are you here?"

"Yes," she said.

"Ramon, are you here? I heard you join us with Manuel."

"Yes, Padre Miguel, I am here. I am happy to see you."

"Hello, Padre Miguel. I am here. Shall we dance?" Manuel said.

The situation did not call for dancing. What about Manuel?

"Raina. Don Luis. Are you here?"

"Yes, we are here."

"Don Pedro?"

"Yes, Padre Miguel."

"Magdelena?"

"I am here."

"Coyitito?"

Why was he asking when he was right there in front of me?

"Coyitito?"

"I, Coyitito, I am here." I hoped we had somehow disguised the scent of the horses.

"Tio?"

Tio nodded.

"And you?"

Who was he talking to?

"You?"

From the back of the line, someone approached.

"Are you alone?"

No answer.

Someone had followed us.

Was it one person? Did they leave a signal for the others? Was it someone dangerous?

"It is I, Padre Miguel. Lucinda."

Lucinda! I hadn't seen Lucinda since we left the school. Lucinda! What was she doing here?

"Lucinda," Padre Miguel said.

"What are you doing here?" he continued.

I felt the others behind me take hold of whatever each of them takes hold of when they ready for something.

"Don't worry about Lucinda," I thought.

But I knew better than that.

I had been to The Closet.

How would we know if she was really Lucinda?

"Are you all right, Lucinda?" Padre Miguel asked.

And then, all of a sudden, Magdelena slipped off Senorita Duende and moved toward Lucinda.

"Lucinda! I have missed you so.

Will you come down and hug me?"

Lucinda came down off her horse and moved to Magdelena with open arms. They hugged each other tightly.

Then Magdelena said,

"I have been given a most beautiful gift, Lucinda."

And she took her mirror from its pouch.

"Here. Look inside with me," she said.

Magdelena held her mirror up, and she and Lucinda looked inside. I saw Magdelena's eyes search Lucinda's face.

Just as Lucinda opened her mouth, Magdelena grabbed her cloth and tied it around Lucinda, preventing the scream from escaping. Magdelena amazed me by doing this.

"I am sorry, Lucinda," she said.

Tio was quick.

His rope flew through the air. He caught Lucinda inside it.

She tried to free herself. She moved until the tight rope stopped her.

"Lucinda, I know a part of you is still yourself. You are still yourself. Did anyone follow you?"

But Lucinda wouldn't answer. She looked into the eyes of Padre Miguel with her own eyes, and he knew from the sight of her that she would never tell.

I looked at Lucinda. What part of her was missing? Tio, Ramon, and Rojo Anita found their own parts before they were moved to The Closet. Some of these No Faces were getting lazy — losing the stolen parts on the way to The Closet. If we knew where Lucinda's lost parts were, perhaps we could bring her back.

"What part is missing from Lucinda's face?" I asked Magdelena. "Which piece is missing?"

"Her eyes," Magdelena said.

Her eyes.

"What if we blindfold her?" I asked Magdelena. "Do you think if we blindfold her, maybe she can talk to us as herself?"

"Maybe, Coyitito, but I don't see why that would matter."

"Because if we blindfold her, maybe we can somehow deceive the eyes she now wears, Magdelena. Maybe we can trick them."

I moved toward Lucinda. I pulled a cloth from my pocket.

"I'm sorry, Lucinda. I don't want to do this. I'm only doing it so maybe we can trick the eyes you see with into losing what they see, and then you can be more of yourself, and you can tell us what is happening."

I placed the blindfold around Lucinda's eyes.

"It can be difficult to read a No Face," Rojo Anita said.

"But in order for us to see if what you are trying to do works, in the event that I can't read her, we will need to free Lucinda's mouth, and if we do that, she may scream, or the others may come.

"Wait! Wait," Rojo Anita continued. "Wait! I hear Lucinda coming through in my mind. I hear her.

"I don't know if what she is thinking is true or not, but I can tell you what she thinks now.

"Lucinda, I am going to tell the others what you are thinking.

"Walking through the courtyard, Lucinda saw a group of men huddled in the corner talking. She pretended she didn't see them, but they knew; they knew she did. She kept walking. They didn't follow her, but she felt something, as if they followed her with their eyes.

"All of a sudden, a strong, strong wind whipped up around her. And she smelled something; the scent was dangerous and disgusting. For some small time, she couldn't see.

"Then she started fighting with herself when she saw some of the others in the courtyard. She wanted to go over and push them. She didn't know what was happening, so she started to run. And she ran to the back of the school where the students do not often go."

Padre Miguel nodded his head.

"She stayed there for a very long time," Rojo Anita continued. "It grew dark. Then she heard the noises. She knew horses were coming. She knew many horses were coming.

"Then the men came.

"They didn't see her.

"They gathered under the dark sky. Then Padre Miguel came. She wanted to cry out to him."

All of a sudden, Lucinda started moving about the best she could. Something was wrong inside; something was happening.

"It is all right, Lucinda. It is fine," said Rojo Anita.

Rojo Anita looked at all of us.

She said, "Lucinda thinks we should all look in the mirror. The last time she saw Padre Miguel, she believes he was a No Face, and she thinks we should all check now to make sure none of us has been taken over. She apologizes."

I looked at Rojo Anita. No one wanted to look in the mirror.

"Lucinda thinks that Magdelena should look inside the glass with each of us."

"And who should look with Magdelena?" I thought.

"You ought to do that, Coyitito" said Rojo Anita.

.

I waited to see what would happen. Was Manuel really Manuel?

We all had our own faces. I was relieved about that.

"Lucinda, how did you get down here in this secret tunnel?" Tio asked her. I had thought about it, but there was so much going on, so I didn't say anything. But Tio did. Tio asked her. Sometimes he would do something like that: tell a whole story, or ask a question, or throw a rope.

Lucinda thought her answer, and Rojo Anita said that Lucinda said she really didn't know. She was out in the grove in the back of the school. When night came, she ran across the yard and entered the grove. She thought no one saw her go there, because no one found her there.

And she was very, very upset. She was struggling with two sets of feelings: one belonged to Lucinda herself, and the other belonged to the No Face that had taken her eyes.

"Can everyone stop thinking for the moment, so I can concentrate on Lucinda's mind.

"Stop thinking. Focus," Rojo Anita said.

I think we all tried our best because, all of a sudden, Rojo Anita said that Lucinda had been leaning up against a tree all night long. She was terrified and brave. She was scared and courageous. But she did cry, and she did say, 'Help me, please. Help me be safe.' And then the tree she leaned against opened. A door opened inside the trunk, and a staircase appeared. Lucinda entered, and here she is."

"Lucinda luckily found the Tree Who Hears Our Needs," said Padre Miguel. "That is one way to enter the tunnel. If we are in earnest need, and we ask for help outside the Tree Who Hears Our Needs, then the Tree will open us to safety.

"Not everyone can do that — open the tree, especially when one is part No Face. But your need must have been greater than the part trying to take you over, Lucinda, because here you are," Padre Miguel said softly.

"Lucinda says that we must hurry, Padre Miguel," said Rojo Anita, who was speaking for Lucinda.

"Lucinda says that the Petition Feast will probably be starting soon. The guests will all be in the yard. All of them will bring food for the feast, asking for the safe return of the ones who are missing. The people will gather and not know that outside the gates, the No Faces will come in large numbers. They will come down the canyon trail, and they will come from all directions.

"The gates of the school will be closed. At first, no one will see the No Faces as they surround the school because, as you know, the school is surrounded by high cement walls all around — except at the gate. The walls are higher than the No Faces on their horses, so they will remain unseen.

"Then, when all the guests are gathered at the tables ready to offer the foods they have all brought to share, the bell will ring three times. After the third ring, the gates will be opened, and the No Faces will enter the schoolyard. They will gather the people. Each No Face will take one or two, however many people they need to take, until everyone is gone. The school will be barren, empty, and the No Faces will take the people to wherever it is they take people, and everyone will be gone."

"Why do they need to take the people when they can just take parts of them instead?" Tio asked Lucinda.

"Lucinda is not completely certain, Tio," said Rojo Anita, "but she did hear a conversation when she was hiding earlier — before she went to the grove.

"They were saying that as they became more powerful, they wanted to overtake the whole person, not just pieces. If they took the whole person, then the Stolen One would not waver back and forth between good intentions and intentions that are not good. The Big One, the One who must have become Padre Miguel, said that it wasn't easy to take over Padre Miguel. It took many of them. He said they didn't have the kind of time it took to completely take over the ones with Faces. They want to capture people; they want to frighten people and capture them, and they want to make the captive ones become part of them: the No Faces.

"When I, Lucinda, came down into the tunnel, the sun was up, and everyone was busy with preparations for the feast. I don't know how long I have been down here, but I do believe that we need to hurry."

Padre Miguel acted quickly.

"Follow me," he said. He gave out the lit lanterns, and moved along the underground tunnel. We followed him. Then he came to a stop and said, "Wait here one moment."

He disappeared, and all of a sudden, from the place where he had gone, something was in the air. All of a sudden, something was flying in the darkness above us.

I thought about bats and other winged creatures in the dark, but Padre Miguel said, "Tio, catch." And Tio lifted up his arm while he pulled his other rope from Lucinda. He caught what Padre Miguel threw. It was another rope.

"Coyitito, catch."

I lifted up my arms, watching the rope traveling from the darkness. I caught it.

"Magdelena, this one's for you." Magdelena opened her arms and caught the traveling rope.

Padre Miguel threw each of us a rope, all except for Lucinda.

"I'm sorry, Lucinda, but you are not completely yourself. Raina and Don Luis, you keep Lucinda with you. And for now, please cover her ears."

Padre Miguel continued, "This tunnel leads to several places at the school. One stop is near my office. Behind the back of the school near my office is a solid brick thick wall: some of the bricks move into a word. If you know the pattern, and how the word appears on the word bricks, you can touch it into doing what it says. Some of the bricks spell the word "Open." I know which ones. If you trace the word, a door appears for you to "open".

"Once inside that space, there are a series of small rooms. Each of the rooms opens to another somewhere somehow. Some have doors; some have floorboards. If you know the doors, you can move quickly. Very quickly. I can move quickly through the openings.

"These rooms will lead to a wall outside my office. Several small holes are along the wall. When we get there, I will look in and see what is going on. When and if I can, I will enter my office and act as though I was never gone.

"Rojo Anita, I will bring you with me, keeping you as close as I can, so you can read my thoughts in case they take me. I will send you thoughts until you can no longer hear me. The rest of you will go to another entrance, the one of which Lucinda spoke. You will go through the door of the Tree Who Hears Our Needs.

"Tell the Tree that you need it to open. It will. Once it does, you will be in the grove. Leave the horses inside the tunnel. Tell the Tree that you will need to get back inside, and when you do, the Tree must listen for what you need. If you need your horses, tell the Tree to release them. The Tree gives what is already there.

"Before you get your horses, climb into the trees with your ropes. There are many more No Faces than us.

"But go into the trees with your ropes. Do not do anything; do not make a sound; do not be visible until you hear a signal from me.

"When you hear my signal, throw your ropes.

"Lucinda, how many No Faces are inside the gates?' continued Padre Miguel.

Rojo Anita answered for Lucinda. "She is not sure; many."

"It is best to be prepared for more rather than fewer. And I'm sure that there are many more outside," said Padre Miguel.

"Wait for my signal, and then carefully, staying very focused, start throwing your ropes. We need to protect all the innocent people who have come to the Petition, and the school.

"Good luck."

Start throwing our ropes? What did Padre Miguel think — that we: Tio, Magdelena, Manuel, Ramon, Don Luis, and Maestra Maria, I mean Raina, and I could take care of — catching all these No Faces?

I hoped Padre Miguel had another piece of the plan when he gave his signal.

"Magdelena," Padre Miguel then said. "Walk straight in the tunnel. Just keep going straight. The others will follow you. Do not make any turns; just walk straight and you will reach a staircase. Climb the stairs; tell the Tree you need to go into the grove and that you need the horses to stay where they are.

"Tio, you go out first, very quietly; be very careful, and look around. If you see it is safe, call the others into the grove. Pick your tree and climb. Be as still as you can.

"Rojo Anita and I leave you all here. Coyitito, come with us. Yes, come, come with us. Once we see what is going on in my office, you can run back through the tunnel to the grove and tell the others."

I didn't want to go.

Why me? Why not pick Tio? I wanted to stay with the group inside the tunnel.

Rojo Anita said,

"Coyitito thanks you for picking him for this part, Padre Miguel."

"Yes, Padre Miguel," I said. "Thank you."

I squeezed Magdelena's hand, then Tio's. "I will see you in the grove," I said.

Padre Miguel ascended the stairs. Rojo Anita paused to let me go in front of her.

"Watch what Padre Miguel does," she said.

"Yes, that is what I was thinking," he said. "Watch what I do, Coyitito."

At the top step, he started touching the bricks.

"This one, see, this one has the O. Here. Give me your hand. Feel it. Circle the O with your fingers, Coyitito.

"Now find the P. It is not the next brick. Your fingers need to search. If you do not find it quickly, I will show you."

But I did find it quickly. I searched with my fingers. I don't know if Padre Miguel knew, but I'm sure Rojo Anita was aware that I had closed my eyes.

O.P.

I continued on my own. Padre Miguel was quiet. I'm sure he was watching me, but he let me find my own way. Here is the E. I moved my fingers down the line of the letter and then three lines across.

Now the N. It wasn't as easy to find the N. I searched several bricks, but no N.

"It can't be too easy," Padre Miguel said. "We always take precautions. Move to the right more. Still more. More."

And then I felt the corner of the letter. And I traced it. And when I came to the bottom of the diagonal line, I waited. Nothing happened.

And then slowly the letters unlocked the door, and it opened.

Padre Miguel stepped out first. I waved Rojo Anita on in front of me. I was trying to be the gentleman Maestra Maria had taught me to be. Oh, Maestra Maria! She was now in the hands of these dangerous men. Maestra Maria …

"Focus, Coyitito. Be present here and now," Rojo Anita said.

Somehow I thought that if I thought about Maestra Maria, I could keep her safe.

"But that is not so, Coyitito. Focus here," Rojo Anita reminded me.

I looked at the room where we were. The only person carrying a lantern was Padre Miguel. We had left ours in the tunnel.

Padre Miguel moved the light around a pitch black room. It felt like we were still in the tunnel, but we had come upstairs, so I think we were above ground, although nothing about this room said so.

"There are twelve rooms to go through before we come to the wall outside my office.

"This first room is not complicated. The way into the next room is right over here.

"See, see this panel here? It has a slight, slight indentation on the side. See if you can find it, Coyitito."

I ran my hand along the side of the panel, and there, there it was.

"Pull it open," said Padre Miguel.

I did, and the three of us bent down, walking through the opening in the door into Room Number Two.

"You must remember to close the passageways, Coyitito. Precaution. Always precaution."

I wondered why Padre Miguel trusted Rojo Anita, and then I wished I hadn't because Rojo Anita said,

"And why do you think he trusts you, Coyitito?"

Magdelena's mirror said we were who we were. Padre Miguel really trusted Rojo Anita.

"Find the passage in this room," Padre Miguel said.

In this room — this was a room of rocks.

I wondered if Rojo Anita was searching for the passage.

"I know where it is, Coyitito. I learned it from Padre Miguel's mind," she said.

"Can you teach me how to read minds, Rojo Anita?"

"Focus on what you are doing. That's not the passageway," she said. "You're getting cold. Go the other way."

So I listened to her and went to the other side of room. It didn't make sense to go to the other side of the room, but I did, and Padre Miguel said, "See the smaller stone."

And I did. And I pulled it. And when I pulled the stone, a rock wall slid open on the other side, leading to the next room.

"Is there a stone on the wall that I can pull from the other side to open this room when I come back, Padre Miguel?"

"Do not worry, Coyitito."

I looked around the third room. It was different from the others. Long, silk maroon and gold curtains hung from the windows. Big tassels tied them back.

Behind the windows was another wall. I wasn't sure what to do.

"Open the window," said Rojo Anita, who, I guess, was Padre Miguel's voice.

When I opened the window, a space in the wall appeared.

"Room Number Four," Padre Miguel said. "Room Four is tricky. Keep your mind focused on your task. If you don't, anything could happen."

All right. Keep my mind focused on my task. Keep my mind … I can't find it. I can't see anything in here. It's just a room. What's that? What's that noise? What was that? Was that a shape? "Padre Miguel, Rojo Anita, what is that sound? Where are you? Where did you go? Don't leave me alone in here! Who's that? Who is that? Oh no. How did he get in here? Oh no.

"Padre Miguel. Rojo Anita. Help me. Help." Where are they? Here he comes. Oh no. Here he comes. Here …

"Focus on your task, Coyitito. Think only of your task," said Rojo Anita.

"So you are in here? How come I can't see you? Oh no. He's coming at me. No. … no."

"Focus, Coyitito. Focus. Be present."

"Stand still," I heard Padre Miguel say.

"But Padre Miguel, he is coming; he is coming at me."

"He is in your mind, Coyitito. Room Number Four is the Room of Fears. Whatever you fear will arrive. To get out, all you need to do is cross the room. The door is right across the room. And it's open," said Padre Miguel, whom I now saw, was standing right there, waiting for me with Rojo Anita.

I tried not to think of all my fears because if I did think of them, I would never cross the room.

I stayed focused as best as I could. I think the room was much smaller than I thought, or it became smaller, because "He" went away, and I reached the door. When I turned the knob, Room Number Five appeared.

Immediately, my feet were wet.

"It is a blessing that you know how to swim," said Padre Miguel, and all of a sudden, I was knee deep in water. And moments later, the water was over my head. But I did know how to swim; Padre Miguel and Rojo Anita were very good swimmers also.

I don't know how the room filled with water, but I did know that we swam toward an opening, and when we entered it, we found a door. Room Number Six. Then I remembered that the No Faces didn't know how to swim.

"Precautions," said Rojo Anita.

The door opened, and I saw that Room Number Six was peculiar. A maze was built in the middle of the room. At first, I thought it was simple, so I entered.

Padre Miguel and Rojo Anita were far ahead of me. I followed them, but I never caught up to them. I kept moving in circles or some other shape I didn't know. Time was ticking away. Padre Miguel and Rojo Anita needed to help me.

"The string," Rojo Anita said.

What string? I thought about what Maestra Maria had taught us in Greek Mythology, about Ariadne and the string in the labyrinth. But I didn't see any string.

And then I looked again.

And there it was. It wasn't really very visible, but if you looked like I looked now, there it was: a thin green string on the sides of the maze, right where the ground met the wall. The ground was green and the string was green, but if you looked, you could see that the string was there.

So I followed it.

I followed the green thread to a door, and when I opened it, Padre Miguel and Rojo Anita stood there smiling.

"Room Number Seven," Padre Miguel said.

Room Number Seven.

I saw a door on the other side of Room Number Seven. I tried not to think frightening thoughts, so no one would come at me.

I started to cross the room very, very slowly. Padre Miguel and Rojo Anita were already at the door. Each step I took brought me closer. I started to think that maybe, maybe, after all the other rooms, it was getting easier to cross through the doors.

And just as I had that thought, the floor opened up right in front of me. I tried not to take the next step, but it was too late. I stepped … and I fell into total darkness. I fell, and I fell. I yelled from the bottom of my feet. My stomach left me as I fell.

Where was I going?

I tried to call Maestra Maria. I thought she could help me. "Magdelena, Tio, help me! Help me, please!"

And then I landed. I must have been miles down in the earth — beneath any tunnel. I thought that maybe I landed in Meme's kitchen, but nobody came out to greet me. No one came to help.

Then I saw it: a door. I saw a door, so I got up. Luckily, I wasn't hurt at all. I walked over to the door, turned its handle, but nothing happened. Nothing at all.

I turned the knob right; I turned the knob left. I pulled, I pushed — nothing.

"Padre Miguel," I yelled.

"Use the secret word," Padre Miguel called to me.

Use the secret word? What word? What was the secret word?

And then I felt it on my fingertips. I felt the secret word: OPEN.

"Open," I said.

The door opened. Padre Miguel patted me on the back.

"You are doing a great job, Coyitito."

I thought I would stay really close to them in Room Number Eight. If I followed them closely, I could get through the door with them. But this time, no one moved. They stood still, and Padre Miguel said,

"Your job is to let us all out of this room."

So that was my job; I had to not only free myself from this room, but free Rojo Anita and Padre Miguel.

"You never said the rooms were as difficult as this," I thought. It seemed like when Padre Miguel explained the rooms, they were tricky, but this was not tricky; it was very, very difficult. And the clock was ticking as the Petition was getting underway.

"Yes, Coyitito. The clock is ticking if you think about it," said Rojo Anita.

What was it with Rojo Anita? "Just focus, Coyitito. Be present, Coyitito," she would say.

"I hear you, Coyitito," she said.

I looked around the room. Hundreds of small doors appeared in front of my eyes.

How was I to know? How could I possibly figure out which door opened to the next room: Room Number Nine.

Why did Padre Miguel choose me for this? Magdelena would have been better, or Tio. But not me. I didn't know what to do next.

"Remember, Coyitito. You have almost gotten through eight of the rooms already. You have figured them out," said Rojo Anita.

Yes, with their help I had figured out the rooms. I looked at all the doors again. And then I just closed my eyes. And when I did that, when I closed my eyes, I saw it. One of the doors in the bottom center had a key. When I opened my eyes, it disappeared. So I closed them again. With my eyes closed, I moved toward the door, reached out my hand, and turned the key.

Click.

I waved to Padre Miguel and Rojo Anita, "Come here." We ducked our heads and entered Room Number Nine.

Room Number Nine was a waterfall, a beautiful flowing waterfall from way up in a canyon.

"What was the trick?" I wondered.

I crossed the room.

And then I knew.

Somewhere behind the waterfall was a door. And when I found the door, I would need to find a way to open it — just like before.

So I stood at the bottom of the clear water. Somehow, something in me wanted to know if the water was cold, how it tasted.

The water was cool and fresh.

Where were Padre Miguel and Rojo Anita? They were gone. I seemed to be alone with the water.

I knew that if I could get behind the falls, the door would be there. But the water was coming down strong, and I would get hurt if I crossed under it.

So I waited.

And felt tired.

And wanted to nap.

I reminded myself that on the other side of the walls, the people I knew and loved were in grave danger. I knew Padre Miguel was counting on me; he had chosen me. But I grew so sleepy; so, so sleepy. Maybe it was the water.

"Coyitito, wake up," I told myself.

"Coyitito, wake up."

I sat down.

Then I tilted my body.

I put my head on the ground and closed my eyes.

And then I heard her. She said,

"Coyitito, you must part the waterfall as though it is hair. Make a part in it, like when Maestra Maria makes a part in my hair before she braids it," and then Magdelena disappeared.

So I stood up again, even though I was very tired, and I approached the waterfall. The water was coming down strong, but I took my two hands, and I pushed a small stream; that was all I could handle. I pushed two slim sides from each other as best I could. The water pounded down on my hands, but the water was with me and enough of a tiny seam opened; I could see a door.

So I did it again — as best I could. And it happened. The waterfall parted in front of me, and I went behind it

And yes, Padre Miguel and Rojo Anita were waiting for me.

"You are doing an excellent job, Coyitito. You have entered nine of the twelve rooms. Three quarters of this job are complete.

"And because you have succeeded in nine rooms, which equals three quarters of your job, you may be allowed to use the secret word for the rest of the doors.

"We will try the secret word," said Padre Miguel.

"If it works, as soon as you get to the last room, you must be so, so quiet, for that is when I will look into my office and see what is inside there.

"When I return to my office, you are to return to the others at the grove, and head into the trees."

"How will I get through all the rooms again, Padre Miguel?"

"The rooms will remember you, Coyitito. On the way back, use the secret word, and they will open for you. You have done the work to learn them. They will remember.

"Here. Try."

I stood in front of the next door, which was right in front of me, and I said, "Open." The door slid open. Room Number Ten was just a room.

"Open," into Room Number Eleven.

And then the last room appeared, the one which led to Padre Miguel's office area.

"Open."

Room Number Twelve was white.

Padre Miguel lifted his finger to his lips: the quiet sign. He moved over to a wall. He then motioned for Rojo Anita and me to follow. Tiny dots appeared on the surface of the wall when I looked closer. He leaned peering into the dots. Rojo Anita and I did the same.

There it was! There was Padre Miguel's office. Oh, my heart yearned to be sitting in there with Magdelena and Tio, sharing a cold glass of water or lemonade with Padre Miguel. How I yearned to sit in there with Maestra Maria, hearing her tell us a story.

But at this moment, the office was not a safe place. I don't even think it was safe for Padre Miguel. He turned to me and said, "I'm counting on you, Coyitito." Then he slid open the wall and quietly stepped inside the room, sliding the wall shut behind him.

Counting on me? Why was he counting on me? What was he counting on me to do?

Rojo Anita looked through the dots in the wall, but I knew she heard me because she removed her head from its peering place, put her mouth right next to my ear, and whispered, "You will know, Coyitito."

I couldn't even think to myself.

I will know. I will know what? What will I know?

But my own thoughts were interrupted by sounds on the other side of the wall.

Rojo Anita moved back into her place. I looked through the tiny dots.

Two men entered Padre Miguel's office. He was already seated behind his big brown desk when they stormed into the room. They both looked intensely at him.

"Where were you?" one of them asked him.

You could tell they didn't trust him. There was no way they trusted the man sitting in front of them.

I started to shake inside myself. Padre Miguel was counting on me; counting on me to do what? I glanced at Rojo Anita; she didn't move.

The other man came right up next to the one who questioned Padre Miguel; Padre Miguel hadn't raised his eyes yet. He seemed to be reading a piece of paper.

The other man stood right next to the first one. They seemed to be threatening Padre Miguel, who hadn't moved from his spot.

Then he did. He moved. Only for a second; only long enough to release the rope he had curled at his waist. His arm hardly moved, but his rope did, and within an instant, the two men were closer to each other than they might want to be.

Silence: neither one of them spoke. Padre Miguel never moved from his chair. His eyes were still looking down at the paper he read.

"I believe you were asking me a question," he said into the open air.

"I do believe you were asking me a question concerning my whereabouts. How interesting that you think you can question me. Explain this to me."

Now Padre Miguel stood up, holding the end of the rope tightly in his hand.

"Explain to me in a language I can understand because so far I do not understand; explain to me why you think you have the right to question me."

The man who had asked the question began to speak, but Padre Miguel pulled tighter on the rope; silenced, the man dropped his head.

"I wasn't finished talking. When I am finished, I will let you know. You see, I was reading my paper when suddenly the two of you burst into my office, and you questioned me about my whereabouts. Is that what happened? Is that what happened?"

The two men were afraid to answer. When Padre Miguel tugged on the rope again, they nodded their heads.

"I didn't hear you," he said.

Behind the wall, I was getting very, very nervous. I had never, ever, ever seen Padre Miguel act like this. Perhaps he was a No Face. Perhaps he was the No Face leader. I looked at Rojo Anita, but she did not take her eyes from the wall.

When I looked back, I saw the men in Padre Miguel's grasp, and they faintly answered, "Yes."

"Louder."

"Yes," they answered.

"Are you fools? Do you consider yourselves to be fools? Do you think of yourselves as fools? Answer me. Are.You. Fools?"

"Yes."

"Yes. What?"

"Yes. We are fools," they both said.

Padre Miguel moved back to his desk.

Now he did something else I had never seen or heard him do.

With his free hand, he pounded on his desk. The blood rose up to his face; the veins in his neck popped.

He pounded his hand on his desk and yelled,

"Yes. You. Are. FOOLS. DO. NOT. EVER. QUESTION. ME. Never question me. Do you understand that?"

Both men looked down and said, "Yes."

"I think it is best if you speak at a volume I can appreciate. What do you think? Do you think that is wise?"

"Yes," they both said.

"Which question were you answering yes to?"

"Any question you ask," said the first man who had spoken.

"Any question you ask," repeated the second one.

"Good. Now you two should stay comfortably close to each other for the rest of our conversation. I will be asking the questions.

"You will be giving the answers."

Then he pulled the rope so hard the eyeballs bulged in the sockets of the men.

He went up close, very, very close to their faces.

"You know, it really, really bothers me that you questioned me. I don't think I will be able to forget it.

"Now, back to business; has everyone arrived for the Feast?" he questioned them.

And that is when Rojo Anita reached her arm out to touch my hand. She waved her hand as if to say, "Go." Rojo Anita's eyes never left the wall, but her hand found mine as I backed away from the place where I had watched Padre Miguel become someone I didn't know existed. She squeezed my hand tightly, and I dashed away.

When I arrived at the door in Room Number Twelve, I whispered, "Open," and it did; it opened just like Padre Miguel said it would.

The next door in Room Number Eleven slid away as I repeated the secret word. I thought about how it wasn't really such a secret word; I mean the word was "open." It had been used before. I was thinking of the book Maestra Maria read with us. The character would arrive at a door and would say, "Open Sesame." It was kind of like that.

But then I remembered that Padre Miguel had said that the doors and the rooms would remember me because I had been through them, and I had been through them with Padre Miguel himself.

"Open," I said to Room Number Ten, and it did. Next was Room Number Nine. Now I was reversing my journey through the rooms. I had just walked through one quarter of the rooms; three quarters were left, and Room Number Nine was where the waterfall existed. I must say that I was relieved not to have to figure out the rooms. I mean, on the way to Padre Miguel's office, I had two guides: Padre Miguel and Rojo Anita. I would still be in Room Number One without their help. But now I was alone, so I was very grateful, very, very grateful that all I had to do was say "Open."

"Open." Door Number Nine popped open. Noise filled my ears. I wasn't sure where it was coming from, but I quickly found its source. I felt the spray against my face, and I knew; it wasn't going to be as easy as I thought. Here I was — with the waterfall in Room Number Nine.

At first, I had hope. I had done this before. "Remember, do not give in to lying down, Coyitito. Do not let the tired feeling overtake you," I told myself.

"Coyitito, move toward the waterfall, and part it like Maestra Maria parts Magdelena's hair before she braids it," I told myself.

My left foot took a step, and then I noticed that I was standing on a very, very small, circular ledge outside the door. The entire room was covered in waterfalls.

The water started falling somewhere above me, and it fell pounding far, far down. Very, very far down — too far for me to dive.

I stood there, stricken with my own nerves. How could I move along? Danger was growing outside. Padre Miguel was counting on me for something; I suppose I would figure that out as I went along, and here I was, standing on a too-small ledge surrounded by waterfalls.

One decision I made quickly was to go back into Room Ten and enter Room Nine all over again. Maybe it would be different the second time.

When I turned the knob on the door, it didn't move. The knob was stuck and wouldn't turn one way or another. I pushed and pulled at the door. And then it happened. I slipped. The platform was so wet; it was now slippery, and I did slip. I started to fall backwards, but then tilted sideways, and within moments, I was hanging on to this small, wet, slippery platform.

"Oh, please help me," I pleaded. "Please, please help me."

I called to Rojo Anita. I thought deep thoughts, pleading to her for help.

"Please, Rojo Anita; it is I, Coyitito, hanging from a small ledge over a dangerous pounding waterfall in Room Number Nine. Rojo Anita! Oh, Rojo Anita, it is I, Coyitito. Help me."

But Rojo Anita didn't come.

Then Padre Miguel flashed before my eyes. I thought that maybe I was dying. I saw him inside my mind; he was at his desk; his arm barely moved, but the rope flew from his hand, and he caught the two men.

I dropped my right hand. My left hand held on tight to a spot that was getting more slippery by the moment. The rope was at my side. It was worth a try. I tossed the rope up toward the door knob. When it was positioned at the spot, or what looked like the spot from where my eyes were, just above the ledge, I tugged, and I hoped the end of the rope would wrap around the knob. The rope followed my lead. I pulled myself up onto the platform.

For a while, I wanted to sit there, where I was. But the danger of falling was all around me. The doorknob must surely open now, I thought. So I turned it, and nothing happened. The door still wouldn't budge.

So I looked around. There is always another door in these rooms. A way in and a way out appears each time. If I found the other door, I might be able to open it.

My eyes traveled around the room. The water fell and pounded against my ears. My clothes were soaked, my face was wet, and then I saw it. Yes, I found the other door. And it was all the way across the room. It was far, far across the room. Directly across from where I was now, the other door appeared in back of a small ledge, just like the one where I was now wilting.

How could I ever get there?

I didn't understand why all this was happening. Why couldn't I just go through the doors, the way Padre Miguel had said? Had he known this would happen? And if he had known, then why didn't he help me? Why didn't he ... and then I remembered the rope that I just used to pull myself up from falling, and how the rope followed my intention. I had thrown the rope toward the doorknob, and it had landed there, and up I pulled myself.

This rope that Padre Miguel had given me, if I threw this rope across the room, would I be able to catch the other doorknob, and then ... what? And then what? Would I be able to crawl across this rope? Could I pull myself?

I never walked a tightrope. Others did. We saw them in books at the school; people walked across big open spaces on a clothesline, but not me. I wasn't one for heights.

What else could I do? Try the door again? Slip over the edge of the ledge as the water pelted it, and lose my balance? Oh, what else could I do?

I slowly crawled to the door. "Open." Nothing happened.

The rope flew across the room when I released it. At first, it didn't seem long enough. But it must have grown and grown as it spread to the other side because the rope I was using, which Padre Miguel had given me, made it across, and when I tugged at the rope, it seemed to be fastened tightly.

Then I knew I had to go. On the door above my head, a large round clock appeared with a yellow bird, and it said, "Hurry. It is time.

"Hurry. It is time.

"Hurry up now. It is time."

That frightened me so much that I almost slipped again. I had to go.

I was on my knees, afraid of sliding off as I approached the rope. Then I saw what happened. The rope didn't only grow longer; it grew wider so that it was wide enough for me to walk, or crawl.

Standing up was scary. I was in the middle of this giant, gaping hole filled with pounding water. "Maybe crawling was best," I thought. And then I changed my mind completely, and I ran across, right across, as fast as I could. I ran right up to the ledge, turned the knob, and the door stayed tightly closed.

I tried again. Nothing.

The rope slipped into my hands when I took it from the knob. Then I remembered.

"Open," I said, and the door creaked me into Room Number Eight.

My clothes were dripping wet; my heart pounded; my eyes were covered with mist. "Here I am," I thought. What was Room Number Eight again? Oh yes, the room with all the hundreds of doors. What would happen this time?

All the doors were there. Maybe I needed to close my eyes in order to see the key, but when I did, no key appeared. I tried again. No key.

So I walked across the room and yelled, "Open," as loud as I could. All the doors opened, and I was released into Room Number Seven.

"Well, that was easy," I thought. So I crossed Room Number Seven, relieved that the doors were back on track to open at my command. I reached for the doorknob, went to turn it to the right, but I missed because in Room Number Seven the ground opens, and there I was, spiraling down in darkness.

I knew what to do. At my side was the rope Padre Miguel had given me. After the waterfall crossing, I curled the rope back up and tied it around my waist. As I now fell, I reached for the end of it. I knew that if I tossed the rope up from where I was falling, I might, oh, I might with *this* rope, hit the doorknob, and I could pull myself back up to the space in front of the door.

I released the rope into the dark space, but within moments, it snapped back toward me. Again I tried, but again the rope fell my way. And this time, instead of making a bridge for me, it fell below me and pulled me down quicker into the dark hole.

Inside myself, I was shaking.

I, Coyitito, was becoming more and more shaken. Some rooms opened; some didn't. Sometimes the rope helped me, and sometimes it didn't. Here I was being pulled down, down — and then plop! I landed on the ground with my rope gathered around me.

"Coyitito, where have you been? I have been trying to get in touch with you."

"Meme! Meme, is that you?"

"Well, of course it's me, Coyitito. You came to my kitchen. Why would you come to my kitchen and wonder whose kitchen you arrived in to visit? Now … help me with these, Coyitito."

Meme stood before a tall, high, thin stack of drawers.

"I can't reach up there, Coyitito. Way up there. Here. Let me get the ladder for you."

"I'll get the ladder, Meme," I said.

But she was already gone and back with her ladder.

"Don't forget your rope," she said.

I just looked at Meme; then I bent to pick up my rope and tie it around my waist.

"Try that drawer, that one there. I've been hurrying to make these cookies; these … and they need … try that drawer, Coyitito!"

Up on the ladder, I opened a drawer.

"Here. Here. Let me turn the light on so you can see. Here. Does that help? What is in there?"

I pulled a purple stone from the piles of stone inside Meme's drawer, which was full of these different shades of purple. When I held the stone in the light, it was like a fire burned inside and changed the color as it sizzled.

"No, no, that's not it. That's for a different batch of cookies, but not for now. I keep the amethyst for special occasions. Shut the drawer. Shut that one, Coyitito."

I put the purple stone back in Meme's drawer and closed it. When shut, I saw that the drawer closed right into the stone wall.

"Try that one, Coyitito."

"This one?"

"No, no, that one. That one there. Yes, that one."

I opened the drawer Meme pointed to. When I pulled out a piece of what was inside and held it to the light, I saw a most amazing blue.

"No. No. That is lapis lazuli. No, no, that's not what I need. That one is good for the poets, but not for this batch of cookies.

"Try that one, three up from where you are now. Yes, yes, that one. Yes. Open that one, Coyitito."

I pulled open the drawer, reached inside, and pulled out what looked like rock — just plain rock. I held it up to the light.

Meme's face burst into a big smile.

"Yes, that's it. That's it. Now go to the drawer above. Don't put that one back. Here, give that one to me."

Meme climbed partway up the ladder to get the rock I pulled from the drawer.

"Go in that drawer, Coyitito."

I opened the drawer and pulled out more rock. Meme seemed excited. When I pulled out the shiny, beautiful stones, Meme wasn't as excited as when I pulled out these dull grey rocks.

"Yes. Yes. Now one more there, Coyitito. There — that one."

More gray rock. "Give me that one and the one you pulled from the other drawer. A little of this is what we need for this batch.

"All right, Coyitito."

Meme disappeared with her rocks. I didn't know if she was gone for good or only for the moment, but she returned with tins.

"Carry these with you, and you will know when to use them."

I don't know why people say these things to me. "I'll know when to use them; I'll know the signal."

Then I said to Meme, "Do you mean I'll know when to eat them?" but she didn't answer me, and I wasn't sure that rock cookies were meant to be eaten anyway.

"This is very important, Coyitito, so do not forget. When you get to Room Two, the Room of Rocks, you must gather some rock dust and sprinkle the cookies in the tins with that dust. Do not forget to do that."

Room Two. I was in Room Seven. Several rooms were between Seven and Two.

I was still standing on the ladder when Meme said to me,

"Open that drawer, Coyitito; the one staring at you."

I opened the drawer. From what seemed like its shallow depth, clear crystals grew into the air. They grew into each other, colliding and making new forms. I didn't at first know what the form was, but then I saw it. The crystals were transforming themselves into a staircase: a crystal staircase grew right before my eyes.

When Meme asked me to open another drawer, I didn't hear her because the glimmering crystals shone in the light and grew up into the center of the darkness toward the door I needed to reach to leave Room Number Seven and enter Room Number Six.

"Coyitito! Coyitito!" Meme called.

I looked at her.

"Open that drawer — that one."

And when I did, the clock appeared, and the yellow bird said,

"Hurry up. It is time."

I stared at it, wide-eyed.

"Hurry up, Coyitito. Take the crystal staircase before it disappears. If you hurry, you will find doors to the other rooms, and you can pass through quickly. Do not forget what I told you about the Room of Rocks, Room Two.

"Now go, Coyitito! Hurry."

I began to climb the crystal staircase.

Up ahead of me, just a few steps, was a door to Room Number Six. I was so frightened to open the door. Who knew? Surely I didn't know. Sometimes the doors opened, and I easily crossed the room; sometimes I was under water, crossing rooms on my rope, or falling and meeting Meme.

Meme. The tins she gave me were tucked into my pockets, tiny tins with one cookie each. I must remember, she said, to get the Rock Dust from Room Number Two.

The door to Room Number Six was right in front of me. I took a deep breath and turned the knob.

If I remembered correctly, Room Number Six was a maze. I hoped, oh I hoped, that the maze wouldn't be there, and I could just walk across the floor and into Room Number Five. "Open," I said.

Darkness. I couldn't tell what was inside the room because it was dark — oh, so very dark. And then, just like that, the light started to appear, just as when the sun comes from way far away in the sky.

And when the light came, so did the maze. There it was — right in front of me. I thought about the string. If the string were there, I would be able to travel through the maze quickly.

I walked to the beginning of the riddled trail. Oh, why was all this happening? I really needed to get back to the others. What was happening to Padre Miguel at this moment? Where was Maestra Maria? How was Rojo Anita going to get back through all these rooms? And where was the string? The green string wasn't there.

I turned around. Again I thought that maybe, oh maybe, I could go back out the door and come in again. But the door was gone, and I had to find another door.

There was only one thing to do: I had to start walking into the maze. So I did. First my right foot, then my left, and I started my journey in search of the door to Room Number Five.

"Remember when you were a horse, Coyitito. Remember how you traveled the maze into The Closet. Be like the horse. Remember the way you traveled," a voice in my head said to me.

So, I did what I sometimes do. I closed my eyes.

Yes, I was so very frightened. In fact, I wanted to open my eyes, and I did. I opened them immediately. Then I reminded myself to keep my eyes closed and see what happened.

The maze was covered by a cement wall, which rose high. A small passageway was in front of me. But several feet away, another path emerged. And that's when it all became so important. Which way should I go? If I went one way, the path would probably lead me out; but if I went the other way, I might be trapped in the maze forever.

Oh no! I might be walking around the maze forever. And what about Magdelena and Tio? And what about all the No Faces surrounding the school? What about that? And all the innocent people who are at the Feast? And Maestra Maria? And what about if there are dangerous things lurking inside the maze, and what if they devour me?

"But, Coyitito," I reminded myself. "This is not Room Number Four, The Room of Fears!"

"But maybe this is worse," I thought. "Maybe there is not just fear in here; this is for real. Real things come."

I worked myself into a sweat. My heart raced. I turned around to run out of the maze, but a cement wall blocked my path to return.

I leaned against it. My head was against the hard cement wall; I felt defeated. My eyes were closed, and that's when I saw it; it all became clear to me, and I started walking.

When my eyes were closed, I saw the door to Room Number Five, and I started walking.

With my eyes closed, I put one foot in front of the other, and within moments, I was in front of a door.

Outside the door was a puddle. "Oh no," I thought: "the Room of Water." Anything could happen in the Room of Water. I took a deep breath before I entered because maybe, as soon as I went into that room, I would be under water. One. Two. Three. Turn. "Open."

The door opened. I waited for the water to rush out at me. But it didn't; instead, the water in that room was refreshing. It felt cool and welcoming like our friend The River.

"Are you our friend The River?" I asked the water. But I didn't receive an answer. Or maybe I did because several feet in front of me, I saw the next door.

I decided to swim in The River, even though it wasn't deep. And then a funny thing happened; as I swam toward the door, the crystal staircase started to rise up into the air from the bottom of The River. Oh, the crystal staircase. Perhaps The

River was sending me an invitation. And the staircase led right to the door where I was heading.

I wasn't sure why the staircase appeared. The door was so close to me that I didn't think I needed help getting there. But maybe I did because, as I swam toward the door, I saw that it was much higher up than I had thought. So the staircase would help me reach it quicker — maybe.

The crystal step was right in front of me. I lifted my foot from the cool, soft water. My dripping leg landed on the step.

I started to climb toward the door, and as I did so, the door moved further away. "Why is this happening?" I thought. I ran up several steps, and the door moved several steps further up into darkness.

"Maybe I should return to The River," I thought. So I started back down the steps. The River was still several steps away, but then something else happened. All of a sudden, the staircase started to turn. It turned in what seemed like a circle. The movement wasn't very fast, but it was fast enough. The room was dark, but the crystal staircase stayed lit. I didn't know where it was taking me; around we spun.

We seemed to go upside down for a moment, but I didn't fall. And then it stopped just like that, and then the light grew brighter in the room. I saw the water below me, and up ahead of me was the door just like before. I thought that when I tried to reach the door, it would move further away from me. I climbed toward it anyway because something needed to happen. I could try to go back to The River and see if there was another door maybe under the water. Or I could try again. I could try to get to that door.

It seemed to be four steps from my grasp. When I climbed to three steps away, it didn't move further from me. Two. One step away, and it was still there, waiting.

I took the step; the doorknob didn't move away when I reached out my hand to turn it. So I turned it: "Open." More water.

Was I back in Room Number Five, the Room of Water? Maybe when the staircase spun around, it brought me back to the Room of Water. Maybe I was supposed to return to Padre Miguel's office and head out into the courtyard through the school. Maybe the No Faces had found their way into the tunnels, and as soon as I got there, they would catch me. Maybe they had already caught everyone else.

Maybe … Maybe …

Where was Magdelena? Where was … ?

Whoosh!

"SooooOOOOOO. YOU. Thought. You. Could. Escape. ME??? HowfoolishfoolishFOOLish of YOU. There is no. ESCAPING. ME!"

Oh no, oh no. I was in the water, and so was Marleena.

"The GREAT MARLEENA is here. To greet YOU."

I was caught in one of her arms.

"HERE. Come see ME. YOUUUUU came to visit. ME, so let's. GETupcloseand PERsonal. Comehere. Come. Say. Hello."

Whish. I was whisked through the water so quickly I thought my skin would come off my bones. I hadn't prepared for this. Yes, I could hold my breath underwater for a while, but Marleena could sink me for hours if she wanted.

And then she brought me face to face with her. Only she was gigantic, and so was her face.

"SOOOOOOOooooo, what brings. YOU here??? Have. You. Missed. Me? What brings. YOUinTOMYwatERS?"

I needed air — quickly.

"Need to. Catch. Your. BREATH, Fella?"

As quick as a lightning bolt, Marleena released me into the end of her arm.

"JOYride?"

She lifted me up and out of the water. I had no idea where I was, but I was able to take one breath, two, three ...

"HEREweGO ... back. Into. The. Water. HERE, try this ARM; it works better. I'VE been workingoutonthisarm." And she tossed me into one of her waiting arms.

"Want to PLAY.CATCH? Here's how WE do it. I TOSS. You. From one arm. To the next. TO the NEXTtothenext. YOU. knowhowthisgoes. I have EIGHT. ARMS, but then I, ALSO, have many, many girls. AND they. Each. Have. Eight. ARMS. This could GOonFORawhile.

"But let's. Start. With. ME.

"I'll toss YOU from arm. To ARM. And if I MISS ... if YOU fall while. I. AMplayingcatchwith YOU, maybe YOU could try andswimaway.

"You got AWAY. From. Me. BEFoRe, but I don't know if youcanGETAWAYthis time.

"Here. Let's trY."

She lifted me in and out of the water.

"I want to keep YOU breathing; it's more FUNthatway."

All of a sudden, I was flying through blackness.

If this was, somehow, the Room of Fears, how come my other fears weren't coming by to visit me in the depths of Marleena's lair?

"Tossssssssssss. CATCH!"

Marleena's slimy arms caught me and curled me right up into her face.

"Gotcha! Let's doITagain."

She stretched her arm and me out all the way. We were in darkness. I couldn't see anything as she whirled me far from her face. She held me in darkness, half submerged in water. I waited for her to throw me or sink me. Terrified, I didn't know how this would end.

Then she lifted me out of the water and up into the air. As I rose into the darkness, I saw something in the water, something lit. What was that? I squinted and then, within an instant, I was hurled through the pitch black.

My stomach tumbled, and I felt sick. Oh no! Then Marleena flung me high, high up into the air.

How would she ever catch me? If she didn't, the fall would be too much for me. I spun downward, straight down headfirst. And then I hit the water. She didn't catch me. And fast, very, very fast, I traveled down, down, down, closer and closer to the light in the water.

Then I saw it; there it was in front of me. The crystal staircase stood up at the bottom of Marleena's waters. I was so close. If I could just step on the stairs, maybe, oh maybe, I would be ...

"Missed YOU, but GOTYOU NOW. Comehere," Marleena almost whispered, but I heard her. Within moments, I was face to face with her again.

"SoooooooooOOO, what are. YOU. Looking. AT?" she asked me. "Whatdidyou SET your EYES on down there? TREASURE? HA. HA. HA!"

And then I was flying in darkness.

"What ARMwasTHAT — the one THAT missed. YOU? Was that ARMnumber TWOorTHREE? I BETTER workoutmore with. THOSE. Arms. Wheeeee!"

And I was whirling through space — falling, falling ...

"Here. You. Are! See, THIS ARM is much better. ThisISoneOFmyFAVorite arms.

"GET.READY because my NEXT. ARM. iS very. HITorMISSSSSSS. I've had SOME PROBLEMS from my past.With this. ONE. Sometimes it CATches; Sometimes. It. MissessSSS. I've been doing a lot of work on. THIS ONE. Let'SSSSssss see. HowIV'EbeenDOing."

Marleena tossed me high into the darkness.

"Not baD," she said.

"Caught. YOU. Justlikethat. My hard work onTHATARM. Is. Payingoff.

"HERE. Why don't. YOUtry? Why DON'T youTRY. TossSSSSSSSSing me around a little??? How. AREyourarms? Are they strong — YOURARMS? How. Strong. Are. You??

"HA. HA. Ha.

"Just. Kidding!

"Get READY because thisONEisssGOINGtoBEtough, TOUGHtough. I feel like. This. Time. I. Am. Going. To. Missss. YOU. And. You. Are. Going. To. Fall. Deep. Deep. Deep. Into. The. Water. And. I. Don't. Know. If. You. Will. Ever. Come. Out. Again.

"LetMEgetTHEgirls READY. In case I choose to MISSSSSSSSSSSS, I don't WANT YOU getting. Too. FAR from my Arm's. Length. HA. Ha. Ha.

"Maybe you're THINKING you. CanGetAaway, but GOOD. LUCK.

"Oh, Girls. GIRLS. GIRLSSS. Gather round. I am goingtobe TOSSING HIM any minute NOW.

"And you, Kar-o-LEENA — get THOSE girls OUT here NOW. We'll MAKE a GAME of it!

"Whoever catches him WINSssaPRIZE!

"If I MISS, and I MIGHT, we'll SEEif someONE else catches him, or he "GETS AWAY," like HE thinks HE mighT.

"HERE. Goes.

"Everyone. READY?"

Then Marleena pulled me up to her by wrapping me in her long arm and whirling me as close to her face as she could get. I felt her slimy skin against my cheek.

"And.How.About.You? Are.You.Ready. For. The.Toss?"

I didn't answer her.

I was too frightened.

"ARE.YOU.READY.FOR.THE.TOSSSSS?"

I still didn't answer.

"I willaskonemoretime — Out. Of. Courtesy. ARE YOU READY FOR THE TOSSS? What — DO I NEED TO SAY EVERYTHING three TIMESSS?"

Nothing. I couldn't answer. I couldn't even bring the words to my mouth.

"How. RUde." Marleena's words hit my ear. And then I was tossed and traveling through the inescapable darkness.

Up, up, and then, all of a sudden, I started falling, like every other time. If only I could reach the crystal staircase. I knew that if I could reach the staircase, I could get away from Marleena. Something told me that. If I could …

But I was speeding through darkness, into arms, and then more arms, and then even more. And she hadn't called her water ropes yet.

"HERE. HE. COMES!!! GET. READY. GIRLS. Kar-o-LEENA. GET THE-GIRLSSSREADY. ARMSSSSSSS UP! EVERYONE —

LIFT YOUR ARMS! BECAUSE.HERE.HE.COMESSS!!!

I felt all the arms rise.

"I. HAVE. A. NEW. IDEA!!! LET'S CATCH. HIM. AND. TOSS. HIM. AROUNDDD, like thatGAME *HOT OYSTER SHELL*. Is. THAT. The. GAME? HowDOESitGO go, KAR-O-LEENA? DoWEsay, "Hotoystershell, hotoystershell, hotoystershell, COLD OYSTER SHELL," and WHOEVER'S ARMS HAVE HIM AT "coldoystershell" WINS — or LOSESSSSS? DO. THEY.WIN.OR.LOSE?"

"It. Doesn't. Matter. For. I. ALWAYS. WIN. DON'T.I.GIRLS???"

And Marleena caught me at that moment.

"GOT. HIM!!!

"NOW, KAR-O-LEENA. I startSAYING, "hotoystershell hotoystershell, HO-TOYSTERSHELL, COLDOYSTERSHELL" andwhenwefinish, WHOEVER IS HOLDING HIM — LET'S.SAY — WINSSSSSSSSSSS!!!

"GOaHEAD, KAR-O-LEENA. START SAYING IT, AND I'LL START TOSSINGSSS!!!!!"

Even in my horrible state of motion sickness and so much fear, I thought about some of Marleena's grammar and usage, and I heard Kar-o-leen-a. She didn't sound anything like Marleena. And I realized she took too long to start because I heard one of Marleena's arms swish toward something, and I knew it was Karoleena.

"DO. YOU. WANT. ME. TO. SQUEEZE. YOUR. THROAT. WITH. MY. ARM. UNTIL. YOU. SAY. THE. WORDS? IS. THAT. WHAT. YOU. WANT. KAR-O-LEENA??? NOW — SAY IT.!"

Karoleena just started to say the words when Marleena threw me into the air to be caught by her or someone else.

I flew again into darkness, started to fall, and was caught in another arm.

"We must hurry, Coyitito."

ROJO ANITA'S ARM was pulling me across the room.

Rojo Anita! From where did she come?

"Coyitito. Come. Hurry. Padre Miguel has moved into the courtyard. Come."

"But Rojo Anita. Rojo Anita. Marleena was here. In the water."

I turned around to look for her.

The room was dry. A door was across the room. When I turned in front of me, as I was dragged by Rojo Anita, I saw another door.

"Coyitito, why is your hand so wet?"

And then Rojo Anita registered my story with her mind.

"Gruesome. She sounds gruesome, Coyitito. Who is she?"

"She is One of Them, Rojo Anita. And she has many, many arms. At least it seems like she must have eighty. And she's in charge of all the girls. And she guards the Underwater Cave of Secrets."

"If I can get close enough to her, maybe I can read her mind and learn the secrets," Rojo Anita said.

"Oh, Rojo Anita. I hope that you never, ever, ever get close to her. I couldn't bear it if she threw you around in her big rope arms. Me, yes ... you, no."

"Be here now, Coyitito," Rojo Anita said.

"Stop all this thinking. We must keep moving through the doors — quickly. I heard Padre Miguel's mind, and he said that we must move quickly, that the danger was grave.

"I know he doesn't know exactly what we will all do, but we will, hopefully, know when I get close enough again to hear him.

"There is bad reception in this tunnel."

A white, small, thin door waited across the room. I didn't trust the rooms or the doors. I felt that Rojo Anita still held my hand and guided me across the room. I wondered if she thought that somehow, by holding my hand and guiding me, we would cross quickly, and the rooms wouldn't be able to trick me.

We stood in front of the white door.

"Open," I said.

I turned the handle. The door opened, and the noise was so overwhelming. It was so loud; I wondered if it was just me, or if Rojo Anita heard it too.

"Yes, I hear it, Coyitito.

"Hold onto my hand, and keep walking straight in front of me."

"What is this?" I yelled to Rojo Anita, but I knew she heard my thoughts more than my voice.

I needed to cover my ears. The noise was so very, very loud, I couldn't bear it. How did Rojo Anita listen to this sound?

I tried to pull my hand from her, but she held on to me tightly.

Then something else happened. Something very, very different happened. The noise started to change. The loud, loud sounds softened almost to a whisper.

And then Rojo Anita did something terrifying. She suddenly stopped moving. Completely. It wasn't totally dark in the room: it was the color of twilight. I could see her: her silhouette moved more than she did. I saw her arm reach toward her side. Her hand dropped down. Then she spun swiftly toward me. So did her rope. I heard the sound of it lash out into the dimly lit air; then it surrounded me. I couldn't move.

Her rope wound me tight against myself. "Rojo Anita, what are you doing? Why are you doing this to me?"

I was afraid to see her face.

"Rojo Anita."

"I hear you with my mind, not my ears, Coyitito. Trust me."

Trust her?

"Yes, trust me."

How could I trust her? I could barely breathe. Her rope was around my chest and arms.

And then she started to pull me along.

"What are you doing?" But this time she did not answer me. Maybe her mind didn't hear me, or maybe she had caught me and was taking me outside to meet my fate.

And then I heard it.

Was it Magdelena?

"Magdelena, is that you?"

Was it Maestra Maria?

I had never heard a sound like this before.

I turned my head toward the sound. And I saw behind me; I saw that fog that I would see sometimes when I woke up early and went outside, crossed over to the trees, went near The River, and the fog would come. It floated up from the ground and covered my feet, my ankles, sometimes my knees. Sometimes the fog went up toward my chest.

I would play games with it, dropping down onto the ground, raising one finger up through the fog. I would kick my leg up and watch it lift from invisible to visible.

Sometimes Magdelena and Tio were there, and we would play hide-and-seek in the fog. It was really hard to find each other with a cover of that small cloud.

When my head was turned, I saw the fog, and it started drifting toward Rojo Anita and me. It wasn't very high at first; it seemed as if it would reach the bottom of my feet. That's all.

"Rojo Anita. Rojo Anita," I yelled.

"The fog. Do you see the fog?"

Rojo Anita ignored me.

"Coyitito. Coyitito. Come play hide-and-seek."

Magdelena! She was coming with the fog.

"Coyitito."

I turned to look for her. The fog grew higher. It touched me. My feet disappeared. Then my ankles.

"Coyitito. Come play in the fog with us. Come on, Coyitito. Come."

I felt the tug. I went to follow. The rope around me tightened.

"Stop it, Rojo Anita," I yelled.

"Coyitito, come. Tell Rojo Anita to come, too. Tell her to come and play hide-and-seek with us."

I looked down. I had no knees.

And then Tio said,

"Come and find me, Coyitito. I am hiding in the fog; come and find me. Are you not my friend?"

"Of course I am your friend, Tio."

"Rojo Anita! Rojo Anita!"

"Coyitito, come this way. Come to us," said Magdelena.

I felt her hand. She clutched for me.

"Coyitito, come with me. Come."

"Rojo Anita," I yelled. "Stop moving. Magdelena and Tio are calling me."

"Remember the song we sing, Coyitito?" Magdelena asked me. "Remember the song about the star, the one we sing at night before we go to bed. How does it start? Sing it with me, Coyitito. Sing it to me. Sing to me," Magdelena said.

I pulled with all my might. I pulled to stop Rojo Anita from pulling me along.

"Stop. Rojo Anita. Stop."

But she pulled harder, and even though I didn't want to, my feet moved along. I thought that if I stopped moving, Rojo Anita could not pull me, and I would fall. Then what would she do?

"Coyitito. Here. Take my hand."

Magdelena reached for me again. I reached for her. I turned around with all my force. Magdelena's fingers reached through the fog for mine. Why wouldn't Rojo Anita let me go? I felt the tips of Magdelena's fingers brush past.

"Catch my fingers, Coyitito. Come."

I reached for her.

"Oh, Magdelena."

"Coyitito, here. Here. Take my hand."

My arms were tied down. I struggled. If I could just somehow find the end of Rojo Anita's rope — or reach mine.

Bam!

I was on the ground. Then I was lifted up, up through the fog.

"Coyitito. Stay. Stay here with me. Sing to me, Coyitito. Are you ready? At three, we will sing our song.

One."

I was lifted higher.

"Two."

I felt her arms.

"Three."

She carried me.

"Stop moving," Magdelena said.

And then she screeched. I never heard Magdelena make a sound like that before. She screeched so loudly I thought something had come through the fog to hurt her.

"Noooooo," she wailed. "Nooooo …."

I didn't know why she was wailing when she had me in her arms.

"Magdelena! Magdelena! What is it? What is wrong? Magdelena."

"Say it, Coyitito. Coyitito. Say it. Say 'Open.'"

Why did she want me to say, "Open?"

"Noooooo, Coyitito, Noooo."

"Say 'Open.'"

"Open. Open. Open," I said.

And the wail of Magdelena pierced through me like spears.

Rojo Anita looked at me. I saw her pull something from each of her ears. Then she unwrapped me. "Padre Miguel said that might happen," Rojo Anita said. "So he told me to cover my ears with these rubber tubes he had on the shelves in the room behind his office. But he didn't realize, no one really can realize, that I hear with my mind; I hear what the others are thinking, so I heard much of what you heard, Coyitito, and I almost let you reach for the hand of the fog."

"Magdelena and Tio were in the fog, Rojo Anita. We left them there inside the fog."

"No, Coyitito. They are outside in the grove with the others. Soon we will join them."

I was still panting; my heart was still aching. I wasn't sure if we had just left Magdelena and Tio in the fog.

When I looked, Rojo Anita was no longer by my side.

I stood in Room Number Two. Maybe I had finally emerged from the tunnels without knowing because here I was on the canyon trail. I was all alone on the trail.

I didn't know which trail, but I hoped it was a friendly one that led me back to the school.

"Rojo Anita," I thought. I didn't want to make any sounds because I didn't know, I really could not be sure if any No Faces were hiding or even walking nearby, and if I made noises, I might bring them to me.

"Look for the door, Coyitito," I reminded myself. "You need to get through this room quickly, so scan the canyon for another door."

Another door! When my eyes started searching the rocks for an entrance, I saw plenty of doors. Many of the rocks around me and the ones going up higher had openings, which could be doors.

I waited. I was very anxious to get to Padre Miguel and to find Rojo Anita, but I didn't move; I just stood among the rocks in the sunlight, waiting to know what to do next.

"Rojo Anita," I called again in my mind and waited.

Rojo Anita did not appear. But then I heard a sound. It was further away when it started, but then it grew louder. I did not know what the sound was, but it did grow as it came my way. I became terrified. I needed to hide because the sound was getting nearer and nearer. I didn't know what it was; it was ahead, somewhere in the sky. Whatever it was would see me, so I ran toward one of the entrances in the canyon wall and entered a cave.

Just in time.

I watched a flock of birds — hundreds of them — fly over me. They were making a sound I couldn't identify. They seemed to be looking for me or talking to me because nobody else was anywhere in sight.

I thought they were gone, so I started to leave the cave entrance where I was. I shuddered with fear. I wasn't sure which way to head, but I didn't think that it was this way. The cave did not seem to be a host to the door that would lead to Room Number One.

Looking right and left, up and down, I stuck my foot out into the sun. Silence. I moved two steps, three, and from out of nowhere, the flock of birds swooped down in front of me. I ran back into the cave. They didn't come in; they stayed outside in the sunlight. And then I heard them; I heard what they said.

"Hurry up; it's time.

Hurry up; it's time."

They chanted the same words over and over again. Frozen in my spot, I covered my ears, but I still heard them.

"Hurry up; it's time."

I knew it was time. Padre Miguel and the others were in grave danger, and here I was being stalked by a flock of yellow birds who reminded me over and over again that it was time.

"Hurry up; it's time.

Hurry up; it's time."

"Stop it," I yelled. I stamped my feet on the canyon ground, unnerved, and yelled as loud as I could.

"Stop it!"

"Hurry up; it's time."

It seemed as if they were mechanical talking clocks, and every second was announced with one of the words, "Hurry. Up. It's. Time." Four seconds of silence and the next four seconds of reminder: "Hurry. Up. It's. Time." Yelling at them did not stop their message. They couldn't stop. This is what they did; they reminded me that time was passing, and the dangers in the courtyard of the school were growing.

Maybe I was already too late.

Four more seconds went by, and there I was, petrified of what was happening to Padre Miguel and unable to move because of the time flock.

I stood staring at them; each word made me more anxious. And then I remembered that I was inside Room Number Two looking for the door. I didn't know what the birds wanted; they kept telling me to "hurry," which made me more and more nervous. So I decided to try to make myself calm. I thought about all the times I was anxious, and I would turn to Magdelena for comfort. I thought of her now; I thought of what Magdelena would tell me. She would say, "Coyitito. Be calm. Be calm and then you will see differently." So I tried very, very hard to become calm.

It wasn't easy. The birds were in front of me announcing that I should hurry, and each time they said that word, I started worrying. But I couldn't go anywhere with the flock of birds in front of me. They weren't leaving, and they weren't becoming quiet, so I needed to do something else.

An idea arrived. "I'll go deeper into the cave," I thought. If I travel further, maybe I'll find the door, which will take me back to Padre Miguel.

I turned around.

And the birds changed their direction, too. They flew *into* the cave. I thought they would stay outside in the open air, but no; they followed me.

I started to run.

They swooped over my head, surrounding me on all sides.

"Hurry. Up. It's. Time."

"No," I yelled. "Stop. Please stop."

I turned back toward the entrance, but it was gone.

I hadn't traveled far into the cave, so where did the entrance go? How could it disappear like that?

The birds surrounded me.

I couldn't move away from them. The sound of their talking seconds beat off the cave walls in echoes. The noise was continuous. I couldn't bear the sound.

"Magdelena, help me, please.

"Maestra Maria; Rojo Anita.

"Padre Miguel. Help me. Please."

Then I sat down on the floor of the cave, bending my head to my knees, covering my ears. The sound was enormous.

I closed my eyes and did the only thing I could do: I surrendered. I took my hands off my ears; I opened my eyes; I stood up, and I looked at the birds. I listened to them. And I stood there, trying very, very hard — very hard — to wait. Maybe they would leave; maybe a message would come; maybe Senorita Duende would come to take me away, maybe …

I listened to them, watching them, looking into their eyes.

No reflection, only the beating of seconds passing.

"Be still, Coyitito." I heard the voice inside me. Whose voice was this?

"Do not listen to what the birds say; just be still."

Who was talking to me?

"Who's there?" I asked, but no one answered. When I looked around, all I saw was the flock of yellow birds.

"Be still. Calm."

Was it Padre Miguel?

I tried to be still.

"Hurry. Up. It's. Time."

I noticed that the birds had no emotion. They said the same thing over and over.

So I stood still. Every time I thought I needed to hurry — and I did need to hurry — the birds came closer, surrounding me tighter. It was like time was a boa constrictor. But if I didn't get as anxious, they seemed to move a bit away from me.

I tried to be as still as possible. The thoughts in my head kept moving: dangers, school, Magdelena, Padre Miguel, Maestra Maria, Tio, oh, oh, oh — and the flock would move so close to me. I felt their wings brush my face and their voices penetrate my ears. I wanted to yell, "Stop," but I knew that would bring them closer. I almost couldn't control myself, and then I did it; I yelled, 'Stop!' and they were right in front of my eyes and ears demanding, "Hurry. Up. It's. Time."

It's time.

"Stop," I told myself.

The voice came.

"Be still, Coyitito."

"Be still," I thought. I tried. I tried very, very hard. "Be still."

So again, I closed my eyes and concentrated on being still. Then I thought about how the birds kept me from moving. Maybe they were protecting me from a graver danger inside the cave. Protecting me! I realized that I needed to go and protect the others. And then I started getting anxious.

"Be still, Coyitito."

Be still.

I stood with my eyes closed. The birds still counted off time, but I stood still. I felt them near me, but I tried to calm my fears.

"Breathe."

"Breathe? Who are you?"

"Breathe."

I tried to breathe. As I took deeper breaths, I noticed that the birds moved away from me.

"Keep breathing. Focus on breathing."

"Focus on breathing!"

I tried. I listened to the voice. Whose voice was that? I knew the voice. Somewhere I had heard that voice before — somewhere.

Deeper breaths and I felt the birds moving further and further. They were still there, but not as close.

"Hurry," still sent shivers up my spine, but I tried very hard, very, very hard because I knew that it was the only way out of here and back to the school yard.

"Breathe," I told myself.

The birds were further away, almost a whisper, when I noticed them again. Still they kept time, but I decided to open my eyes. Slowly, I let my eyes open into the cave. At first, it was so dark I couldn't see anything. Startled, I became anxious, and I heard the birds make their chant louder.

"Close your eyes and breathe," I thought to myself. And I did. I closed my eyes, and when I opened them, a frame of light appeared around a door.

When I reached for the handle, something stopped me. What was it? A nagging thought was in my head. I needed to do something — what was it? What was this thought?

"Just say, 'Open,' Coyitito," I told myself.

"You are forgetting an important ingredient," I heard inside myself. An important ingredient. Ingredient.

I reached inside my pocket and took out the tin from Meme. Rock dust! I needed to get some rock dust. I reached toward the ground, and scooped dust from the floor of the cave. I didn't know if it was rock dust, but rocks were lying around on the ground. To be certain, I kicked some of the rocks with my foot, gathering whatever dust flew and throwing it into the tins. Then I put the covers on and said, "Open," turning the handle.

Cement steps appeared in Room Number One.

"Let's go, Coyitito," Rojo Anita said to me.

"Rojo Anita!"

And we quickly went out the door. "Open," I said, and we fled down the steps.

We needed to turn left to go through the tunnel into the grove to meet the others.

But Rojo Anita went toward the door that led us into the Rooms, which led to Padre Miguel's office.

"Rojo Anita, we need to go left."

"You go. You go, Coyitito. Join the others. I am going this way."

"No, Rojo Anita. No. You cannot go out there. You need to come into the grove."

"Coyitito. Go. Go. Padre Miguel is talking to me. I have reception, and I hear him. I must go this way. You go through the tunnel. I will meet you when I can. Padre Miguel tells me that you will know what to do. He tells me to tell you to check your pockets. Now go."

Check my pockets! What do I have in my pockets? The only objects in my pockets are … cookies. Rock cookies from Meme. Check my pockets.

I put my hands into my pockets.

Rojo Anita opened the door, entered, and disappeared.

I knew I had to get to the grove quickly, but I followed Rojo Anita. And then I wished I hadn't.

When I opened the door, the sunlight almost knocked me over. I felt like I had been in darkness too long. The strong sun that flooded my eyes told me noon was near. And at noon, the No Faces were going to storm into the courtyard and take everyone, kidnap all the village people and all of us. Soon, I could tell by the heat and the light, very, very soon, they would begin.

I didn't know what to do. I kept waiting to figure out what it was I was supposed to do.

Everyone was at the Petition to ask for our safe return. Special foods were prepared; some were our favorites, hoping the scents would bring us back to the school. People dressed in our favorite colors and painted signs with our names on them. The Feast looked festive, but really everyone there was quite, quite concerned for our safe return.

Some of the guests had cooked our favorite meals, which took several days. Dona Clara had made the chili Tio enjoyed so much. She cooked the meat for six hours with tomatillos she grew in her garden. She made a green hot sauce. I smelled it from where I stood. I saw that Dona Williams had brought the ice-cream, which she made from her goat's milk: that ice cream was a favorite of Magdelena and mine.

Later, the music would start and some would hope that Manuel would come dancing to them. And they would dance with him because even though he was young, he was the best dancer! He would spin them and twirl them.

And then he would dance with Magdelena and Tio and me. And the stars would come out. And the lemonade would be cold. And Maestra Maria, Maestra Maria would even dance with Manuel and laugh. Like in the past.

"He is missing!"

I heard the terrible shout.

"He is no longer in the Closet. He is Gone. Seize him."

What was this?

I turned my eyes toward the gates. Men crossed the road toward the entrance of the school. I looked at them. One of them, Pepe, had ridden on Magdelena's and my back when we were a horse. He was mean. What was he now talking about as he yelled? The gates opened.

I froze.

Were the No Faces going to come now? Right now? And here I was, peering from the door. I started to turn toward the tunnel. I knew I had to go to the grove. I knew that was where I needed to be.

And then it all happened so quickly.

The gates opened and instead of the March of No Faces, only three entered through the opening.

The two imposters on each side of Padre Miguel, who had entered the courtyard, getting ready to toll the bell, those two men each grabbed an arm of Padre Miguel.

One of the Mean Ones rode up to Padre Miguel — right up to him. I couldn't move from my spot. I knew I needed to, but there I was — frozen.

People at the Feast turned toward the gates. Silence spread.

"His body is missing from The Closet — so — you — you are an imposter!"

No, Padre Miguel wasn't an imposter. He was Padre Miguel.

"Take him to the office."

One of the riders looked at all the stricken people at the Feast and said, "Continue. Continue as you were. We have this under control. Continue doing what you were doing."

But no one moved.

"It is fine. It is fine. Continue. Strike up the music. Band — play!"

And the men turned Padre Miguel around, leading him back to his office.

I DON'T KNOW whose rope flew first, but all of a sudden, the ropes wrapped around the Ones on either side of Padre Miguel. And each of the men stumbled to the ground, rolled in rope.

My rope flew straight to the gates and wrapped around the iron posts, keeping the gates fastened. I couldn't hold the strength of the No Faces on the other side by myself. I needed to find something to hold my rope, in case it didn't show the powers it had inside the Rooms.

"Open the gates," yelled the Mean One.

"Open the gates now!"

During the commotion, Padre Miguel started to run across the yard when a rope flew from the crowd of guests and brought him to the ground. No Faces were spread among the guests.

Where was Rojo Anita? She had just been with me. Where were Magdelena and Tio?

A group of No Faces on horses appeared at the gates. All of a sudden, another rope flew across the sky and coiled around the iron entrance gate. I looked around me quickly.

Guests scrambled. Some yelled. The Mean One was wrapped in ropes when I looked his way, but his mouth was open, barking orders.

I saw the guests running for shelter as ropes braided the sky.

Padre Miguel was on the ground. I watched as someone somewhere pulled him, and he was a rolling tumbleweed heading toward someone's hands.

Where was Maestra Maria?

What were they doing in the grove?

I think I had seen several ropes circle around the gates, but the No Faces were right there ready by the large iron opening. At any minute, they could start scaling the walls. Even though the walls were built high, I'm sure they could make human ladders on each other's shoulders and climb into the schoolyard. And how many were in here already?

People ran around the yard; some were chased by ropes. To the left of me was a column. Struggling, I took my rope and tied it around the column. I wasn't the only one holding the gates closed. I could never have done it alone. I wondered who was helping me, but I needed to stay focused — very, very focused.

My rope coiled around the column. I knotted it closed. Padre Miguel had invited a man to school several months ago — was that several months ago? — and he had showed us how to tie different knots. This was a simple knot, but I think it was a strong one.

The knot was intact, but at some point, with all those No Faces outside, the gates wouldn't hold.

I scanned the crowd for Padre Miguel, but I did not see him anywhere.

Then I heard it. I heard it before I saw it, and I ducked inside the entrance from which I had just emerged. I didn't want to go back inside the tunnel, even though I knew I needed to get to the grove, because I was frightened that somehow I would wind up in those Rooms, and once inside, I might never get back out to help the others.

"Magdelena, where are you?"

"Tio?"

The rope that flew toward me hit the side of the building instead of me; I knew whoever was throwing the rope would try again and again until the rope caught me.

I watched the rope from where I stood in the doorway. It dripped down the wall, hit the ground, and continued looking for me. I didn't think it would come inside this entranceway.

And then it did.

It waited at the entrance, waiting for me to come back into the light.

Every second mattered.

I heard screams outside.

"Rojo Anita, where are you? I have a rope here waiting to get me; it is guarding the entrance." Maybe I was supposed to turn into the tunnel.

"You'll know what to do," Rojo Anita and Padre Miguel had said. Well, I didn't know what to do.

"Rojo Anita! Do something. Can't you hear me?"

I watched the entranceway, and the rope disappeared. Either Rojo Anita had heard me, or the rope would be back to get me in a moment. I had to get back out there.

"Why didn't I just go through the tunnel into the grove?" I asked myself. And then I knew I had to go back out into the yard. I put my foot through the door, and right away, a rope flew, caught my foot, and dragged me.

I was being dragged across the dirt — toward where? Who was pulling me? I tried to scramble, but it was no use. The one who caught me held me tight, and I was on my way to danger.

How could I help in this position?

All of a sudden, I was pulled to the side of the school. My fate waited. "I'm sorry, Padre Miguel; I'm sorry that I am caught," I thought to myself, hoping he would hear me.

My captor was close. I shuddered. And then I stopped moving. My eyes were closed, and I didn't see anything: no visions of what to do next. I did not want to open my eyes. I heard the shouts; the ropes were flying across the sky. And here I was, helpless.

"Coyitito. Get up. Hurry."

She was my captor.

"Coyitito."

Magdelena was covered in dust.

"Hurry."

I was free from her rope.

"We must do something. What do we do? What did Padre Miguel tell you?"

"He told me I would know what to do."

"Well then, what is it that we do?"

"I don't know, Magdelena."

All of a sudden, Tio appeared from around the corner.

"I have my rope around the tree, but I think they will soon be stronger and open the gates," he said.

My rope was around the column.

"Coyitito, we must do something," Magdelena said.

Yes, we must, I thought. What is it? What do we do? I looked up into the sky.

The sun was blazing.

Any moment, the gates would not hold. The No Faces inside were beginning to capture the guests.

I saw something fly over our heads, then land near our feet.

"Coyitito!"

"Dreamer!"

Gold and Dreamer landed on the ground in front of us.

"Coyitito! There are many, many, so many outside the gates, lining the road. They are getting ready to come in and take over. What can I do to help? We are here if you need us."

"Are there others like Gold?" I asked her. "Can you call others?" And while I waited for her to answer, I looked up at the sky, hoping somehow that they were on their way.

"Coyitito," Dreamer began, but then something else happened.

Snap.

When I looked up, I didn't see other horses with wings in the sky; I saw Meme. And she wasn't happy. Her arms were crossed; she was tapping her foot and looking down at me.

"Meme!" I thought. I wanted to ask her to help me, but I knew better. She would not answer me with that scowl on her face.

And then it dawned on me. I reached inside my pocket, felt Meme's tins, took one into my hand, opened its cover, and lifted one of her rock cookies. When I bit down, it just about broke my tooth. The vision of her disappeared. I did not want to take another bite out of this cookie. I felt the rock dust in my mouth, and then the cookie started to grow heavier and heavier in my hand.

What have I done? I wondered. For some moments, I couldn't concentrate on anything happening around me. For these moments, I couldn't concentrate on Magdelena, Tio, Dreamer, Gold, the schoolyard, the danger — for these few moments I only felt the weight of the rock cookie in my hand. And soon I couldn't hold it any longer — not even with both hands. And soon I had to drop it.

And when I did, the ground shook.

I knew everyone felt it because, for a moment, all the sounds stopped. All of them. The shouting, the yelling — it all stopped.

And then the horses started. The horses knew. Outside the gates and inside the yard, the horses started rearing.

Everyone waited to see if another tremor would follow.

And then we heard the shouts before the ground moved again.

Above the rock wall closest to the school, I saw something. It looked like a man. Yes, it was! It was a man. I knew Tio and Magdelena saw it too. They knew; they knew who it was.

Then he seemed to walk over to a large rock near him and roll it over the edge from where he stood.

Canyon Joe! "Magdelena. Tio. It's Canyon Joe! Look. Look. It's Canyon Joe." And then we saw him and his horse. And he did what he had shown us when we first met him: he climbed onto Midnight, and together they jumped from the canyon surface, landing on the ground, heading our way.

And then I heard it! I heard the sound of the water. Everyone heard it. All movement stood still as the sound of water gushed into our ears. Even the No Faces heard it, and they didn't know how to swim. Some of them ran toward the horses, but the horses were fearful of the tremor in the ground, so they did not stop for the No Faces.

Outside the gate was a loud, loud commotion.

And then I heard her.

From where we stood in the courtyard, we saw the huge wave come from the canyon trail. It sped down the road toward the front of our school. At first I thought that the ocean spilled over with the quaking of the ground, but then I knew; I knew what was happening.

Riding on the wave's crest, dazzling in the sunlight, sat Marina Teresa in the pocket of Aphrodite!

Her blue hair flew out to the sides as they rode toward us.

"Magdelena! Tio! Look! It's Marina Teresa and Aphrodite."

Tio ran to the gates. Inside the courtyard, everyone stood still, but we knew. We had met Marina Teresa and Canyon Joe and Aphrodite and Midnight before.

"Hello Coyitito! Magdelena! Tio!" Marina Teresa yelled. "Stop here, Aphrodite." The wave stood still right in front of the gates, never spilling from its path.

"Hey, you," Canyon Joe yelled ahead of himself. "Hello, Coyitito, Magdelena, and Tio! Helloooooooo!" he shouted as he neared us.

He turned toward us.

"These No Faces think that they can run away from us! They can't get away from us! The water will follow them. Remember: they can't swim, but their horses can. Marina Teresa, can you pick up these No Faces and take them for a ride?"

Marina Teresa looked at us.

"You three are covered in dust. Soon, go down to The River and wash it off; we'll take care of this now."

"Hey, Coyitito," Canyon Joe yelled. "As soon as I heard you call, when your rock hit the ground, I knew you needed some help from Canyon Joe and Marina Teresa.

"I am Canyon Joe; I know the rocks; they talk to me. I heard your rock, Coyitito, loud and clear. So I started a small earthquake, enough to cause a stir, and Marina Teresa joined me.

"Tio, didn't you once have a shell to call the water?" Canyon Joe asked him.

Tio looked at him; I thought about my key. And Tio's blanket. Yes, we *used* to have them.

"Well, do you have any No Faces in there that need to come with us?"

"Yes, Canyon Joe," I said. "No Faces are here, but we are not sure who is who."

"Open the Flood Gates! I'm coming in. We'll do the best we can!" said Canyon Joe.

Marina Teresa spread out her wave, and Canyon Joe and Midnight rode the water over the fence and into the yard. As soon as Canyon Joe was close to the ground, the water retreated to the other side of the fence.

"Now, where are those No Faces?" Canyon Joe boomed.

And then I watched as, all of a sudden, Padre Miguel, Maestra Maria, Rojo Anita, Don Pedro, and again Maestra Maria and another Don Pedro came walking across the courtyard carrying ropes.

I couldn't believe it. I couldn't believe they were all No Faces.

Padre Miguel led the crowd right up to Canyon Joe. My heart sank. How could he still be an Imposter? Maybe he had tried to get rid of me in those rooms. And Rojo Anita. And Maestra Maria? How could Maestra Maria ever be a No Face?

And then Padre Miguel reached out his hand.

"Canyon Joe." Then Padre Miguel looked out over the fence. "Marina Teresa — thank you. Thank you for your help. Midnight. Aphrodite. Thank you."

"We've rounded up as many as we could. We have them wrapped up over there."

And over there — where Padre Miguel pointed, No Faces were wrapped in rope.

"Should we try a swimming test to find the others?" Canyon Joe's eyes roved around the crowd. Mostly everyone had learned how to swim at some point or other. Except the No Faces, of course; they hadn't yet learned.

"Come on everybody," Canyon Joe called. "Let's go for a swim. Marina Teresa, can you send some of your waves in here?"

Marina Teresa's water slipped under the gate. Puddles formed at our feet. The water rapidly grew up to our knees. I was hoping we could catch a wave as the water built, but as the water rose, a few of the guests starting running from it. Not many, just a few, ran away from the gates.

"Looks like you're coming with us," said Canyon Joe.

"Coyitito, Magdelena, Tio, you want to get those three running away from the water?"

Padre Miguel, Maestra Maria, and Rojo Anita threw each of us a rope.

We let the ropes fly.

"Three more non-swimmers," Canyon Joe said.

It seemed like no one else feared the water.

"Round em up," said Canyon Joe.

"You might need some horses to save you because we're taking you on a water ride," he said to all the captured No Faces. "Find someone to ride with — or swim."

Marina Teresa held the wave steady outside the gate.

"When Marina Teresa says 'release,' the water will come right your way," Canyon Joe said as the No Faces walked toward the gate; the water inside was retreating just steps ahead of them.

Then Padre Miguel called to the guests:

"Come out. It is safe now for you to come out from your hiding. If any of you witnessed any activity, which went against one of us, if any of you saw someone who tried to hurt or capture any of us, please, let us know now."

Everyone in the yard gathered, coming closer and closer.

Padre Miguel waited to see if anyone said anything.

We all looked at each other.

Noone moved or said anything.

"Well, let's get them over there, the ones you have tied up with your ropes," Canyon Joe said. "Want to help me?" He looked at Tio, Magdelena, and me.

I got goose bumps. I didn't want to be near the No Faces, but Magdelena and Tio marched right along with Canyon Joe, so I had to go, too. And so we walked over to the line-up of No Faces wrapped in rope.

"Whose ropes are these?" I thought.

"All of ours," said Rojo Anita.

And I realized that Rojo Anita was back in the reception area.

The No Faces shuffled toward the gate.

The Mean One turned to me and whispered, "We have broken through your Protected Zone. We will never cease. We will be back for you. Remember that."

I shuddered next to Magdelena and Tio. I looked to see if they heard The Mean One, but they didn't seem to. I would ask them later. Maybe Rojo Anita heard him.

All of a sudden, the yard filled with cheers. We had safely returned. The guests formed a Circle of Gratitude. Breaking the circle to join hands with Magdelena came Manuel and Lucinda. Was Lucinda safe? Had she somehow been returned? I would ask Magdelena to get her mirror out later and check, just for safety.

Then someone stepped between Tio and me on one side, and Magdelena and me on the other.

Ah, Maestra Maria held my hand on one side — and then on the other.

Two Maestra Marias!

Guess who heard my thought!

"The Twins," Rojo Anita said as she slipped between the Maestra Marias and me.

Padre Miguel joined the circle next to Dona Williams.

The Circle of Gratitude was in full swing.

Dreamer and Gold lifted off into the sky above us, heading back to the Dream-time.

The Circle's offering was complete. Now we would all eat the foods that had been prepared for our safe return.

All of a sudden, Padre Miguel II and Senorita Duende ran through the yard.

Tio looked at us; we looked at Padre Miguel. He saw us and nodded his head. We followed our horses. For the moment, it seemed safe to go out of the gate. The No Faces had gotten inside the Protected Zone, but they were riding a wave at the moment, so it seemed safe to go the way of Senorita Duende and Padre Miguel II.

I looked for Maestra Maria in the crowd. I saw one; then the other. They both smiled my way.

Magdelena, Tio, and I left the gate together.

The road was no longer flowing. When I looked down, I saw that something caught the sun and shone. I bent to look closer.

My key; my key sat in the middle of the road. I reached for it, putting it inside my pocket.

Then I saw something else in the road: a shell. But no blanket; Tio's blanket had not been returned to us.

I looked at Tio. He looked at me, reached down for his shell, and then he was gone, running as Padre Miguel II joined him.

Magdelena was no longer standing next to me.

Senorita Duende started moving, and then she turned her head to look my way. It must be difficult for her when Magdelena and I aren't moving together.

"The River is calling, Coyitito," Magdelena called to me.

"Hurry."

And I ran after them toward The River's invitation.

www.ingramcontent.com/pod-product-compliance
Lightning Source LLC
Chambersburg PA
CBHW072205170626
46813CB00003B/799